Unexpected Pregnancy

RED GARNIER
JACQUELINE DIAMOND
TANYA MICHAELS

MILLS & BOON

HarperCollins
PUBLISHERS
Since 1817

First Published in Great Britain 2017
By Mills & Boon, an imprint of HarperCollins*Publishers*
1 London Bridge Street, London, SE1 9GF

UNEXPECTED LEGACY © 2017 Harlequin Books S. A.

Once Pregnant, Twice Shy, A Baby For The Doctor and *Her Secret, His Baby* were first published in Great Britain by Harlequin (UK) Limited.

Once Pregnant, Twice Shy © 2014 Red Garnier
A Baby For The Doctor © 2014 Jackie Hyman
Her Secret, His Baby © 2013 Tanya Michna

ISBN: 978-0-263-92965-2

05-0517

Printed and bound in Spain
by CPI, Barcelona

ONCE PREGNANT, TWICE SHY

BY
RED GARNIER

Red Garnier is a fan of books, chocolate and happily-ever-afters. What better way to spend the day than combining all three? Traveling frequently between the United States and Mexico, Red likes to call Texas home. She'd love to hear from her readers at redgarnier@gmail.com. For more on upcoming books and current contests, please visit her website, www.redgarnier.com.

As always, with my deepest thanks to everyone
at Harlequin Desire—who make the best team
of editors I've ever come across! Thank you
for making this book shine.

This book is once again dedicated to my flesh-and-
blood hero and our two little ones, who, it turns
out, are not so little anymore.

Prologue

He was the sexiest best man the maid of honor had ever seen, and he wouldn't stop looking at her.

Stomach clenched tight with longing, she stared into his gorgeous obsidian eyes and wondered how she was going to have the courage to tell him that their one incredible night together, that night that should have never happened but *did,* had resulted in a little surprise on the way.

That the stork would be paying them a visit in eight months or so.

The thought alone made her legs tremble. Clutching her white orchid bouquet with trembling hands, Kate Devaney forced herself to focus on her sister, Molly, and how stunning she looked up on the altar in her snow-white wedding gown next to the drop-dead-gorgeous groom.

The fresh noon sun lit her lovely pink-cheeked face, its warm rays illuminating the couple as they stood before the priest. They were surrounded by an explosion of white casablancas, orchids, tulips and roses. The train of the bride's wedding gown reached almost to the end of the red velvet carpet, where the guests sat in rapt attention on rows and rows of elegant white benches. Molly's voice trembled with emotion as she spoke her vows to Julian, her best friend for forever, and the man she'd always loved.

"I, Molly, take you, Julian John, to be my husband…"

Kate's heart constricted with emotion for her little sister, but no matter how much she fought the impulse, her eyes kept straying to the right side of the groom…to where the best man stood towering and silent.

Garrett Gage.

Her tummy quivered when their eyes met again. His eyes were hot and tumultuous, his jaw set tight and square as a cutting board.

He'd been looking at her for every second of the ceremony, his palpable gaze boring pinprick holes through the top of her head.

What a pity that his fiancée wasn't at the wedding, so that he could go and stare at that blonde and leave Kate alone, she thought angrily.

But no, he haunted her. This man. Day and night she thought of him, wanted him, ached for him, while every second of the day, she tried futilely to forget him.

For the past month, it had been a struggle to ignore the enticing memories of the things he'd said to her, a struggle not to remember the way he'd held her in his strong, hard arms like she was more precious than platinum.

She'd told herself, every night for the past thirty nights, that they would never work, and when she'd finally heard of his upcoming marriage, she'd had no other choice but to believe herself.

It was fine. Really. She hadn't wanted to marry him. She would never marry unless she could have what Molly and Julian had; if Kate couldn't have a little piece of real love for herself, then she'd rather be alone.

So tomorrow she was leaving. She had a one-way ticket to Florida. Miami, to be precise. Where she could begin a new life and never have to see the man she loved with another woman again. But before she left, she must let him know the truth. A truth she had been carefully keeping to herself for a month, not wanting to detract from the joy of Molly's big day.

Molly was her only sister; Kate had practically raised her since they had both been orphaned as little girls. She wanted Molly's wedding day to be perfect.

Yes, Kate was pregnant, but there was still plenty of time to find the right moment to tell Garrett about it. If only he'd stop looking at her like he wanted her for lunch, making her insides twist and clench with yearning.

"You may now kiss the bride!"

Startled, Kate couldn't believe she'd missed so much of the ceremony, and then she watched as the handsome, blond-haired Julian lifted Molly in his arms as if she weighed no more than a feather and kissed the breath out of her.

Arms twining around him, Molly squeaked in delight as Julian swung her full circle, still kissing her. But he pulled back with a frown and murmured, "Oh, crap!" when he realized Molly's train had gone round and round both their bodies.

When they looked down to the coil around them, they both burst out laughing, then they started kissing again, Julian's open hands almost engulfing all of Molly's petite face as he cradled it.

"I got it," Kate said, laughing as she easily detached the train from her sister's dress. With Molly in his arms, Julian hopped out of the tulle and carried her down the aisle to the cheers and claps of their guests and the blaring sound of the "Wedding March."

They looked so happy, so in love, as they headed for the beautifully decorated gardens where their outdoor wedding celebration was to take place, leaving Kate behind with a pair of stinging eyes, the train and the best man.

As Kate began gathering what felt like a hundred miles of tulle, Garrett came over, bringing her the other end of the train. She couldn't seem to look up at him. "Thanks," she said, and felt her cheeks burn. God, why was she even blushing? They'd grown up together. He should be a man she was comfortable with and instead she was a wreck just wondering how she was going to tell him.

Despite how much it hurt her to know he was marrying someone else, she didn't want to ruin his life, because he'd always protected and cared for her. Always.

And she feared this news was going to be a whopper for him.

Suddenly his tan, long-fingered hands captured and stilled hers, and she held her breath as the warmth of his palms seeped into her skin. She looked up and into those riveting onyx eyes, her lungs straining for air.

"Tell me if I'm mistaken—" his voice was low, his eyes so unbearably intimate she could die "—but did my brother just marry your sister?"

She wouldn't stare at his beautifully shaped lips as he spoke. She wouldn't. But, oh, God, he was so handsome she could burst from it. "It only took a full hour, Garrett. You couldn't have missed it," she said, trying to keep her voice level.

And yet, maybe she was hallucinating, but…was he staring at *her* lips? "Apparently I did."

"You were standing right there. Where were you? Mars?" She straightened and rolled her eyes, ready to leave, but his voice, the intensity in his words, stopped her.

"I was in my bedroom, Kate. With you in my arms."

She went utterly still, her back to him, while every inch of her body fought to suppress a tremor of heat that fluttered enticingly down her spine. His words seduced her body and soul in ways she couldn't even believe were possible. Her legs felt watery, and every pore in her body quivered with wanting of him. His words transported her to his bedroom. To his arms. To that night.

No, no, no, she couldn't do this here. She just couldn't.

Shaking her head almost to herself, she started down the beautiful red path that led to the Gage mansion, painfully aware that he followed.

"Kay, I need to talk to you," he said thickly.

That low, coarse timbre managed to do sexy things to her skin, and her physical response to him irritated her beyond measure.

"If it's to tell me about your wedding, I already know. Congratulations," she said in a voice as flat as the bottom of her shoe.

"Then maybe you can tell me the details, since apparently you know more about it than I do? Dammit, I need to talk to you somewhere *private*."

He grabbed her elbow to halt her, but she immediately yanked it free. "I need to talk to you, too, but I'm not doing it here. Nor am I doing it *today*."

He followed her again with long, easy strides, the determination in his voice nearly undoing her. "Well, I *am*. So just listen to me." He stopped her again, forced her to turn and stared heatedly into her eyes. "I don't know what happened to me the other day, Katie.... What you told me left me so damn winded, I swear I didn't know where to begin...."

She covered her ears. "Not here, please, *please not here!*"

He seized her wrists and forced her hands down. "I know I hurt you, I know you don't want me to apologize, but I need to say I am sorry. I am sorry for how things have gone down and for hurting you. I'm sorry how it happened, Katie. I wish I'd done it differently. If I could take it back, I would, if only to get you to stop looking at me like you are just now."

His apology was the last straw. It really was. The last. Straw. "You wish to take the night back, that's what you wish?" The pitch of her voice was rising, but she couldn't control the hysteria bubbling up inside her chest, couldn't stop herself from incredulously thinking, *How can I take back the baby you gave me, you ass!* "Oh, you're something special, do you know that? You're something else. I can't even believe I let you put your filthy paws on me, you no-good—"

"Goddammit, I really didn't want to do it this way, Kay. But you're giving me no choice!" Teeth gritted, he scooped her up into his arms and stalked across the gardens toward the house.

"Wha—" The tulle train fell inch by inch from her grasp and trailed a path behind them as she kicked and squirmed and hit his chest. "Garrett, stop! Put me down! What are you *doing?*"

He kicked the front doors open and carried her up the stairs, his jaw like steel, his hands blatantly gripping her buttocks. "Something I should've done a long, long time ago."

One

Two months earlier...

This was hell.

The Gage family mansion was lit up with light and music and flowers tonight. All the movers and shakers in San Antonio seemed to be having a good time, a good wine and a good laugh. But Kate had gone well past purgatory an hour ago and was now sure that this night, this endless night, was nothing other than hell.

With a sinking feeling in the pit of her stomach, she watched the striking couple across the glittering marble floor.

"Garrett," the slight, sensual blonde gushed to the tall dark man, "you're just like fine wine, better and better with age."

Garrett Gage, the sexiest man on the planet, and the

devil in Kate's hell, ducked his head and whispered something into the woman's ear with a wicked gleam in his dark eyes.

How many nights had she dreamed Garrett would look at her like that? Not like a little girl, but like a woman?

In a black suit and blood-red tie, with his dark hair slicked back to reveal his chiseled features, standing proud and imposing like the media baron he'd become, Garrett Gage could cause lightning to strike. He could make butterflies rise in your stomach. Make the earth stop. Make your heart thump. He could make you do *anything* just for a chance to be the one woman at his side.

For years, Kate had thought that feeding him, seeing him enjoy and praise her creations, was good enough. The next best thing to having sex with him, she supposed. But now it just pained her to cook and cater for a man who didn't even notice that *she,* Kate Devaney, the woman who made the chocolate croissants he so loved, was on the menu, too.

If only one of her waiters hadn't failed her at the party tonight, Kate might have showcased her new dress with just the right amount of hip sway to finally draw Garrett's discerning eye. But with a tray fixed permanently to her shoulder, no one spared a glance at the glossy satin dress she wore; she was just passing the food.

"Darling, be a dear and bring over some of those cute little shrimp skewers with the pineapple tips," a woman said as she swept up a crab-and-spinach roll and guided it to her lips.

"Orange-pineapple shrimp? It'll be right over," Kate said.

Grateful for the distraction, she swept back into the kitchen to load up a new tray. Usually the sight of her workers milling about the three-tiered cake and pulling out mouthwatering snacks and hors d'oeuvres from the oven would fill her with satisfaction. But even that didn't lift her spirits tonight. *Eight more weeks, Kate. Just two months. And then you never have to see him with another woman again.*

As she carried a new tray into the busy living room, it struck her that she was going to leave behind this house with so many good memories, and this family who'd practically raised her as one of their own. She'd been so happy here; she'd honestly never imagined leaving until her feelings for Garrett had become so...painful. Moving to Florida was the best thing to do—the healthiest. For her. To be away from that hardheaded *idiot!*

"Mother tells me you're leaving." Julian John fell into step beside her as she navigated past a large group. Kate had been so deep in thought that she started at the low, sensual voice.

She glanced up and into the gold-green eyes of the youngest Gage brother, a beautiful man with a heart-breaking smile who was known to be guarded and quiet—except with Molly. He was only two months away from marrying Kate's perky and passionate younger sister and officially becoming her brother-in-law. But if Julian already knew about her departure—*who else did?* Her stomach cramped in dread.

"I can't believe she's told you. I asked her not to tell."

Julian plucked a shrimp skewer from the tray and popped it into his mouth. Like all Gage men, he had massively broad shoulders, and his symmetrical, masculine face looked as if it had been cast in bronze. "Knowing

my mother, she probably thought you meant not to tell
the press—and that would exclude its owners."

Kate smiled. At seventy, still stout and active, the
Gage matron was a force to be reckoned with. She was
the proud mother of three strong, successful media mag-
nates—not that Landon, Garrett and Julian John were
powerful enough to keep the sassy woman from having her say.

She glittered tonight in a high-end ruby-colored dress,
which was completely undermined by the plain black
bed slippers she wore. Comfort, to her, was everything.
She didn't care what others thought and had enough
money to ensure that everyone would at least *pretend*
they thought the best of her.

She'd been the closest thing to a mother to Kate,
who'd grown up without one. At the tender age of seven,
she and her bodyguard dad had moved in to this very
house where Garrett's birthday celebration was being
held. Her father had died shortly after, leaving Kate and
Molly orphans, but this house had remained their home.

"Nothing Molly and I can do to change your mind?"
Julian asked, gold-green eyes flicking across the room
toward Molly.

Kate could melt when she saw the glimmer of pride
and satisfaction in his eyes when he looked at her sister.

It only reminded her of what she herself wanted in
her future.

A family of her own.

Which was why she had to leave and rebuild her life,
find other interests, and find herself an actual love life
with a man who *wanted* her.

"I really have to do this, Jules," she told him as she
shook her head and extended the tray to the people stand-

ing opposite him. Within seconds, the shrimp skewers started to disappear, one by one.

She had to get away, before she ended up watching the man she loved marry another, form a family. Before she became the dreaded "Aunt Kate" to children she'd always wished would be hers.

"But don't tell Garrett yet, okay? I don't want him on my back already."

"Hell, nobody wants that man on their back. Of course I won't tell him."

Smiling at that, she stole a glance in his direction, and yes, he was still there, as gorgeous as he'd been a minute ago, the blonde looking completely absorbed in him.

The woman was some sort of business associate of his who clearly enjoyed raising men's temperatures. Kate didn't know her, but already she abhorred her.

Seeming distracted, Garrett glanced around the room, and his liquid coal eyes stopped on Kate. Her heart stuttered when his gaze seemed to trail down the length of her silky form-fitting dress—the first male eyes to take in her attire tonight—then came back up to meet her startled stare.

Suddenly the look in his eyes was so dark and unfathomable, she almost thought that he—

No.

Whatever emotion lurked in his eyes, it was swiftly concealed. He raised his wineglass in the air in a mock toast, and added a smile that, although brief and friendly, went straight to her toes.

But that smile had nothing on the one he gave his companion when he turned away from Kate. His lips curled wide, with a flash of white teeth, and Kate just knew the poor woman was done for.

So was Kate.

Damn it, why hadn't she gotten one of those wolf-ish smiles?

Garrett had been there for her for as long as she could remember. A permanent fixture in her life. Steady and strong as a mountain. Her father had died for him. And Garrett had taken the promise he'd made to the dying man to heart.

Now Garrett protected Kate from raindrops and hail, from snow and heat, from kittens with claws and barking dogs. He even protected her from bankruptcy by ensuring the family always had a catering "event" around the corner. But Kate did not want a father.

She'd had one, the best one, and he was gone.

Garrett couldn't replace him; nobody could.

"He's not going to be pleased when he learns, Kate," Julian warned her.

Kate nodded in silence, watching Garrett's mother walk up to him. The elderly woman said something he didn't seem to find particularly pleasant to hear, and a frown settled on his handsome face as he listened.

If only she didn't love that stubborn moron so very, very much...

"Lately he's not pleased about anything," Kate absently said. She remembered the times she'd caught him looking at her with a black scowl during the family events, and just couldn't see why he seemed so bothered with her. "And I don't want him to stop me."

Her father's job had been to protect the Gages. And he had. But somehow, with his death, the family had ended up feeling like they should protect Kate.

They'd made her feel welcome and appreciated for almost two decades. But after receiving so much for so long and giving back so little, Kate felt indebted to the family in a way that made her desperate to prove to them, to all of them, that she was an independent woman now. Especially to Garrett.

"Fair enough. Sunny Florida it is," Julian agreed.

He had always been the easiest to talk to. There was a reason everyone, possibly every female at this party other than Kate, had a little crush on Julian John.

He seized her hand and kissed her knuckles, his eyes sparkling. "I guess this means we'll be buying a beach house next door."

She laughed at that, but then sobered. "Julian. You will take care of Molly for me, won't you?"

His eyes warmed at the mention of his soon-to-be wife. "Ah, Kate, I'd die for my girl. You know that."

Kate gave him a smile that told him silently but plainly how much she adored him for that. Witnessing their love for each other and how it had started out of friendship had been surprising and inspiring, and yet also heartbreaking for Kate. She loved seeing her sister so happy, but couldn't help wish…

Wish Garrett would look at her in the way Julian looked at Molly.

Stupid, blind Garrett.

Blind to the fact that the little girl who'd grown up with him had become a woman.

Blind to the fact that she would gladly be *his* woman.

And even blinder to the fact that before he could say *yay* or *nay,* Kate Devaney was moving to Florida.

"What do you mean, Katie's moving to Florida?"

Stunned, Garrett stared in disbelief at his mother,

his date and business associate completely forgotten at his side.

"Only what I meant. Little Katie's moving to Florida. And no, there's nothing we can do about it. I already tried. And hi there," she said to the blonde pouting at his side. "What did you say your name was?"

"Cassandra Clarks." The woman extended a hand that sparkled with almost as many jewels as his mother's.

But Garrett was too preoccupied to pay attention to their sudden conversation, a conversation that was no doubt about the promising possibility of merging Clarks Communications into the Gage conglomerate. He spotted Kate across the room, and a horrible sensation wrenched through him. *She was leaving?*

When her gaze collided with his, the grip in his stomach tightened a notch. God, she looked cute as a ladybug tonight, too cute to be waltzing around in that dress without making a man sweat.

Then there were her eyes. Every time she looked up at him with those sky-blue eyes, pain sliced through his chest as though that bullet had actually hit Garrett, instead of her father. He'd never forget that he was living now, breathing now, because Kate's father had stepped into the line of fire to save him.

He'd tried to make it up to her. The entire family had. A good education, a roof over her head, help with securing her own place and encouragement so she'd open her catering business. But lately Kate seemed sad and discontent, and Garrett just didn't know how to resolve that.

He felt sad and discontent, too.

"But…she can't go," he said.

Eleanor Gage halted her conversation with Cassandra and turned her unapologetic expression up to his. "She says she can."

"To do what? Her whole *life* is here."

His mother raised a perfectly plucked brow that dared him to wonder *why,* exactly, she would want to leave, and a sudden thought occurred to him. He frowned as he considered it. Kate's distance would be good for him. He might even finally be able to get some sleep. But no. Hell, no.

He'd made a promise to her father, years ago, the tragic night of his death. Kate and her little sister, Molly, had become orphans because of Garrett. They would always belong here, with the Gages. This was their home, and Garrett had done everything in his power so that they would feel comfortable, protected and cared for.

Molly was marrying his younger brother now. But Kate?

Garrett had always had a weakness for her. He respected her. Protected her. Even from things he himself sometimes felt.

His whole life he'd ignored the way Kate's hair fell over her eyes. The way she said *Garrett* an octave lower than any other word she spoke. He'd ignored the way his chest cramped when she spoke of having a date, and he'd even done his best to try not to count all the freckles on the bridge of her pretty nose.

It wasn't easy to force himself to be so damned ignorant. Of that. But he'd done it by force and that was exactly how it would remain.

Kate was like his sister and best friend. Except she was truly neither....

No matter.

He would still do all kinds of things to protect her—

and this included making her see that moving to Florida was not a good option. Not an option, period.

Scowling, he snagged his mother by the elbow and pulled her closer, so that Cassandra didn't overhear. But the woman took the cue and easily began to mingle— leaving him to talk to his mother in peace. "When did she say she was leaving?"

"The day after the wedding."

"Eight weeks?" His brain almost ached as he tried to think of ways to keep her here. "Long enough to change her mind then."

"My darling, if you manage to—" his mother gently patted him on the chest "—you'll make me a very happy woman. I don't want Katie anywhere in the world but *here*."

Garrett bleakly agreed and snatched a wine goblet from a passing server. He almost downed the liquid in one gulp, wondering how in the hell one could change the mind of a stubborn little handful like Kate. She could teach old, grumpy men a thing or two about sticking to their guns, and Garrett wasn't looking forward to being on the opposite end of the field from her. Or then again, maybe he was.

It was always fun to pick a fight with Kate.

It seemed the only way he could vent his frustrations sometimes.

Frustrations that seemed to grow by the minute as he stalked over to Cassandra, who was engaged in a conversation with two other women Garrett knew but couldn't remember the names of.

He was interested in securing her family's company to consolidate the Gages' grip on Texas media, but he couldn't even think about that now.

Kate was packing her bags and flying out of his life in eight weeks, and he was so determined to stop that from happening that, if he had to, he would run to Florida after her on his own two feet, and come back carrying her like a sack of potatoes on his back.

Which might even be more fun than fighting with her now.

"Something's come up," he apologized as he brought the blonde around to look at him. "I'm afraid I'll need a rain check on our talk."

He smiled down at her to ease the blow, marveling that he could, and he was glad to find there was no hostility in her eyes. She didn't tell him to go take his apology and shove it where it hurt, but instead she said, sounding alarmed, "When can I see you again?"

"Soon," he said with a nod, his mind already on Kate.

Two

He spotted her out on the terrace, and his insides twisted painfully tight. Tall and slender, Kate leaned against the balcony railing outside of the French doors, peacefully gazing out at the gardens. Her dress dipped seductively in the back, exposing inches and inches of flawless bare flesh and the small, delicate little rises of her spine. Something feral and dangerous pummeled through him. *She's leaving me...*.

She'd been avoiding him tonight. And now he knew why.

He clenched his hands, hauled in a breath, then yanked the doors open and stepped outside.

A warm breeze flitted by as he approached her. A slice of moon hung in the sky above her, bathing her with its silvery light. It was the kind of night lovers waited for. A night for whispers, for promising forever...

"Why?"

She spun around in a whirl of silk and red hair, her lips slightly parted, her eyes wide and bright. "Don't tell me," she said with a disappointed shake of her head. "Your mother told you."

"Why, Kate? Why am I always the last to know?"

For a moment, she didn't seem to have an answer. *She's leaving you. She's leaving you and won't tell you. Won't look at you.*

Restlessly, she pulled at her small earring as she gazed out at the majestically lit lawns. "I...uh, planned to tell you."

"From where? *Florida?*" he scoffed, unsure whether he was wounded, angry, amused or just plain damn confused.

"Okay, maybe yes, from Florida," she admitted. "But you've been grumpy lately, Garrett. I can't handle you right now. I'm too busy."

His lips twisted into a cynical smile as he leaned on the balustrade next to her. He eyed the length of her glossy hair, wondering what it would smell like up close. Raspberries in the summer...? Peaches and cream? And why in the hell did he need to know? And what did she mean, he was grumpy? "I don't *need* to be *handled.*"

With a pointed stare that told him that he really *did,* Kate studied him with mischievous blue eyes. "You haven't exactly been easy to be around lately."

"Come on, I can't be that bad!"

She shot him a wry smile, and Garrett found himself responding to that captivating grin. He nudged her elbow up on the railing. "Kate. What did you think I'd do? Tie you to your kitchen to keep you here? Steal your damn plane ticket?"

"The fact that you've already thought of that makes me wonder about your sanity."

"The fact that you're leaving makes me want to check your head, too. You belong here."

He sensed—rather than saw—the smile on her lips, but when she refused to look at him, Garrett wondered why Kate seemed so absorbed by the dark gardens it was as if she'd never seen them before—as if she'd never played outside in that yard when she was growing up. His heart jerked as an awful suspicion struck him.

"This is because of a man, isn't it?"

"Excuse me?"

"You don't just dump a life like yours and go away for nothing. So why are you running? Is it a man?"

"Does it matter?" she asked, thrusting her chin up a notch. "I'm leaving, Garrett, and I'm certain."

The rebellious note that crept into her voice only confirmed to him that it was a man.

A toad Garrett wanted to kill with his own two hands.

Pushing away from the railing with sudden force, he plunged his hands into his pants pockets and paced in a circle on the terrace, lowering his voice when he stopped at her side again. "Who's going to protect you?"

She scrunched her pretty nose with a little scoff. "I don't need protecting anymore. I'm grown up, in case you missed it."

He was struck by a memory of holding his jacket over Kate's head while they rushed into the house, soaked and laughing. They'd both been just teens. His chest turned to lead as he wondered if he'd never do that again. Laugh with her again. Laugh, period.

"Adult or baby, you still need to know that someone's got your back," he grumbled.

She glanced down at the limestone terrace floor, and for a nanosecond, he detected a flash of pain in her expression. "I know you've got my back," she said softly.

She sounded as sad as he felt, and suddenly he wanted to punch his fist into something.

Because *nothing* in his life felt right anymore.

Everything he did felt pointless. He felt restless. Angry. So angry at himself.

He imagined her all alone in a new place, with no one to help her with anything. Not if she got lost. Not if she was lonely. Not to unload her stuff. Not if there was thunder outside—she hated thunder. He clamped his jaw, loath to think of how many Florida men would be out there just ready to use and discard her, and then continued his attempt at persuasion. "What about Molly? You two are close."

"And we still will be. But Molly has Julian now. Plus she's promised to visit, and so will I."

"Then what about your catering business?"

"What about it?"

"It's taken off during the past couple of years. You worked your butt off to make it happen, Kate."

She lifted her shoulders in a casual shrug, as if leaving her entire life behind were just an everyday occurrence to her, as if she couldn't wait to leave the shadow of the Gages behind. "Beth's my associate now. Trust me, if Landon married her, it means she's very capable of handling things by herself. We'll hire a couple more helpers, and I can start a new branch in Miami."

Frustrated at her responses, he ground his molars as he thought of a thousand arguments, but he predicted she'd have a retort for each one. How in the hell was he going to change her mind?

Her smile lacked its usual playfulness as her pretty blue eyes held his. "So that's it? Those are your arguments for me staying?"

Her lips...they looked redder tonight, plumper. He wanted to touch them with his thumb and take off her lipstick. See her all fresh and pure like he was used to seeing her. Not all made up. Just pink, fresh-skinned, with those seven freckles on her nose, and that soft coral mouth that he—

Damn.

He stiffened against the heat building in his loins.

But Kate... She made him feel so damned protective it wasn't even funny. Her smiles, her personality, her alertness... There was no part of Kate he would ever change. No part of her he wouldn't miss when she left for Florida.

Luckily, she wouldn't be going anywhere.

"What am I going to do to change your mind?" he asked, more to himself than to her.

"Nothing. Honestly. My mind's completely made up."

He noticed the tray of wineglasses she'd set down nearby. She was taking a short break from making the rounds, he supposed. So he seized one and offered her another.

"Here's to me changing your mind," he said with an arrogant smile. He would find out what she was running away from, and he would eliminate it from the face of the planet.

She laughed, and the sound did magical things to him even as she declined the wine he offered her. "Oh, no, I don't drink when I'm working."

He snorted. "I should've stopped seven glasses ago, and yet here I am. Still going strong. Drink with me, Freckles."

"Well it *is* your birthday. You might as well enjoy."

"Come on. Join me on this toast. I relieve you of your duties." He pressed the glass against the back of her fingers, glad when she finally took it. He felt cocky and arrogant as he lifted his glass. "Here's to me changing your mind," he repeated.

Kate's eyes gained a new sparkle as she did the same. "And to me, and my new life in *Florida*."

They knocked glasses in toast, and it was on.

It was *on*.

Like when they were kids playing Battleship…hell, yeah. Garrett was going to sink Kate's Florida ship to the bottom of the ocean.

As though mentally plotting, too, Kate quietly sipped, watching him over the rim with a little glimmer in her eyes. A glimmer that told him she was definitely onto his plan.

Think what you want, Freckles. But you won't be going anywhere.

"I'm not backing out until I get my way, Kate. You know this, correct?" Garrett warned with a smile

Kate shook her head, but was smiling, too. "See? And you asked me why I didn't tell you? There's your answer. I can't *deal* with you right now, Garrett. I need to pack and make plans, help Molly with preparations so I can leave after the wedding."

"You don't need to *deal* with me. I will be the one dealing with *you*," he countered as he finished his glass. He snatched another and then gazed out at the gardens, the alcohol already slowing his usually sharp brain. Oh, yes, he was determined.

He just couldn't imagine his life without Kate in it. Every family celebration—hell, every family dinner, gathering or festivity—she would be there. Every morning in his office, her delectable croissants would be there. In his mind, his very dark soul, every second of the day, she was *there*....

"Will you be spending the night here?"

The lights in her eyes vanished at his question, and she nodded sadly. "Your mother said I could use my old room. She doesn't want me driving alone so late. You know what happened..."

To our fathers, he thought. They'd taken Garrett to watch a rock concert.

Neither had returned.

The reminder made his stomach twist and turn until he thought he'd puke.

He wanted to discuss Florida, take back control, make her promise she would stay and settle this here and now. But he didn't feel like he was in control of all five senses anymore; he'd drained the second glass already, which brought tonight's drink count to almost a dozen, so perhaps he could save this for another day.

Setting down the empty glass on the tray, he said, "All right, Kate. Sleep tight. I'll see you in the morning."

"Garrett." Her voice stopped him, and he turned from the terrace door. There was regret in her eyes, and he worried she'd see the truth of his torment in his. Then she sadly shook her head. "Happy birthday."

"You know what I want from you for my birthday, don't you?" he asked, his voice so low she'd probably barely heard it.

For a long, charged moment, their gazes held. The wind rustled the bottom of her dress and pulled tendrils of hair out of her bun. Watching the way the breeze caressed her, he felt unraveled on the inside with crazy thoughts about tucking that hair behind her ear, feeling the material of her silky dress under his fingers.

"What?" she asked, sounding breathless. "What is it that you want for your birthday?"

Her eyes had glazed over. Now her chest heaved as though his answer made her nervous and, at the same time, excited, and for a moment, Garrett felt equally nervous, and equally excited. For that fraction of a second, he just wanted to say one word, just one word, that would change their lives unequivocally in some way. But he forced himself to say the rest.

"You," he whispered, barely able to continue when he noticed the way her cheeks flushed, the way she licked her lips. "Here. I want you here on my next birthday. I want you here every day of the year. That's all I want, Kate."

You...

Kate felt strangely melancholy, lying in her old bed, in her old room, with its decorations still left over from her childhood. She didn't want to think that this was the last time she'd be sleeping here, a door away from Garrett. She didn't want to think it'd be the last birthday she spent with him and that some other guy she'd meet in Florida, a cabana boy or whatever, would be the one she'd settle down with.

She'd been barely seven when she buried her dad, and in that strange reflective moment when a grieving child gains the maturity of an old person, Kate had realized that her chance to be loved, to belong to something and someone, was now buried six feet under, in a smooth wood coffin.

She'd never blamed Garrett for anything, at least not at first.

She hadn't been told what had happened in the beginning. She'd only learned that two men had been murdered and the killers had been caught and would spend their lives behind bars. Which had seemed like such an easy punishment, compared to how her father and Garrett's had lost their lives. Garrett and his brothers had grieved their father, and Kate and Molly had quietly grieved their own. But then she had overheard a conversation Garrett's mother had had with the police, and Kate had found out what really happened. She had felt betrayed, kept from the truth by their whispers. Garrett's betrayal had hurt most of all.

She'd always had a soft spot for that dark-haired boy, and she'd felt like he hadn't even cared enough for her to tell her the truth. That her father had not died to save his dad. He had died to save Garrett. She'd rushed up to him one day and told him he should be ashamed of himself. She'd asked him how he could stand there with that poker face, and laugh, and try to pretend nothing had happened, when it had been his fault! Her father had died protecting Garrett from the gunshots. All because Garrett hadn't run for cover when he should have. She'd been angry because they'd all lied to her, to her and poor innocent Molly, who was merely three and lonely. But she had been especially angry at Garrett.

She'd regretted the words instantly, though, when she'd seen the way his neck had gone red, and his fisted hands had trembled at his sides, and his eyes had gone dead like she'd just delivered the last blow that he'd needed to join the two men down under.

The death wish the boy had developed afterward

had alarmed the family to such an extent that the Gage matron had asked Kate to please talk to him. Horribly remorseful, Kate had approached him one day and apologized. She'd realized that her father would have done that for anyone, which was true. No matter how painful it had been to speak, she'd said that it had been his job, and he had done it well. He was a hero. Her hero, and now he was gone.

Garrett had listened gravely, said nothing for long moments, and Kate had felt a new, piercing sense of loss when she realized in fear that she and Garrett would never be friends again. They would never be able to cope with this huge loss and guilt again.

"I wish it had been me."

"No! No!" She'd suddenly hated herself for having planted this in his head, for not coping well with this strange anger and neediness inside her. Maybe she'd been so angry because all she'd wanted was for someone to put his arms around her and Molly and say it would be okay, even if it was a lie and it would never be okay.

But Garrett had tossed a small twig aside, and gazed down at her hand like he'd wanted to take it. She hadn't known if she wanted him to hold it or not, but when he had, a current had rushed up her arm as if the tips of her fingers where he touched her had been struck by lightning.

"I'm gonna be your hero now," he'd said.

And he was.

He'd protected her his entire life, from anything and everything. He'd become not only her hero…but the only man she'd ever wanted.

He could feel Kate in the house somehow.

Of course his mother wouldn't let her drive so late

back to her apartment alone. Garrett also had an apartment of his own in a newer neighborhood, but tonight he'd also planned to stay in his old room so he could get blissfully inebriated without having to drive. And yet even after all the wine he'd drunk, he didn't feel so high.

The news of Kate's plans to move had sobered him.

Now he lay in bed with just a little buzz to scramble his brain, not enough to numb his thoughts. He couldn't stop thinking about her.

He might as well have been eighteen again, staring at the ceiling, sleepless with the knowledge that Kate slept nearby. Except now, Molly no longer slept in Kate's same room, and Kate wasn't a teenager anymore. Neither was Garrett.

With the vivid imagination of a man, he imagined her red hair fanning out against the white pillow, and the mere thought of her in bed caused his muscles to tighten.

His chest became heavy as he grappled with the same feelings of guilt and solitude that he always did when he thought of her.

Garrett had also denied little Molly of a father. But Molly had never looked at him with resentment. She had never really looked at him like she *wanted* something from him, like Kate did.

Sometimes, when he got drunk and reflective, he wondered if that night had never happened, would things have been different for him? He might have been happier, like his younger brother. He could have also waited until Kate was the right age, and then, if there had been any hint of her having any special feelings for him, he might have let himself feel them back for her. But it was pointless to imagine it. Pointless torture and torment.

Because that night *had happened,* and Garrett could still feel the dank air, hear the gunshots and remember it as if it had happened less than twenty-four hours ago.

Yeah, he remembered exactly how those gunshots had exploded so close to him, how they'd burst between the buildings of downtown San Antonio like an echo. He remembered his father's grip—which had been firm on Garrett as he guided him into the concert entrance—and how suddenly he'd jerked at his side and his fingers had let go. His father had crashed like a deadweight to the asphalt.

"Dad?" Garrett had said, paralyzed in confusion for a second, only to be instantly shoved aside by Dave Devaney, whose expression clearly told Garrett he'd already figured out what was going on.

"Get down—run!" the man had shouted, reaching for the weapon Garrett knew he carried inside his jacket. But Garrett could hear his father sputtering, struggling to breathe, and he had been paralyzed for a stunned moment. The world could have been crashing over him. As far as he'd known, it had been. But all he had been conscious of was his father. In the middle of the street, clutching his chest, where blood spurted through his open fingers like a fountain.

Instead of running away, Garrett had run back to him. He hadn't known what he planned to do. He'd only known his father was covered in blood, choking on his own breath, and that his eyes—dark as coal like Garrett's—looked wild and frightened. As wild and frightened as Garrett felt.

He'd dived back for the figure on the ground and gripped him by one arm, trying to drag him aside, when he'd heard Devaney's "No, boy! Dammit, no!" A half dozen more gunshots had exploded, and in that instant, the weight of a man had crushed him to the ground.

Garrett had cursed in front of his father for the first time in his life and squirmed between both men. Something hot and sticky had oozed across both his chest and back as he'd tried to push free, which had proved immensely difficult being he was only ten, and Dave Devaney had been a big man. His father had sputtered one last time beneath him, and when Garrett swung his head around, Jonathan Gage's eyes had been lifeless.

Garrett had gone cold, listening to sirens in the distance, footsteps, chaos around them.

Suddenly he'd heard Dave's voice, saying, "Garrett," as he rolled to the side to spare Garrett his weight. He'd blinked up at the man, shocked, mute when he realized the man had stepped into the line of fire to save him. Him. Who hadn't run when he'd been told to.

The man had reached out to pat his jaw, and Garrett had grabbed the man's hand and attempted a reassuring squeeze. He'd shaken uncontrollably, felt sticky and startlingly cold. "My daughters… They have no one but me. No one but me. Do you understand me, boy?"

He'd nodded wildly.

The man had seemed to struggle to swallow. To speak and breathe. But his eyes had had that wild desperation Garrett's father had worn, except his gaze had also been pleading. Pleading with Garrett. "Help me…. Be there…for them…"

He'd nodded wildly again.

"So that they are not alone…taken care of…safe. Tell 'em…I l-love…"

Garrett had nodded, his face wet and his eyes scalding hot as he tried to reassure the dying man. His chest had hurt so much he'd thought he'd been shot, as well. "Yes, sir," he'd said low, with the conviction of a ten-year-old who'd suddenly aged to eighty. "I'll take care of them both."

But how *could* he take care of Kate now, if they would be miles and states apart?

Kate was jolted from her thoughts when the door of her bedroom crashed open. She sat upright on the bed, her heart hammering in her chest. A huge shadow loomed at the threshold.

Garrett.

"I don't want you to leave," he said gruffly.

Shock widened her eyes. His voice was slurred, and she wondered how many more drinks he'd had after they'd last seen each other.

From the light of the hall, she could see he was still partly dressed in his black slacks and button-up shirt. His tie was loose around his collar. His hair rumpled. His sleeves rolled up. Oh, God, he looked adorable.

"I've made up my mind," she told him.

"Then unmake it."

He shut the door behind him and strode into the darkness, and her heart beat faster in response.

"I can't unmake it," she said, her voice raspy. Her throat was aching and she thought that the night of no sleep yesterday and the marathon to get everything set up today had just set her up to fall ill. "Look, I made up my mind. I can't stay here."

"Why?"

"Because I'm unhappy, Garrett. I've got everything I ever wanted, and yet don't. I make money for myself,

I've got great friends, and Molly, and I've got you and your family...and I'm so unhappy."

The mattress squeaked as he sat down, and suddenly she felt his hand patting the bed as though to find her. "Why are you unhappy?" he asked. He found her thigh over the covers, and when he squeezed, her stomach tightened, too.

She couldn't remember ever being in a dark room with him, or maybe she could, decades ago, when he had been sick and she would help Eleanor nurse him and feed him soup. But now she was no longer a girl. Her body was a woman's, and her responses to this man were purely feminine and decidedly discomforting. Her blood raced hot through her veins as her body turned the same consistency of her pillow behind her. Soft. Feathery. Weightless.

"Why are you unhappy?" he murmured. She felt the mattress squeak again when he edged closer. He seemed to be palpating the air until he felt her shoulder; then he slid his hand up her face. The touch of his fingers melted her, and she closed her eyes as he cupped her jaw and bent to her ear. "Tell me what makes you unhappy and I'll fix it for you."

He smelled of alcohol. And his unique scent.

She shook her head at his impossible proposition, almost amused, but not quite. More like unsettled. By his nearness, his touch.

She had promised herself, when she'd decided she had to move away, that she would forget this man. And now all she could think of was reaching up to touch his hair and draw his lips to hers. She couldn't see him in the darkness, but she knew his face by memory. The sleek line of his dark eyebrows. The beautiful tips of his sooty eyelashes. The strikingly beautiful espresso shade of his eyes, dark brown from up close and coal-black from afar.

She knew his strong face, with that strong, proud forehead, as strong as his cheekbones and jaw, and she knew the perfect shape of his mouth. She might not have touched his face with her fingers in her life, but her eyes had run over those features more than they had touched any other thing on this earth.

"You can't fix it. You're not God," she sadly whispered. Her throat now ached with emotion, too.

"You're right. I'm a devil." He cupped her face in both hands and stroked his thumb across the flesh of her lips, triggering a strange reaction in her body. "Why did you wear lipstick tonight? You look prettier bare."

Her breath caught as she realized he was stroking her lips with his thumb like he wanted to kiss her. He'd called her pretty. When had he ever called her pretty? Decades ago, maybe by accident, he'd blurted it out. But it had been years since he'd ever complimented her. Or touched her.

He'd just done both.

And suddenly the only thing moving in the room was her heaving chest, and his thumb as it moved side to side, caressing her lips, filling her body with an ocean of longing. She swallowed back a moan.

"You're right to want to leave here, Kate." His voice thickened as he bent his head, and he smelled so good and exuded such body warmth and strength, she went light-headed. "You should run from here."

It took every ounce of willpower for her to push at his hard shoulders. "You're drunk, Garrett. Go away and get out of my bed."

His hands tightened on her face as he nuzzled her

nose with his, the timbre of his voice rough with torment. "Kate, there's not a day I don't remember what I
took from you—"

"Garrett, we can talk about all this tomorrow."

"There's nothing to discuss. You're staying here.
Here, Kate. Where I can take care of you and I know
you're safe. All right, Freckles?"

"Even if I'm miserable?"

He dropped his hands to her shoulders and squeezed.
"Tell me what makes you miserable, Kate. I'll take care
of it. I'll make it better for you."

Kate wanted to push him away, *needed* to push him
away. He was drunk and she didn't have the energy to
deal with him tonight, not like this. But the instant she
flattened her palms on his shirt, they stayed there. On
his chest. Feeling his hard muscles through the fabric,
his heart beating under her hands. Between her legs, she
grew moist and hot.

When she was little, she'd wanted him because he
was strong and protective, and her favorite boy of all the
boys she'd ever met. But now she was older and a new
kind of wanting tangled up inside her. Her breasts went
heavy from the mere act of touching his chest through
his shirt, and her nipples puckered against her nightshirt.

"Do me a favor, Kate?"

His voice slurring even more, Garrett sounded
drunker by the second as he stroked her face with unsteady fingertips. Every pore in her body became aware
of that whispery touch, causing shivers down her nerve
endings.

"Stay with us. My mother loves you. Beth loves you,
and so does her son." He seemed to wrack his brain for

more to say. "And Molly. Molly loves you, Kate. She needs you. Julian, Landon, hell, everyone."

But not him?

She didn't know if she wanted to laugh or cry or hit him for excluding himself, but she already knew that she was a weight on him, a responsibility to him. That's what she'd always been. Forcing her arms to return to her sides, she sighed. "Garrett..."

"What will that obsessed client of yours, Missy Something, do without your currant muffins? What will I do? Hmm, Kate? It's a tragedy to think about it."

"I don't want to argue about this now, Garrett." She rubbed her temple.

"All right, Katie."

She blinked.

"All right?" she repeated.

Confused by his easy concession, which was not like Garrett at all, she suddenly heard him shift on the bed and spread his big body down the length beside her.

Eyes widening in horror, she heard him plump one of the two pillows.

"All right, Katie. We'll talk about it in the morning," he said in that deep, slurred voice.

She heard him shift once more, as if to get more comfortable. Sitting on the bed, frozen in disbelief, she managed to sputter, "You're not planning to *stay* here the night, are you?"

He made a move with his head that she couldn't see but rustled the pillow.

"Garrett, you moron, go to your *room*," she said, shoving at his arm a little.

He caught her hand and squeezed it. "Relax, you little witch. I'll go back to my room when I stop spin-

ning. Come here and brace me down." He draped his
arm around her shoulders and drew her to his side, and
Kate was too stunned to do anything but play rag doll.

Minutes passed as she remained utterly still, every
part of her body excruciatingly aware of his powerful
arm. Garrett was not the touchy-feely brother; that was
Julian. In fact, Garrett seemed to do his best not to touch
her. But his guard was down and he seemed not to want
to let *go* this time.

She frowned when he tightened his hold and slid his
fingers up beneath the fall of her hair. Cupping her scalp,
he pressed her face down to his chest.

"Garrett," Kate said, poking on his abs. They were
hard as rocks under his shirt.

He breathed heavily. Oh, no. Seriously. Was he
asleep?

"Garrett?"

She groaned when there was no response and wondered if she should move into Garrett's room and leave
him to sleep here, because she was certainly not dragging him to his own room. He must weigh double what
she did, even if he was all muscle, judging from the hardness of the arm around her and the abs she'd just poked.

Instead, she grumbled and complained under her
breath, and ended up using her pillow as a barrier between them. She eased his arm from around her, setting
it on the pillow. His hand was enormous between her
fingers, and for a moment, she seemed to be unable to
let go, kept her hand over his just to feel that he was not
a figment of her imagination. Then she realized what
she was doing and that it was stupid and foolish, and she
yanked her hand away.

Damn him.

He was going to do everything possible to keep her in Texas, she knew.

But he wasn't going to take Florida away from her.

Oh, no, her life had stopped revolving around Garrett Gage ever since she'd decided she didn't want him anymore, and now she'd be damned before she let him screw up her perfect plans, too.

Three

Monday morning, business at the *San Antonio Daily* was more intense than normal.

Usually Landon, the eldest Gage brother, would bark about the grammar mistakes in that day's print edition. Julian John, the youngest, was no longer working at headquarters since he'd started his own PR firm, but he still occasionally dropped in and offered his services in weekly status meetings. Lately, Garrett had been focused on maneuvering their assets to make one of their greatest takeovers, one that would absorb Clarks Communications into the *Daily* and the rest of their holdings.

Which was why Cassandra Clarks was visiting today. She sat in Garrett's office, quietly eating the remaining muffin from the batch Kate had sent to the office this morning.

It made Garrett grumpy to see that muffin go.

But he feigned indifference as he flipped to the next page of the current stock statistics for Clarks Communications. Still, he wasn't really paying attention to their impressive growth numbers. Instead, he kept going back to Saturday night and Sunday morning.

He'd woken up alone, dressed in the most uncomfortable way possible, with a stiff back and the scent of Kate in bed, which had made him hard as marble.

Then he'd realized he was lying on Kate's old, frilly pink bed. Which he'd apparently decided to take over during the night while on a semidrunken spree.

Damn.

He'd immediately texted her Sunday morning, and even now, he kept glancing at his phone, replaying their conversation.

Sorry for crashing in last night.

You mean that was you? That's all right, at least u didn't break anything.

But my pride. And my back.

Ouch. Ok, but it's nothing my muffins won't cure.

Holy hell. Was she flirting with him?

I'm going to savor every bite.

He wasn't sure if he'd been flirting, too. *Savor every bite.* The alcohol had still been running through his system, clearly messing up his head. Thank God Kate hadn't replied after that last one. But she'd sent a dozen muffins this morning and he had gobbled three up with barely a drink of coffee. His experience with Kate's food was almost sexual.

He couldn't help it; it had always been like this since the beginning.

The first time she'd made chocolate-chip cookies on her own, Garrett had been fresh out of bed on a Sunday in his randy teen years. He'd been scouring the kitchen for breakfast and had shoved a warm cookie into his mouth, nodding when she'd asked if it was good. Then Kate had laughingly stepped up and brushed a crumb from the side of his mouth, and he'd almost swallowed the cookie whole.

Sometimes he waited until he was alone to eat her stuff. And he imagined he was licking her fingers when he wrapped his tongue around her sugary frostings. And when they had little sprinkles, he pictured her freckles.

He really should look into therapy.

Suddenly he heard Landon sigh and slap his copy of the report shut, and he was jerked back to the present.

"So if your brother is still not aware of our plans," he asked Cassandra, "why are you chickening out on selling?" The chair creaked as he leaned back, folding his arms over his chest.

Cassandra Clarks may have had the appearance of a blonde bombshell, but behind that "bimbo" facade, Garrett had learned, there was actually a brain. The woman was not only smart, but about as flexible on her terms as a damned wall.

Today she exuded casual confidence, slowly shaking her head as Landon explained his position.

"We're supposed to keep buying the stock until we get over twenty percent," Landon told her. "In a week, two at most, your brother's company will be ours before he even realizes we're in bed with him. No pun intended."

"None taken," Cassandra said, eyeing Landon judiciously as she finally stopped shaking her head and allowed him to continue.

"Once we secure your remaining thirty-two percent, it puts us in control, and it leaves you a very wealthy woman, Cassie."

"That's the problem. My brother will know I sold to you. He will destroy me and anything else I have," she said, her entire countenance clouded with worry. "What I wanted to propose to Garrett on Saturday before he cut me short was a marriage of convenience. My brother has control of my stake in the company now, but if I marry, he won't have control over financial decisions regarding my stake anymore. My husband can take over the shares and compensate me discreetly. It would be an easy arrangement, and over in six months, where we'll both happily walk away with what we want. Me with my money, you with the stock."

Garrett remained silent as he absorbed the proposal.

He met Cassandra's gaze unflinchingly, the ambitious businessman in him wanting to say yes. But in his mind, he went back to waking up to Kate's scent on the pillow, to the memory of somehow holding her in his arms.

He tugged at the collar of his shirt several times, aware that his frown was pinching into his face. "I'm afraid that's not an option, Cassandra," he said, signaling for his assistant to refill all their coffees.

Hell, he might even start drinking whiskey at this hour. Because *marriage?*

"Like Landon said, we're willing to buy those shares up front. No need to get dramatic about it."

"I'm afraid selling out front is not an option. My brother is… You don't know him. Marriage is the only way I can free myself of his control. You take the shares, transfer the money to me, and then we walk six months later with irreconcilable differences. It's a marriage in name only and we have nothing to lose. That's the only way it's happening: you marry me and by right take my thirty-two percent."

Landon's and Garrett's eyes met across the conference table. Landon's gray gaze almost looked silver in his concern.

"Look, Cassandra," he started. "We're almost at twenty percent already. We'll buy your position outright at way above market price. At fifty-two percent, we'll be in control and can get your brother out of there. He won't have a say in the matter anymore."

She shook her head, her eyes tearing up. "You don't know him. He has a say in a lot of things in my life. I don't get real financial independence until I marry— can't you understand?"

She reached across the table and squeezed Garrett's hand as if she were falling from a precipice and he'd been appointed the task of hauling her up.

"It'll be a marriage in name only, but I can make it sweet for you. I can. I know I'm pretty. I think you're an incredibly sexy man."

His stomach turned, and he was amazed at how calmly he looked back at her. Several years ago, he'd probably have done it without thinking. He was a businessman, after all. She was an attractive woman offering something and he had nothing to lose. People got married and divorced for other reasons; why not for business?

He just didn't have the energy for it right now. What

he'd told Kate at his party had been the truth. All he wanted was for Kate to be home. He would dedicate every waking moment to making that happen. Life without Kate to him was…unimaginable.

He was selfish when it came to her.

He was stupid, unreasonable and stubborn when it came to her.

But Cassandra Clarks didn't know this. She didn't know that as he sat in this chair, and let her squeeze his hand, every cell in his body was burning with yearning for another woman. He'd burned for so many years, it was a miracle he hadn't turned to ashes by now.

"We'll talk about this during the week, see what we can come up with," Landon finally said. In silence, the Gage brothers both stood up to dismiss her.

Cassandra went over to shake Landon's hand, and then returned to Garrett, giving him a hug that crushed all of her assets against his chest. He could see she was trying very hard to look seductive, but he saw fear and frustration glowing in the depths of her eyes as she eased back.

Cassandra was blonde and beautiful, and she also appeared desperate. If Garrett had an ounce of mercy in him at all, he'd find a way to help her. "You'll let me know?" she asked hopefully.

He nodded. "You'll hear from us in a week or two."

"Marriage," Garrett grumbled as the door closed behind her. He fell back on his chair and rubbed his temples as he tried to think of a way they could free Cassandra from her brother's grip and get their hands on Clarks Communications.

"In name only," Landon said, gazing out the window with a thoughtful frown.

"I'm not interested in a fake marriage, Lan."

Landon sighed and spun around, coming back to the table. "Do you have any other ideas?"

Garrett lifted his shoulders. "We find another fish in the pond, let go of Clarks," he said bitterly, glaring down at his coffee.

The silence that followed made it clear that neither Landon nor he was ecstatic at the possibility. Clarks was the biggest fish in their pond, and if they were smart—which the Gage brothers were—they would secure it at all costs.

When evaluating the big picture, six months wasn't a lot of time, if it meant getting Clarks into their pocket. And Garrett had everything riding on this project. Currently, Clarks posed a threat. But once they'd acquired the company, it would be a huge asset for the Gage conglomerate.

But at the cost of a fake wedding?

Hell, it's not like you plan to ever marry. Why not at least do some business?

The two large doors of the conference room knocked open, and in strode Julian John, casual as could be, blond and Hollywoodesque, an hour after the scheduled meeting time. Behind him, one of the secretaries rushed to close the doors.

Jules never said good-morning, but then they were brothers. They didn't have to.

He regarded the pair of somber men seated at the conference table and remained standing. "I had something to do, so drop the long faces, both of you."

Landon arched a challenging brow and leaned back in his chair. "I hope it was business and not you play-

ing around while we try to take over Clarks Communications."

"Do you even remember I no longer work here? I'm
here to offer my assistance, that's all. Molls needed me
this morning."

"Tell Molly to leave the baby-making for the evening," said Landon with a devilish smile.

Heading to his chair, Julian rolled his eyes at his
brother. "I picked up some medicine for Kate, idiot, after
Molly took her to the doctor. And if I want to make babies in the morning with my Molls, I sure as hell will
make them without your permi—"

"What the hell is wrong with Kate? Is she sick?"

Julian's attention swung back to Garrett, and his
blond eyebrows flew upward. "Why? Are you a doctor?"

"Is Kate," Garrett slowly enunciated, "sick? Ill? Feeling badly?"

Julian's eyes twinkled like they did when he was up to
no good. "Don't you think it's about time you did something about how you feel for her, Dr. Garrett?"

"I feel responsible for her, that's how I feel," he gritted out. "And right now I'm going to punch your face if
you don't tell me what's wrong with her."

Plopping into his chair, Julian grabbed his folder and
started scanning the contents. "She's running a fever.
A high fever. Molly took her home to stay with her,
and I was the guy who picked up the prescription and
dropped it off."

Garrett's overwhelming protectiveness surged with
a vengeance. Kate was never sick. Ever. He didn't like
knowing she was sick at all, and now, he felt sick inside.
"I could've picked it up for her."

"And tear you away from Cassandra Clarks and our

plans for world domination?" Julian said. "No, bro. If that girl is selling anything, she'll sell it to you. I saw her with you at your party. I think she digs you even if you don't dig her."

"She digs him enough to marry him." Landon filled his brother in, then broached the topic currently setting Garrett's brain on overdrive. "Is Kate still planning to move to Miami?"

"As far as I know, nothing has changed her mind. But Molly's privately freaking out about it," Julian said, his expression going somber. Garrett knew his younger brother was intensely territorial and protective of Molly, and even if he was usually cool as a cucumber, it must irk him not to be able to do anything to spare her any pain.

"So is Beth," Landon murmured sadly.

Garrett looked down at the conference table and scowled. Nobody in this goddamned world could be as freaked out about it as he was.

He pictured Kate in Miami, sick and alone. Who would take her to the doctor? Who would even know that she was sick? The thought was so disturbing he pulled at his tie, feeling choked to death.

But as much as he loathed that she was sick today, maybe this would provide an opportunity to make Kate see how indispensable family that protected and cared for you was. Also, her stubbornness might be at a low point because of the fever, and he might be able to talk to her without putting her on the defensive.

"You guys don't mind if I take the rest of the day off? If there's even a chance of making her stay, I need to filter through her defenses and find out why the hell she wants to *leave*."

"You mean you want to bulldoze through her walls,

without any tact whatsoever, and screw everything?" Julian teased.

"Jules, I happen to think Kate is the one who's bulldozed through Garrett's defenses with her imminent departure," Landon said.

Both his brothers looked terribly amused.

Garrett shoved his arms into his jacket and grabbed his iPhone. "Screw you. You guys know how hotheaded Kate is when she gets something in her mind—at least today she won't have all the energy to fight me. Hell, you took two months off for your honeymoon, Landon, and you don't even work here anymore. Jules. I'm taking a day off, no matter what you both have to say."

Julian answered, with a laugh, "We have a lot to say about it, bro. We just won't be saying it to you."

"So I know you're going to find all sorts of things wrong with my stupid soup, but it's still chicken and broth and I'm not the baker here, okay, Kate?"

Molly set the tray with the steaming bowl on a chair by the window and parted the drapes.

Kate almost hissed as she raised her hand to shield herself from the sunlight.

"Wow. You look so bad, Kate."

Molly's blue eyes brimmed with sisterly pity as Kate sat up in bed and tried to peel her sweaty T-shirt off her skin. The cotton was soaked from when the fever had started dropping during her nap. Her hair was plastered to the sides of her face as if with glue.

"I feel worse than I look, I guarantee," Kate rasped out, her throat raw.

She had strep throat. Which meant she had nausea, a

throat that ached like hell and a fever that was kicking her fanny. *Wonderful*.

"Let me run a bath for you."

Molly disappeared into the bathroom, and Kate groaned when she heard the loud chime of the doorbell.

"I'll get that, Kate. Don't even move a finger. I'll be back in a bit. In the meantime, you can eat my sucky soup," Molly said, poking her head back into the bedroom. Kate smiled weakly and nodded.

As her little sister went down the hall to the front door, Kate marveled at how sharp and efficient she was being.

Molly had always been a red-hot mess, but today Kate truly felt Molly's motherly instincts surge to the forefront as she tried to pamper her big sis.

It was a rare event when Kate succumbed to being sick. She just didn't have time for it. What the hell was wrong with her?

The stress of her move had her sleepless and anxious and now, apparently, had left her with no defenses against strep.

Sighing and plopping back on her pillow, she heard voices in the living room. Then she heard footsteps approaching. Kate opened her eyes, and her stomach dropped when she saw him.

The last man she wanted to see.

Or to be more precise, the last man she wanted to see *her* like this.

She flew upright to a sitting position, her cheeks warming in an awful blush when Garrett stopped at the threshold. Her blood bubbled in her veins, and the feeling was unbidden and unwanted. He looked positively beautiful, his shoulders about a yard wide, his patterned tie slightly undone. His dark hair stood up on end as if he'd been pulling at it on his drive over.

He was honestly the most beautiful thing she'd seen all day.

She indulged in a small moment of grief as she realized that while he looked so excellent, she'd never looked worse.

"Did you lose your GPS? Your office is the other way," she said, merely because attitude was the only thing she had left now.

"I followed another compass today." A tender look warmed his eyes as he stepped inside and shut the door behind him.

He removed his jacket, and her pulse jumped at each flex of his muscles under his snowy shirt.

"How do you feel, Freckles?" He draped his jacket on the back of her desk chair and rolled his sleeves to his elbows. "We should've made you drink tequila Saturday. That would've killed anything off."

All the grogginess fled from her when he seized the tray with the soup and brought it to the bed.

"Molly suggests you eat her sucky soup."

Kate grimaced. "I'm not hungry, Garrett," she said in her slightly raspy strep-throat voice. "There's no need to check up on me."

He settled down on the edge of the bed and lifted the spoon, his eyes glimmering in pure devil-like mischief. "Starve the virus, feed the fever."

"And that means, Confucius…?"

"You need to feed your immune system. Come on. Open your mouth."

After a brief hesitation, she parted her lips and Garrett offered her the soup. Her stomach was warmed by the intent look on Garrett's face as she curled her lips around the spoon. He tipped it back, and she swallowed. Then he lowered the spoon, watching her.

"It's not that bad," she said. The soup slid down her throat and coated her sore spots. "But it's still a little too hot."

He immediately set the tray at the foot of the bed. "Molls said you're about to take a bath? Would you like to hop in there now?"

Before she could even nod, he disappeared into the bathroom, where she heard the water stop, and then he returned. He looked so sexy but at the same time, so domesticated; she almost felt giddy at all this sweet male attention.

"While you relax in your bath, I'll go get my laptop and briefcase, all right?" He signaled toward the window at his Audi parked outside. "Since she's having such success as an artist, I told Molly I'd stay here so she could go to her studio and finish up her pending works before the wedding."

"Wh-what? No! No! I don't need a babysitter!"

"Good because I didn't hire one." The smile he shot her was rather wolfish, and he looked very damned pleased about himself. "It's just you and me now. I can see you're excited about it."

"As I am about having strep!" she countered.

He burst out laughing, and once again she felt things she didn't really want to feel. Kate was going to kill her sister. Kill her. But of course Molly must've been thrilled about this turn of events. She kept insisting that Kate should stay in town until some miracle happened and Kate and Garrett finally became an item. *Ha.* She was clearly still such an innocent.

And right now, especially, not even a miracle would make someone want Kate. Only a thing called strep throat wanted her.

And just then, she remembered the exquisite feel of Garrett, big and warm, in bed with her Saturday night.

As the thought rushed through her, Kate ducked her head to hide her blush, never wanting Garrett to know the effect he had on her. On the night of his birthday, she'd been so angry and frustrated. She'd felt all kinds of unwanted arousal while he'd slept soundly next to her. So she'd promised herself she would get over him. And she would. No matter what. She merely wished that he, of all the men in the world, hadn't seen her in this state.

"You want help getting to the tub?" He gestured toward the bathroom. She was still in bed, holding the sheets to the top of her neck like a shield.

"I can walk," she answered the moment she realized how silly she must look. Frowning in annoyance at her own prudish attitude, she kicked the sheets aside, then realized that her T-shirt had ridden up to her hips. As she struggled out of bed, Garrett got a perfect view of her pink panties.

He whipped his eyes away, but not before she saw that he *saw*. Her pink panties. And her toned thighs.

Garrett's face hardened instantly, and he rubbed the nape of his neck as Kate felt a red-hot flush creep up her body.

"So, you have strep?" he asked, looking away quickly.

"It's very contagious. You should leave." In fact, she'd probably even had it incubating when he'd slept in her bed the other night. The thought of giving him strep made her insides twist in foreboding. "You should really leave, Garrett."

"I'll leave when your fever's gone, Katie."

Groaning in disgust at his stubbornness, she went into the bathroom and locked the door behind her. Oddly, she felt acutely aware of her nakedness when she stripped. Aware, also, of only one measly door separating her from him.

After double-checking the lock, she settled in the tub. The water felt so warm. She closed her eyes and sighed as she dunked her head and slowly surfaced, starting to relax.

As the minutes passed, she couldn't stop wondering what Garrett was doing out in her room. She definitely heard noises, and she figured he must be setting up a miniature office. The thought both annoyed her and… didn't. He looked extremely good today. But she couldn't help but wonder what the purpose of this sudden attention was. Of course something sneaky was going on. She had no doubt this all had to do with her leaving for Florida—and Garrett intending to convince her not to.

No way are you going to stop me, Garrett Gage.

She scowled at the thought. She hadn't even had boyfriends because of him. Directly or indirectly, he'd been responsible for Kate waiting to lose her virginity until she was over twenty-one and then she'd lost it to someone she didn't even like all that much. Even then, though, she'd kept expecting him to one day realize they were meant for each other. Now she was determined to stop waiting for anything Garrett-related.

Fiercely resolved, she came out minutes later, wrapped in a towel, bathed, refreshed and wet.

She found, not to her surprise, that Garrett was already settled in her room. He lounged back in a chair with his laptop open on her small desk before him. He'd also turned the chair so that it was facing the bed, rather than the window. He looked as out of place in her feminine bedroom as a bear would.

He glanced up when she padded barefoot toward her dresser, and an irresistibly devastating grin appeared on his face. "You already look better."

"Actually, I feel tons better." Clutching the towel to her chest, she rummaged through her drawers and was about to try to get dressed under the towel when she remembered to say, "Look away for a second, please."

As she selected her new panties, purple this time, she asked, "Are you looking away?"

"What do you think, Kate?" he asked, annoyed.

She took that as a yes and quickly let the towel drop and slipped into her panties. Even though he was looking away, her cheeks flushed red at the thought of him being so close when she was naked. She quickly slipped on her bra, still feeling hot inside, but then she realized he would probably be as moved by her nakedness as a sofa. The man was completely immune to her.

Then again, her butt was quite nice thanks to her Pilates classes. As she was thinking these thoughts and smoothing her panties over the curves in question, a strange silence settled in the room.

Garrett's voice was deceptively calm when she reached into her drawer again.

"Did you really think I'd look away, Kate?"

Kate's stomach clenched, but she went about the task of selecting a T-shirt.

And now she could feel his eyes were definitely on her.

Boring holes into her bottom, actually.

And suddenly she really prayed that it was, indeed, a very nice bottom.

"Please don't tell me you were looking," she threatened, starting to panic. She broke out into a fresh sweat as the fever continued dropping after her bath.

As she grabbed a T-shirt with a Minnie Mouse image on the front and pulled it on, she heard a deep male groan.

"Freckles, I'm not made of stone you know."

Garrett sounded grumpy, as if he was in danger of getting strep, too.

"Really? I thought you were." Instead of being embarrassed, she was suddenly amused as she pulled the T-shirt as low as possible and turned around. But her smile froze on her face.

Garrett sat like a marble statue on the chair, his muscled arms crossed, his forearms corded with veins, his lips hard and completely unsmiling. His face was harsh with intensity, and his eyes were the blackest she'd ever seen them. There was such an unearthly sheen in them, Kate stopped breathing.

They stared at each other for a heart-stopping moment, and the atmosphere seemed to morph, becoming heavy and thick with something inexplicable. There was a deeper significance to their stare that she couldn't quite pinpoint, but it felt like a delicate thread between them was pulling tight.

It hurt. This strange link. It felt threatening.

It hurt, and ached in all kinds of places inside her.

Garrett put his forehead in his hand for a moment, then sighed and ran a big, tanned hand down his face in pure frustration. "Look, Katie."

"Look, Garrett, you need to stop this now."

"Stop what?"

They stared once more, and the atmosphere in the room continued feeling heavy and odd. Kate's nerves could barely handle it.

"I know what you're trying to do, and it's not going to work," she finally said.

His eyes remained almost predatory in their intensity. Finally he raised one sleek black eyebrow. "My plot to save the world, to keep Kate in Texas, won't work, even if I put in some good hours of doctoring time?"

"It won't work."

"So you didn't mean it the night of my birthday when you said that we would talk about it later?"

"We'd both been drinking. Whatever we said that night was the alcohol talking."

"All right, so today the strep is talking. When is Kate going to talk to me?"

"I'm talking to you now."

His eyebrows fell low over his eyes. His shirt stretched over his square shoulders as he sat back, his muscled arms still crossed over his chest. "Then tell me if you're leaving because of a man. First. And second, you're going to tell me who."

"Ha. This is my house. I run it. So I say who has firsts and seconds here, not you."

She bent to put on some socks. A rivulet of water slid along her toned legs, and when she straightened, she saw his eyes had darkened even more. He continued to stare at her legs for a wildly erotic moment.

Her pulse jumped at the thought of him touching her—of him even *wanting* to touch her—and her hands trembled as she bent her head and slowly wrapped the discarded towel around her wet hair.

When she straightened, Garrett's expression had turned bleak as a funeral, and he pushed to his feet, stalking over like a pissed-off predator. "What do you need so you can get back in the damned bed, Kate?"

"I don't want to get into bed. I've been there all day. My fever is dropping and I'm sweating. I feel hot."

"Then put something on, would you!" He signaled at her long legs, and a wash of feminine awareness swept through her when his eyes raked her up and down as if he couldn't help himself.

She laughed nervously and glanced away so that he wouldn't notice his effect on her; then she hopped into a comfortable pair of white cotton shorts she used for yoga sometimes.

Garrett seemed completely disturbed and grumpy... but more than that, he seemed alert. Did this mean she'd finally gotten past one of Garrett's walls?

She almost laughed. She'd always tried many subtle ways to get his male attention. Who would have thought she just needed to do a little striptease?

It's too late, Kate. You don't want him anymore. You want a new start—without him.

Turning in sudden annoyance, she shoved at his chest so he stepped out of her personal space. "Just go home, Garrett. You don't have to do this. Aren't you working on that big deal all your brothers are talking about?"

He looked agitated and started pacing around, scowling down at the carpet. "There's nothing I can do about it today. We're ironing out the details."

"Well, go iron them out somewhere else."

"On the bed, Freckles! Unless you like your soup cold!"

With a complaining sound, Kate plopped down on the

bed and crossed her legs under her body. He expelled a breath, as if finally appeased; he was just so handsome her heart ached. She propped her head back on the headboard as he brought back the tray, and she quietly studied him as he fed her.

Garrett Gage was one of the least emotionally accessible men Kate had ever met, and to see him do something so honestly sweet for her triggered a wealth of unreasonable emotions in her chest.

She didn't want to feel giddy and protected and cared for. But she did. She felt safe. And fiercely achy for so much more. His dark espresso eyes wouldn't stop watching her mouth as he guided the spoon inside, and out, and it made every time she wrapped her lips around the spoon unbearably...intimate.

Suddenly all she could hear was the sound of their breathing in the bedroom. Hers was not all that steady. His was inexplicably slow and deep, his chest extending slowly under his shirt as those dark, thick-lashed, half-mast eyes remained on her face.

"Poor Jules. I swear Molly doesn't cook for anything," Kate whispered, anxious to break the silence.

Now that she was able to taste the soup better, she definitely knew her little sister could use a little cooking advice from her.

Garrett chuckled. The sound was rich and male as he set down the spoon. "He's in love with her, Katie. She can feed him cotton balls and he'll be content."

"I love how they love each other."

Suddenly feeling drained, she shook her head when Garrett offered more soup. She slid down the bed a little so that the back of her head could rest on her pillow.

The thought of Julian and Molly made the ache in her chest multiply tenfold.

"They're not afraid to," she added.

Garrett didn't respond. He merely set the tray aside and turned thoughtfully back to her. "I wouldn't let fear keep me from someone," he said then, his voice a low murmur.

"No? Then what would?"

His powerful shoulders lifted in a noncommittal shrug, and then he said, "If you love someone, you want what's best for them. Even if it means it's not you."

Something in his words caused a little ribbon of pain to unravel within her. Had he ever felt anything for her, and thought that he wasn't good enough for her?

No. How could he not be good enough for anyone? He was honorable and dedicated, fiercely passionate about those he loved, as protective as an angry panther.

"Garrett, you don't have to stay. I know you told Molly you would but I'd rather you go," she said, getting sleepier by the second. "The antibiotics and steroids make me dizzy anyway, so I'll probably sleep all afternoon. And if you stay here I'm going to give you strep."

The tenderness that liquefied his gaze suddenly made her feel even more soft and languid. "You're not giving me anything. Relax and I'll be here when you wake up."

His voice was so soothing and gentle she couldn't help but nod and close her eyes. As she heard him take the tray to the kitchen, she snuggled into her pillow, her stomach warmed with Molly's sucky soup, which, even if tasteless, had served its purpose well. Ever since Molly had moved in with Julian, the house had seemed so quiet. Just knowing Garrett was around right now made her feel safe and protected.

The steroids were kicking in as well as the antibiotics, and her fever seemed to be breaking.

New beads of perspiration popped onto her brow, and a new, unexpected heaviness settled in her chest as she thought of her move to Florida and how she wouldn't see Garrett and Molly and all her loved ones as frequently as she did now.

She sighed when she felt something cool and damp slide along her forehead. Her pulse skittered when she realized Garrett was stroking her face with a cool towel, and she felt out of breath as she murmured, "That feels good."

He dragged the damp cloth along her cheek, and the cool mist on her skin made her nipples bead under her T-shirt. His voice was low and sensually hypnotic. "So of all the states, why Florida?" He ran the towel along the length of her bare arms, and her nipples turned hard as stones.

With a delicious shiver, she sighed and leaned her cheek to her right, into his chest. "Some of my college friends live in Miami Beach. And I'm a sun person."

She hadn't realized she was grabbing onto his arm, but she knew that she didn't want to let go. He smelled so good and felt warm and substantial, so she kept her arms curled around his elbow. God, she'd done the impossible to get this man to notice her. The impossible. She'd dated men she hadn't even liked. She'd said she'd marry other men. Ignored Garrett and paid attention to everyone else. It had made him scowl, but that had been the whole extent of his reactions to her efforts.

It had been infuriating and disheartening.

He really did see her as some sort of friendly sister, while Kate had fantasized about him for decades. She

hated that she never could really enjoy sex with her partners because a part of her heart had always belonged to
this man.

This man who now caressed her neck with that cloth,
and made her new purple panties damp with wanting.
Even if she'd convinced herself she didn't love him anymore, her body was still hazardously attracted to his.
Hell, if she weren't sick, she would open her eyes and
kiss him even if he didn't want her to. She'd just go crazy
and kiss him, because that was the only thing she'd never
tried, of all the crazy stunts she'd pulled to get him to
notice her. She had his attention with Florida. But this
was no longer a stunt.

She had to leave. And she had to leave now.

So that when she came for a visit, she would have a
new life, a steady boyfriend and an equally great catering business in Miami, and when she saw Garrett, she
would see what she had been meant to see all along. A
friend and a brother figure.

"Do you want me to bring my laptop here?" he whispered in her ear, his voice strangely husky. "Kate?"

She nodded, not opening her eyes as she released
him and waited, with a new kind of fever, for him to
come back.

Garrett was hard as granite and hated that he was,
but he was trying his damnedest to ignore it as he set
his laptop on the nightstand. He kept the computer shut,
and instead kicked off his shoes and plopped down on
the bed next to Kate, stretching his legs out as he put his
arm around her shoulders, sensing her need for comfort.

She'd been holding his arm so hard, he hadn't wanted
to move.

Hell, his back had gone stiff as a board as soon as her fingers had curled around him. He'd desperately wanted her touch and at the same time, he'd been distressed over the way his body responded to it. In the end, he'd wanted it more than he'd disliked it, and he'd come back. For more. Like a needy dog wanting a bone.

When she'd been getting dressed, he had thought he'd have a heart attack at the sight of that beautiful bare bottom. Kate was willowy and slim, and her wet hair had so temptingly caressed her shoulders. In a fraction of a second, he'd visualized about a dozen things he wanted to do to her, a dozen ways he wanted to kiss and feel her.

Now she was cuddling against his side, with that cute little T-shirt, and that soft, almost dreamlike smile on her lips.

He put his arm around her shoulders, and she sighed in contentment and snuggled into his chest, clutching a piece of his collar. The gesture was so possessive and sweet his chest knotted with emotion as he set his head back on the headboard and held her to him.

What would it be like to marry someone like Kate? Someone he cared for. He wanted. Not for any other purpose but because he needed her by his side.

Flooded with tenderness, he felt her squirm to get closer, and her T-shirt rode up to reveal…those purple panties that made his mouth water.

Just give me something to think about other than those long legs. Those sweet purple panties…

Her hair was still wrapped in a white towel, and Garrett gently unwound it and ran it slowly over her scalp, seeing her lashes resting on her cheekbones as she let him dry her hair, her skin pale in the sunlight.

He wanted to kiss those soft lips, which were natu-

ral and bare today, peachy in color. He wanted to slide
his hands up her arms, touch her bare skin and memorize its texture, its color, its temperature. He wanted her
eyelashes to flutter apart, so he could stare into her eyes
and say something about the things roiling inside of him.

Instead, he finished drying her hair and tossed the
towel onto the chair by the window. He shifted back
to her side, noticing how she stiffened and tightened
her hold on his collar until he wrapped his arm tightly
around her again, and she relaxed.

He yanked off his tie and set it on the nightstand,
and then wrapped his other arm around her waist and
set his jaw on the top of her head. Her hair smelled of
raspberries. He'd wanted to know? Yeah. He had his
answer. And now his blood heated with one whiff. He
grabbed the bed sheet and pulled it up over them both,
not wanting her to notice his painfully pulsing erection
if she opened her eyes.

She sighed and turned to him, snuggling closer. Her
breasts brushed his ribs, and his body went crazy. He
dragged his fingers down her shoulder and to her waist
and stroked the little bit of skin exposed from her raised
T-shirt.

He kissed her forehead. She didn't stir. Sweet baby,
she looked so vulnerable today. He knew she was strong,
but he still wanted to coddle her. He looked at her lips
and ran a hand down her damp hair. He'd never wanted
anything more than to make this woman happy. And
right now, he wanted to kiss her.

"You awake, Kate?" he asked, his voice barely rec-
ognizable, it was so gruff.

She was breathing evenly, which confirmed she'd
fallen asleep. Garrett slid his hand up and down her

arm, his heart pounding. He bent his head and kissed her freckles, a light, dry kiss, and then he stole a kiss from her soft, marshmallow mouth.

Intoxicating. Soft. Female. *Perfect.*

Coming undone, he drank in her expression. Her eyes remained shut, her lashes forming titian-colored half-moons against her cheekbones.

He stroked the back of one finger down her jaw. She was everything he'd wanted and never allowed himself to have, and she was breathing like a baby, sleeping like one. He heard his own haggard exhale as he tried to draw back. He bent down again, softly brushing his lips over her forehead, then her nose, her cheekbones, her jaw…until he fitted his mouth back over her lips and whispered, "Kate."

She remained asleep, but sighed at her name and opened her mouth under his, her breath blending with his. Desire exploded in the pit of his stomach. The urge to splay his body over hers, open her lips wider, search her tongue with his, bury himself inside her, was so acute, he had to drag his jaw up her temple as he fought for control, completely infuriated with himself.

What was he doing?

Since when had he become a masochist?

He'd always known he couldn't have Kate. He'd done everything in his power to stay away from her. He'd hurt her enough, and he didn't truly feel he could ever make a woman happy when he had so many regrets on his shoulders.

It was hard to believe you were ever worthy when someone had died to give you your life.

But the thought of Kate leaving had set a beast loose inside him. He wanted to protect her and look after her, and just imagining that she could meet a man in Florida, a man she could have powerful feelings for, made him feel rabid to stake a claim.

Even now, when there were no states separating them and he was holding her snug in his arms, it just didn't seem like he could get close enough to her. He'd spent years pushing her away, and now it felt like she wouldn't ever let him back in.

And if she did, he didn't even know what he'd do with himself or this wanting.

Four

More than a week later, Kate's wood-paneled kitchen was a mess of cooking utensils as she, Beth and Molly fiddled around on the kitchen island. Kate and Beth had a looming deadline to cater a baby shower this afternoon. Worse, now only Beth would be going to set up, since Kate had had a last-minute change of plans.

Molly had been the one to deliver the plan-altering news less than an hour ago, when she'd casually mentioned that Julian had been asked to fill in for Garrett at the *San Antonio Daily* this morning. Garrett had come down with strep.

Kate had been floored. How could she not go and take care of him?

"You love that man like crazy, Kay. Just look at how you're running to his side at the first sign of trouble! I just can't see why you're so determined to leave Texas,"

Molly complained as she licked the remaining vanilla topping off a discarded spatula. Her cheek was smeared with a streak of red.

Since she was an artist, Kate's little sister always had smudges on her clothes, hair or face, but it only enhanced her bohemian style and made her look even cuter—especially to Julian, who would always tickle and poke her whenever she was "messy."

"You know, I thought you guys would bond over your strep throat," Molly continued with a frown. "You still could now that you gave it to him. Did he kiss you?"

Kate clicked the oven light on and peered through the window to check on Garrett's muffins. "Molly, please start supporting me a little more in my decision. I've told you I'll fly over here to see you as much as I can. We can talk on Skype all the time, too. And of course we didn't kiss. I'm not stupid! Who kisses a sick person?" Kate said in disgust.

"Someone who loves them."

She snorted. "We're not you and Julian."

"Kate, the day Julian and I got back together, he and Garrett had a talk. Julian tells me that the man is severely and painfully in love with you and doesn't even know it."

Kate's heart stuttered, and at that moment, her chest felt as spongy as the muffins she was watching through the oven window. She remembered the way Garrett had taken care of her the day she'd come home with strep.

He'd checked in on her every afternoon afterward, but that first day, he'd spent the night with her. A quiver raced down her skin when she remembered how they'd cuddled all night. He'd stayed dressed, like he had when he'd been drunk and crashed in her bedroom the night of his birthday, but he'd held her as if she was precious.

When she'd woken up in the middle of the night to realize he was holding her, she had been engulfed with such a feeling of happiness beyond what she'd ever felt before. On impulse, she'd stroked her fingers along his stubbled jaw, and he'd made a strange, groaning noise as he'd turned his face into her touch, his voice deliciously groggy. "You feel all right? Do you need anything?"

"Sorry. I'm perfect. Go to sleep."

She'd cuddled back down to hear his heart beat under her ear, and she'd wanted to stay awake just to memorize its rhythm. She'd never, ever, felt so whole. Which only made her feel sorry for herself now. Because they hadn't even kissed. Had he made her melt over some snuggles?

It wasn't just the snuggling. It was also that they'd known each other for so long they didn't even need to talk. When she'd woken up, he'd been awake and watching her with a smile on his handsome face, and his eyes had seemed to turn liquid as he'd run a finger down her cheek. "Fever's gone," he'd whispered.

And she'd almost swallowed her tongue and nodded. Because she'd known there was nothing she could do for the other kind of fever inside her. She'd had to remind herself that this was Garrett, a very stubborn, hardheaded Gage man, and that he wasn't her lover or a Prince Charming. Garrett had some serious baggage to deal with, and Kate had once loved him—too hard, and for too long, and too painfully—to allow so much as a little flicker of hope to linger.

Julian might think that Garrett had feelings for Kate, but all he surely felt was the same thing he'd always felt. Guilt and responsibility.

Beth spoke up from her corner of the island, where she busily worked her artistic skills on a tray of cookies for the shower. "You're shaking your head at me now, Kate, but now that I think about it, I also suspect Garrett has always had a thing for you."

"No, he doesn't. And I'm sick and tired of chasing after him like some tramp," Kate countered as she dumped the egg shells in the trash and wiped the granite counter clean.

Molly laughed. "Kate, you've never chased after Garrett, at least not blatantly. Men are sometimes stupid about those things—you need to be frank with them."

Frank?

All right, so let's be frank.

Kate had stripped in front of him. She had almost kissed him in her bed when he'd dragged that cool cloth around her body. Hell, she was pretty sure if she hadn't been sick, she would have thrown herself at him. And she'd done this with her plane ticket to Florida already sitting in her night drawer. That just couldn't be good. Could it?

She'd lain there with her eyes closed as he ran that cloth over her, and she'd been shaking in her bones as she'd imagined what it would feel like to be kissed by him. She'd even had dreams about it all during the week. Heat had spread through her at one particularly erotic one, when she'd felt him touch her aching nipples, then kiss them....

That night in her bed, she'd wanted to dissolve into his strong arms when he'd held her, and when he'd dried her hair, she'd been so affected and felt such desire pool between her thighs, she'd almost released an embarrassing sound that only her raw throat—abused by the strep—had been able to stop.

No. If she stayed here, she wouldn't be able to stay

away from Garrett, and seeing him while not having him would be torment. It had always been so, but after the night of his birthday, when he'd cradled her face and tried to tell her he'd do anything to fix her "dilemma," and after he'd nursed her when she was sick, it felt doubly so.

It.

Hurt.

The man might not love her as his mate, but he cared about her, and Kate knew this was exactly why she'd never be able to ever come clean with her feelings. He'd either feel awful about not responding, or feel pity for her and do something gallant like keep on sacrificing himself for her to make up for what he "took."

She. Had. To. Leave!

And start fresh, without Garrett's shadow tormenting and taunting her.

She knew it would be difficult. But she still had to leave. She had to give herself the chance, and Garrett his freedom.

Thinking about him, sick and bedridden today, made her stomach knot as she put on a floral-print oven mitt and bent over to pull the tray of muffins out of the oven. She'd made this particular recipe because it had lately become her favorite. The muffins were healthy and yummy, made of almond flour, with orange zest and black currants and walnuts. She set them on the cooling grill and prepared a small basket while the chicken soup finished.

"Food. That's how you guys make love, I swear. Those sounds he makes when he eats your cookies."

"Whoa!" Beth said from the corner, where she was now adding the decorations to the pacifier-shaped chocolate lollipops. "You're getting wicked, Molls!"

Molly laughed, fairly radiating mischief.

Beth laughed and shook her head, but then turned sober as she watched Kate stir the chicken soup. "Kate, it's not a bad idea. If you're taking that over to his apartment, you could totally seduce him. I mean, clearly the man wants you. Every time you're not looking, he's staring in your direction. Maybe if you guys work it out, you wouldn't be so determined to leave?"

"You're confusing him with Landon looking at you, Beth," Kate countered, turning off the stove. "Plus, I won't begin with the way Julian looks at you, Molly— oh, Lord, that man loves you."

"Does he?" Molly said with a cheeky grin, twirling the tip of her ponytail in one finger. "I don't ever tire of him telling me he does. God, I can't wait to marry him and make him all mine."

Looking thoughtful, Beth followed Kate to the cupboard as she pulled out a glass container.

"Kate, if Garrett didn't want you he wouldn't spend all day taking care of you when you look like leftovers."

Kate rolled her eyes. "Thanks, Beth. With friends like you, who needs an enemy?"

"Kate! Come on, listen to us. We're dishing out good advice here."

"Even if he *'wanted me'* for one crazy night and I managed to get him to drop his guard," Kate said, facing them, "I want love. If I can't have what you guys have, I'd rather be alone."

Molly sighed. For the first time since her Florida announcement, Kate could tell that the possibility of her moving to another state was truly sinking in. It hurt, too. To hurt them. She knew they didn't want her to leave, but she also knew that deep down, they understood.

"I still think you could find love here in Texas." Despite her words, Molly sounded more dejected now. "Garrett would make a *great* husband once he realizes everything that happened is *not his fault*."

"Molly, please, I can't talk about this anymore. I don't love him anymore, and he's not interested in me. When will you guys understand? Garrett always gets what he wants. He's not a subtle man. If he wanted me, don't you think he'd go for me?"

When Beth and Molly exchanged sad looks and fell silent, Kate's stomach sank. Well, what had she expected? Had she wanted one of them to lie and contradict her? Maybe so, but the truth was the truth, and they couldn't change it.

Molly attempted to lighten up the suddenly somber ambience. "I still think it's sweet, you going over with soup and muffins."

"Well, he's obviously sick because of me. I have to repay the favor. I was thinking of doing something nice for him to say thank-you for taking care of me, anyway."

For holding me and watching my fever break and just making me feel like he cares at least a little bit.

Even if the devil's ultimate plan had probably been to remove Miami from Kate's agenda.

She sighed as she glanced at the muffins. Without further hesitation, she put them in a small basket, then poured the soup in a large glass container. This might be the last time in her life she nursed Garrett back to health, so she had to make it count.

The doorman recognized Kate as she walked into the marble lobby with her goodies in her arms. She told him that she was here to drop the stuff off for Garrett, and he allowed her to go up to the penthouse.

Trying not to make noise, she entered the palatial bachelor pad. It was simple and modern, with dark leather furniture with chrome accents, glass tables and dark walnut flooring. But what she most loved was the stainless-steel, state-of-the-art kitchen. It almost seemed to be merely decorative, since she knew Garrett rarely ate at home, but it was still worthy of a five-star restaurant.

Heating up the hot drawer, Kate slid the chicken soup container inside, and then set the muffins on a covered cake stand. Satisfied with her work, she resisted the urge to go primp herself, but did take a peek at her appearance in the mirror over the entry console.

She looked…quite nice, actually.

Now that she was no longer sick, the color had returned to her cheeks. Her eyes had a nice shine, as though she were excited about something, and the soft cotton sundress with blue-and-white stripes almost made it seem like she was ready for the beach. She'd bought it specifically with Florida in mind, but, oh well, today she'd felt like wearing something he hadn't seen her in before.

And she wasn't even going to dwell on her reasoning either.

It was only that he'd looked extra good when he'd come to see her and she'd felt and looked like crapola, and now she wanted him to…well, to think she looked like a fresh piece of sunshine.

"Garrett?" She called his name softly down the hall, her stomach turning leaden at each tentative footstep she took toward his bedroom. She didn't know what she'd do if she found him in bed with someone. Nothing, probably, but she would definitely cry about it later.

She knew he slept with women. A man like him had his choice of girls all the time. But Garrett had always been discreet about it and he'd never really paraded a lot of women in front of Kate. She couldn't begin to imagine how much it would hurt if she saw him kissing someone, or lying in bed with someone, or putting his arm around someone....

She paused at his open bedroom door, holding her breath. The drapes were wide open, letting the sun inside. His bedroom was done in different shades of gray and black, the nightstands made of ebony wood with chrome accessories. It was all so manly, she couldn't imagine any design more fitting to Garrett's dark good looks.

Something warm flitted through her when she spotted his prone figure on the bed. Her heart almost stopped when she realized he was only wearing a pair of black boxer briefs, the rest of his body covered in his natural golden tan and nothing else. Suddenly he looked very large, very dark and very powerful.

"Garrett?"

He stiffened almost imperceptibly, but Kate couldn't miss the tensing of the muscles in his back. "I'm going to kill my mother," he growled into his folded arm.

"She didn't tell me. Molly did."

"Then I'm going to kill Julian."

He rolled to his side and pulled the satiny gray bedspread up to his waist.

It was hard not to notice how beautiful his muscled torso was, and how sexy he looked with his dark hair all rumpled.

It was also hard not to notice his scowl.

Kate bit back a smile and stepped in with her arms up in feigned innocence. "Me. Come. In. Peace. Bring food. For. Grumpy. Man. May I pass?"

"Freckles, get away or you will get strep again."

"I will not."

"Get out of here, Katie."

She shook her head. "Katie. No. Understand. What. Grumpy. Man. Says."

"Grumpy man says *leave,*" Garrett said, but all of Kate's maternal instincts had flared to life with just one look at him, and she couldn't suppress the need to coddle this man like she had when they were younger and she'd helped Eleanor take care of him.

She kicked off her shoes, and before thinking about it, jumped onto the bed next to him, taking care not to touch any part of his body. "You're not the only bed crasher, you know. I have full authority to crash your bed now that you've crashed mine twice."

He sighed and closed his eyes, banging his head on the headboard. "Get out of my bed."

"Not until you let me feed you. Starve the virus, feed the fever? Sound familiar? My part-time doc told it to me."

"Docs are renowned for failing to take their own advice."

"This one is special. Hey, have they medicated you?"

"I'm already drugged as hell. I don't want to eat, Freckles. Just get out of here."

Now Kate scowled, too.

"Garrett, why won't you look at me? Are you in pain? You look like you are."

"Yeah, I'm in pain."

"What is it? Is it your head?" She felt his forehead and he was definitely hot. And she noticed he'd stiffened.

"Don't," he murmured, seizing her wrist and returning her hand to her lap.

Eyes widening at the lines of agony carved in his face, she curled her fingers into her palm because they tingled after his touch.

He inhaled long and deep before his lids finally lifted open, and her heart melted when he looked at her with that dark, tired gaze. His glassy look killed her, but something there, something she couldn't decipher, made her stomach constrict. His pupils were fully dilated and his eyes held a strange awareness.

"Please just leave," he said, and there was something very desperate in his voice that almost made her hesitate.

"Come here, Garrett." She slid closer until her back was against the gray suede headboard, and she urged his dark head to rest against her chest and ran her fingers through his hair. "If you don't want to eat, just let me keep you company."

He groaned on contact, and wrapped his arms around her waist. "Kate, I don't have the energy to do this with you today."

"This what? I'm not planning to fight you."

"This… Damn." He made another deep noise when she lightly massaged his scalp. As her fingers twined in his hair and he pressed closer and tightened his hold around her, her body experienced all sorts of chemical reactions. He was adorable. She wanted to hug him. To tuck him into her suitcase and take him with her.

Crazy girl. The point was to get away from him, wasn't it?

She continued caressing his hair until he relaxed

against her, and her body also turned mushy. When his voice reached her ears minutes later, she started, for she'd almost been falling asleep with him.

"You used to bring me soup when I was sick." He spoke in a murmur against her chest, and his warm breath slipped seductively into her cleavage. "I liked getting sick because of you."

She laughed. "You're a very troubled man, Garrett."

"I was a very troubled young boy."

He angled his face so he could peer up at her, then raised his hand and absently ran his thumb down the bridge of her nose. "And you? You weren't Little Miss Perfect. When you heard the thunder and lightning and that huge storm one night, you lost your marbles completely. Do you remember?"

She dropped her hands as he sat up.

"I'm not sure, since I lose my marbles with all the storms."

"The one that made both you girls run into the boys' room. Before we knew it, Molly had jumped into Julian's bed and you were in mine. But Jules tried to hide her under the covers, and you and I immediately went all around the house looking for Molly, thinking she was somewhere else."

"Okay. Now I remember."

He sat back with his temple propped against the headboard, his eyes suddenly warm with the memory. "You and I ended up splitting up to find Molly, and I found you asleep in the living room after I found out Julian had hijacked her and was hiding her in his bed. Do you remember what you said?"

Kate was so riveted by his retelling, by the way his

smile flashed as he remembered, she'd lost all power of speech. He looked...happy. And also sad?

And devastating.

When she didn't answer, he tipped her head back by the chin, and his voice acquired a strange note. It was deeper. Especially with that strep-throat rasp. "You asked me why I hadn't hijacked you, too."

A strange tingle was growing in the pit of Kate's stomach, and she couldn't stop it, couldn't control it.

"I was probably more asleep than awake."

The atmosphere around them felt heavy with something unnameable and untamable. She became fiercely aware of every point of contact of their bodies. Her knee against his thigh. Her shoulder against the side of his arm.

"Do you want me to hijack you now, Kate?"

Her stomach tightened at the question. "What do you mean?" She narrowed her eyes and told herself his husky tone was due to the strep throat, but it was too thick, too heavy, as heavy as those coal-black eyes.

He cupped her cheek in one huge, dry palm. "You always took care of Molly until she found Julian. You always put her first, before anything else. Didn't you?"

When Kate could only nod, he continued.

"This is how I am with you, Kate. It's instinctive in me. Putting you first. I'd never take advantage of you, that's my number-one priority. But if I knew you might want something from me, I would like to give it to you. So..."

Suddenly he looked as hungry as he did when he ate her food.

"Do you want me to hijack you?" he asked. "Want

me to come after you? Is that why you're leaving for Florida? Do you want me to give chase?"

His stare was so piercing and primal, he didn't look weak or sick at all.

He looked predatory and male, and she felt fragile and female. Inside her, a dozen words rippled with the need to come forth.

I want you. Please give me your love. Yourself.

But how could she tie him up this way? Was this really the answer he wanted? Or was he seeking for her to appease him by saying that she didn't need anything else from him? He'd given her so much already. For his whole life.

A sound of protest tore from her chest, and it sounded so sexual, Kate swallowed it back in horror.

He smiled slowly, almost seductively, as his thumb trailed down the curve of her jaw. "Cat got your tongue?"

Kate couldn't think. Speak. Breathe.

His thumb went lower, and now slowly brushed over the sleeve of her dress. Then it trailed down her bare arm, the touch a shivery, silken whisper that made her insides quiver with yearning. Her heart galloped as pure need kicked in. His other fingers joined his thumb to caress the inside of her left arm, and her skin broke out in goose bumps as her lungs strained for air.

Garrett was quiet as he watched her reactions. She realized she hadn't pulled away from his touch, but instead had leaned closer.

He slid the fingers of his other hand into her hair, softly tangling them inside the loose mass. He watched her with somber expectation, as though wondering if she would stop him.

She didn't.

Oh, why didn't she?

What on earth was he doing?

What was she doing?

Intense sexual thoughts began to flicker through her mind. Garrett's lips, his beautiful body naked against hers...

Their gazes held, both of them silent, their eyes almost questioning but also on fire with desire. His breath, slow and deep and slightly uneven, bathed her face.

Suddenly, he tugged her dress up her thighs and then slid his hand under the fabric, up her panty-clad bottom, then up her back, his fingers slowly tracing the little dents of her spine.

Kate sucked in a mouthful of air.

She probably should stop him. She probably should. Instead, she trembled and bent to brush a kiss across his lightly stubbled jaw. Then she drew back and noticed that his eyes were closed, his face almost in an expression of pain. She cupped his jaw and kissed his forehead, her insides melting when he groaned, encouraging her, so that she kissed the tip of his nose.

His hands were suddenly on her hips. Pushing her away? No. He drew her over his lap, guiding her so that she straddled him, and suddenly his fingers stole under her panties to caress her buttocks as his nose slid down the length of hers. She should pull away, but she was breathless, waiting for something, anything, as he buzzed her lips with his. "Kate, stop me," he said softly.

Five

Holy hell, what was he doing?

He blamed the seven freckles on her nose. They made him do stupid stuff.

He blamed the strep, the fact that he was on steroids, antibiotics and some strange tea his mother had made him this morning. He blamed the fact that Kate smelled like spring and raspberries. He'd never been so hungry, and he didn't know if a thousand men could tear her away from his arms today.

He was fixated on her lips. It was surreal, so surreal, having Kate in his bed. "Stop me, Katie," he found himself saying, as he continued to run his hands up and down her thighs, and grip her lovely bottom.

He wanted to squeeze her so tight he feared he'd break her bones. He shouldn't be touching her buttocks, but he was too tired to fight the urge and too sick to care. They felt too good. *She* felt too good.

He'd wanted to do this since he'd seen her slide into those purple panties and he'd been haunted ever since. Why had she done that little striptease? He couldn't stop thinking she'd wanted him to see her. She'd wanted him to want her.

And he did, he really did.

"You think I'm blind? That I don't know?" he murmured against the top of her head. He drew back and stared into her face, noticing how soft her lips looked parted. "What you want is right here—and you'll want it whether you're in this room with me or all the way in Florida. You'll want *me*."

He didn't know why he was testing her like this. But he wanted to see…

If she feels anything for me.

Anything even remotely resembling this madness that I feel.

He caught her closer when she squirmed and tried to push herself away. "You have no idea what I want!" she angrily spat.

"I know exactly what you want! I notice it every time you look at me, like I'm everything you've ever wanted. But I'm not, Kate. We both know I'm not. There's not a day I don't remember what I took from you—"

"Shut up, Garrett! You're sick and…medicated and clearly out of your mind."

He caught her back against him and stroked her cheeks as tenderly as he could, but knew his hands were shaking. "I know you'll probably hate me for this, but I still won't let you go to Florida. I want you close to me, where I know you're safe."

"I'm not asking for your permission!"

He frowned and stared into her beautiful shining eyes, wondering why he couldn't have this girl, why he felt like he was poison for this girl.

"So you'll make me follow you? Hmm? Is that what you want, Kate?"

She glared at him, and he couldn't stand that little glare. He set a kiss on her forehead and rubbed her back under her dress, and she shuddered and pressed closer. Her need seeped into him, warming him to the core, until he felt like a torch was blazing inside of him. Blazing for her. He could feel her need of him like you'd feel rain pelting your back or the sun on your face. There were days when he could successfully ignore the pull between them, the undeniable chemistry. But tonight, his heart beat like a crazed drum for her. His muscles strained with aching desire. He could hardly stand not to touch her, felt dizzy with temptation, weak from fighting it.

"Do me a favor and say you'll stay?" He nuzzled her face with his own. "Stay with your family. With me."

His chest cramped as he thought about what he felt for her. What he felt for Kate was like a storm, and it was always there, consuming him from the inside, tormenting his every living moment.

Her voice sounded resentful. "Why? So I can keep on playing my Oscar-worthy role of the good little—"

He lost it. It was the anger and need in her voice, the closeness of her body. It was Kate. Driving him past the point of obsession, past the point of reason. He curled his hands around the back of her head and growled, "Damn you, the only one playing the role of a freaking wallflower, pretending not to want you like this, is *me,*" and his mouth pressed, scorching and hungry, against hers.

He hadn't meant to kiss her. He hadn't planned to crush her body against his and part her lips with his own. He hadn't planned to hungrily push his tongue into her soft mouth, but he did all that, because he needed to. And when she responded by twining her arms around his neck and releasing a soft moan that nearly drove him to his knees, he did more.

He wanted her, wanted her more than air, more than food, water, anything.

Blood boiling in his veins, he grabbed her curvy buttocks and molded her body tighter against his as he twirled his tongue around hers, wildly tasting every inch of her warm, giving mouth. The kiss was fire, lightning, electrifying to him, surpassing his every dream and fantasy about her. Surpassing any other kiss he'd ever had.

He was thirty already, and he had never felt so out of control, gotten so carried away with a woman before. His arms, his legs, his every muscle shook uncontrollably with pure, raw lust, as if one mere taste of Kate alone was enough to make him addicted to her. And he was, he *was* addicted.

Her luscious flavor, the erotic little moans she poured into his mouth, stimulated his thirst to levels far beyond quenching. He wanted her so much he could eat her up alive and still not be satiated. He could lick every inch of her creamy skin and be still ravenous for more. Because she was everything he wanted and everything he couldn't have. *Dammit.*

It took an inhuman effort for him to draw back, and he did it with a pained sound from deep within his throat.

"Kate, do you know what's happening here?" He

panted hard for his breath, and dropped his head, unable to resist her.

His hungry mouth opened wide around the fabric of her dress and he sucked hard, mindlessly, as his hand cupped her breast from beneath and squeezed the tip even farther out for him to suck.

"Garrett," she gasped as he drew her nipple, fabric and all, deeper into his mouth.

He groaned in ecstasy, turning his head to nuzzle the tip of her second breast. "Kate, if you don't want this— stop me…stop me now…."

She palmed his jaw and drew his mouth up to hers, searing him with her eager kiss, her lips trembling with desire.

He groaned and shut his eyes when she dragged her mouth up to kiss his nose, then his eyelids, and an out-of-control shudder wracked his large body.

He knew he was losing himself in the fragrant scent of her arousal, in the feel of her small body trembling against his, in the sound of tears in her voice. He should make her leave, so he could go back to hell. But some demon was shouting at him that he was losing her, that she would be out of his life in weeks, and suddenly he couldn't take it.

"Three seconds," he rasped as he opened his eyes, his hands unsteady as he cupped her breasts and used his thumbs to circle the budded peaks. "You have three seconds to tell me to stop."

To emphasize his words, he gave her another branding kiss, praying that she would resist him.

And that somebody would just whack his head from behind, tie up his hands and gag his mouth, so that he didn't use them all over her body like he was aching to.

Because he just couldn't withhold his desire any longer. He didn't care if he was going to hell. As far as he was concerned, he'd been living there for years, and every one of those years, he'd wanted her.

Yeah, he must be a devil to be here with this angel in bed, ready to have the best sex of his life with her. Ready to make the fantasies he'd had for hours and days and weeks and months and years come true for him. For both of them.

I'm going to hell and it will damn well be worth it....
"One," he warned.

Kate only watched him, as though waiting for him to get to three to kiss him again. The thought made him grind out, "Two."

She looked thoroughly kissed and ready to be taken. He'd never in his life wanted anything so much.

"Three."

When she sighed in outward relief and never made so much as a move to stop him, he went crazy. He pulled her dress over her head and tossed it to the floor, then trailed his lips down her flushed face as his hands coasted down the sides of his newly revealed treasure. She was smooth, slim and curvy, and she made him want to kneel at her feet and revere her. Adore her. Make love to her until they died from it.

With a little sound of frustration, Kate reached to the waistband of his underwear and tugged down his boxer briefs.

He helped her, and once he was naked, rolled around immediately, almost crushing her with his weight as he flattened her back on the bed and held her by the hair. His tongue plunged into her mouth, flooding him with her essence, feeding his reckless thirst.

Her bare skin slid against his as she suckled his tongue, and the unexpected act triggered ripples of pleasure through his system. She rubbed her breasts against his chest while he slanted his head for deeper access to her. Crazy good. She tasted crazy, crazy good.

Warnings shot across his mind as he pulled open her bra. This was the time to stop, but he was past stopping.

He did not care about anything else except branding her, taking her to a place where there would be no talk of Florida, no talk of leaving; there would be nothing but the two of them. Together.

He shoved the fabric aside and exposed her nipples. Perfect and pink.

He cupped one in his big hand and licked his way down her throat, down to the pebbled nipple. He groaned at her taste, then slid his fingers between her parted thighs and easily yanked down her panties. Squirming restlessly, she pulled him up by the hair, to her lips, and kissed him while she breathlessly murmured, "Hurry."

He cradled her head and angled her back for his devouring kiss. Murmuring her name softly, he blanketed her body with his, his erection nestling between her legs.

He ducked his head to nibble hungrily on her lips and reached between her legs again, stroking his fingers along her slick folds. She was so hot and wet. He groaned, then stuck his finger into her channel only to bring it up and stick that finger into his mouth, tasting her before he stroked and penetrated her again. "How long has it been for you?" he asked, her tightness closing around him.

"A long time," she gasped.

"How long?" he pressed.

"Years."

He closed his eyes as his chest swelled with emotion. *Mine, mine, mine,* he thought, noting how tight she was, how hot she was, as she rocked her hips to his caress.

The fact that she had also not been with anyone for a long time made him wild. He already felt dangerously close to orgasm as he added his thumb to caress her tender spot. He watched her toss and turn in pleasure, his erection throbbing painfully between his legs.

She's going to be just yours from now on....

He couldn't think beyond sinking himself inside her, taking something no one would ever take from her. Her sex was slick against his fingers as she curled her legs around him and locked her ankles at the small of his back, urging him on with a sensual rock and a breathless, "Please. Garrett, please, I hurt."

She wants me so much she's hurting for me....

Groaning softly out of pure sheer overwhelming need, he slid his hands up her arms and intertwined their fingers as he pinned her hands at her sides.

"Are you ready, Katie?"

Her voice got strangled in her throat, thick with need and desire. "Please, yes."

His body tensed in anticipation as he teased his hardness along her entrance. She was slick and wet and swollen—so damned perfect. He closed his eyes and savored her body as he gently prodded her entry, inch by inch, slow and deep, releasing a growl of pure animal need. "Ahh, Kate."

"Garrett," she cried out and stiffened. A killer wave of red-hot ecstasy whipped through him, tensing his muscles that already strained for release.

He groaned when he realized he wasn't wearing any protection.

"Kate…damn…"

She cried out when he dragged out, grabbing his shoulders and saying, "Don't stop, don't stop!"

He groaned in torment and eased back in, totally lost in her heat. The sound she released was slow and dark, as if the pain were morphing into pleasure. "Better?" he rasped.

He took her answering whimper in his mouth and kissed deeper until her body was writhing wildly underneath his.

He drove inside her once more.

Kate gasped, moaning out his name, and it was the sexiest thing he'd ever heard her say. And when she said, "More," he snapped and began a frantic pace.

They kissed like crazy for several minutes, and then she clutched his hard shoulders and gazed up at him with cloudy blue eyes.

She was so damned beautiful like this—this was how he wanted to have her every night in his bed. Red hair. Coral lips. Rosy cheeks. Thickened, recently kissed nipples.

He didn't even remember that his body hurt, that his throat was raw. All he knew was that Kate watched him, her breath rippling from between his lips as they moved together. All he knew was that he was shattering with pleasure as he gripped her waist and increased the pace. He thrust deeper, harder, lost in her grip, her heat, in *her*.

A knot of ecstasy pulled inside him and shot him off to outer space, and with three more thrusts, he pushed her past the precipice into an explosion that made her shout his name as he sank all the way home, spilling himself inside her.

For minutes they lay there, entangled and sweaty. He was breathless, sated and frankly, awed as hell.

He'd never felt so whole. He'd never made love like this. He shifted to look at her, then groaned at the sight of her languid body and dewy face, so beautiful and so taken.

"I'm sorry I lost control, Katie," he murmured, kissing her cheek, loving how warm and loose she felt as she snuggled closer. "I should've worn protection. What day are you in your cycle?"

"I don't know. Eight maybe," she said, tucking her face in his neck, as if hiding from his prying eyes. "Please don't worry, Garrett."

"Eight. Is that even safe...?" Man. He'd been as careless and excited as an adolescent to touch her. Not using protection had been inexcusable, made his chest churn with disgust at himself. "Freckles, damn..."

She sat up and pushed his hands away, shaking her head. "Please just...please stop apologizing for it, Garrett. I wanted this to happen, so did you. We had fun, it was great, it's done. There's no need to get all serious about it, and there's certainly no need for you to add it to your guilt bag."

Garrett sat back, so stunned at her words, his mind came up blank. Guilt bag? So she thought he had a guilt bag?

"What the hell is that supposed to mean?" he demanded.

"It means it was no big deal! It was just sex. You've had it with millions of women and I plan to do the same with other men in the future. I don't want you to apologize and I definitely don't want you considering...thinking that it could possibly…everything is all right here, okay?"

"I'm trying to be responsible. If there are repercussions—"

"Stop! Just stop! Even if there *were*…"

"If there were, I need to fricking *know* before I enter into any sort of agreement with Cassandra Clarks!" he angrily barked.

Kate stiffened. "What do you mean? What agreement?"

His lips formed a thin, angry line.

"What agreement, Garrett?"

He groaned and raked a hand through his hair, then let his hand fall. "She wants to marry me as a condition for selling us her share of Clarks."

"Marry…*you?*"

A thousand expressions crossed her face, until hurt ended up on the forefront, and Garrett felt like an ass.

"You! How dare you touch me when you're thinking of…I would *never* marry for anything other than love!"

He winced as she angrily jumped out of bed and searched for her dress.

He'd just had sex without a condom and honestly? He didn't even care.

He wanted her. He just wanted her. If it meant taking responsibility and doing something about it now, he would. But now it felt like the last thing she wanted was to be tied to him.

She'd basically told him that she thought the worst of him, that she wouldn't marry him if he were the last man on earth. Of course she didn't want him. He'd mucked up her entire life, and if she got pregnant, he'd muck it up again, taking her dream of Florida away from her.

The realization hurt him so much, he could only watch her from the bed, wondering if he'd actually stayed away from her all these years out of duty, or because he was a coward and knew, deep down, that he just didn't deserve her.

"Do you want some of the food I brought over, or should I just go home now?" she asked, and as if she'd already decided on the latter, she slipped back into her dress. Then she resumed searching on the floor for her panties.

He held them out to her with a scowl. "You were trembling in this bed with me, Kate. You. *Begged.* For me."

"You're right." She covered her face with shaking hands, then plunged her legs into her panties. "I even started it."

He was baffled. She looked very perturbed by the fact that she'd slept with him. He didn't know what to make of it when he'd just felt her writhe beneath him, wet and wanton.

"No. *I* did, Kate. I started it," he said, gentling his voice, standing up to embrace her. "Hell, I've been thinking about doing this with you since…"

Her eyes widened as though he'd just divulged something completely damning. "Since when? Since I said I was going to Florida? Ohmigod, are you trying to use sex to get me to bend to your will and stay here? Why else would you touch me when you haven't your whole life!"

She suddenly looked enlightened, while he stared blankly at her, puzzled and confused. Her cheeks were reddening by the second, but Garrett was growing too angry at her accusation to care. "Kate, do you seriously believe I'm that cold and calculating?"

Did she think anything even remotely redeeming about him, and was there any chance in hell she could ever love him when she was holding their past against him?

"Of course I do! You're a man who just confessed to be considering some sort of weird business marriage with some bimbo you barely even know!"

"She's not a bimbo, Kate," he said, just to be fair to Cassandra.

Kate's cheeks went redder. "You still haven't told me why you went behind your beloved's back and slept with me."

"Why don't you first tell me why the hell you slept with *me?* Were you just horny or did you just pity me tonight, or were you apologizing for giving me strep?"

"Who do you think you are to judge? Garrett, you *slept* with me even while thinking of marrying some stranger in the name of…business. I swear that's the most disgusting thing anyone's ever done to me!"

"You're just goddamned playing with me! You've teased me your whole life, parading around with other men! You just gave me a little taste of what I want, and once you got what you wanted, you're ditching me!"

She glared and stomped to the door. "Go to hell!"

"I'm already there, Kate. It's been my damned zip code since I was ten!"

As she stormed out of the room and slammed the door behind her, Garrett punched his fist into the pillow and yelled, "Goddammit!"

Six

"We're sitting at twenty-eight percent today…" Landon said. As usual, the man droned on and on about business.

Garrett made it a point to occasionally nod as if he were listening while he scrolled through his last text conversation with Kate. He'd texted her in the middle of the night after the debacle of their argument four nights ago. He'd been lying awake at midnight feeling medicated and as low as a dog. All he'd needed was for someone to put a bowl of Alpo out for him. Instead he'd found her food in the kitchen, cursed himself over and over again, heated up his soup and chowed down on several muffins, then grabbed his phone and texted her. Despite the fact that it had been past one in the morning, she'd replied. Which meant she'd been lying awake, too, as sleepless as he was.

Thanks for my food. When can I see you? I want to talk.

Everything is fine. I've already forgotten about it.

Garrett wasn't so stupid as to believe this, but had answered.

K. So I hear you're getting your dresses fitted Wednesday. I'll drive you.

Won't your girlfriend get jealous?

I'd like to explain to you about her.

It's fine. The fitting is at five so I'll see you before then.

"Are you even listening, Garrett?"

He lifted his head to Landon's confused gray gaze. "Hmm? What?"

Landon scowled and then continued, raising his voice as though to be clearer. "Clarks...new strategy..."

So, Kate thought Garrett had planned it all?

How could she believe that he'd planned to get sick, so that he could get her to bring over some food for him, get her into bed, seduce her like some out-of-control adolescent and conveniently forget a condom so she might have to stay? Well, hell, it sounded so brilliant, he felt like an idiot for not thinking of it before.

"Garrett, dammit, did you hear?"

"Yes. Clarks. A new strategy." He set his phone aside, but putting thoughts about Kate aside wasn't that easy.

"You're the last single Gage. Will you or won't you go through with this?" Landon asked.

With a major wrench of mental muscles, Garrett

pulled his scrambled brain together and tried to focus on the topic today.

"All three of us know that I'm not really the last single Gage, Lan." Garrett leaned back to survey both his brothers' expressions across the conference table.

Landon's eyebrows shot up. "Don't go there."

"Why not?" He shrugged. "He's still a Gage."

"Mother wanted nothing to do with him. Hell, we paid him millions to get out of our lives for good, and you want to bring him back?"

"How badly do you want Clarks?" Garrett countered.

"As badly as you want it," Landon returned.

Garrett scraped a hand along the tense muscles at the back of his neck. He wanted Clarks, but not as bad as he wanted something else.

"Plus who's to say that selfish bastard will want to help us?" Landon rose to pace by the wall of windows. "He will want a big piece of the pie, and he'll want even more than that. Do you remember Father refused to recognize him?"

"But we know he was Father's son, no matter how many times he denied it to Mother," Garrett countered. He'd been wracking his brain for other options and this was, fortunately or unfortunately, the only one he'd been able to come with.

To bring their illegitimate half brother, Emerson Wells, back into the fold.

Julian chewed on the back of a pen before he lowered it and spoke. "We could entice him with money. Stock. Something. Maybe we should call just him."

"He's trouble," Landon said pointedly, his face furrowed in thought. "What does he do now anyway?"

"Last I heard he was in the personal security business here in San Antonio. Started as a bodyguard."

"Seriously?"

"What can I say? He likes beating people up."

"All right then." Crossing the room, Landon clicked the phone intercom and rang his assistant. "If you'd please get me Emerson Wells on the line. You should be able to do a Google search and find his number. He owns some sort of personal security business here in town."

Hanging up, Landon rubbed his chin thoughtfully, his gray eyes on Garrett. "If he denies us...would you still go through with it?"

Kate's face and words surfaced in his mind with a vengeance, and his chest cramped. *I would never marry for anything other than love!*

For one painful moment, he wondered if she'd even care whether he married someone else, for whatever reason. But although her words had cut through him, her body had spoken another language. He'd lost control, and so had she. They'd both been so needy he hadn't even been able to stop to put on a condom.

What had he done?

Perhaps Garrett hadn't technically broken his promise to her father, but he felt like he had. There was probably no man more undeserving of Kate's affection than he.

Clearly, you blew it, Gage.

But she had wanted him. Hell, she'd not only wanted him, she'd melted under his touch. Was he supposed to turn his mind blank and forget about a moment like that?

"Molls said they have a fitting this afternoon that you insisted on driving them to?"

He glanced up at Julian in confusion. "Molly? I told Kate I'd drive her. I didn't know it included Molly."

"And Beth," Landon added with a grin. "They're all going together."

Garrett almost groaned. So much for talking to Kate one-on-one.

"Fine, then. I'll drive the three of them," Garrett reluctantly conceded. An infuriating hunch told him that Kate was doing this on purpose. Clearly, she had no desire to discuss anything with him.

Julian dropped his pencil on the table and angled his head, his eyes sparkling in amusement.

"You know, bro, I can't help you here. Molls would strangle me if I see her in *the* dress."

"That's fine." He plunged a hand through his hair. He'd wanted to spend some time with Kate and talk, but he would manage somehow. "I'll drop Kate off last and see if she'll do dinner with me."

"So I take it this means whatever Emerson says, you're not keen on the marriage of convenience?" Julian queried.

"Would you be?" Garrett countered. "Keen to marry a stranger? When your every thought is consumed by someone else?"

"Why don't you just tell Kate how you feel and get it all out there?"

Garrett shook his head.

Because he didn't deserve her.

Hell, the way things stood, even if he were to tell Kate how she made him feel, she'd probably tell him to stick his declaration where it hurts. She resented him for having taken her father from her, no matter how much she tried to pretend she didn't. He still couldn't forget those words she'd lashed out at him with when they were young: *How dare you!*

He'd never forget the hurt betrayal in her eyes when she'd found out her father had died because Garrett hadn't run as he'd been told to. And now, to top it off, she believed he'd deliberately slept with her just to make sure she stayed in San Antonio. True, it might have been the catalyst, but that was so not the reason.

"You know, Garrett," Landon said, coming over to pat his back, "we all get the love we think we deserve…and you *deserve* it, man. No matter what you think. You both do. So you better own it before she leaves for Florida, brother. Neither Julian nor I, nor for that matter, Mother, has any desire to watch what her departure does to you."

Seven

Kate checked herself in the mirror for the tenth time. She wore a plain khaki skirt and sleeveless halter top. She knew that it would be silly to try on another top, so she grabbed her purse and her phone, then glanced down on impulse at Garrett's last texts.

He'd said he wanted to talk and tell her about the "bimbo," but just thinking about the way he'd defended her made Kate's blood boil. Worse was that every time she went back a little further, to his kisses, little bubbles of remembrance shot through her system. She didn't want the bubbles. Or the tingles. Or any of the gut-churning jealousy she felt when she thought about him and Cassandra Clarks.

She hadn't slept a wink last night; she could still feel his touch on her traitorously sensitive skin. Now, Beth and Molly were waiting in her living room for him to pick them up, and Kate was grateful for the buffer they would provide.

Coward. That's why you asked them to come over.

Yes, yes, so fine, she was a coward. She just didn't trust herself to be alone with him. She feared she'd either do something sexual, which she had to put a stop to, or say some other cruel things that she didn't mean. She regretted getting so defensive when he'd started apologizing. Garrett was actually the most unselfish man she knew. He'd always thought ahead to how he would protect her if something unexpected happened. But the last thing Kate had wanted was to add to his burdens when it came to her. She hadn't ever imagined they'd end up naked and entangled. But he'd been there. So available. So sexy, tan and bare-chested. How could she resist? And the bastard had broken remorselessly through her walls, all in his stupid attempt to bend her to his will and liking!

But then he'd pretended to be hurt by her accusation, and accused her of being a tease. The reminder made her frown. She'd never considered that she was. Did she tease him? She'd tried to make him jealous for years, but she'd never known it had even had an effect.

Maybe it had more than he'd let on.

"Landon thinks he's going to do it," Beth was telling Molly.

"Do what?" Kate asked as she came back into the living room.

Molly turned to her with a sad, moping face. "Marry Cassandra Clarks. Jules told me yesterday. I just didn't know how to bring it up."

Kate's stomach clenched.

"It's got something to do with acquiring Clarks Communications," Beth said, shaking her head. "Kate, I'm sorry."

Once again, Kate felt the painful stab of jealousy inside her. "All the more reason I should leave," she whispered.

"You'd let the man you love marry another woman?" Beth asked uncertainly.

"If he wants her, yes. And I don't love him. I might have had a crush, but I'm over that. I'm in love with the idea of Florida now."

"Kate, I think it's hard for him to let himself want something, with what happened to your father, but I've always seen that he's got it bad for you," Beth said.

"No. *I* had it bad for *him*. And now I've promised myself to forget him. I should find a man with no baggage who actually makes me feel loved, Beth."

Both women quietly watched her pace to the window and then back.

"So there's nothing going on between the two of you? The boys say he's distracted. And so are you," Beth insisted.

Her best friend's eyes twinkled all of a sudden, and Kate wanted to groan when she saw Molly's mischievous smile also appear. Did they suspect Kate had totally gone sex-crazed at Garrett's place several days ago?

"There's nothing going on. We're...normal. Friends." *Who slipped up once,* she mentally added. Through the window, she watched his silver Audi pull over to the curb. Little bugs tickled the insides of her stomach. "He's here."

"I guess I'll just slide into the back with Molly," Beth offered as they went outside, and Kate locked up behind her.

She hated how her heart pounded when she walked up to the shiny silver car. Garrett stood holding the door open, his eyes sweet and liquid chocolate as he smiled. "Hi, Katie."

Her bones went mushy every time he called her Katie. "Hey, Garrett." His broad shoulder brushed hers as she got in, and her pulse sped with his nearness as he bent to kiss her on the cheek.

Oh, God, please don't be nice today, she thought miserably.

She could handle fighting with him. But this?

The thought of him marrying anyone, touching anyone like he'd touched her, tortured her.

He settled behind the steering wheel. She watched his hands on the gearshift as they sped off, and her core warmed and boiled hot as she remembered the ways he'd caressed her. Every part of her body wanted to do it again except her mind, where warning bells were ringing at full volume.

She couldn't let it happen again.

He was talking *marriage* to another woman.

She was only too glad she wouldn't be here to watch it.

After forty-five minutes at the dress shop, Garrett could now totally understand his brothers' amused grins from only hours ago.

He'd never gone to a dress fitting before.

Torture.

He sat on a chair outside a line of dressing rooms and watched as the ladies came out to stand before a huge mirror, where a busy little woman picked and poked and stabbed the material until she'd shaped it to her liking.

He'd been doing fine, answering emails on his iPhone, until Kate came out and took his breath away.

He watched her hop onto the platform and model the dress, exposing her slim, creamy ankles as she discussed the length with the short, busy-bee shop attendant. He felt as if a grenade had just exploded in his chest. His blood heated as he remembered the hell of watching her grow up, grow breasts, wear her hair longer, develop those curves. He'd seen her in her prom dress, in a barely there black bikini that hugged her silken curves in all the right places and made Garrett hurt in all the wrong ones.

He'd seen her naked in his bed…writhing in his arms….

And once he got her back there, he never wanted to see her dressed again.

He wanted to touch her, hold her.

He wanted to hear her breathe next to him at night. He just knew if she slept at his side, the mere feel of her would make all his nightmares vanish.

He suddenly saw, clearly, how he'd be complete and whole with her. How he'd feel worthy and needed in a way he had never, ever felt before. But at the same time, he'd be vulnerable. Because, holy God, he needed this woman so much.

He saw her eyes go bright when the girls came over, squealing in delight.

"That blue looks so good on you," Molly gushed.

"Oh, your date is going to be so thrilled!"

Garrett cocked a brow as he pushed himself off the chair and came over, listening to her ask if they were sure.

He stood next to her and caught her gaze in the mirror. "Date?"

She spun around to face him and her lips trembled in a smile. "I don't know. We won't be catering so I'll have some time to spare."

"Exactly. Flirt around with a man. Have a little fun," Molly said from nearby. Garrett couldn't miss the mischievous glint in Molly's eyes as she surveyed Garrett for a reaction.

He gave her none.

"Do we want this fitted…?" The saleslady maneuvered Kate's skirt, and Garrett watched in rapture as the woman tucked the fabric around her waist to enhance Kate's luscious curves even more.

He studied her breasts, how lush they were, tightly constrained by the corsetlike bodice. His mouth watered and his hands ached. He was in hell and heaven at the same time, and it was the most puzzling feeling he'd ever experienced.

Kate stared at his reflection, her blue eyes shining in concern and somehow pleading for a compliment. "Do you like it?"

They both stared at one another, and for that one moment, nothing mattered but her. She held his gaze, and he held hers. His world centered around this one woman he'd always tried not to want.

His eyes trailed along her body, taking her in, and he heard the soft, amusing sound of her breath catching. The gown was sapphire-colored, consisting of a tight corset top clinging to her body like second skin, then flaring into a wide skirt. He wanted to toss it up in the air and bury himself between her legs. Her arms were toned and slim, her breasts perky and tightly constricted, making him want to free them. Her glossy hair, too long and beautiful to keep restrained, hung down her shoulders.

She was gazing at him nervously, wetting her lips. "Garrett...do you like it?" she repeated.

He nodded while his body burned under his skin.

Smiling tremulously, she hopped off the platform and started toward the changing rooms, but within three steps, he caught her wrist and spun her around. As if shocked, she looked down at his fingers curled around her flesh, then watched him, wide-eyed, as he lifted her hand in his and kissed her knuckles, one by one. "Speaking of dates," he whispered when he was done, "do you have one?"

Surprise and excitement flickered in her gaze, and his smile widened as he watched her struggle for a reply. He should probably ask Cassandra out on a date, start playing up appearances, but the hope he saw in Kate's pretty eyes... He wanted to kiss her eyelids, and track her jaw with his tongue. Then go to the shell of her ear, where he would whisper all sort of things to her, naughty and nice. He wanted to have what his brothers had; he wanted all of that, with Kate.

This talk of marriages of convenience and business mergers...

Did any of it matter to him? If he didn't have Kate?

He didn't deserve her, but he was damned ready to work to get her. He wanted to stop punishing himself, stop blaming himself for people dying, and just dream of all that life and love he felt when he looked at Kate.

"I..." She hesitated, then shook her head, her cheeks coloring pink. "It's best I go on my own."

She quickly pried her hand free and disappeared behind a velvet curtain to change once more.

* * *

Garrett Gage asking her out on a date?

No. Not a date. Garrett Gage asking her out to the wedding.

And he hadn't really asked her. He seemed to be checking whether she already knew whom she'd go with, which was different.

Still. In her heart, her gut, in the way he'd looked at her...*oooh,* how it had felt when he'd asked her that question.

Kate was still reeling at the possibilities as they dropped off Beth and Molly and then rode in silence back to her place. Rain caught up with them by the time he pulled over in front of her one-story house. The drops were so big, they made huge splattering sounds on the windshield and the top of the car.

"Oh, no," Kate groaned.

Garrett reached into the backseat and grabbed his suit jacket. "Remember this? Something like this has saved your pretty head from getting wet before."

The memories surfaced, and when his teeth flashed wide in a white smile, there was no future in Florida, no painful past, only Garrett and his coat, and the rain outside.

He grabbed the door handle. "All right, Kate, here we go."

Heart pounding with emotion as she remembered other times he'd saved her just like this, she watched him sprint around the car and jerk the door open, holding his jacket over both their heads as he pulled her up against his side and onto the sidewalk. As her flats began getting soaked, she pressed close to his massive chest and suddenly his arm slid around her waist, his eyes glinting. "Ready? On three."

She nodded breathlessly, a gasp already poised in her throat.

"One, two, three!"

They ran for cover to the door, the fresh puddles at their feet splashing at each step as they both burst out laughing. Kate knew this wouldn't have happened if her catering van hadn't been parked in the middle of her driveway, but rain in Texas was truly rare and she hadn't expected it at all.

Once at the door, she struggled to fit the key into the doorknob, and she could hear Garrett breathing at her back as he hunched his shoulders over her, the jacket covering them both.

"Katie, be any slower, and we could just shampoo here already."

"I'm getting it!" she cried, laughing at her own awkwardness as the angle of the rain managed to get them both wet from the sides. The door clicked open at last, and she hurried inside, turning to see him standing just outside the door, getting wetter by the second. She couldn't bear to leave him there like that, so she motioned him inside and slammed the door after him. His white shirt clung damply to his back and right side.

She squeezed a couple of raindrops out of the tips of her hair as Garrett shook his jacket in the air and hooked it on the coat stand. When Kate kicked off her shoes, their shoulders touched, and she realized Garrett smelled of fresh rain.

She couldn't miss the way his broad chest jerked and stretched his white dress shirt with each breath. And she knew her nipples were poking into her dampened blouse;

she caught his dazzlingly sexy white smile as he stared down at her. "Someone looks wet," he said laughingly.

"You should see yourself."

"I'm perfectly aware that I'm wet."

"Take your shirt off, and I'll dry it for you. I'd do the same for your jacket, but I assume it's dry-clean?"

"So is the damn shirt."

"Then at least let me hang it." Without thinking, her hands flew up to start unbuttoning him, and by the time she started to undo the last button, she realized that he'd gone utterly still. His eyes had darkened completely, and emotion clogged Kate's throat as their love-making vividly came back to her mind.

"Katie, if you don't want this—stop me...stop me now...."

He seemed to notice that something had made her hands fall still, for he angled his head downward and peered mischievously into her eyes. "Just say you want me naked and I'll take it all off."

"You're so easy," she scoffed, but she dropped her hands when she realized the danger, and his shirt fell open to reveal his beautiful tan abs. She shouldn't be talking to him. She shouldn't even want to, need to, be close to him. She could have almost kicked herself when she asked, "Do you want some dinner?"

He didn't hesitate, even when the tension between them as palpable.

He followed her through the living room. "I don't want to put you to work."

"It's not work to me. I'll cook us something easy. I hate eating alone and miss Molly terribly," she said.

But was that really why she'd asked him to dinner? Or was it because she knew that as soon as she left San

Antonio, she would never be able to enjoy his company like this again?

"I'm sorry, Kate."

For a moment, she didn't know what he was sorry about. *He's sorry about you missing Molly, Kate. Get your head in the game.* "But she's so happy," she finally answered. She smiled as she eased into the adjoining kitchen, quietly slipping on an apron.

"Aren't you a cute one," Garrett murmured.

His gaze was so openly admiring that Kate's stomach squeezed. She grabbed a knife and gestured dramatically with it. "Flattery will get you equal portions, so don't waste your breath."

"I'm not wasting it. I'm holding it."

Ignoring the butterflies in her stomach, Kate rummaged through the fridge and pulled out her almond flour, eggs, milk and a bunch of vegetables. She set the veggies on a cutting board and transferred them to the kitchen island. "Help me with these while I work on the dough?"

"Of course. Just tell me what to do."

"Cut the mushrooms, red peppers, onions and zucchini into small but pretty slices."

"I can do small, but I don't guarantee pretty." His lips curled upward as he grasped the knife that she offered and his fingers closed warmly over hers.

Shivers of delight shot from the place he touched, and she couldn't suppress the shudder that ran down her limbs. "They're not going to a beauty pageant. Just small will do," she whispered, impulsively pressing in behind him and leaning to watch as she showed him how. She shifted her hands so that he held the knife, and she held *him,* and then she slowly guided him to cut in the size she wanted.

Garrett stood utterly still and compliant, letting her guide him, and suddenly her nipples pressed painfully into his hard back as she realized how intimately her arms were going around his narrow waist.

"What are we making?"

She swallowed when he turned slightly and glanced directly at her. His voice was smooth and calm, but when she spoke, Kate's wasn't. "Vegetable goat-cheese pizza."

He turned back to watch her cut a slice of pepper. "Kate, you're going to kill me."

"Why? I thought you liked it?"

"Exactly. My mouth is watering."

Her cheeks flamed up as she thought of his mouth, and she instantly released him and went back to her spot to prepare the dough. Moments later, she lifted her head when the rhythmical sounds of Garrett's chopping stopped. He was watching her massage the dough. A lock of his dark hair fell over one eye. Her legs weakened at the sexy look, and her heart grew wings in her chest. Garrett looked incredibly beautiful in her kitchen. As beautiful as he did in bed with her.

She opened her mouth to say something, then closed it when her cheeks burned at the memory. She really shouldn't have slept with him. Now she couldn't even look at him without becoming hyperaware of the electricity between them.

A smile slowly formed on his lips as if he could read her thoughts. Then he turned his attention back to his chopping, his profile hard and square, but the expression on his face also thoughtful. Kate swallowed and mixed her dough, then slammed her fists into it and rolled it a couple of more times.

"Bring the veggies once they're cut so you can help me arrange them."

He didn't answer, but soon, he brought over the cutting board. He set it on the counter, and as Kate began to arrange all the little pieces on the flattened pizza crust, his hands gripped her waist from behind. Her breath was knocked out of her when his fingers squeezed her and his lips brushed against her ear.

"Why'd you sleep with me, Kate?" he murmured.

Heat arrowed from her ear straight to her toes, and she stiffened against the dissolving sensation in her bones.

He didn't sound angry. He sounded confused, but patient, much as he did when he wanted to get to the bottom of something.

He surprised her by pressing into her body, trapping her between the counter and himself. Kate had nowhere to go, her spine arching up against his chest as she closed her eyes and tried to still her racing heartbeat.

His voice sounded in her ear as his fingers started a trail up her rib cage. "Did you feel pity for me because I was sick—?"

"No." She could barely utter the word.

"Then why?"

His breath was warm, and damp, and it made her shiver. "It was a mistake. We weren't thinking clearly." Trying to gather her wits, she nervously turned in the cage of his arms, gripped the tray and slid the pizza into the oven, forcing him to step back as she bent forward.

When she shut the door and turned, Garrett had stepped back and merely stood watching her. His snowy-white dress shirt was still parted at the middle, and her saliva glands went crazy at the sight of his bare chest, his flat, hard abs and his belly button.

"Maybe it was a mistake, Kate, one I've spent all my life avoiding. But what if it isn't a mistake?"

Her blood started heating in her veins as she remembered the delicious way he'd moved in her. Kissed her. Gripped her.

She knew they had to talk about this, no matter how much she wished they would pretend nothing had gone on that day. And now that he'd brought up the topic, she could barely think straight. The look in his eyes was beyond intimate. It was downright proprietary, and she almost drowned in the darkness of those eyes that haunted her dreams. With an inhuman effort, she made her way around the kitchen island, putting some distance between them.

His voice stopped her as he followed her around.

"Kate. Answer me. What if it wasn't a mistake?"

Her breath caught in disbelief, and suddenly, she did a one-eighty to face him. "You just want to keep me here, Garrett. You'd do anything to win—that's how you are. And you want to keep me from going to Florida."

"You know me better than that, Freckles."

"I know you're the most stubborn man I know."

He lifted one lone eyebrow. "And you aren't stubborn? You're stubborn *and* proud, Katie. The combo makes for a very difficult lady."

She shook her head but couldn't help smiling. Then she signaled at his damp shirt; it was still driving her crazy how it stuck damply to his beautiful brown nipples. It was about as sexy as him being naked or, strangely, even more so. "Are you taking that shirt off? I can still dry it for you."

He whipped it off, and it gave her something to do as she hooked it on a high kitchen cabinet close to the oven heat. "So that's how you get men naked," he roughly teased.

"Of course. I make it rain, then I strip them." She smoothed her hands down the sleeves to unwrinkle them.

"What do you do after you strip them?"

She stopped fussing over his shirt and realized he was coming closer. His smile was overtly sexual, his dark eyes glimmering in liquid mischief. "Do you kiss them?"

"Maybe," she said and slid past him to go back around the kitchen island. There was something very predatory in his eyes, and she began backing away more quickly as her heart kicked wildly in her rib cage.

"Do you caress them with those hands of yours? Look up at them with those pretty eyes?"

She blinked for a moment, then burst out laughing. "*What* do you mean? These are the only eyes I have. Which others should I use?"

"It's the look in those eyes I refer to. Do you use that doe look on them, too? The one that makes me want to chase you?"

When she laughingly shook her head and backed away farther, he charged and she squealed and sped around the kitchen island, managing two rounds until he caught her and spun her around, both their smiles a mile long. His grin faded before she could even bask in the beauty of it, and his expression fell deathly somber. "I want to kiss you very badly," he whispered, bending his head, his chest heaving.

"Garrett, no," she murmured, struggling to pull free. She spun around and went to check on the pizza, her pulse throbbing in her temples as she pretended to be busy watching the cheese melt.

He came up behind her again and stroked a hand down her hair. "What if I asked you for what you wanted, and you told me exactly what it is that you *want?*"

"Florida."

His stare almost bored holes into her profile, and through the corner of her eye, she noticed his jaw clamped, hard as granite. "Be real with me, Kate. For once in our lives, let's stop playing games."

She shook her head, feeling panicked and afraid of opening up to him. "Whatever it is, you can't give it to me."

"Just try me."

Gnawing on her lower lip, she studied his face, his features carved fiercely in determination, as if he truly did care for her. Well...did he? Had he seen her like a woman all along and had she not noticed because she'd been too busy pretending she didn't love him? She wanted him. All of him. A family of her own. She knew it was too much to want of him, to *ask* from him. Especially after what she'd heard.

"Everyone knows about you and...that heiress you're planning a wedding with."

His eyebrows lifted in mock interest. "Like it's a fact now?"

Ignoring the dangerous purr in his voice, Kate put on an oven mitt, pulled the pizza out and set it on the stove top. "I can't believe you'd marry for business." She couldn't look at him while saying that, so she occupied herself with preparing the food.

He was silent as she used her cutter to slice the pizza into perfect pieces.

Then he murmured, "I wasn't going to marry at all. So why would it matter if I just used it as means to an end, if it's what Cassandra's asking for and it will all be over in six months anyway?"

"You're better than that, Garrett," she whispered.

"But not good enough for you," he mumbled, watching her closely.

Her throat tightened on a reply that she just refused to give as she put a slice on a plate for him, and another on one for herself, staying quiet. What was the point? Flirting with him? Playing with fire? He never wanted to marry, he'd just said, and if he did, it was purely for business. She had to believe she deserved a family of her own. Especially since she'd had her own family torn apart when she was so young.

Quietly, she carried both plates to the kitchen island. He sat down on the stool beside her, then took a large bite, munching.

"Freckles, this is so good." He shook his head and took another bite, making a groaning noise that made her remember…sex. With him.

"It is, isn't it?" The sweet vegetable flavors combined with the toasted-almond flour and goat cheese melted in her mouth, but her insides melted more at the sounds he made. She squirmed on her stool and watched him get up to pour two glasses of water from the pitcher in the fridge.

He set hers down next to her plate, then continued eating. When he licked up a crumb from the corner of his lips, her heart raced in a strange mix of fear and anticipation. He'd asked if she wanted him to give chase… and suddenly she couldn't imagine anything more exhilarating than being hunted, chased and claimed by him.

Shaking her head, she washed down her pizza with the water. She was surprised when he spoke again; he'd already finished his slice. Now his attention seemed fixed solely on her again.

He stroked a finger down her jaw.

"What about me?" he asked.

She frowned and set her half-eaten pizza down. "What do you mean, what about you?"

"You say you'd only marry for love. Do you feel nothing for me? If I go through with this marriage to Cassandra, how would you feel about it?"

The meal suddenly wasn't sitting too well in her stomach. "If she's what you want…"

"I'm very interested in something that she has, but I want to make it clear that I don't want her." There was no mistaking the steel in his voice as he set a hand on her thigh as if it belonged there. "What I want to know is if there's even a chance that I can have what I most want on this earth."

Her pulse skyrocketed when she saw the stark hunger in his gaze, a gaze that ping-ponged from her eyes to her mouth and made her pulse race erratically. But when he began to get close, she stood up for some reason. Garrett laughed darkly, quietly, as if to himself. Then he followed her up and began to back her into a corner with purpose, his eyes blazing.

"Where are you going, Kate?"

She quickened her steps, but he followed closely until she stopped when the back of her knees hit a wall.

He smiled delightedly. "You do want me to catch you, don't you?"

With painstaking slowness, as though to torture her, he raised his hand and set it on her hair, and it was as if she could feel his fingers tangling inside her, tangling around her heart. "Do you want to be with me again?" he rasped, using his fist in her hair to tip her head back.

Every instinct of self-preservation warned her against reaching out to him, giving him this power over her again, but there was no pulling away from him as his hand wound deeper into the fall of hair at her nape, his piercing onyx eyes drowning her in their depths.

"I've been inside you once—and it wasn't enough. I wanted to wake up and look into your eyes and see you smile at me. I didn't want you to leave. Not like that. Not like it was a mistake."

Her breasts rose and fell with each strained breath. "It wasn't a mistake to me. I loved every moment of it."

"Then why don't you put your arms around me now? Why don't you touch me? Was I too rough?" His voice dropped even lower as he tightened his fist, his eyes holding a sexy, primal shine as he drank in her face. "Katie, I promise you that next time I'll take it so much slower. I'll kiss you from the tip of your toes to the top of your lovely head. I'll move slowly inside you…"

He bent his head, tipped up her face with a crooked finger and kissed her parted lips. The gasps stealing out of her were impossible to hold back. He opened his mouth as though to breathe them into his body, drag them into his lungs.

"I'll prepare you for me again. Prepare you for hours, Kate. Hours. I don't regret it happened, Kate, only that I didn't do it right."

He grasped her hands and placed them on his shoulders, and Kate didn't take them away. Her nails gouged into his skin as she pressed against him, her eyes drifting shut. "Please don't do this."

"How long will you hold out, Kate? If I do this…"

Expert fingers traced the tips of her sensitive breasts through her damp shirt, and Kate gasped as sensations stormed through her.

"Will you say no? If I do this…?"

He undid her halter top and let the fabric pool at her waist, and then eased one breast out of the material of her bra. He bent his head and kissed one straining nipple, laving it expertly with his tongue, priming it before he latched on and suckled her with his warm mouth.

Moisture pooled between her legs, red-hot desire rocking to her very core.

She clasped his head, thinking to pull him back, but instead she just clutched his silky hair as he turned his head and performed the same expert torture on the other puckered tip.

She struggled weakly, halfheartedly, until he pressed her arms down at her sides, their fingers linking in a tight grip as he took her mouth in a wild, stormy kiss. Her lips opened, allowing him entrance with a soft, welcoming moan, and she was undone by his taste. "Garrett."

Not even thinking what she was doing, Kate clung to him and curled one leg around his hips, her skirt hiking up as she nestled his hardness between her open thighs.

He curled a hand around the back of her knee to keep her leg up, and he rocked his hips and pulled back to stare into her wide, sparkling eyes. He bent down to take her lips softly. "You want that, Katie? You want that from me?"

The feel of him, the reminder of what it felt like to have him, hot and hard, inside her, made her feverish.

She wanted to nod, to say yes, to tell him not to ask

and just take her, but instead she wedged a hand between their burning bodies and palmed his erection. He hissed out a breath and nipped her earlobe, the closest thing to his mouth, then swept down to devour one aching nipple again.

She moaned feebly and began to pant. Arching her back, she pushed her breast up, as if craving a deeper kiss, so he opened wide around her flesh and sucked hard. "Garrett!" she cried.

A groan rumbled up in his chest as he seized her hands and pinned them over her head, trapping her as he looked at her with wild, hungry eyes.

"I want this so much." He ducked his head and his lips brushed the tip of her breast, his hand tightening on her wrists.

She felt a new surge of dampness in her panties, her breasts weighing heavily with the need to be cupped by his palms. Kate couldn't believe how many times she'd dreamed of this, wanted it. She moaned softly and arched her back in invitation once more.

"Garrett…" She pressed herself up to his mouth, and his lips returned to her nipple. Fire swept through her.

Fisting her flowing, flaming hair in his hands, he pulled her face back to look at him. "Tell me you want me." He spoke in a dangerous tone as his hands slid downward to unzip her skirt.

"I want you," she gasped.

He kissed her hard, blindingly, as he shoved the material down her hips, then slid her clinging halter top off, as well.

His lips softened on a groan as he cupped her sex in his big palm. His voice was but a breath in her ear, shaking her world like a cannon blast. "I want you, too. I can't stop wanting you."

He pressed the heel of his palm to the bundle of nerves hidden at her core, and she released a soft cry.

He dipped his hand into her panties, then watched her as he parted her folds with his fingers and pushed the middle one inside. Her hips rolled while her eyes searched his face and he pushed her arousal even higher.

"Does one feel good? Or would you rather have two?" he rasped.

He watched her expression dissolve as he added a second finger into her snug grip. A surge of moisture drenched his hand, and he bent his head and prodded a taut nipple with his tongue.

That's when he heard voices out in the living room.

Kate snapped out of her daze and stiffened when she heard the front door slam shut. She practically flew away from Garrett, jumping as the voices became clear and the two figures appeared in the living room—which adjoined the kitchen.

"—so just be quiet and let me get it real qui…"

Molly and Julian froze in their tracks.

Molly's eyes flared in mute shock as Kate struggled to right her bra and panties and used the vegetable chopping block to cover what she could. Julian's eyes widened like saucers as he took in Garrett's bare-chested state and Kate trying her damnedest to hide behind one miserable little cutting board.

"Okay, I'd rather not have seen that. What about you, Molls?" Julian smirked.

Molly blinked, her cheeks about as red as her hair, but Kate was sure she wasn't nearly as red as Kate. "Seen what? I didn't see anything. I think I'll come visit with Kate another day."

They shuffled backward through the living room, and even after the front door slammed shut behind them, Kate just couldn't look at Garrett. Her face burned in embarrassment. They were panting, the sounds of their haggard breaths echoing in the silence. Slowly, he reached out, but she stepped back and shook her head.

"What is it you want from me, Garrett?" she asked brokenly.

His voice was low and textured with wanting. "I want you to stay in the city, Kate."

"Is that all?"

"For now, yes." His face tightened with emotion as he watched her slip back into her skirt, and his eyes flashed as he saw her reach for her discarded clothing. "Fine, no."

"Then what?" Her arms shook as she shoved them back into the arm holes.

"I want you in bed with me." His eyes raked down her body almost desperately, and she hated how easily her blood bubbled again when he grabbed her hands to stop her from dressing. "Please. Kate. Don't."

"So this is about sex," she said. She pushed his hands away.

"You make it sound like that's a bad thing. Katie, I know you want me, too. You were just trembling in my arms."

"For how long do you want me in bed? A week? Two?" she dared, her heart twisting in her chest when she tried to recall if Garrett had ever really even been with anyone for that long. "What about Cassandra? Don't you think she'd like to know about your little side plan here?"

His mouth dipped into an even deeper scowl than usual, then he restlessly raked his fingers through his hair. "Damn, Katie, I keep feeling like I'm falling short here. What the hell is it that you *want* from me?"

"You're talking about marriage with another woman, Garrett! And you stand here telling me you fall short? You damned well do fall short! If I'd wanted an affair, I'd have it with someone other than you. I want a shot at having the family I've never had, that's what I want!"

In the instant she spoke those last words, Kate wished she could take them back. It was as though she'd slapped him; Garrett suddenly looked like that young boy, that dark, tormented young boy, so forlorn after what had happened the night of the murders.

"Well, then you were right about one thing," he said, a tinge of angry frustration in his voice. "I can definitely not give you back what you want."

"Garrett, you misunderstood me—"

But he was gone, the bang of the door that followed his departure making her wince.

Eight

Garrett knew that their half brother, Emerson Wells, harbored no love for the Gages. Even though the Gage patriarch had apparently been screwing Emerson's mother for years, he'd refused to recognize Emerson as his son and bought the woman off to stay quiet and away from them—something the family had discovered when their father's lawyer, upon his death, disclosed the existence of another heir who could contest part of the inheritance.

He never did, though Eleanor Gage had thought it wise to pay him a few million dollars to go away for good.

Naturally, if Emerson had half the clout and pride of a Gage—which he apparently did—he would have no intention of ever catering to a Gage's wishes. So he'd denied Landon's summons six times during the past several weeks, something that didn't surprise Garrett. But now, they were running out of time to make concrete decisions about the Clarks Communications deal, and Garrett finally had it with begging the imbecile for a meeting. This limbo was putting everyone on edge, especially him, since not only his two brothers, but Cassandra herself, seemed to believe Garrett was the only one who could make the deal possible now.

He'd been so close to just saying, "To hell with it, I'll do it."

Kate would never have him anyway.

And yet a little part of him knew that he could never stop trying. Not now. Not when he knew that she wanted him, knew the delicate feel of her body against his, knew the fragrance of that devilishly sexy red hair. Kate might not know it yet, and hell, Garrett might have spent his entire life fighting it, but they belonged to one another.

The recent times they'd seen one another at his mother's Sunday brunches, they'd spoken of trivial things, their last argument forgotten—or at least, not mentioned. But the air crackled between them. Her eyes seemed bluer when they rested on him. They softened when she saw him. He wasn't blind to it, couldn't be blind to those looks anymore. He had to do something, and fast.

So that's how he'd found himself sitting in his office yesterday, dialing Emerson's mother. He was surprised that she'd picked up after a few rings.

"This is Garrett Gage, and I realize Emerson doesn't want to hear from us, but it's imperative we talk to him. I assure you he'll be happy to hear us out, if you could—"

The woman had hung up.

But Garrett hadn't given up. He'd then punched in some numbers and got Emerson's secretary on the line.

After a moment of silence, she'd put him on hold. When she finally came back, she'd reluctantly conceded, "He'll give you ten minutes tomorrow morning."

Now, as he presented himself at his half brother's office downtown, he marveled at how well his brother seemed to be doing for himself. Garrett strolled through the floor containing the executive offices and found his brother's secretary waiting for him. "Mr. Wells will be here shortly, Mr. Gage. You can go right in."

He grabbed a mint from the plate on her desk as she continued typing on her keyboard, and instead of taking a seat, he paced around while the woman continued typing. After taking a phone call, she hung up and left her desk, and Garrett knew exactly where he would wait for his brother. He strolled directly into the sumptuous office with the plaque EMERSON WELLS, PRESIDENT on the door. He took the seat in front of Emerson's desk and laced his fingers behind his head as he waited, taking in his surroundings with an admiring eye. Apparently his half brother appreciated art—he had a vitrine full of pre-Columbian artifacts that stretched across an entire wall. There were no photographs on his desk; in fact, there were hardly any personal effects at all.

After a few more minutes the man arrived, and his murderous expression told Garrett he didn't like seeing him one bit.

But he *had* agreed to the appointment, at last.

Emerson sighed and crossed his arms. "Which one of the three brothers are you?"

"The middle one," Garrett said.

Emerson's expression softened somewhat at the news, and for a moment, Garrett even sensed that he'd dropped his guard a little. His voice was still wary, though. "So you're the one who was there when Father died."

Garrett's insides went icy cold at the reminder, but he still managed a curt nod, though Emerson hadn't seemed to phrase it as a question anyway.

"He say anything about me?" Emerson asked, and Garrett flashed back to the sidewalk, the street, the concert they'd just come from that night.

Chest knotting up painfully, Garrett dragged in a long, steadying breath. "He tried to speak, but he couldn't get much out."

The talk about his father made the memory so goddamned fresh now, his stomach roiled. He thought back to Dave Devaney's last breath, and to Kate. The way her face had crumpled when the police had brought Garrett home and he'd told everyone that both men were dead.

Kate wanted a family. A family she'd never had, because of *him*.

There hadn't been a night since she'd said that when he hadn't recalled her words. He hadn't been able to face her a moment longer. She'd torn him open and apart, and for weeks he'd been grappling for ways in which he could ever make it up to her. Would he never be able to put it behind him? Was she leaving because Garrett reminded her too much of what she couldn't have? Or because she'd never forgive him for repeatedly screwing up her life?

Shaking the disturbing thought aside, he stood up and stuck his hands into his pants pockets, assuming a casual stance as they faced each other. "I can tell you want me gone, so I'll happily drop the chitchat. My brothers and I want to make a deal with you. We're not interested in making friends, and we know you aren't either. What we're interested in is business, and judging by the luxurious surroundings and the Picasso on the wall, you're a man who thinks of business just as we do. Am I right?"

Though he was dark-haired like Garrett, Emerson's eyes weren't the same. He had Landon's silver eyes instead, and they glowed eerily with warning. "My father ran me over like a goddamned mongrel without a tail. I won't allow the same from you."

"I'm sorry that he felt he had to," Garrett said, but he understood what his father was trying to protect. He hadn't wanted his wife to ever find out he'd strayed. So he'd cut off his illegitimate son and lover from his life, only to die so soon afterward that his lawyers had still been paying off the woman for her silence when it happened.

It had been tragic, to watch his mother find out she'd been betrayed. When she could do nothing about it.

She'd been broken at the funeral—crying nonstop at first, already having found out from the accounts, and the lawyers, her husband had not been the faithful, loving man she'd always imagined. Garrett had had his own grief on his shoulders, and he'd blamed himself for the pain he saw on her mother's face. His mother would have never found out about Emerson, or another woman, if her husband hadn't died so abruptly and she hadn't been forced to take over the financials of the family. The records of money sent to another woman's account, regularly, sparked alarm, confusion, until finally, the truth had sunk in.

"He freaking ruined my life. He broke my mother's heart and mine, too," Emerson grated, his teeth tightly clamped as he curled his fingers into fists.

Garrett was taken aback by the hard anger in his half

brother's eyes. Would Cassandra Clarks be able to handle
being married to this guy for six months? He appeared
only half-civilized, and dangerous, to boot.

"Emerson, I'm sorry if the measures he took were not
to your liking, but your mother liked them very well,"
Garrett said. He was referring to the three million-dollar
payments she'd received for her silence—after his father
died. Not to mention that he'd already been providing
for her to have quite a healthy living while he was still
alive. Emerson couldn't have been more than twelve at
the time. Julian had barely been ten. Garrett had been
fifteen and Landon eighteen.

If their father hadn't died, Emerson would be walking the streets without the Gage brothers ever knowing
he existed.

Maybe they should have tried to contact him. Maybe
Emerson resented that, too. But just seeing the grief on
their mother's face had been enough to make them want
to keep him as far away from the family as they could.

Maybe, all hell would break loose when Mother once
again realized they were dealing with him. But Landon
had said that he'd take care of Mother. Enough time had
passed that hopefully she'd look beyond her dead husband's transgressions at this point. And their mother was
shrewd when it came to business, too.

"Will you meet with me and my brothers to discuss
our business proposition? We really need your help."

Impatient, Garrett waited for Emerson's answer, but
his half brother only glared at him as he slowly headed
over to resume his place behind his desk.

Emerson was more rugged than all his brothers, and
even with his well-groomed appearance in that gray suit,
there was an air of isolation around his tall figure that

made Garrett somehow relate to him. He knew that Emerson was somewhere between Julian and Garrett in age, so that put him around twenty-eight or twenty-nine. His hair was dark as Garrett's, his face as square and tan, but personality-wise, he seemed to be a wild card.

"I'll give you a half hour," Emerson finally conceded, his expression unreadable as he dropped into his chair and powered on his computer. "But not today. I have too much to do."

"Fine," he agreed. "Tomorrow then. Be at the *Daily* at nine a.m."

"No can do. I'm afraid I can only do it Friday."

Friday wasn't ideal. It was three days from now and only a day before the wedding. But Garrett ground his molars, shut the hell up and took the offer. Something in Emerson's angry expression when he looked up and gestured at the door to signal the conservation was over told Garrett this offer was the best he'd get from him.

"Don't be late," Garrett growled as he left.

"Kate, I'm calling and calling and no answer, then I come to get the things for the shower and they're not even baked! What is wrong with you? It's ten in the morning and we have work to do. This is our last gig before we're swept away with all this wedding stuff. You didn't talk to anyone all weekend. What's the matter? It's Tuesday. A new day awaits!"

Kate groaned when a chirpy Beth yanked open her bedroom curtains and a shaft of sunlight sliced between Kate's eyelids. She waved a weak hand in the air and rolled onto her stomach.

"Go away, Beth."

"No, I'm not going away. You, my sleepy little chef, will stand up, take a shower and—"

"I'm pregnant," Kate groaned.

"—get to work. What did you just say?"

Kate covered her face with the pillow and screamed into its feathery depths while kicking off the sheets tangled around her ankles. "I'm pregnant. *God!* I'm such a fool. Fool, fool, *fool.*"

"You're pregnant as in…you're with *child?*"

Kate sat up and cracked open her puffy eyes. "Three tests, Beth. Three. And they all agree on the fact that I'm preggo. What am I going to do?"

Sighing in misery, she covered her face with her hands, refusing to answer the string of startled, quick-fire questions Beth bombarded her with next. *"Well, whose is it? When did this happen? Why didn't you tell me? When did you find out, damn it? Are you sure?"*

Oh, Beth. She was like a bright little shooting star today—a bright little shooting star in Kate's dark gray world.

Was Kate sure? Yes, she was sure. The test stick couldn't get any pinker! The two lines, almost neon in their brightness, had been clear enough to spin Kate into a whirlwind of despair all through the night.

While miserably pondering what to do, Kate heard Beth shuffle around the room, no doubt in search of the pregnancy tests. Beth was big on evidence and that sort of thing. This came from being married to a douche bag before she'd fallen in love with Landon.

When her friend couldn't seem to find them, Kate muttered, "They're in the trash, Beth."

"Oh."

Beth disappeared into the bathroom. Kate glumly

wondered what Garrett would do when he eventually found out she was carrying his baby. She remembered how handsome he'd looked two Sundays ago at brunch. He had been thoughtful and dark as sin, and staring at her so intently and so intimately, Kate had barely been able to eat anything. She'd felt eaten by *him*. He'd stood to follow her when she'd gone to pretend to fill her plate at the buffet, and she'd felt his hand at the small of her back. "You all right?" he'd murmured.

"Of course. Why wouldn't I be?"

"You've been so busy with work, I keep wondering if you're avoiding me."

"I'm sorry. We can talk at the rehearsal dinner…that is, if you don't…if you're not bringing…"

"I won't bring anyone if you won't," he said, staring at her intently.

"I won't," she assured him.

"Then I won't," he said back.

And oh, how she wished she had the courage to say she was sorry for what she'd said to him that day in her apartment, but the continued talk she heard from Molly and Beth regarding the Clarks and Gage wedding was driving her insane with jealousy and anger.

It killed her. How could he? How dare he tell her he wanted her in his bed while he was planning his brilliant and very convenient wedding? The desire that had whipped them up like tornadoes had now dropped them hard on land, and the whirlwind and the emotions in the air had been reduced to nothing.

Nothing but a one-night stand, that's what it had been.

But of course, good ol' Murphy's law had come for a visit and made *sure* Kate got pregnant.

And now they were going to have a child together.

"Yes. You're pregnant," Beth agreed when she came back out of the bathroom.

A silence settled bleakly in the room.

You're pregnant....

Her chest gripped with yearning. Along with the inexplicable fear of dying alone, without a family or anyone to love her, Kate had harbored another kind of fear for years. It was one of those little fears that took root in you and you never really knew why you had them—only that you did.

She'd feared she'd prove infertile when she grew up, and that she'd never be able to have the family she'd always longed for. She'd imagined, on her best days, that if she ever got pregnant, the thrill she'd feel would obliterate anything else.

Now, maybe a little kernel of thrill had taken up residence somewhere, in some quiet, motherly part of her, but it was too hidden to recognize.

Kate had proven fertile, yes. Physically capable of having a family, yes.

But she had conceived this baby with Garrett Gage.

And her considerable pride already smarted like *hell* since she knew she would have to tell him. Especially after this past month, when they'd both pretended at the family Sunday brunches that they were still just friends.

Kate saw that Beth had her cell phone in her hand and leaped out of bed. "No! What are you doing?"

Beth held the phone out of Kate's reach, her expression stern as a concerned mother's. "I'm calling a doctor. Unless you want me to call Garrett, Kate. It's his, isn't it? You look pale, Kate. I think—"

"Call anyone and die. Do you hear me?"

The thought of Garrett knowing this so soon, before

she had time to build up her emotional walls against him…the thought of him finding out that just the thought of carrying his baby inside her made her queasy and restless…and the thought of him demanding to *marry* her out of duty and honor and all he held dearer than Kate…

No. God, it was worse than she could imagine.

Her worst nightmare come true.

Beth paused when she noticed the angry flush spreading up Kate's neck. Lips pursed, she hung up, and started dialing again.

"No! Beth, don't you *dare*."

"I'm calling Molly, okay? We need to figure out how we're handling this with the family. Don't even try to stop me this time."

Kate groaned. "Molly's getting her paintings shipped to New York, and she's got enough on her plate with a wedding in five days!"

"Fine, then Julian. Julian will help us with this, Kate, you know he will."

An image of hunky, easygoing Julian, never judgmental, always one for cool-headed thoughts, flitted through her mind. Julian had always been the perfect coconspirator. Not only did he know how to stay quiet, it was his nature to.

But Kate still shook her head. "Beth, the wedding is in five days. Let's just…drop this for now. Please. Please don't tell anyone until I'm ready."

Beth met her eyes dubiously. "But what are you going to do when you see Garrett at the rehearsal dinner? At the wedding? When are you going to tell him?"

"After the wedding. I can't do it before. I want Molly to enjoy her day," she said miserably.

"No, no, no, that's not a good plan. It might be too

late, Kate. He might be engaged by then to another woman!"

Pain wrenched through Kate's insides. "I don't expect him to stop his plans for me. Honestly. We could be better parents if we weren't together than if we are forced to be together."

"You're afraid, Kate, and that's okay. But you're turning into a coward. Where's the girl I know? The Kate I know would fight for him. Stop being afraid that he will break your heart. You're breaking it yourself without even letting him know that he has it."

Kate couldn't reply.

But the words replayed in her head like an echo of a truth she wasn't sure she was prepared to listen to when she had a pregnancy to deal with.

Was Beth right?

Was Kate so afraid of letting him in that she was running away, not from being hurt by him, but from *loving* him?

Oh, God. And now what was she going to do about Miami?

Nine

Kate was turning out to be one of those pregnant women who had nausea every morning, and it wasn't fun at all. But at least by Thursday evening at Molly and Julian's rehearsal dinner at the Gage mansion, she felt better. The wedding was to be held this upcoming Saturday at noon, and the gardens had been bursting with activity all day as contractors had started delivering tables, chairs…the works. Through the windows on the other side of the living room, Kate could see the beautiful white trellis that would serve as the chapel, halfway to being fully erected.

It was going to be a beautiful wedding.

Her heart soared as she watched Molly and Julian laugh while talking to the minister. Julian towered behind Molly, who seemed to be leaning back against him as if he were a pillar. His arms were loosely around her, his chin resting on the top of her head.

There was no doubt in Kate's mind when she saw them that they belonged together. Molly had always loved Julian, but Kate hadn't realized that Julian had loved her sister back until a couple of months ago.

She'd always believed in having one soul mate…until, at eighteen, she'd realized that the man she thought might be her soul mate didn't seem to agree. He'd never openly touched her like Julian had touched Molly, but now she kept remembering the way he'd made love to her.

Did he *care* about her? Or was this all about her leaving?

"There you are!" Kate heard the booming voice of Eleanor Gage from nearby, and in the same instant, spotted the person she was speaking to as he came into the room.

Dressed in a black suit and gleaming silver tie, Garrett made such a striking figure that the atmosphere altered dramatically with him near. His beautiful face looked thoughtful and intense as he kissed his mother on the cheek, then lifted his head and seemed to be scanning the area for something. His gaze stopped roaming when he saw her, and she couldn't breathe.

With an expression almost of relief, he came over. He had such purpose in his step, and her heart almost stopped when she saw the way his eyes glimmered with…happiness?

Oh, God, she was going to die when she had to tell him.

"We should've driven over together."

His liquid black eyes raked her figure, and her pulse skyrocketed as though he could suddenly see with some sort of X-ray vision the little baby growing inside her.

For a moment she thought he knew. He knew her secret and it would all be out in the open.

Drawing in a deep breath, she blew a loose strand of hair out of her face. "I hitched a ride with Beth and Landon." The thought of being alone with him in the close confinement of his car again both terrified and excited her.

The more distance she kept from him, the smoother her plans would run.

He seized her elbow and pulled her along the room, leading her to the terrace doors. "Come with me outside."

"Why?"

"Because I want to talk to you, Kate."

She let him lead her to the exact spot they'd visited on his birthday, when he'd found out she was leaving. Rather than release her, his hand stayed on her elbow as he smiled and took in her dress with the thirsty eyes of a man who intimately knew her.

The situation worsened when he bent his head and his voice caressed her ear, its texture a seductive black velvet. "So what have you been up to? Besides avoiding me?"

She ducked, not wanting him to know he still made her knees weak, her insides mushy. She wished—goodness, she wished—that Garrett wasn't considering marriage to another woman, so that Kate wouldn't dread the moment she'd have to mention a child was on the way so much.

"Working and...packing."

"Packing," he repeated without any inflection whatsoever.

The fact that his hand was on her elbow, causing all sorts of ripples of want inside her, made her drop her gaze to take in the contrast of his tan skin with her fair complexion. As though that were an instruction for him to let go, he dropped his hold.

His eyebrows pulled low over his eyes—eyes that were hard with frustration.

"Kate, honestly, what the hell are you running from?"

Anger flared inside her. What else would she be running away from but him? "What do you care if I leave? Why are you so hell-bent on stopping me? Go and worry about your heiress!"

"I will, but you come first, Kate. You've always come first for me. Before anything in the world. And I happen to be responsible for you, Kate."

"Oh puhleeze! Responsible, my fanny. I'm a grown woman, Garrett, a fact that you can attest to yourself. Why do insist on continuing to treat me like your sister?"

"Sister? Kate, I freaking *slept with you!*"

Her eyes widened in shock. Her throat clogged with emotion, and she spun around toward the glass doors. "I can't do this right now. Not here. Not now."

He stopped her with one hand. "I'm sorry, I didn't mean to upset you. But it would be very damn simple for me to marry an heiress right now if it weren't for the fact that you and I made love, Kate."

"We had se—"

"We made love."

His eyes glowed down at her fiercely. Crazily, she even thought she saw longing there. But if he longed for her, why would he even consider marrying anyone else?

"I told you it was a mistake. Please just carry on with your plans, and I'll carry on with mine."

"God, you're so stubborn, Kate." He propped his elbows next to hers on the balustrade and gazed outside, his expression pained. "You'll never be able to forget your father died because of me, will you?"

She swallowed and shook her head. "No. That's not true. I don't blame you, Garrett. You were just a boy, and you wanted to help your father. Like you always want to help everyone. You misunderstood what I said. I might have blamed you for a time because I needed someone to blame. I was so angry."

"Me, too." He leaned forward and stared at the cluttered tables and chairs out on the lawn, and Kate watched his profile as the urge to touch him began to consume her.

"But my anger isn't about that now. It's about me. It angers me to want something that I can't have."

He glanced at her curiously, his head cocked to the side as he patiently waited for her to explain.

"Having a family is something I've wanted my whole life," she admitted, softly.

He dragged her into his arms, and she was so exhausted from learning she was pregnant, she closed her eyes and let him. His thumb stroked her arm, causing goose bumps to jump along her bare flesh.

"I never thought I'd have one of my own, and now I can't stop thinking about it," he whispered.

Fighting to ignore the sensual stirring inside her, Kate closed her eyes, her connection with him too great to ignore. She suddenly wanted to cry, right here in his arms, at his confession. Because she was sure he was imagining having a family with someone else, with a woman he might marry for convenience. Not with Kate. Still, she loved him so much she couldn't hate him for wanting the same thing that she did.

"You deserve to be happy, Garrett. You've tried to take care of all of us for so long. Even Julian and Molly."

He rubbed her back and she rubbed his. "They hate me for making them keep their hands to themselves until now." His whisper stirred the top of her hair.

His scent made her light-headed but instead of drawing away, she drew closer and inhaled, happy that he had an arm around her. "You've always tried to do the right thing."

His lips twitched against her scalp, and he edged back and glanced down at her, searching her expression. "You've always trusted me, Katie. To do the right thing. But you don't trust I'll make the right choice with Cassandra?"

Her stomach twisted uncomfortably, and when she attempted to pry free, Garrett kept her pinned to him. Even his eyes held her trapped. "Relax. Let's not fight, all right? Let me just hold you like this."

His body emanated heat, and her every cell perfectly recalled the night she had belonged to him. Kate's throat closed so tight she couldn't talk, especially when she settled down against him once more. He ran a hand tenderly down the back of her head, and she relaxed her muscles despite herself.

"Katie, let me make it better for you," he whispered against the top of her head.

Kate closed her eyes. She knew he felt compelled to watch over her, but Garrett had been tied to his promise and had looked at her as a *duty* his whole life.

Kate would rue the day she ever trapped him any further.

But now she was carrying his baby.

"If you leave—" he tipped her chin back to look at

her "—who's to tell me it isn't your way of making me come get you?"

She edged back, wide-eyed, then scowled. "I would never do that! I don't want you to…do anything. Plus, it would be hard for you to follow me with a new wife attached to your arm."

"A wife I will not have if I choose not to," he said. "Why don't you tell me why you're so interested in her if you're not interested in staying here?"

She glared, and suddenly it was just too painful to look at him.

She shook her head, and turned to walk away but he wasn't letting her go just yet.

"Where are you going, Katie?" he taunted. "Do I frighten you? Is it me you're running away from?"

She was struggling, but he caught her and looked fiercely into her eyes. His breath fanned her face, slow and steady, warm and unexpectedly sweet.

"Garrett…" she whispered, dying with want as she clutched his shoulders.

He squeezed her. "Kate, I've known you all my life. I've been there for you all my life—I have to be there for the rest of it. You have to let me. We need to talk about what happened. We can't just pretend that it didn't when I'm consumed with knowing that it *did*."

Her eyes were fastened to his mouth, and all she could think of was that his mouth was *there* for her. His lips were there to sear her again, brand her again. Kate trembled with the need to wrap herself around his shoulders and neck and never let go. She wanted to crush his mouth with hers and do all the things she hadn't done with anyone else because she'd been waiting for the boy she secretly loved to *look* at her.

Now he was looking at her. His gaze hungry, missing no detail of her features. Almost seeing into her soul, discovering her secret, aching love for him.

"Tell me why you're leaving. Is it because of me?" He couldn't seem to help himself as he lifted his finger to trace her lips. Her breath caught, and his face darkened as he watched.

Kiss him. Tell him it's him and that he's going to be a father! But while all these impulses rampaged through her, she drew back an inch and considered it a good moment to retreat before she truly lost her senses. She'd lost them once. Now she was pregnant. She didn't want to castigate him for that night, a night she had been wishing and praying would someday happen. She didn't want him to pay with his whole life. She simply loved him too much.

Kate shook her head and glanced away. "No, it's not you."

Spinning away before she could lose her head, she hugged herself and stared into the house, where there was light and music and smiles everywhere.

"You could be carrying my—" Garrett cleared his throat behind her "—you could be pregnant, Kate."

The air felt static as she turned back to him in alarm. "Excuse me?"

The intensity in his eyes terrified her. "We didn't use protection, Freckles."

She shook her head. Fast. Almost too fast.

"You'd tell me if there were consequences, right?" he asked meaningfully.

Her world tilted on its axis. What if she went ahead and told him that she was having his child? Her stomach cramped at the thought.

She was loath to worry Molly a day before her wedding. Kate was the eldest and had cared for her like a mother, had always set a good example. How could she bear detracting from her sister's joy right now?

She had to wait until after the wedding.

She bit her lip, glancing away. "Whatever happens, I meant what I said. I'm not marrying ever without love."

"Why? Do you love another man?"

Swallowing, Kate met his stormy black gaze. "No, Garrett. It would have been hard for me to love anyone, when my whole life I've been in love with you."

He blinked at her words.

God.

She couldn't believe she'd said them.

But she had.

She had to come clean.

She glanced away, blushing. "That's why I slept with you that night, Garrett. And that's why I'm leaving. I want to be loved back."

He stared at her as though flabbergasted, motionless and unmoving.

"We need to go. Dinner is about to be served," she murmured and went inside.

He didn't follow her for minutes, and from inside, she saw him leaning on the balustrade with his face in his hands, breathing hard.

Her insides knotted with pain for him. Maybe she shouldn't have confessed it. But Beth was right. Kate was a coward, afraid he'd hurt her. She'd had to at least let him know that all the time they'd spent together had meant everything to Kate, even when she knew he had not ever been emotionally available to love her like she wanted him to.

Garrett was a fair man. He was a man who recognized his own flaws, maybe even to the extreme extent that he saw flaws where none existed. She knew he felt…unworthy. That he believed a man had died because of him. But he was also generous and giving, and he wouldn't be able to stand the idea of causing Kate any pain.

He'd let her go so she could find what she was looking for, especially once he recognized that he wouldn't be able to give it to her himself. And he'd marry his heiress, for whom he wouldn't need to feel anything. But at least Kate had stopped lying to him and to herself about not loving him anymore. At least she'd told him her real reasons for leaving.

Baby or not, she would still go.

Once they were seated at the tables in the formal dining room, she felt him stare at her as intently as ever from across the floral centerpiece.

Waiters brought over the salads first—arugula, organic pear, goat cheese and candied pecans, topped with a soft vinaigrette dressing with a hint of pomegranate. That was followed by an assortment of lamb, duck, beef tenderloins and chicken medallions, accompanied by the most deliciously spiced vegetables Kate had ever tasted.

She ate whatever she was served and almost still felt a little hungry. But most of all, she was conscious of everything Garrett did on the opposite side of the table. Under the table, she held her hands over her stomach, where she could feel and sense her baby, feeling almost nostalgic that the father was so close, and didn't even know what he'd just given her.

She stole peeks at him throughout the night as idle conversation abounded. When their eyes met, emotions and confusion flooded her.

Once they were enjoying a variety of sorbet, cheese, and sweet desserts, Landon pushed his chair back and stood. "Cheers! To Julian and Molly," Landon said, and glanced at Garrett.

Kate saw the manner in which Garrett nodded somberly at Landon, almost as though saying, "You're next," and Kate jerked her eyes down at her plate, the nausea suddenly coming back with a vengeance.

But no matter how fervently she wished it, there was no taking back her *I love you*.

The next morning, all three Gage brothers sat across the conference table from their half brother. Garrett noticed how Landon and Julian were taking stock of their brother. Emerson was beastly in size, very large and muscled. As president of his personal security business, it seemed fitting, but today Emerson was also proving to be a very moody man. He'd seemed impatient to leave from the moment he arrived.

It seemed truly unjust to Garrett that his father had treated Emerson and his mother the way he had. And when he'd died, he'd ended up hurting everyone, for the truth easily had come to light. Their lawyers had had to explain to the Gages, once they took over all the financial accounts, why there were so many transfers and payments made to an unknown woman.

When they'd learned it was because this woman had borne a Gage son, Garrett's mother had entered a wild depression for years, and he didn't even want to think of how it had been for Emerson and his mother. It had hurt the Gages to lose their father to death, but the pain of losing him while he was living might possibly be even worse.

Now every bit of pain and resentment marked Emerson's hard, unyielding features. Garrett couldn't know the true extent of his resentments, but he'd bet they ran deeper than the man let on. His energy was too controlled, and his eyes were too ruthless and sharp to reveal his emotions.

Garrett knew it would hardly matter to Cassandra which man she married as long as she got out of her brother's clutches, and he and his brothers would be happy to compensate Emerson for the task.

If, that was, they could convince the stubborn man to agree to this whole scenario.

With a bleak, tight-lipped smile, Emerson finally spoke after Landon explained the situation. "If this chick is as hot as you all say, why don't *you* marry her?" he asked, silver eyes trained on Garrett.

"Garrett's not inclined to marry," Landon answered. He sat calmly in his leather chair on the opposite side of the conference table.

"Well, that makes two of us," Emerson said with a growl. "I'm never marrying, especially no damn heiress."

"You might like to reconsider with what we're offering," Landon said, signaling at the open folder sitting before him on the table. "You'll be a very rich man, Emerson, if you agree to this."

"I'm already very rich without needing to deal with any of you."

"Emerson, we're talking fifty million for your take *alone.* That's almost ten million a month for just marrying her."

"Why don't *you* do it?" he persisted, glaring at Garrett.

Garrett wasn't going to tell him why.

But he still remembered Kate in his arms on the terrace last night. He'd been so damned excited to have her in his arms. He'd wanted to make love to her again, had been more than ready to physically. He could have moved back so that she wouldn't notice, and perhaps she hadn't, but instead he'd remained in place, his every sense attuned to her, to the contact of their bodies—the press of her belly against his erection. He'd wanted to press harder into her, to devour her and break her every resistance until she gave him everything he wanted, and admitted to everything he needed to know. At the same time, he wanted to protect her from everything and everyone.

He hadn't pushed, but he knew the thought of leaving was killing her. He knew Molly's wedding had to get to her. Kate was a woman. And she was the older sister, almost like a mother to Molly.

He wanted her. Needed her with a force he'd never needed anyone in his life. Physically, he wanted to be with her again, but it was more. It had always been more with her. *She loved him....*

But he wasn't going to tear his guts open in front of Emerson, not even in front of his other brothers, so when silence reigned, Emerson sighed and rose.

"Sit down, Emerson. I'm planning to marry someone else," Garrett snapped, scowling because he'd had to let the cat out of the bag.

Emerson plopped back down and cocked a brow. "Should I start renting a tux?" he asked, his cockiness reminding Garrett of his younger brother, Julian, somehow.

"Rent it for your own wedding. You won't be coming to mine."

"*My* own wedding is tomorrow and we need this engagement settled. So are you in, or are you out, Emerson?" Julian demanded.

Emerson eyed Julian, then Landon, then Garrett, then Landon again. "There's only one thing that would ever tempt me to agree to this farce."

"Name it and it's yours," said Landon with his business voice.

"I want the Gage name. I'm as much his son as you are. My mother provided a paternity test, and he refused to acknowledge me. I want it acknowledged today. If I get my rightful name, you have a deal."

Garrett crossed his arms and eyed Landon, who seemed to be the one most reluctant to grant Emerson's wish. Garrett wasn't against it. The Gage brothers had no right to withhold something their own father should have granted his kid in the first place, but they would need to talk to their mother first. She was a just woman, but she might need some time to get used to the idea of a fourth Gage in town.

In a terse but quiet voice, Landon spoke at last. "When you go through with the marriage and quietly walk away from Cassandra without trouble, we'll amend our former agreement so you can become a Gage."

Emerson rose to his feet. "I'll need to get it in writing."

"Of course," Landon assured him.

"So do we arrange for them to meet?" Julian queried, rising, too, probably eager to leave to get his other business in order before his wedding and honeymoon.

"Do whatever the hell you want," Emerson snarled. "Just tell me when and where I get to meet my wife."

"So, it's done then," Landon concluded, still keeping

up his cool facade. But once Emerson stalked out of the conference room, Landon sighed wearily and scraped a hand along his face.

"Mother's going to throw a fit."

"Let's not tell her yet. He's not a Gage until he carries through...and he might fail," Jules said. Then he swung his full attention to Garrett. "So do you have something to tell us, bro?"

Garrett knew what he was referring to, of course.

It would have been hard for me to love anyone, when my whole life I've been in love with you.

She'd killed him with those words. He'd been replaying them in his head all night, dying in his bed, aroused and pained when he relived them. He wanted her by his side. He wanted every inch of her. Now, his chest swelled with emotion as he reached into his jacket pocket and pulled out a small blue velvet box. He opened it and extended it so that both his brothers could see the ring nestled at its center.

Julian chuckled and swung his head up with a look of incredulousness. "That ring is obscene, man. I've never seen anything as obscene in my life."

Garrett scowled at him. "Tiffany and Company doesn't do obscene."

"But *you* do."

Ignoring the jibe, Garrett studied the brilliant rock. It was the whitest, the purest and yes, the biggest he could find in seventy-six hours. An 8.39 carat, D, internally flawless round brilliant, in a solitaire platinum band. And he had every intention of putting it on Kate's ring finger.

"I need to make a statement," he murmured at Julian,

who seemed to be amused by the fact that Garrett had gotten himself in this mess in the first place.

"Statement. You mean like 'I'm a jerk and I had to make up for it with a big rock'?"

"Go to hell."

"Tsk, more respect, old man. You're marrying my fiancée's sister."

"If she'll have me," he grumbled.

"A little drastic of you to do this just so she doesn't move to Florida, don't you think?"

Garrett snorted.

He just wouldn't let her leave.

For years, he had seen that need in her, calling to him like a siren song. He had needed to summon more self-control every year not to cave in. He had prayed she would one day realize she was too good for him and move on. Now, he needed to prove to her the opposite. He needed to remind her what that night had meant to him, how it could have been between them all along if two deaths and a lot of regret hadn't stood between them.

He freaking *loved* her, too. More than anything or anyone.

He wasn't letting her go.

He was ready to chase her to Florida if he needed to.

He held the ring between his fingers and watched it catch the light. The man at the store said it was guaranteed to make a statement, and when Garrett had said, "Guaranteed to make her say yes?" he'd nodded amiably. If only the man knew half of it. That she could be pregnant with his child.

His stomach roiled once more at the thought, and he snapped the velvet Tiffany box closed.

If she wasn't pregnant, he couldn't wait for her to be.

She wanted a family. He hadn't realized how much he wanted one, too, until now.

He imagined being a father in eight months.

She didn't seem to want to consider the possibility, but he did. Hell, he even hoped she was pregnant. *Because she'd have to take me no matter what.*

It had been years since he'd had a father. Kate herself probably no longer remembered what her father had smelled like, felt like. Garrett barely remembered his own. But he could remember how good it had felt to have him around, and he burned with the desire to be one himself. Protective and just, but he wanted something their fathers hadn't given them.

He'd once thought he'd never marry. For Kate was out of his reach.

Now he would marry no one else. And he wanted a litter of little kids for them. Girls and boys.

He would bond with his boys over cars and planes, money and business....

As for girls, a picture of a red-haired little girl like Kate popped into his mind, and his toes almost curled with the love he already felt for that little thing he'd pamper like a princess.

Then he thought of Kate when she was young, the age when her father died. His chest constricted at the reminder. Garrett still dreamed about that night, and woke up drenched in sweat, hearing the sounds of gunshots. Sometimes in his dreams they were shooting at Kate and Molly. Sometimes at his brothers. And the worst part was that Garrett survived every time.

And somehow it was always Garrett's fault.

Would he never do things right? Would his actions always hurt the people he cared about?

He breathed out through his nose as he shoved the ring box into his suit pocket. It wasn't time yet. But it would be. And once he put that ring on her finger, it would never be undone. She would be his.

And he'd spend his life making things right for her. For them both.

Ten

Molly was freaking out in the bathroom of Eleanor Gage's master bedroom, waving her hands in front of her face as her cheeks turned crimson. "It's too tight, it's too tight. Kate, it's too tight."

"Molly, you just had it altered."

"Kate, I'm pregnant."

Kate's eyes widened with joy and disbelief. "You are? Molly!" Kate squealed and hugged her, and Molly crushed her in her arms. "Does Jules know?" Kate demanded.

"No! I'm saving it for tonight. I'm almost bursting with excitement and bursting out of this damn dress! I wish I'd just married him in my boho skirt. I know he'd love it because it's more me."

"Yes, but you've already bought this beautiful designer dress, and now we want you to wear it," Kate said, shushing her and trying to see where she could loosen the material to give her some air while Molly hyperventilated.

The dress had a lovely bell skirt and a tight top—very much like the bridesmaids' dresses that Kate and Beth wore, except the bridesmaids' dresses were blue.

"Molly, relax, you look stunning," Kate assured her. Molly nodded, and their gazes locked in the mirror. Kate's eyes began to tear up. "I love you, you know that?" Kate said softly, patting Molly's bun, which needed only the veil to be perfect.

Molly turned and squeezed Kate's hand, then placed it over her stomach—where she carried Julian's baby. "I want to beg you not to go, Kate. Especially now."

Kate could almost feel the connection between both their babies as she touched her sister's belly. Her throat constricted with the need to tell her sister she was pregnant, too. She imagined sharing all things pregnancy-related with Molly and her heart swelled. "I don't want to go, Molly. The thought of not seeing my niece or nephew and not being here for you…" *And of my child not being close to people who would offer so much love.* "I'm just afraid."

Sympathy flooded Molly's blue eyes. "Kate, I know… I know you don't want to see him, especially with him getting ready to marry someone else."

The reminder that the man she loved would marry someone else while she would be alone with his beautiful baby, somewhere else, set a new world of pain crashing down on her. Her eyes stung.

It might be her pregnancy hormones. Or the fact that time was galloping closer, ready to slam into her. It would be time to leave soon. It was time for her sister to marry. This morning Beth had told her she'd heard that Garrett had proposed to Cassandra already, and she'd wanted to warn Kate to be strong during the wedding in case he appeared with her.

He'd told her he wouldn't bring anyone. But if they were engaged, he'd bring her, of course.

Yes. Soon, it would be time for Garrett to let her know that it was done, that he was engaged to another woman. But then, she already knew from Beth.

She helped Molly with the veil, all the while blinking back the tears, and then she softly kissed her cheek. "You're the most beautiful bride I've ever seen."

"Kate, I want this for you," Molly said, gesturing at her wedding dress.

Kate nodded. "That's why I might just go after all, Moo. To find love and hopefully a family of my own."

They shared a forlorn smile, until Eleanor's shout from the bedroom snapped them out of it.

"It's time, my little Molly dear!"

Molly's eyes widened in excitement and she immediately puckered her lips into an O and drew in a series of little panting breaths that made Kate laugh. Poor Molly would probably be anxious for Julian to get her out of that dress tonight.

Molly smacked Kate's derriere. "Come on, sis. Let's go make that man mine," she said cheekily, and Kate adjusted her train around her arm and told her she'd be right out.

It was definitely the hormones. Or maybe a broken heart. Or the sentiment of watching her baby sister in a wedding gown.

Whatever it was, Kate sobbed quietly in the bathroom stall for a quick minute, and then wiped her tears and patted her makeup dry. Once her eyes didn't look so swollen, she went out into the gardens.

It was a perfect day for a wedding.

A breeze rustled through the oak trees. The sun blazed high in the sky, and it seemed the entire elite from Houston, Dallas, Austin and San Antonio was congregated at the Gage estate, all sumptuously dressed, many of the ladies wearing high-fashion hats on their heads.

Flowers framed the beautiful arched trellis, and the orchestra began softly with their violins while Kate quickly lined up behind Molly. She hadn't even thought she'd have the courage to see Garrett today, but he stood at the other end of the red-carpeted aisle next to Julian, whose smile was mesmerizing, his green eyes staring possessively at Molly.

Kate's gaze was magnetically drawn to Garrett, so stunning in his black tuxedo that her heart almost cracked with emotion when the "Bridal Chorus" began and Molly took the first step forward. Because this would never be her, walking up to him, like this.

Garrett's mouth was watering like crazy. He was supposed to watch Molly make her grand entrance but he could focus only on one redhead, and even from afar, he could see that Kate's eyes were full of tears, which just worried him and made him feel an insane need to go to her and embrace her and offer her support.

His thoughts filtered back to the day he'd met her. She and Molly had been brought up to the house by their father, the Gages' new bodyguard. Molly had been a little bitty thing, toddling over to give her lollipop to Julian. Kate had been just a tad older, but she'd been as open and chatty as a teenager, immediately warming up to his mother, asking why this? Why that?

She'd made him scowl, and when she'd turned to talk to Julian and warn him not to take Molly's lollipop, Garrett had immediately wanted her to pay attention to him, too. It had been the story of his life. Wanting her attention, her eyes on him, wanting everything from her and hating that he wanted it. He'd wanted to be the apple of her eye, and instead, he'd been the idiot who took away her father.

He'd promised himself he'd be her hero, and he'd tried like hell to protect her from everything he could—especially himself. When all he'd wanted was her. He'd withdrawn with ruthless self-discipline, telling himself that he'd never deserve Kate like Julian deserved Molly.

Today Garrett's eyes were wide open. True, the past was loaded with regrets, but when he thought of the future, one without Kate at the center of it was unfathomable. No man on this earth would ever love and care for Kate and fight for her happiness more than Garrett would. Chest bursting with emotion, he watched the woman he loved walk behind her sister. He saw how her soft smile trembled with emotion, and God, he wanted to hug her and kiss those tears away, telling her whatever changed in her life, he'd always be her constant.

He couldn't take his eyes off her as she came up the aisle. He imagined her walking up to him and his heart stuttered in his chest, he loved her so much.

Now she took her place across from Garrett as her sister tied the knot with the love of her life, and all Garrett knew was that he wanted to do this with Kate. He'd have Kate. Or he'd have no one.

"Dearly beloved, we are gathered here today…" The

priest began the ceremony, and for several minutes, Garrett waited for Kate's gaze to turn to him. Finally, her eyes flicked over to his, and his gut seized with need. She looked so beautiful. Her lips shone in a coral color, her blue eyes highlighted by the sapphire fabric of her dress. A silent plea brimmed in the depths of those eyes, and whatever it was she wanted, Garrett wanted to give it to her.

Not because he'd promised her father that he would. But because he was selfish and he got high on her smiles, got completely drugged and deliciously drunk with her happiness.

"I, Molly, take you, Julian John, to be my husband…"

As soon as he heard Molly speak, Garrett imagined Kate speaking that same vow to him. His chest squeezed as their gazes held across the altar, Kate's blue eyes continuing to tear him to pieces.

She still wanted to leave, didn't she?

But he wouldn't let her.

Not after he'd had her trembling in his arms and whispering his name and giving him everything he'd always wanted.

He'd told himself every night for the past thirty nights that she might have felt pity for him, or that they were just a man and a woman in bed together, getting caught in the moment. It was bull. What they'd been caught up in had been years and years of denied attraction. Burning chemistry. Heated glances. And he was sick and tired of denying himself *her*.

The day she'd made love to him had been the best day of his existence. And he wanted to have her in his arms, where she belonged, every day and night in his future.

"You may now kiss the bride!"

Kate blinked and tore her eyes from his, looking startled as Julian grabbed Molly and twirled her around.

"Oh, crap!"

They ended up tangled in the train, and Kate came instantly to the rescue. Kate. Always taking care of Molly.

"I got it," she said, laughing as she detached the train and Julian proceeded to carry a laughing Molly away, the blaring sound of the "Wedding March" following them.

Watching Kate struggle, Garrett stalked down the aisle, grabbed the other end of the tulle fabric and brought it over, watching her duck her head to avoid his gaze.

"Thanks," she said, and he wanted to kiss her. God, why was this so difficult? They'd grown up together. She was the only woman who knew him, truly knew him. What he liked and loathed. That he would never truly feel like he deserved a life of his own.

If he was going to open up with someone, it should be easy to do it with her.

But the way she was acting skittish and defensive filled him with dread. And he knew that this was going to be one of the hardest things he'd ever done.

She struggled with the tulle. When he reached out and captured her small hands, she sucked in an audible breath. His heart pounded as she looked up at him, those blue eyes wide and concerned.

"Tell me if I'm mistaken—" his voice was low "—but did my brother just marry your sister?"

She didn't smile, but looked intently into his eyes as if she was as entranced as he was. "It only took a full hour, Garrett. You couldn't have missed it," she said.

Her mouth, the way it moved, drove him insane. "Apparently I did."

"You were standing right there. Where were you? Mars?" She straightened and rolled her eyes as she started walking away, the tulle clutched against her chest, and he had to raise his voice a bit to be heard.

"I was in my bedroom, Kate. With you in my arms."

She went utterly still, her back to him, and he knew she remembered. He could feel it in the air, burning between them.

But she didn't turn. Instead, she started down the path that led to the Gage mansion. Garrett fell into step beside her.

"Kay, I need to talk to you," he said.

"If it's to tell me about your wedding, I already know. Congratulations," she said.

He cocked a brow. "Then maybe you can tell me the details, since apparently you know more about it than I do? Dammit, I need to talk to you somewhere *private*."

He grabbed her elbow to halt her, but she immediately yanked it free. "I need to talk to you, too, but I'm not doing it here. Nor am I doing it *today*."

Simmering with frustration, he followed her again,. "Well, I *am*. So just listen to me."

Stopping her, he forced her to turn and gazed into those accusing blue eyes, trying to find the words to begin the wrenching of his damned black soul. "I don't know what happened to me the other day, Katie….What you told me left me so damn winded, I swear I didn't know where to begin…."

Her hands flew to her ears. "Not here, please, *please, not here!*"

He pulled her arms down, scowling. "I know I hurt you, I know you don't want me to apologize, but I need to say I am sorry. I am sorry for how things have gone down and for hurting you. I'm sorry for how it happened, Katie. I wish I'd done it differently. If I could take it back, I would, if only to get you to stop looking at me like you are just now."

She whipped around to face him, her eyes flashing in fury. "You wish to take the night back, that's what you wish? Oh, you're something special, do you know that? You're something else. I can't even believe I let you put your filthy paws on me, you no-good—"

"Goddamn it, I really didn't want to do it this way, Kay. But you're giving me no choice!" Jaw clamped, he grabbed her and swept her into his arms and stalked across the gardens toward the house.

"Wha—" The tulle train fell inch by inch from her grasp and trailed a path behind them as she kicked and squirmed and hit his chest. "Garrett, stop! Put me down! What are you *doing?*"

He kicked the front doors open and carried her up the stairs, his jaw like steel, his hands blatantly gripping her buttocks. "Something I should've done a long, long time ago."

Kate froze for a second, and then struggled with more effort. "Put me down!" she screeched.

He squeezed her bottom as he charged down the hall and into his old bedroom, kicking the door shut behind him. "I'm not apologizing for the night I made love to you. Dammit, Kate, I'm apologizing for being responsible for your father's *death!*"

He put her down on the bench at the foot of his old bed and stepped back so she didn't kick him in the groin.

She went utterly still, but her chest heaved up and down, and damned if that wasn't an attractive sight.

He expelled a long breath and continued. "Kate, I'm not going to apologize for the time you were mine. I won't. I apologized once, but I didn't mean it. I don't regret a second of that time with you. Except not being more careful with you and more than anything, for not doing it sooner."

She sat there, stunned and panting, and Garrett was only just beginning. His necktie was almost choking him as all his emotions surfaced like a hurricane gathering force.

"I apologize for not listening to your father that night, Kate. For being stupid and not listening—"

"Don't!" she pleaded, raising her palms. "Garrett, please don't apologize for that. Or for anything. Please stop apologizing to me. It was an accident. And it was his duty. My father would have…gladly died for you, for any Gage, for any reason. He was passionate about his job, and he was as passionate about you boys as if you were his children. He'd have done it over and over for you, Garrett. He loved you and I love you. I've always loved you."

Her words were like a salve. They might never absolve him, but they appeased him, tamed the dark regret inside him. And stoked the little flickering flame of new hope there.

"You do love me, don't you, Freckles?"

She met his gaze in silence. My God, *her face.* The blush spread everywhere, it seemed, and Garrett trembled with the urge to undress her and see that flush crawl along her skin.

When she didn't say a word, neither affirming nor denying it, he knelt.

* * *

Kate's eyes almost popped out of their sockets as Garrett Gage knelt at her feet.

"You asked me what I wanted from you—Kate, I want everything. The works. Yes, I want kids, I want to be your husband. I know I robbed you of a real family, and I want to give you one. I want to be the father of your children...not because I promised I would take care of you. Because I'm crazy-sick in love with you."

His words sucked the wind out of her.

She sat there, clutching her stomach, not even remembering where the tulle had ended up falling on their way here. Runaway tears streamed down her cheeks as the things Molly and Beth had told her about a Clarks-Gage wedding vanished from her head and she realized with a fluttering heart that Garrett Gage was proposing to her.

"Kate, I've never felt like this before. I can't think clearly when it comes to you. I've been trying to make you stay and at the same time that has driven you away. Don't go, baby. Stay with me. Here. Be my wife. Let me love you like you deserve."

She cried even harder, not believing this was happening. She had dreamed about this. For years. To the point that now her entire life and all her decisions revolved around forgetting it. Around trying not to want what she could *never* have.

And now Garrett Gage knelt, dark and beautiful at her feet, his face somber in its intensity, his gaze like liquid fire.

"If you think this has to do with the promise I made to your father, it doesn't," he murmured as he took her smaller hand within both of his. "I made that promise a long time ago and I've tried to keep it as best as I could.

No, this is about me wanting to promise you, the woman I love, my future."

She wiped her eyes, and squeezed one of his hands with hers. "What about C-Cassandra…?"

"She's marrying Emerson. Our half brother."

"Wh-what do you mean h-half—?"

A movement in the doorway made them both look up in surprise.

"Kate! What…?" Beth blinked. "I'm sorry…uh. This is a bad time, isn't it?"

Garrett nodded, but Kate shook her head and wiped the rest of her tears away. "What is it, Beth?"

Beth pointed in the direction of the stairs behind her. "They're all seated at the tables. And the maid of honor and best man need to speak before the toast."

Garrett dropped his head and cursed under his breath.

"We'll be right there, Beth," Kate said, trembling from head to toe as she rose to her feet.

Garrett held her up and stroked his thumb along her jawline. "You can answer me later," he said softly.

She nodded and rushed to the bathroom to pat her face dry with a tissue, making sure her mascara wasn't dripping all over her face. Garrett waited outside in the hall for her, and every cell in her body screamed at her to fling herself into his arms when she realized he was still there. But she didn't.

In silence, they went downstairs and into the gardens, and halfway there, after the backs of their hands bumped several times, he took her hand within his and led her across to their table.

Her throat closed, and she tried very hard not to think about the gesture and how many times she'd wanted it. It screamed "boyfriend" in her mind. Lover. Love.

Feeling as though five hundred pairs of eyes were on them as they made their way through the tables to the far end of the room, Kate held her gaze on the bride and groom.

Her fingers tingled when her hand unlatched from Garrett's and they each headed to their places on opposite sides of the long table, where Molly and Julian sat watching them with wide smiles. Garrett went to stand at Julian's side, and Kate stood next to Molly. Eleanor had indicated that she didn't want to speak, and she seemed to be hiding behind a tissue right now, but Kate remembered how the groom's mother always thought it proper that ladies go first. So Kate was the first to speak.

Regrettably.

She cleared her throat several times and shakily grabbed a small microphone, struggling to keep her voice level as she tried to quiet her racing mind. "Molly had a favorite story she liked for me to read," she said into the microphone, keeping her eyes on Molly to keep herself focused. "There was a part she loved to hear, when Piglet asked Winnie the Pooh, 'How do you spell love?' And Pooh answered 'You don't spell it…. You feel it.'"

She blinked back her tears as she studied the delightful little bundle by the name of Molly, the only blood family Kate had known for over two decades. Seeing her sister so happy as she started a family of her own with Julian, while Kate herself had a baby in her tummy from the man she loved and a proposal she had always dreamed of, made her suddenly feel weightless with joy. Laughing to herself, she lifted her glass with her free hand.

"Molly and Julian, you guys felt that love for each

other before you could spell it. And I'm just glad you didn't listen to me, Moo, when I filled your head with warnings and my own fears. I'm glad you listened to your heart."

People clapped and drank, and Kate sat down only to hear Garrett's sexy voice coming through the microphone next. "For the better part of my life I've thought it my duty to protect Molly from your claws, little bro."

Julian threw back his head and let out a great peal of laughter, soon joined by all the other guests, and Garrett winked at Molly. "I got to be the ogre separating you two for years, for which I hope you won't always hate me, Molly."

"I forgive you if you finally kiss my sister!" Molly shot back, throwing him a white rose she'd plucked from the centerpiece.

Garrett caught it and laughed, then glanced at Kate and held it in the air, as if promising to give it to her. Tucking it into his pocket, he glanced back at the groom.

"There's no denying that I got to be the voice of reason when Kate and Molly came into our lives, Jules. Because I knew better than you that we were both done for."

He turned his attention to his new sister-in-law next. "Molly, my brother loves you more than anything in the world," he told her, lifting his glass now. "And if you take care of my brother, I promise I will not only kiss your sister, but I will not rest until I make her my wife."

The guests whooped and cheered, as Julian stood to slap him on the back and everyone seemed to glance at Kate for a moment. Their smiles almost pleaded with her not to be stupid and just snatch up this man for herself.

And she would.

Of course she would.

She knew Garrett would want an answer, but before she could give him anything, he would need to know that she was pregnant.

Oh, God. She was having his child, and he loved her. He. Loved. Her.

The hours sped by. Soon, they were served the artichoke hearts with a special tangy mustard sauce, a variety of meats, an assortment of vegetables and desserts to spare.

By the time Molly and Julian were ready for the first dance, Garrett made his way to Kate, and she rose to her feet, anticipation making her heart race. She didn't know if she could postpone her answer until she had a chance to talk to him about the pregnancy. There was impatience etched across his features, as though he'd been waiting too long already to hear her acceptance and he wouldn't wait anymore.

He would want an answer now—she could see it in his eyes. Eyes that wouldn't stop staring at her.

Garrett's heart crashed into his rib cage as he approached Kate, who looked so warm and inviting as she waited for him to get close.

He let his gaze drift down her body, taking in the perky breasts encased in that corset dress he'd seen her try on, the form-fitting fabric that hugged her shapely hips and the skirt that flared over her legs. She wore her hair loose. Long and wavy and so damned glossy it looked like satin, it tumbled past her shoulders. Feather earrings clung to her little ears. And her eyes…

When he looked up at her eyes and found them staring at him with shy vulnerability, he almost couldn't take it, he wanted her so much.

He wanted these people gone, wanted her intimately, in his arms.

"Dance with me," he said quietly as he gently pulled her into his arms. She hooked her arms underneath his, and her hands curved over his shoulders from behind as she pressed her body to him and tucked her face under his chin.

He closed his eyes and savored the feel of her as she drew an invisible pattern with her fingertips along his back. She moved fluidly against him, like she belonged in his arms.

His insides thrummed with impatience as he held one arm around her waist, then slowly reached into his jacket pocket and pulled out the velvet Tiffany box. He clasped her left hand and slid the ring onto her finger, then lifted her hand so that she noticed the jewel as he kissed her knuckles, one by one.

He'd never been so impatient in his life.

He couldn't understand how he'd waited to claim her for so long, for he couldn't handle another second of wondering if she was still planning to move somewhere else.

"I need to hear you say yes," he murmured, tucking her hand under his arm as he kissed her ear softly. Her hair caressed her shoulders as she angled her head backwards an inch or two, and she looked at him with those blue eyes, shining with tears and emotion.

I love you, she'd said.

He was burning to hear it again.

"Say it, Kate," he pressed her, cupping the back of her head in one hand. Impatiently he fitted his lips to hers and hungrily searched inside her mouth for her response. When her tongue pushed back thirstily against him, she set him on fire. He splayed his hand at the small of her back and pressed her tightly to him as he dragged his mouth up to her ear. "Tell me yes."

She grabbed his jaw and turned his head so she could whisper, "I need to tell you something first."

He groaned, already burning with desire, needing to be with her. "Tell me after you've said yes."

She smiled. "You'd take me anyway? Whatever I have to say?"

He shot her a solemn gaze. "Yes, Kate. I would. Tell me yes, and then tell me what you want to say to me."

"Yes, I'll marry you. We're having a baby."

He drew back, staring wordlessly. His astonishment was so complete, his disbelief so overwhelming, he wasn't even breathing. "What baby?"

"Our baby, Garrett. We're having a baby."

"You're pregnant," he said, as if in a daze.

She bit her lower lip, her eyes shining with wariness and excitement and concern.

He shook his head to clear it, but it was full of one thought. Baby. Father. Parents. *She'll give me a child.... She loves me.... She'll give me a baby....*

"Kate...when were you going to tell me this? When?"

"I'm telling you now."

"And you were still going to Florida *without me?*"

Kate wiped away her tears.

"Were you?" he demanded.

"No," she admitted. "I'm not going anywhere. This is my home."

He was shocked. Suddenly he bent and kissed her stomach. "You're not joking me?"

"No. Molly's pregnant, too, but don't say anything."

He straightened again and seized her by the shoulders. "Holy hell, you have to say yes now."

"It was yes before, Garrett. It's…always yes. I've dreamed this. I've wanted it for so long."

He was reeling.

He looked at her and felt that same hot punch to his solar plexus. Then he pulled her back against him, infinitely closer.

He raised a languid hand to stroke the shell of her ear with the back of one curled finger. "Kate…" he murmured adoringly.

She gave him a smile, her eyes glowing. "Yes, Garrett?"

Jamming his fingers into her hair, he tipped her head back so she held his gaze. "God, we've wasted so much time, Kate."

"You said you weren't afraid. To love somebody." She cupped his jaw. "I am. I *was*. I won't be anymore. I'm going to love you like crazy if you let me."

"I'll not only let you, I'll encourage you. I'll do anything possible to make it true." He stroked her belly with one hand, and her scalp with the other. "Have you gone to the doctor?"

"I was going to. I kept hoping Beth and Molly were wrong. That you wouldn't marry Cassandra. And maybe… I'd try one more time to make you love me. Be honest with you this time. No more sneaky tactics to get your attention."

"Kate, you couldn't be sneaky if you tried."

"Garrett, I didn't want to trap you into marriage, please know that."

"I know, Freckles. You don't need to tell me this. But didn't you know? You trapped me with these ages ago…."

He stroked her seven freckles that he adored, then let his finger drift down to the flesh of her lips. "Trapped. Caught. I hardly ever got to chase you and I know you wanted me to."

"I didn't."

"You did."

"All right then, I did." She started running across the gardens, and for a stunned moment, he didn't realize she was heading back to the bedroom where he'd just proposed. Then everything in him burst to action and he chased after her.

Eleven

Garrett drove them over to his apartment, and their excitement made the air crackle between them.

She loved how he'd chased her, and caught her. The crazy man had *tickled* her. They'd danced together, laughed, enjoyed each other. Kate had never felt so free or happy. Garrett had never looked so content, his face never faltering from the dazzling white smile that curled her toes and warmed her tummy.

Now he led her down the hall of his apartment, and her body was going crazy from wanting him.

Their footsteps were rushed as she tried unfastening her dress and Garrett tossed his tux jacket on the floor, then left a trail of clothing to his room—bowtie, shoes, socks, vest.

"I can't wait," he said as he jerked off his snowy-white shirt.

Kate was breathing in little pants at the sight of him bare-chested. He watched her struggle to unlace her dress from the back for a moment, then said, "Turn around, let me get that."

His voice was gruff with desire, and her legs trembled as he got her dress undone. He eased the top half of her dress down to her waist, and then she caught her breath when his thumbs caressed her back in slow circles. She shuddered when he set a kiss at the nape of her neck as he started easing the dress off her hips, then splayed his hands over her rib cage and pressed her back against him before turning her around.

She wasn't wearing a bra and she mewed softly when his hands covered her aching breasts. Then she tilted her face upward as his mouth searched for and found hers.

He teased her with his tongue and rubbed her nipples with his thumbs. His body rocked against her, and Kate couldn't stand the agony.

"Garrett…"

All her emotions had spun and churned for days and weeks, and now she needed him inside her.

With her dress pooled at her ankles, he caressed his hands along the sides of her stockinged thighs. "Do you want me?" His low, erotically textured voice drove her insane.

"So much," she gasped, pushing against him so she could feel how much he wanted her, the proof in the erection straining against his dress slacks.

"Do you love me?" He palmed her between her legs, where a pool of heat had already gathered at the apex.

"Like nothing in my life."

He squeezed her sex in his palm. "I love you, Kate." He dragged his tongue along her neck and down her shoulders as he hooked his fingers around the waist-band of her stockings and tugged off the clinging material. He urged her onto the bench at the end of the bed as he removed them, and she sat and watched his dark head as he bent to tongue a wet path down her bare legs. Tingles of pleasure raced through her body. He tossed the stockings aside, and Kate edged back onto the bed, tossing away some of the decorative pillows as he unfastened his slacks and got naked.

He was beautifully masculine, tanned and hard, and swollen with desire for her.

"The last time I was with you has haunted me," he whispered as he started lowering his body over hers, his arm muscles flexing. Swallowing with a little sound of need, she spread her thighs to welcome him and he settled between them, his urgency matching hers as their tongues tangled heatedly.

"I haven't stopped thinking about it for a second, either," she admitted, nipping his mouth, then kissing his jaw, anxious to claim him like he was claiming her.

He teased her breasts with his thumbs, then grazed the straining peaks with his teeth. She moaned, and he lapped her with his tongue to make her delirious.

"You like that, Freckles? You like my mouth all over you?"

"I love everything you do to me."

He chuckled softly, his breath bathing her nipple tips as he mouthed her breasts, alternating from one to the other. He caressed them until she couldn't wait and was pumping her body eagerly for his penetration.

He primed her with one finger, then two. "I'll be careful with you," he vowed, and kissed her lips. "And you." He kissed her stomach, and Kate's heart unwound like a ribbon when she realized he was talking to their unborn child. "Freckles, I wanted this. You. I wanted something of ours."

"Then make me yours," she whispered.

He gripped her hips and meshed his mouth to hers as he entered her. She arched up for his thrust, clutching him. "Garrett."

He grabbed the sides of her thighs and kept them slightly raised as he inched deeper into her body. She tossed her head back with a grimace of pain that became absolute, exquisite pleasure when he was fully inside.

She was so turned on that every time he pulled out, her sex muscles clung to him, preventing him from leaving her. She wanted more of him, all of him, inside her.

She cried out when he started thrusting harder and deeper, and an explosion of colors rushed through her mind, stretching her nerve endings until they snapped and released. He growled and strained above her, and they rode out the pleasure together.

"That was amazing," she gasped when Garrett rolled over to the side and pulled her up against him. "You're so amazing." She hugged him, and he returned her hug, his arms hot and tight around her.

He clasped the back of her head and stared meaningfully into her eyes. "Every night from now on I want you sleeping in my arms."

"I'm not complaining."

He adjusted her against him so that he was embracing her from behind and his hands were splayed on her stomach. He spoke close to her temple. "If he's a boy, we'll name him after our fathers. Jonathan David Gage. And a girl...you'll drive me crazy if you give me a girl."

"You're the one giving it to me," she laughingly answered, and he turned her face by the chin and brushed her freckles with his lips.

"Always so contrary, my Kate."

"Garrett? Pinch me." He pinched her bottom, and she squealed.

He chuckled, clearly liking it. "Ask me to pinch you again."

"One's enough. I'm convinced I'm not dreaming now."

"You have a lovely bottom. If you let me pinch it again, I'll kiss it afterward."

She laughed. Feeling little tingles in her body, she nodded, and she felt the pinch that made her squeak, and then she felt his kiss, with tongue. It made her moan softly and cuddle back to him, wondering when she could have him again.

"Convinced it's no dream?" he murmured, brushing her hair behind her forehead.

With a smile that almost hurt, she turned over and pressed her face into his chest and stroked her fingers absently across his nipples, growing thoughtful. "Now what was it you were saying about a half brother?"

"You'll meet him soon," he told her. "He looks like me, actually."

"Wow, that good?"

He laughed. "Don't even think about staring for a moment longer than necessary."

"Why would I when I have you?" She tucked her head under his chin. "Why didn't we know about him?"

"Mother didn't want to know about him. But I think it's time we set the past behind us, don't you, Kate?"

"Yes, Garrett. I agree wholeheartedly."

Twelve

Sitting on her front stoop, Kate spotted Garrett's silver Audi turning around the corner and her smile widened. As soon as the car came to a stop, she started for the passenger door.

He couldn't even get out, she got in so fast. "Hey," she said.

His car smelled of him, of leather and spices, deliciously male, and it almost made her dizzy.

"Hey." He reached out and squeezed her hand, bending over and kissing her lips softly. "You look good."

She smiled. "So do you."

Once they arrived at the clinic, Kate filled out the paperwork while Garrett sat, enormous in the little chair out in the waiting room, pulling and pulling at his tie. There were pictures of babies and pregnant women hanging on the walls, but he only had eyes for Kate as she walked back toward him.

Soon, they were led inside to the ultrasound room.

Kate was lying down patiently as the doctor came inside, greeted them and pulled up her robe. After the doctor smeared a cold gel on her stomach, a little blob appeared on the screen.

Garrett had been standing back, but now he approached, his eyes on the screen.

"There we go," Dr. Lowry said.

Garrett peered at the screen, and Kate reached for his hand and squeezed, suddenly extremely excited. He squeezed back even harder, and smiled down at the screen.

"That noise you hear is the heartbeat," the doctor explained.

They were both silent as they registered this. Then the doctor took some measurements, and estimated the date of conception to be…of course, the night she accosted Garrett in his bedroom when he was sick.

"Thank God for strep," he said to himself, and his eyes glittered when he looked at her, as though that was the best thing that could have ever happened to him.

Sharing this with him was incredible. Irrevocable. She could feel the connection as they watched their child on that screen together.

The doctor gave them the estimated delivery date. "So we will be seeing you in two months to find out what you're having."

"Do we really want to know?" Kate asked Garrett.

"Hell, yes, we do."

She smiled and nodded.

The doctor slapped the folder shut. "In the meantime, everything looks fine, Mr. and Mrs. Devaney. You have yourselves a good rest of the day."

"It's *Gage*."

The doctor turned to Garrett. "Oh?" He quickly checked his folder, flustered and confused.

"I filled my name in as Devaney," Kate whispered to Garrett as she wiped the gel off her stomach. His eyes homed in on her bare skin like he wanted to lick the gel up and bury his face in her belly button.

"You're a Gage, too, starting tomorrow," he said flatly.

She rolled her eyes. "Of course I am. I just felt odd using the name before we go to city hall and church."

He helped her down from the examining table and kissed her softly but quickly. "You've always been a Gage, Kate. You've been mine from the start. I didn't need to sleep with you to show you that."

"Maybe you did." She smirked, patting her stomach, and he laughed.

Outside the clinic, he pulled her up against him when they got to his car. "Thank you, Freckles."

"For what?"

"For that night you spent in my arms," he whispered, framing her face in his hands and kissing her. "For agreeing to spend a lifetime of nights with me."

"No, Garrett," she said, cupping his face right back. "Thank *you* for asking."

* * * * *

A BABY FOR
THE DOCTOR

BY
JACQUELINE DIAMOND

Delivered at home by her physician father, **Jacqueline Diamond** came by her interest in medical issues at an early age. Later, during her career as a novelist, Jackie was inspired to follow medical news after successfully undergoing fertility treatment to have her two sons, now grown. Since then, she has written numerous romances involving medicine, as well as romantic intrigues, comedies and Regency historicals, for a total of more than ninety-five books. She and her husband of thirty-five years live in Orange County, California, where she's active in Romance Writers of America. You can see an overview of the Safe Harbor Medical series at www.jacquelinediamond.com and say hello to Jackie at her Facebook site, facebook.com/JacquelineDiamondAuthor.

For Jennifer, Steve, Jessy, Mickey and Courtney.

Chapter One

"That was unbelievable." Exhilarated, Dr. Jack Ryder stripped off his surgical gown, folded it inward to contain the soiled part and stuffed it into the specially marked laundry receptacle.

He wished his mentor, Dr. Owen Tartikoff, hadn't already left the operating suite so he could thank the man for letting him take the lead in today's microsurgery, a procedure known as pain mapping. Instead, he shared his high spirits with the anesthesiologist, Dr. Rod Vintner.

Rod quirked an eyebrow at the younger man's excitement. "Don't let it go to your head. In the Middle Ages, surgery was performed by barbers. By the way, I could use a trim." Pulling off his cap, he displayed a shock of graying brown hair.

"Getting a little thin in the middle," Jack responded. One of the techs, obviously new at Safe Harbor Medical Center, seemed startled at this exchange, so Jack explained, "Rod's my uncle."

"Barely," said the anesthesiologist, removing his glove from the edge, inside out to protect his skin from the contaminated surface. "We're the same age."

"Except that you're eight years older," Jack corrected mildly.

"Anything less than ten years is negligible." Rod slid his bare fingers inside the second glove and pulled it off, also inside out.

"In your fevered brain."

"I have much more interesting things in my fevered brain."
Rod replaced his surgical cap with a fedora. The look, combined with his short beard and sharp eyes, reminded Jack of
a college professor he'd once studied under, a fellow who'd
also been quick to pounce on a student's vulnerability but
was kind at heart.

As he washed his hands, Jack mentally replayed the surgery. The minimally invasive microlaparoscopy technique
involved making an incision about the size of a needle stick.
Then the patient had briefly been brought out of anesthesia,
and he'd used tiny instruments to touch the organs, allowing
her to react so he could identify the exact source of her pain.

After she was again under anesthesia, he'd removed the
endometriosis, excess cells from the uterus lining that had
spread to the abdominal cavity. The small amount might not
have troubled another patient, but each individual perceives
pain differently, and this patient had been in agony. Hopefully, she would now feel much better and be able to pursue
her goal of having a baby.

"I can't believe I hesitated to apply for this surgical fellowship," he commented to Rod as they left the suite. "Thanks
for nudging me."

"You'd been away from Southern California long enough,"
his uncle said. "Anyway, I needed a roommate and I like
your cooking."

Jack took a quick glance around the second-floor hallway. A couple of young nurses must have been watching for
him because they immediately made eye contact and flashed
him warm smiles. He gave what he hoped was a friendly but
distant nod in return. "Could you keep your voice down?"
he murmured.

"Why is it such a big secret that you cook?" Rod strode
alongside him toward the twin elevators.

"I learned a long time ago that if women find out I have
domestic skills, they'll never leave me alone," Jack said.
He'd unwittingly earned a reputation as a ladies' man in his
younger years simply by responding to women's interest.

Whether they were attracted to him as a doctor or as a single male, he'd never been certain, but the discovery that he was a good cook acted like an accelerant on a fire.

He'd soon realized how quickly some ladies made assumptions about having a future with him and how easily feelings could get hurt. So he'd done his best to avoid involvement. Until recently...

"Women never leave you alone," his uncle commented.

"Some of them do." *Especially the one I didn't mean to drive away.*

And there she was, waiting by the elevators, freshly scrubbed after surgery. Wavy brown hair tumbled around nurse Anya Meeks's sweet face, but her full lips no longer curved when Jack appeared and her intense brown eyes avoided his even while she'd been smoothly assisting him in the operating room.

He should have followed his own rules about not hooking up with a coworker. Yet something about Anya had drawn him to her from the start—her dark, humorous gaze, her quirky energy when they joked and the anecdotes she'd shared during operations about helping raise the younger siblings in her large family. After growing up longing for a stronger family connection, Jack had found those stories especially fascinating.

Which was why when he'd run into her at a New Year's Eve party five weeks ago and learned she was ready to go home before her designated-driver roommate, he shouldn't have offered her a ride. He'd been well aware of an undercurrent of attraction between them. Still, because they lived in the same apartment complex, the suggestion had made sense. But then he really shouldn't have walked her to her door, and then walked through her door, and then noticed the leftover mistletoe and claimed a kiss and then...

The experience of being with her had been so unexpected and powerful, he'd wanted to proceed with caution. Plus, Anya had urged him to leave before her roommate came home. "Let's just keep this light, okay?" she'd said.

Jack had agreed. After all, they *were* still coworkers and neighbors, and too much closeness too soon could spell disaster. He did want to see her again, but he'd figured they'd gravitate to each other naturally and let whatever happened, happen. But she'd avoided him ever since. During the past month, he'd done his best to throw himself into her path, but that had led exactly nowhere.

Anya pushed the down button, which was already lit. Jack searched for a casual opening that might persuade her to turn around. Nothing occurred to him that wasn't unbearably clunky.

"Got any plans for the weekend?" Rod asked him.

Jack didn't want to answer such a question in Anya's presence, even though his schedule was extremely boring. "It's only Thursday."

"The lady next door mentioned baking pies with the apples her sister gave her," Rod continued. "I think she was hinting. With a little encouragement, you could…"

"She's a real-estate agent," Jack said between gritted teeth. "She thinks we're rich doctors and she can sell us a house."

Anya kept her back to them, but he saw her shoulders hunch. Didn't Rod realize she could hear every word?

Jack wasn't trying to put the moves on her. He simply regretted that, for some unknown reason, she'd taken a dislike to him after what he'd considered a thrilling encounter that had left them both deliciously sweaty and breathless. She'd moaned louder than he had, he'd be willing to testify.

Scratch that. No testifying. No public testimonials of any sort.

Anya pressed the button again. This floor didn't show the lights from all six stories, so they had no idea where the cars were.

"Must be a lunchtime holdup," Rod remarked. "There's always a chatterbox who can't stop gossiping with her coworkers."

Anya turned, finally. "Why do you assume it's a she?"

"Women usually have the best gossip," Rod replied without hesitation. "Heard anything good lately?"

Long dark lashes swept her cheeks as she glanced down. "This is ridiculous. I'm taking the stairs."

Before she could leave, Jack said, "Why don't you drop by for dinner tomorrow night? I'm broiling pork chops with an orange-rosemary dressing."

Rod stared at him, then spread his hands in a what-the-hell-gives? gesture.

"Tempting, but no," Anya replied, flicking the tiniest of glances at Jack but otherwise keeping her eyes on the ground. "See you around, doctor."

Off she went, a cute figure in that blue-flowered uniform. Even cuter without it…

Stop that, Jack reprimanded himself and started after her. He caught the heavy door to the stairs before it could close in her wake. "Hold up!"

She halted. "What?"

"I…" *Think fast.* "I want to apologize if I've offended you. I didn't call you…afterward…because, well, you gave me the impression you wanted to take things slow."

"That's right," she said.

"You're not mad?"

"No, and thanks for the African violet. Zora and I will give it a suitable burial." She began her descent.

Jack paced alongside. "You killed it already?"

"Not yet, but the light in our unit is terrible," Anya said. "Also, I know you don't usually do laundry on Sunday mornings, so don't pretend otherwise."

"I ran into you by accident." *Weak, Jack, weak.* "Spilled stuff on my clothes the night before."

"While cooking?" Beside him, she lifted a dark eyebrow. Much more effective than when Rod did it. He had no quick comeback with her.

But he'd better speak before they reached the bottom, which was coming up fast. "New recipe. Kind of exploded."

"Sorry I missed the fun."

"So everything's normal between us?"

"Why wouldn't it be?" With that nonanswer, she shouldered the exit door.

Although not completely reassured, Jack hoped that in a few days she might reconsider joining him for dinner. He wanted to be alone with her, to have her bright spirit focused solely on him.

One problem: he'd have to get his uncle out of the apartment. Jack supposed he might encourage Rod to go out with their Realtor neighbor or join an internet dating site. One lousy marriage shouldn't sour the guy on women forever.

"If you're headed for lunch, we could share a table," he said to Anya just as a muscular guy in a dark blue nurse's uniform materialized. He had dark hair, a confident swagger and a couple of tattoos extending from beneath his short sleeves.

The bar pin disclosed the stud's name as Luke Mendez, RN. Jack had never seen him in surgery or labor and delivery, so most likely he worked in the adjacent office building.

"Hey," the man said to Anya. "New developments. You won't want to miss this."

"Miss what?" Jack asked.

"Nothing important," Anya told him. "See you around." Off she went with Nurse Tattoo in the direction of the cafeteria.

Well, damn. Briefly, Jack considered buying lunch at the cafeteria, too. He wouldn't sit at the nurses' table, of course; the only doctors who did that were married to nurses, and even then they usually respected each other's separate social circles. Still, he was curious about what he might overhear.

Don't be an idiot. She'd said everything was fine between them. Furthermore, having been up since before dawn, he could use a nap. The shortage of office space at Safe Harbor forced newcomers like Jack to see their patients on evenings and weekends in shared quarters. It was after one o'clock now, and he had to return by five.

Why should he care about Anya and her chums? Whatever they were doing, he'd find out soon enough via the hospital grapevine and his uncle. So why did he feel as if he was missing something?

So JACK COOKED, Anya mused. It gave him a certain domestic appeal—as if a guy with bright green eyes, thick brown hair and a million-watt smile needed or deserved any further advantages.

As she accompanied Luke—Lucky to his friends—to the cafeteria, Anya felt propelled by her own mental kicks in the butt. Downing two drinks on New Year's Eve was no excuse for jumping into bed with her handsome neighbor. His clumsy attempts to score a second time—which is what she assumed he was doing, given his reputation—were mildly amusing, but she wasn't that big a fool.

She had a more pressing problem—her period being three weeks late. The pill was 99.9 percent effective when used properly, which she did. She ought to take a pregnancy test, but she was almost certain it would prove negative. When it did, Anya preferred to have expert advice on hand because there was definitely something wrong with her.

She doubted it was stress. She wasn't *that* upset about her stupidity in bedding Jack, nor about her roommate pressuring her to move to a cheaper place rather than renew their lease. So was this a hormonal imbalance? An autoimmune disease? At twenty-six, surely she was too young for early menopause.

She checked her phone. No text from Dr. Cavill-Hunter's nurse about working her into today's schedule.

In the cafeteria, Anya studied the posted menu. "What's the special? I don't see it."

"They're out of it," Lucky told her. "It's nearly one-thirty. Just grab a sandwich, will you?"

Anya folded her arms. "What's the rush?"

"People have to get back to work."

She hated pressure. It usually inspired her to go even slower, but she was hungry. Also, across the busy room, she spotted a halo of short ginger hair that identified her roommate, Zora Raditch, sitting across from patient financial counselor Karen Wiggins. Karen's hair color this week: strawberry blond with pink highlights.

The third woman at the table, Melissa Everhart, projected pure gorgeous class with her honey-blond hair in a French twist. Melissa worked with the hospital's recently opened egg bank as egg donor coordinator.

They weren't sharing a table by accident, nor from long-standing friendship. They had serious business to discuss, and it included her.

By now, Lucky was jogging in place. Anya chose a pastrami pita sandwich with avocados and sprouts, sweet-potato chips and iced tea. She paid the cashier and followed her impatient companion.

The three women huddled over a sheet of paper. "You could have this room in the front and Anya this one on the side," Karen was saying as they approached.

Glancing over her roommate's shoulder, Anya saw the floor plan of a two-story house. "I thought you were all set for renters, Karen."

Zora swung around, braced for action. "We're getting a second chance, Anya. Come on! We'll never find a more fun place to live than Karen's house, and it's really quiet and backs onto a park."

Here we go again. For the past year, Anya had relished both the close companionship and the comparative privacy of living with just one friend. Having grown up in a crowded household where her family's expectations, assumptions and criticisms weighed on her constantly like a heavy coat in summertime, she had no interest in sharing quarters with a group.

"That isn't a park—it's wetlands. Mosquito central," Anya responded, setting her tray on a clear spot. "What happened to the two guys who'd signed on?"

"Ned Norwalk decided he prefers living alone." Ned was a fellow nurse. "I wish he'd told me sooner." Karen scowled at Lucky.

"I had nothing to do with that." Turning a chair backward, he sat at the other open space. "I like him."

"But you hate Laird," Melissa noted.

Lucky shrugged. "Karen, I'm sorry, but you know how he is. A few drinks and he's making passes at random women." Catching Karen's eye roll, he added, "*Unwelcome* passes."

"So you chased him off," Karen grumbled.

"Once you come to your senses, you'll thank me," Lucky replied.

Quietly eating her sandwich, Anya conceded that she didn't like Laird either. He might be a psychologist and family counselor, but in her opinion, he could use some counseling of his own.

"How'd you get rid of him?" Zora asked.

Lucky addressed his response to the others, ignoring Zora, as usual. "I may have implied that I'd make his life miserable if he moved in. That's all."

Karen smacked the table. Anya had to grab her iced tea to prevent a spill. "This may be a game to you, Lucky, but I can't make the payments by myself. Now that the renovations are finished, I need a full house. Otherwise, I either have to raise everyone's rent sky-high or sell."

For years, Karen—now in her early forties—had cared for her ailing mom while medical expenses ate up their savings. They'd had to defer all but the most essential maintenance on their five-bedroom home. A few months ago, though, following her mother's death, the counselor had taken out a loan to upgrade the electrical, plumbing and appliances. Then she'd solicited her friends and coworkers to move in for what Anya had to admit was a very reasonable monthly rent.

"It's perfect timing. I understand Anya's lease is up for renewal." Lucky didn't mention Zora. Anya wondered how the two of them expected to share a house. The potential for conflict added to her distaste of the idea of moving in with them.

"You can have the bedroom on the side," Zora wheedled. "I'll take the noisy one in the front."

Everyone stared at Anya. The combined pressure was so

strong, she half expected her chair to tilt. Fortunately, she
was used to resisting pressure. "Zora and I will discuss this
in private," she said.

"Coward," Lucky teased.

"Sharing a kitchen shouldn't be a big deal because you
hardly ever cook," Zora pointed out. As Anya had explained
to her friend, she'd grown up shouldering more than her share
of household duties in her large family. Heating a can of soup
and eating a premade salad felt like a heavenly indulgence.

"And I gather the rent will be considerably lower than what
you're paying for your apartment," Melissa added.

Anya calmly started on the second half of her sandwich.
She had shared her objections with Zora, and the polite
refusal she'd voiced several times previously ought to be
enough for the others.

Karen drummed her fingers on the table. "Contrary to
what you may believe, a wetland is not a swamp. It's a vibrant
ecosystem. A healthy wetland actually reduces the mosquito
population thanks to the thriving birds, frogs and fish."

"And other insects that feed on mosquito larvae," added
Lucky, who'd clearly heard this speech before.

"I just love frogs, fish and insects." Anya's irony didn't
extend to birds. She did enjoy those, except maybe pigeons
in the vicinity of her car.

Zora widened her eyes in mute appeal. Fortunately, there
was little danger of her jumping ship on Anya. Until recently,
Zora, an ultrasound technician, had occupied a pariah-like
status around the hospital because she'd stolen a popular
nurse's husband a few years back. Then, a year ago, Zora had
needed a place to go after her husband cheated on her, too,
and Anya had agreed to move in with her. Zora had burst into
tears of gratitude and they'd had each other's backs ever since.

"I can give you until Sunday night to decide," Karen said.
"Monday, I'm posting the vacancies on the bulletin board."

"Oh, come on, Anya," Lucky said. "You haven't given us
a good reason. My bedroom's downstairs. You ladies will

have plenty of privacy on the second floor, and I can do guard duty."

Anya ignored him and moved on to her sweet-potato chips.

The others shifted to regard someone approaching, as if the short, uniformed woman with thick glasses might be their salvation. Instead, Eva Rogers zeroed in on Anya.

Smiling and holding up her phone, Eva said, "Just got a cancellation. Dr. Cavill-Hunter can fit you in at 6:45. How's that?"

"Fine," Anya replied, trying to keep the bite out of her voice. The other nurse should have more discretion than to approach a patient in front of others, but Anya was grateful for the appointment.

"See you then." With a wave, Eva sauntered off.

Around the table, four very interested faces turned to Anya. "Is anything wrong?" Lucky asked.

"It can't be routine or there'd be no reason to jump at a cancellation," Karen observed.

"Need me to come along for moral support?" Zora asked.

Anya stood. "That's the other reason."

"The other reason for what?" asked her roommate.

"The other reason for not moving into the house." Anya picked up her tray. "Gossip."

She left without waiting for their reactions. Although she'd rather not offend anyone, she had bigger issues to deal with.

Chapter Two

"How is this possible?" Sitting on the examining table, Anya hugged herself through the thin gown.

Mercifully, Dr. Adrienne Cavill-Hunter had broken the news without Eva in the room. Anya's skin was prickling with apprehension so one skeptical look, or even a sympathetic murmur, and her blood pressure might soar to dangerous levels.

The blonde obstetrician rolled her stool over to sit beside Anya. She had chosen this doctor not only because she saw patients in the evening, but for Adrienne's quiet, rational manner.

"Are you taking any over-the-counter medications that might interfere with your birth control pills?" the doctor inquired.

Now, there was a question Anya hadn't considered. It was almost reassuring in its medical focus. And it didn't imply that she'd screwed up by missing any pills.

"The only thing I took was St. John's wort after spending Christmas with my family," she said.

The obstetrician tilted her head questioningly. "Why St. John's wort?"

"It was kind of a depressing experience, and I heard it might help." Anya had chosen the herb, widely available in capsule form, after reading that it was as effective as standard antidepressants with fewer side effects. "Can it interfere with birth control pills?"

"Yes, it can." Dr. Cavill-Hunter—who'd expanded her name after her marriage last month—answered in a level, nonjudgmental tone. "St. John's wort decreases the level of estrogen in the body, which reduces the effectiveness of the pill."

Anya smacked her forehead. "That's why I'm pregnant."

"Not entirely," the doctor said wryly.

True, there'd been no immaculate conception. If only she and Jack had used a condom, too. But in the heat of the moment, they hadn't been able to find one.

Now here she was, stuck in a massive, life-changing situation that Anya couldn't wrap her mind around, except for one important point. "I can't have a baby by myself."

"Many women do," the doctor said gently.

"Not me." Just supervising her three younger sisters had often overwhelmed Anya.

She still had nightmares about one afternoon when she was twelve. After her mother's arthritis had worsened, it had been Anya's responsibility to walk the seven-year-old triplets home from school each day. But Anya's period had arrived unexpectedly and she had to borrow a pad from a teacher, causing her to be late. When she finally arrived at the elementary school, there'd been no sign of Andi, Sandi or Sarah. For a painful half hour, as she traced the path they should have taken home, frightening scenes from TV newscasts had rolled through her mind. What if someone had taken them?

Realizing they might have stopped for a snack at their grandmother's house around the corner, Anya had run there and rung the bell with her heart pounding. Her grandma's gaze had been reproving, but she'd been greatly relieved to find her sisters safe.

Until she faced her father's fury later that night. *You need to take your responsibilities seriously. Why can't we depend on you to do things right?*

Dr. Cavill-Hunter asked a question, jerking Anya back to the present. The doctor had asked about the father and was waiting for an answer. Anya said sharply, "We aren't even dating. It was a mistake. Do you have any resources about adoption?"

"You can take several avenues in that regard." Choosing her words carefully, the doctor continued. "But there's no reason to rush this decision. This is a shock. It's wise to consider what it means to have a child and what kind of family support you might receive."

Anya shuddered at the thought of her family. Returning to Colorado this past Christmas to visit her parents and six siblings had reawakened painful old feelings and reminded her forcefully of why she'd moved to California. "Forget that."

The obstetrician didn't argue. "All right. You can choose a private adoption—either open, with continuing contact, or closed. Or perhaps you have a family member who might take the child."

"No family." Nor did Anya care to deal with a social worker. This was her decision, and she wouldn't be lectured or questioned about her motives. "Can you recommend a lawyer?"

"The hospital's staff attorney could give you a list of family attorneys in the community." The obstetrician cleared her throat. "I'm adopting a child myself, a relative. We're using a lawyer named Geoff Humphreys."

That name rang a bell. "His associate is handling Zora's divorce." She'd have to tell her roommate anyway, so that seemed convenient. "Thanks for mentioning him."

"There's something else." The doctor laced her fingers. "As I'm sure the attorney will inform you, the father has to sign a waiver of parental rights before the child can be released for adoption."

"He what?" Anya would pull all her hair out by the roots before she'd involve that—what was the legal term she'd read?—*casual inseminator.*

Okay, that wasn't fair to Jack, although other nurses *had* described him as a playboy. In her observation, his dramatically good looks simply attracted a lot of women. In her case, despite their joking around in the O.R., he'd always kept a respectful distance. Until New Year's Eve.

That night, while they were dancing at the party, she'd imagined she saw a spark of tenderness in his gorgeous, sparkling green eyes. That, combined with a couple of unaccustomed drinks, had worked magic on her nervous system. Plus, she'd been feeling lonely and estranged from her family after that unhappy Christmas visit.

Jack had been wonderful in bed, fierce and gentle and very skilled. Too skilled, maybe. Anya hadn't had much time for men in her younger years, and her college boyfriend had been sweet but fumbling. Now, her vulnerability scared her. Losing control of her emotions reminded her of how little power she'd had over her life until she left Colorado two years ago.

So over the past few weeks, she'd kept things cool with him, strictly business. He'd gone along at first, as embarrassed as she was, she supposed. Then he'd started flirting again. But she doubted he meant anything by it. He was notorious for avoiding relationships.

And now she needed his permission to choose adoption for her—their—baby? "It's outrageous," she added for good measure.

"It may seem unfair, but that's the law," Adrienne said. "Discuss this with your lawyer. I'm sure he can handle the paperwork."

"So Doctor...Mister Dad gets the news via the U.S. mail?" That was likely to provoke unpleasant repercussions. "I'll deal with him some other way."

Judging by the obstetrician's expression, she hadn't missed the reference to a doctor. She let it go, returning to the pregnancy.

"Based on the dates you gave me, you're about six weeks along, which means you're due in mid to late September," she said. "In case you're interested, the baby's eyes and limb buds are starting to appear at this stage."

Too much information. Anya performed the mental equivalent of closing her ears and skipped to a more bearable topic.

"Six weeks? It's only been five weeks since we…since conception."

"We measure pregnancies from the date of the last menstrual period," the doctor reminded her.

"Oh. Right." All this theoretical knowledge seemed quite different when you were the patient, Anya reflected glumly. "I haven't had any morning sickness. Well, maybe a tiny bit. I thought it was some chorizo I ate."

"Let's talk about a healthy diet during pregnancy," the doctor said, seizing on the topic. "Or are you already familiar with all this?"

Being a scrub nurse, Anya didn't deal with maternity on a regular basis. Also, in her state of shock, she could scarcely recall her own phone number, let alone the rules for moms-to-be. "Refresh my memory. Do I have to eat anything weird?"

"Depends on what you consider weird."

"Seaweed?"

Adrienne smiled. "That won't be necessary, although seaweed is quite nutritious. It's a rich source of antioxidants and vitamins."

Anya wrinkled her nose.

"You can skip it, though," the doctor said. "Be sure to include plenty of fruits and vegetables in your diet. No alcohol or tobacco, no raw fish such as sushi, and avoid soft cheeses. They can carry bacteria."

"I can't eat Brie?" That sounded cruel to Anya. Another mark against Jack. Someone ought to deprive him of Brie for the next eight months.

Oh, don't be childish.

"If the milk's pasteurized, it should be safe," the doctor said. "Cut out caffeine, or at least cut back. No undercooked meat or paté, and limit your fish consumption to twelve ounces a week in case of mercury contamination."

This discussion set Anya's stomach churning. "Can you give me a list?"

"I'd be happy to." From a drawer, the obstetrician fetched several pamphlets and a prescription pad. "Also, we advise that you avoid changing kitty litter because of toxoplasmosis, a disease that sometimes infects cats and can harm the baby. Do you have a pet?"

"Just an African violet." Which Jack had given her. "I hate him," Anya burst out.

The doctor paused, brochures in midair. "The father? Understandable."

"It isn't his fault," Anya conceded. "But that only makes me even madder. I want revenge on somebody, and he's nominated."

"You might write down your revenge fantasies," Dr. Cavill-Hunter responded. "You can always shred them later."

"Can I post them on the internet?" Anya didn't seriously expect an answer. She was simply venting. "Is this what people mean by pregnancy hormones making you cranky?"

"I'd say it's a legitimate emotional response to a difficult situation."

Did the doctor have to be *this* rational? Right now, Anya would prefer a friend to share her righteous wrath.

The rest of the office visit passed in a fog. The doctor answered routine questions. Eva produced a packet of sample vitamins and pregnancy-related goodies and set up the next appointment. Tactfully, she refrained from commenting.

All the while, Anya's emotions seethed. *Revenge. Revenge. Revenge.* Only how did you do that? Especially because she was the one who'd messed up her contraception.

Worse, she had to get the father's stupid John Hancock on the adoption paperwork. Her anger shifted toward the idiots in the state legislature, who she presumed had mandated this. Busybodies. Nanny government.

Don't think about nannies.

In the lobby, her mood didn't improve on finding that the pharmacy had closed minutes earlier. Not that she needed to fill the vitamin prescription in a hurry, but it left yet another pain-in-the-neck detail to take care of.

As she turned away, a twinge of nausea ran through her. Suddenly morning sickness was striking in the evening.

As Anya pressed her hands over her stomach, reality hit like a blast of icy wind. She was pregnant. Carrying a child. About to become a mother. Frequently, she assisted at surgeries for women desperate to conceive and willing to undergo complex, expensive treatments. How unfair this situation was to them—*and her*.

Anya wished she could bless one of them with this miracle because it had happened to the wrong person. She was utterly unready to take on the tremendous job of raising a helpless little person. She was sure to screw up.

Now she also had to deal with the practical side of pregnancy. She faced nearly eight more months of fluctuating hormones and a variety of body aches and pains. How long could she keep working as a surgical nurse? What would her parents say?

Nothing. Because she didn't intend to tell them. To them, it would be yet another sign of her immaturity, of her not being able to do anything right.

Grumpily, she shouldered open the glass exterior door and stopped at a real blast of cold air. February. Ugh. Accustomed to mild Southern California midday temperatures, she'd worn only a light jacket.

Behind her, the elevator doors slid apart and heavy male footsteps smacked across the lobby. "Hold up!" A pushy man—*was there any other kind?* her hormones demanded—reached above her head to hold the door.

It was Jack. Of course. Could this day get any worse?

As always, he smelled like soap and masculinity with a splash of lime. His dark blue coat fit his broad shoulders and strong body as if designed for him. Oddly, she realized, his scent had a soothing effect on her stomach, making her crave more of his nearness. All the more reason to hate him. She trudged on.

He halted on the front walkway. "Anya!"

"Yes?" She wondered what the correct etiquette was for

this situation. You couldn't just blurt, *"I'm pregnant, so sign the parental waiver,"* could you?

That would be efficient but not very diplomatic. Out loud, she said, "We should talk." There, that was better.

Before she could say anything else, though, he asked, "Can you give me a ride?"

They lived in the same complex, so why not? Plus, they'd have a chance to talk away from prying ears. "Okay. What happened to your car?"

"I loaned it to my uncle." He walked alongside her toward the parking garage.

"Where's *his* car?"

"In the shop, as usual." Jack's body partially blocked the wind, cocooning Anya. "He was supposed to pick me up after my office hours, but we had a family emergency."

Anya had never heard about any other members of Jack's family, aside from Dr. Vintner. "I hope it's nothing serious." Much as she'd like for him to suffer, she only wanted him to do so on her terms and without involving innocent third parties.

"Long story."

"Yeah, don't bother to tell me," she grumbled. "Never mind that I'm doing you a favor."

Anya couldn't believe she'd said that out loud. She never snapped at doctors. She hardly ever crabbed at anybody, in fact, except Zora, who could take it.

When they reached the car, Jack put his hand on her arm. The warmth lit a tiny flame inside Anya, a reminder of how comforting it would be to nestle against that strong chest. *Sigh.*

"You're right. I'm being rude." He withdrew his hand as she clicked open the car. "I'll give you the details on the way."

She'd meant to use the ride to talk to *him*. Maybe instead she'd drop her bomb as they parted company at the apartments. Good idea. Not exactly primo revenge, but a satisfying poke all the same.

"I can't wait," she said.

"HAVE YOU HEARD the story about Rod's kids?" That seemed a good place to start, Jack decided as he adjusted the passenger seat to accommodate his long legs.

Backing out of her parking space, Anya frowned. "I didn't know he had any."

Better cut this story short. They only lived a five-minute drive away. "Two daughters. Or so he thought."

"What do you mean?" The pucker between her eyebrows was adorable.

Jack took a moment to organize his thoughts. As they left the garage, he noted only a few cars in the circular drive. Traffic dropped off rapidly in the evening because there was no emergency care aside from labor and delivery at Safe Harbor. Five years ago, the former community hospital had been remodeled to specialize in fertility and maternity treatments, along with a range of gynecological and child services. Most recently it had expanded into treating male infertility, too.

On the opposite side of the compound stood a now-empty dental office building. Someday, with luck, the hospital would acquire it for additional office space. Then Jack could treat patients at more convenient hours.

He resumed his tale. "When my aunt Portia demanded a divorce and my uncle sought joint custody, she revealed that she'd cheated on him." Jack would never forget the heartbreak on Rod's face as he'd shared that discovery. "Neither of the girls was genetically his."

"How awful." She turned the car onto Hospital Way.

"It was a mess." Jack had been living in Nashville, Tennessee, at the time, completing medical school at Vanderbilt University. However, he'd spent most of his holidays with his aunt and uncle.

Technically Tiffany and Amber were his cousins, but he'd always thought of them as nieces. He'd loved playing with them and watching them grow into toddlers and preschoolers. Then they'd been yanked out of his life, leaving a painful void for him, too.

"Your aunt married the girls' father?" Anya tapped the brake at a red light on Safe Harbor Boulevard. The broad avenue bisected the town from the freeway to the harbor that gave the community its name.

"He was long gone, but she found someone else, a rich guy unable to have kids of his own who wanted to adopt hers. They pulled one legal maneuver after another to keep the kids from Rod." Jack still burned at the memory. "Rod was supporting the girls financially, and he went into debt fighting for them in court. If he'd been their genetic father, he'd have stood a chance, but as it was, he lost all rights." And was living in a small apartment and driving an unreliable car as a result.

"What an ordeal." When the light changed, Anya transitioned onto the boulevard, passing a darkened veterinary clinic and a flower shop that supplied the hospital gift boutique.

"We haven't seen the girls for six years. Then, this evening, Rod got a call from my older niece, Tiffany. She ran away from her home in San Diego and asked him to pick her up at the Fullerton train station." That was about a two-hour journey from San Diego.

Anya swung onto a side street. "How old is she?"

"Twelve." He only had a few photos of Tiff from years ago, a little girl with Orphan Annie red hair and a big smile. "It's hard to visualize what she must look like now."

"Twelve is awfully young. Why'd she run away?"

"No idea." His phone rang. Plucking it from his pocket, Jack saw his uncle's name on the screen. "Hey."

"Change of plans. I'm taking Tiffany to her grandmother's house." Rod must be speaking into his wireless device because it was illegal in California to hold a cell phone while driving. "Less risk of legal complications that way. Can you meet us there? You remember where Helen lives?"

"Vaguely." Portia's mother had joined the family for holiday celebrations and had once hosted a Fourth of July party at her bungalow. Jack recalled Helen as a kind, quiet woman overshadowed by her forceful daughter.

A girl's voice piped up in the background. "Is that Uncle Jack? Hi, Uncle Jack!"

"Hi, pumpkin."

"Hi to you too, squash-kins," his uncle said drily. "I mean, as long as we're using vegetables as terms of endearment."

"Very funny. What's the address?"

Rod provided it. Jack's phone showed it to be in the northwest corner of Safe Harbor near the freeway. "Anya, I have another favor to ask."

"Anya's driving you home?" His uncle sounded peevish.

"Who's Anya?" Tiffany piped in. "Can I meet her?"

"End of conversation," Jack said and clicked off. This was far too confusing, and, besides, he needed to focus on winning Anya's cooperation. "How about lending me your car after I drop you at home?"

"How far away is this?" she asked.

"Just a few miles." The alternative was to call a cab, which meant waiting heaven knows how long. In Southern California, where private vehicles outnumbered people, taxi drivers concentrated their efforts on servicing airports and hotels.

And he didn't have the time to waste. No doubt Helen was already dialing her daughter. Portia and her husband, a private equity investor reported to be worth close to a billion dollars, would take a private plane or helicopter to collect the runaway, which left only a window of an hour or so for Jack to connect with her.

Anya hadn't spoken again. "I don't want to lose this chance to see Tiffany." The ragged emotion in his tone surprised Jack. "It's important she understands that she's welcome here and that we love her. I'm afraid that next time, *if* there's a next time, she might go off on her own."

The fate of young runaways in metropolitan areas had been the subject of a recent lecture at the hospital. Staff pediatrician Samantha Forrest had presented a horrifying picture of predators trolling for young girls and boys who'd landed on the streets.

Now that he thought about it, he'd seen Anya at the lecture, too. Surely she understood his concern.

She appeared to be mulling the request as they reached their complex—a half-dozen two-story apartment buildings separated by tree-shaded walkways. In the carport area, Anya halted, her expression shadowed in the thin lighting.

"I'd like to meet her," she said.

"Not a good idea." This was private family business.

"She might talk more freely to a woman than to a couple of guys," Anya said.

"Her grandmother's there."

"I wouldn't discuss anything personal or uncomfortable around *my* grandmother," she replied. "Jack, I remember what my sisters were like at that age. You and your uncle are great guys, and I'm sure her grandmother loves this girl like crazy, but it's important right now that she be able to open up. What can it hurt to have me there?"

Anya did have a point. And he had to admire her willingness to step into such a delicate situation. Jack glanced at her profile: shapely nose, full mouth, firm chin. He needed her help and, besides, he wanted to spend more time with her. Why not seize the opportunity?

"Thanks. I'll navigate, okay?" he said and relaxed as he saw her nod.

They were on the same page for once. That was a nice change.

Chapter Three

Spotting Jack's hybrid sedan in front of a tidy bungalow, Anya knew this must be the place. She wedged her car into a slot at the curb.

What a pretty neighborhood, she thought as they got out. Some of the houses had a fairy-tale air, thanks to their gingerbread trim. Although of a simpler design, the grandmother's cottage had appealing, old-fashioned shutters and an extended porch lit by a sconce-style lamp.

But as Anya hurried to catch up with Jack's rapid pace, she noticed spiderwebs festooning the corners of the front windows. Surely the elderly lady would keep those wiped clear if she were physically capable of it.

The door flew open and a young girl's eager face appeared, her red hair in thick braids. "Uncle Jack!" She threw her arms around him with such enthusiasm that he had to step backward.

"Tiff? I can't believe that's you." After hugging the girl, he took a long look. "You've grown into a young lady."

She smoothed down her navy blazer and tan skirt, evidently a school uniform. "Come in."

"Somebody's blocking my path," he teased.

"Okay, okay." As Tiffany danced inside, her gaze fell on Anya. "Is this your girlfriend? She's pretty! And you're handsome, isn't he, Anya?"

"Most of the nurses seem to think so," she replied, slipping into the room behind them.

Inside, Rod's eyes glittered in the light from the chandelier as he greeted them. Surely those couldn't be tears. Anya had never seen the sardonic anesthesiologist show so much emotion.

The rectangular room encompassed both living and dining areas and had antique-style furnishings. Dusty curio cabinets displayed a charming collection of china plates and cups, while a built-in counter in the dining area held a nativity scene. As the girl's grandmother approached, her small, arthritis-curled hands revealed why she hadn't packed the holiday decorations or removed those outside spiderwebs. Why didn't her married-to-a-billionaire daughter spring for a housekeeper?

"Anya's a nurse who works with Rod and me," Jack explained as he introduced her to the grandmother, Helen Pepper. Slim and silver-haired, Helen wore a mint-green embellished top and pull-on pants that would be easy for those gnarled hands to manage.

"I'm very glad to meet you," she told Anya earnestly.

Anya took the extended hands gently. "You have a beautiful home."

"Anya was kind enough to give me a ride," Jack added. "Since Rod commandeered my car."

"When I heard my little girl's voice on the phone, I couldn't think about anything but rushing to the rescue," his uncle admitted. "It's a good thing the CHP didn't clock my speed on the freeway."

"I'm sorry I had patients, or I'd have driven you," Jack said. "Tiff, I want you to know that Rod moved heaven and earth to try to gain custody, or at least visitation. These past few years have been torture."

Tiffany nodded vigorously. "I was convinced Mom and Vince must have lied to me."

"Lied about what?" Jack asked.

"Well, I didn't get it at first. I was only six." The girl took a deep breath. "They told Amber and me our dad rejected us because we weren't really his."

The anguish on Rod's face tore at Anya's heart. "They dared to say that after I nearly went bankrupt fighting them in court?"

"That's not only a lie, it was cruel to the girls," Jack observed.

"I'm sorry I didn't speak up sooner," Helen said. "I always felt like I was walking on eggshells when I visited them. Please, everybody, have a seat."

She gestured the group into the living room, its walls brightened by colorful framed floral embroideries. She must have loved creating them before arthritis crippled her hands, Anya thought.

"Why did *you* stop visiting, Grandma?" Tiffany nestled beside Rod on the couch. "You hardly come anymore."

Helen lowered herself gingerly to the sofa. "My hip got so bad, I can't travel." To the others, she said, "I don't mean to complain. Portia hired a limo to bring me for Thanksgiving and Christmas."

"Big of her," Rod muttered.

It seemed to Anya that everyone was avoiding the central question of why this child had run away. However, being a not-very-invited guest at a family crisis, she held her tongue.

"How's your little sister?" Jack beamed at his niece, apparently as overjoyed to see her as she was to see him, Rod and her grandmother. "Amber must be ten now. She was a bold little thing. I'm surprised she didn't come with you."

"Don't give them ideas," Helen said tartly.

"Oh, she isn't bold anymore," Tiff said. "She's shy."

"Unlike somebody I know." Rod quirked the girl a smile. "Sweetheart, as Jack said, I fought for both of you."

"I figured you must have." Tiffany lifted her chin proudly. "I kept remembering you reading us bedtime stories and cracking jokes, and the older I got, the weirder it seemed that you stopped caring about us."

"I always cared!"

"How'd you get his phone number?" Helen asked. "I'm

sure your parents don't keep it around, although I guess kids can find anything on the internet these days."

"Mom and Vince only let us use computers for school-work." Tiffany made a face. "They won't let me have a cell phone either. My friend's big brother dug up Daddy's phone number."

Rod tweaked one of Tiffany's braids. "You should have called before you left home, squirt. Taking the train by your-self, that's scary."

"It was fun," the red-haired girl proclaimed. "And if I'd called, you might have said no."

Jack regarded her sternly. "Tiff, what if he'd been out of town? Dangerous people hang around train and bus stations watching for runaways. Please don't take a chance like that again."

"Then you'd better give me *your* number, too," she replied, then added mischievously, "just in case."

"Sure." Fishing a prescription pad from his pocket, Jack began writing on it. "Honey, call me before you put yourself into a potentially dangerous situation, okay?"

"I'll try."

"Don't just try." He also gave her a business card. "That's my office number. If for any reason you can't get through on my cell, make sure the receptionist understands it's an emergency."

He certainly was acting fatherly, or like an uncle, Anya thought. Another woman in her situation might be thrilled, but to her it raised a whole bramble bush of unwanted pos-sibilities. If he cared this much about his nieces, how might he feel about his own child?

"I hate to bring this up, but I have to call your parents and let them know you're safe," Helen said.

"Not yet!" Tiffany begged. "I'll go home on Sunday, okay?"

"It's only Thursday, and you've already missed a day of school," her grandmother chided.

With obvious reluctance, Rod backed Helen up. "They've

probably notified the police. We'll all be in trouble if we don't report your whereabouts."

"They're mean." Tiffany slouched down. "If my grades aren't perfect, they ground me for a whole weekend. They make me play soccer because that was Vince's sport. I had to drop dance class, which is my favorite."

"Too many organized activities," Helen commiserated. "It's not healthy."

Anya wondered how Tiffany would have responded to *her* family's demands. At twelve, Anya had hurried home every day after school with her seven-year-old triplet sisters, assisted her disabled mother, cleaned the house and fixed dinner.

Her older brothers had spent their after-school hours assisting Dad in the feed store. The only escapee had been her older sister, Ruth, who'd married and moved out by then. But she'd soon had kids of her own to care for.

"Children deserve a chance to develop at their own pace," Rod was telling Tiffany as Anya tuned back in. "But if you were still with me, you'd probably complain about how strict I am, too."

Anya admired his effort to be fair. He could easily seize on this chance to whip up his daughter's resentment toward her parents.

"No, I wouldn't because I'd know you loved me." The girl's lips trembled. "When I asked them if I could visit you, Vince said if I ever mentioned you again, he'd send me to a boarding school in Switzerland."

Rod looped an arm around his daughter's shoulders. "Honey, I'd hate for that to happen. But after the court ruled in his favor, Vince adopted you. I have no legal rights."

"He treats Amber and me like he owns us. Like we're pretty objects for him to show off to his friends."

We're still missing something, Anya thought. The girl was unhappy, but why take action *now?* "Why did you run away today?" she ventured. "Did something happen?"

"Good question," Jack murmured.

"It's because of last Sunday." The girl sniffed. After a deep breath, she resumed. "They make me take piano lessons even though I'm terrible because their friends' kids play instruments. I had a recital on Sunday and I messed up."

"What do you mean 'messed up'?" Helen asked.

Tiffany's hands clenched. "I forgot part of my piece in front of all those people. It was embarrassing. As soon as it was over, Vince dragged me outside and yelled at me where everybody could hear. He called me stupid and lazy." Tears rolled down her cheeks. "Daddy, no matter how hard I practice, I still suck. When I try to memorize music, it falls out of my brain."

"It's good to play an instrument, but not if it makes you miserable," her grandmother noted.

"I was great in dance class!" Tiffany burst out. "And I enjoyed it."

"That's why you ran away?" Jack asked.

"I had to see Daddy," the girl said. "I knew he'd love me for who I am."

Rod drew her close. No question about it; those were definitely tears brightening his eyes.

Anya understood how it felt to long for the freedom to be oneself. In a sense, she, too, had run off, although she'd waited until she was an adult with a nursing degree.

Rod's gaze met Helen's, his frustration obvious. "I wish I had the power to intervene, but legally, I don't."

"I should get a choice about who I live with," Tiffany insisted.

"When you're older, you might," her grandmother said.

"How much older?"

"Fourteen, I believe." Jack recalled that information from the lecture about runaways. "But you'd need your parents' consent and your own money."

"That'll never happen!" Tiffany flared. "And what about Amber? They're mean to her, too."

"In what way?" Rod asked sharply.

"Since she's a good swimmer, Vince took her to this competitive coach. Now he and Vince both yell at her when she doesn't do well at meets," her sister said. "She hardly talks to anybody anymore except me. When I told her I was short on money to buy my ticket, she gave me her savings."

"Amber knew about your plans?" Rod sighed. "They'll squeeze the truth out of her. They could have me arrested if we don't report right away that you're here."

"We love you guys," Jack put in. "But nobody's above the law."

"If they stick me in boarding school, I'll run away from there, too." Fire flashed in Tiffany's eyes. Anya shuddered at the prospect of the girl wandering alone in some foreign city, an easy target for a predator.

"Please don't put yourself in danger," Rod said.

"If I can't live here, they ought to at least let me visit," Tiffany responded. "I'm going to tell them that when I get home."

"Oh, dear." Helen's shoulders slumped. "I heard Vince say to your mother…"

"What?" Tiffany demanded.

"That I'm a bad influence because I indulge you girls. And once Vince's mind is made up, he's a bulldozer. I'm afraid he'll cut me off completely."

Vince was clearly a control freak. He couldn't stand sharing the girls with anyone.

"My opinion of that man isn't fit for polite company," Rod growled.

"I did talk to a lawyer in town," Helen said. "I could file with the court for visitation rights. But they'd fight it, and you know how much money Vince has. He'd bankrupt me before he'd give in."

Unless they found a solution, Tiffany faced a difficult and possibly disastrous adolescence, Anya thought. Although it wasn't her place to interfere, she did have an idea. "May I make a suggestion?"

Mixed expressions greeted this remark. Rod spoke first. "I appreciate your concern, Anya, but you're not familiar with any of the people involved."

"She was a teenage girl herself not long ago. Let's hear what she has to say." Jack's encouragement finally drew a nod from his uncle.

Anya addressed the girl. "They won't let you visit your dad, but your grandmother isn't getting any younger. You and your sister are old enough to spend a week or two with her during vacations. And then you can discreetly visit your dad."

"Vince won't let us do anything that isn't his idea," Tiffany replied bitterly.

"Surely your mom has some influence. Play the guilt card," Anya persisted. "Grandmothers are precious, and I'm sure she could use two helpers for spring cleaning. It would give your parents a break, too, during vacation."

"They already get a break. They stick us in camps, like music camp and swim camp and soccer camp." Despite the objection, a note of hope brightened the girl's voice.

"I would love to have them here. They're growing up so fast." Helen gazed fondly at her granddaughter. "And it would be wonderful to do some spring cleaning together."

"I'd like that. Amber would, too," Tiffany replied. "Could we visit Daddy and Uncle Jack while we're here?"

"Not officially," Rod told her. "If your parents get wind that I'm involved, they'll forbid you to come. They might even file a restraining order against me."

Jack leaned forward. "I'll bet we could arrange something if we're careful, though."

That was exactly what Anya had had in mind. She wondered if she should speak again or let the others carry the ball from here.

Helen clasped her hands in her lap. "But if Portia and that husband of hers found out I let you spend time with the girls, they'll cut off all contact with me."

"I suppose that's a risk," Jack conceded.

Anya cleared her throat. Everyone turned to her, with varying degrees of curiosity and skepticism.

"As I said, you have to be discreet," she ventured. "But, Helen, surely you have friends who could take the girls on outings. It wouldn't be your fault if they happen to run into their dad."

"You're a sneaky little thing," Rod said appreciatively.

"I grew up in a family that tried to run my life even after I was grown," she explained. "I learned the less I told them, the better."

"Some of the hospital staff have school-age children," Jack remarked. "There are lots of possibilities for playdates at a park or the beach."

Rod grinned. "If I ran into them, naturally I'd offer to spring for lunch."

"Thanks for the idea," Helen told Anya. "I don't suppose you have children, do you? You'd be a splendid parent."

"Not yet." With a twist of pain, she remembered the news she'd received this evening. *I will have a child for about five minutes—until her forever mom claims her.*

A dozen years from now, how would her child feel about being adopted? Anya supposed different kids had different responses. Tiffany had been torn up about Rod's supposed abandonment, but that was because they'd formed a bond. A birth mother who relinquished her baby wasn't rejecting her. Exactly the opposite. You had to do what was best for the child.

"I have another idea! Amber and I could go to the movies with Anya and Jack. Like a double date." Tiffany clearly assumed they were a couple, despite their denials. "And he could cook dinner for us. Do you still cook, Uncle Jack?"

"Rumor has it," he replied cheerfully.

More soberly, Rod said, "None of this is guaranteed. But you should make your case, Tiff. The fact that you ran away might show them they can't keep you under lock and key. Let's hope Amber hasn't mentioned that you planned to contact me."

"I swore her to secrecy." The girl toyed with the end of her braid. "She knows Vince would go ballistic."

"When you talk to them, don't forget to lay on the guilt,"

Anya reminded her. "Emphasize how unfair they're being to your grandmother."

"Their poor *aging* grandmother," Helen said lightly. "Who can't do a proper spring cleaning anymore."

"Not that anyone could tell." Anya wasn't about to mention the spiderwebs on the front windows. Even if the detail reinforced Tiffany's case, it would only embarrass her grandmother.

The girl bounced with excitement. "I'll act totally pathetic. This is great! Thank you, Anya. I can't wait till you're my aunt."

Heat rushed to her cheeks. "Jack and I aren't dating, sweetie. We just work together."

Rod studied her. Anya hoped he hadn't changed his mind about her so drastically that he might play matchmaker. She hadn't meant to be *that* helpful.

"Now that we have a plan, I'll go call your mother," Helen said.

Taking that as her cue, Anya stood. "It's been great meeting you and Tiffany."

"Do you have to leave already?" the girl asked. "I like you."

"I like you, too." And truthfully, Anya hoped she'd see Rod's daughter again. "But I have to hit the hay. Surgical nurses start work at 7:00 a.m. That means rolling out of bed by 5:30 a.m."

"Does Uncle Jack roll out of bed by 5:30 a.m., too?" his niece asked mischievously.

Anya blushed. "I wouldn't know."

"You're grown-ups. That means you can sleep together, right?" Tiffany teased.

"Where'd you pick up that idea?" Rod demanded. "I thought your parents monitored your media access."

"Everybody knows about that stuff." Tiffany patted his arm. "Don't worry, Daddy. I don't have a boyfriend yet."

"That's one thing I approve of," he said with mock gruffness.

Anya said her goodbyes. "Back in a sec," Jack told the others, then followed her outside.

"We have something to discuss," she began as they walked toward her car.

"Maybe tomorrow."

She'd prefer to get this over with. "It's important."

He didn't seem to hear her, though. "What was my aunt thinking, shutting Rod out of the girls' lives? Rod's their father in every sense that counts. You can't sever a bond like that, no matter how many lawyers you hire."

In this state, Jack wouldn't take her news well, Anya conceded. "Tomorrow night, then. Let's find a moment to talk, okay?"

"I remember flying home from college right after Tiffany was born," he continued, oblivious. "Holding her in my arms... She was a little cutie with her red hair. I got this wild rush, like it was my job to protect her from the world. Isn't that nuts? I was twenty years old."

"Kind of a strong reaction." In the glow of a streetlamp, Anya clicked open her car lock. "You're only their uncle. Or cousin. Or whatever."

"Yes, whatever," he said dourly. "But it doesn't matter that we aren't genetically related. We're family. And families mean more to me than to most people."

She stopped. "Why?"

"Because for most of my childhood, I missed out on having one." Jack dug his hands into his pockets.

He hardly struck Anya as the product of a deprived upbringing. "You grew up in foster homes?"

"Not exactly."

"What does that mean?"

"My dad was a firefighter who died in a fire when I was three." Jack stared down the dark street. "My mother wasn't the domestic type, and after Dad died, she stopped trying to be. She adopted one cause after another and travels all over the world, saving the subjugated women of India and Africa.

And South America. And Central America. And probably the South Pole."

"Surely she took you along." Anya had no idea how anyone could raise a child under those circumstances, but it might be exciting and educational.

"She dragged me here and there until I reached kindergarten. Then she dumped me on my grandparents." Bitterness underscored his words.

At five years old, his mother had left him? That was harsh. With a shiver, Anya tried to relate his mother's actions to her own situation. To her, it seemed an entirely different matter. But Jack might not see it that way.

"Grandparents are family, too," she said.

"Mine weren't even prepared to have Rod, a surprise midlife baby. He's thirteen years younger than my mom, and they certainly weren't eager to add a grandchild to the mix." Jack seemed lost in his painful past. "Physically, they took care of me, but I grew up feeling as if I wasn't wanted there. It was lonely."

The opposite of me. Anya had often longed for less family. "Wasn't your uncle like a brother?"

"A much older brother. He was a teenager when I was in grade school," Jack said. "It was later that we got close."

She shook her head. "I had no idea. Are your grandparents still around?"

"They died a few months apart while I was in high school." A hurt look shadowed his face. "It felt like the end of the world to me. They may not have been perfect, but at least I had a home."

"What about your mom?" Surely the woman had stepped up to the plate at such a critical point.

"After the funeral, she offered to fly me to Central America, where she was living in a jungle hut or something like that," Jack said tightly. "She was vague about her circumstances, which I took to mean she'd rather I stayed here."

"What did you do?" Anya wished she could soothe his

sadness. She'd always pictured Jack as a secure person from a solid, supportive background.

"I moved in with Rod. He was in medical school by then and too busy to spend much time with me, but we got along. I received my father's survivor benefits from Social Security, so that covered my share of expenses, and I did my best to be useful."

"That's why you learned to cook?"

"Along with other household skills." He shrugged. "That's how my childhood went. Better than for a lot of kids, but not exactly storybook." Jack glanced toward the house. "That's why it tears me apart to see Tiffany and Amber growing up like this. Being rich doesn't compensate for feeling unloved and unvalued."

"Surely their mother loves them."

"Not enough to put their interests ahead of hers," he said grimly.

Anya had no intention of discussing *that* subject. Instead, she sent forth a small feeler. "I don't suppose you want children of your own, considering how unhappy you were."

Deep green eyes bored into hers. "If I'm ever lucky enough to have them, I'll be there for them one hundred percent. They'll be the most important things in my life."

What a devoted father he'd make, Anya thought, but how realistic was his promise? As a surgeon, he had to work long hours. The person who'd really be there morning, noon and night was the mother.

Still, seeing his hurt, feeling his unhappiness, Anya couldn't help wanting to fix things for him. But she knew where that path led. She had the best of intentions but eventually her patience wore out, and she made dangerous mistakes.

She'd tried to be the perfect substitute for her mom with her younger siblings and to help at home as her mother's rheumatoid arthritis grew progressively worse. Molly had put on a cheerful face for her husband and the triplets, but Anya had noticed the swollen joints and profound fatigue, the weight loss and the discouragement as one promising medication after another proved disappointing.

Anya had been exhausted by the extra work and—much as she regretted it—sometimes resentful. During her senior year in college, she was studying for exams one weekend and had decided to ignore her mother's call for assistance from downstairs, just for a few minutes. *Please, let someone else help her this once,* Anya had thought. Unaware that everyone else had gone out, she'd concentrated on her textbook until she heard a sickening crash.

Trying to go to the bathroom alone, Molly had fallen and sprained her hip. Aching for her mother and filled with guilt, Anya had spent the next few days sleeping in her mother's hospital room to make sure no such accident happened again. She'd also endured furious lectures from her father about failing those who relied on her yet again.

Then on the exams she'd received her lowest grades ever, losing a chance at a grant for a graduate program. Anya had given up her goal of becoming a nurse practitioner with her own practice. Instead, she'd taken a job at a hospital in Denver, continuing to make the hour-long commute from her small town until she'd gained enough experience and enough self-confidence to move out of state.

It was only two years later, and Anya wasn't ready to tackle a lifelong commitment to a child or a man. Her baby would have as close to an ideal childhood as she could arrange, though—with an adoptive family. As for how Jack might react when he learned about her pregnancy, she'd rather not be there.

She'd learned the hard way that avoidance was often a wiser tactic than blunt honesty. She'd admitted to Dad what had happened that day with her mother and had received a tongue-lashing.

Yes, she'd let Jack calm down on his own rather than lash out at her out of shock. In fact, the more distance she put between them, the better. Suddenly, Karen's house seemed like a haven.

"It was great meeting your niece," she told him.

The tension eased from his body. "You were great. Thank you."

"Glad to do it." As she slid into the car, Anya added, "By the way, my roommate and I are moving."

"Moving?" Dismay replaced his warmth. "What about your lease?"

"It's up for renewal, and this will be cheaper," she said. "We're only going a few miles, to Karen Wiggins's house. See you at work!"

Quick escape: turn on the ignition, pull out from the curb, wave blithely and *go!* In the rearview mirror, she saw Jack staring after her, openmouthed.

As she drove home, Anya processed the fact that she'd just committed to living with four other people, including Lucky, who was annoyingly nosy. And she still had to deal with informing Jack about his impending fatherhood.

Look on the bright side. Literally. In Karen's airy house, her African violet had a better shot at survival.

And so did Anya's hard-won peace of mind.

Chapter Four

"Manager or police?" Jack asked.

His uncle studied the dented blue van blocking their carport spaces. "I'm guessing the driver hasn't gone far. It'll be faster if we wait."

"I'd rather call someone, but you're probably right." At 11:00 a.m. on a Sunday morning, Jack's stomach was growling for brunch at Waffle Heaven. "I figured now that you have your car back, we'd be bulletproof. If one doesn't start, we could take the other. Then this jerk blocked us both."

"Shall we punch him when he shows up?" Rod asked drily.

"You do the punching," Jack said. "A surgeon's hands have to be protected."

"It takes dexterity to insert my tubes and syringes," his uncle replied. "How about I sit on him while you administer the beating?"

"What if he is a she?" Jack asked.

"Let's do rock paper scissors," his uncle proposed.

"To decide whether we call the police or to decide which of us messes up our hands?"

They broke off their nonsensical discussion when they heard voices from around the corner of the nearest apartment unit.

"Angle it to your left! No, your other left," a man ordered.

"It's tilting!" squawked a woman.

"Hang in there, Anya. Zora, get over here!"

Shoes shuffled on the sidewalk. "Okay, I have it."

They came into view on the walkway, navigating the narrow path between low-growing palms and bushes. With Anya and Zora was the male nurse Jack had met a few days earlier. Even though the temperature had barely reached the low sixties, he was wearing a sleeveless undershirt, displaying his expansive tattoos.

Behind him, Anya helped her roommate support the other end of a faded purple couch. She'd tied back her dark hair and donned an oversize T-shirt that ought to be shapeless. But on her, every movement reminded Jack of the tempting curves underneath.

"That," announced Rod to the group, "is a truly ugly sofa. Dare I hope you're taking that purple monstrosity to the Dumpster?"

"It isn't purple," said Anya. "It's orchid."

Her roommate's thin face poked out from behind the couch. "It's for the second-floor landing." She blew a curl of reddish-brown hair off her temple. "Nobody has to see it but us."

"Hauling it upstairs is going to be a fun job," Lucky muttered. Served him right for playing rooster in the henhouse, in Jack's opinion. "Are we blocking you doctors?"

"Yes, and we're hungry," Rod answered.

Show no weakness in front of Anya. Especially not while this guy was hefting furniture and rippling his muscles. "I'm not that hungry. We can pitch in." As if to defy his speech, Jack's stomach rumbled. Hoping no one had heard, he marched over to boost the women's end of the couch. They released it willingly.

Reaching the van, the men maneuvered it inside. A few minutes of grunting and shifting later, they'd fitted it in place. By then, Anya and Zora had disappeared between the buildings.

As Jack jumped down, the male nurse said, "I'll get the van out of your way. We don't want to inconvenience you lords of the realm."

Did the man resent all physicians or just the two of them

specifically? Jack had learned—more or less by chance—that Lucky worked for the distinguished head of the men's fertility program. He doubted the fellow leveled snide remarks at the famed Dr. Cole Rattigan. But apparently an anesthesiologist and an ordinary ob-gyn were fair game.

"Don't bother," Jack said. "We're fine."

Rod rolled his eyes. "What if they run out of waffles?"

"Honestly!" Jack growled.

"Go ahead. I can handle this," Lucky assured them.

Jack refused to let Anya see him as a lazy slug who whisked off for a leisurely meal while others, especially her, labored. "With a few more hands, you'll finish faster."

Lucky rolled his shoulders, producing loud cracks. "Suit yourself."

The women reappeared, arms full of mismatched towels and sheets wrapped in clear plastic bags. "Amazing. The ladies copied our color scheme," Rod said.

Zora peered dubiously at the linens in hues ranging from pink to purple to olive-green. "This is a color scheme?"

"Dr. Vintner has a dry sense of humor." Anya lugged her towels to the open van.

On the upper level, Lucky took them from her arms. "Didn't I mention we should bring out the chairs and table before the small stuff?"

The women exchanged glances. "Huh," said Anya. "Did he?"

"Maybe, but these were on top of them," Zora responded.

"And you couldn't put them on the floor?" Lucky asked.

The guy was blowing his opportunity to appear heroic, Jack thought. And although the man's peevishness appeared to be aimed at the redhead, Anya was the one who spoke up. "Don't make a federal case out of it. Pile them on the couch."

With an annoyed click of the tongue, Lucky obeyed.

Rod, still planted on the sidewalk, smiled pleasantly and said to him, "It's nice when roommates get along so well."

"I'm sure they'll work it out," Jack told him. "Once they've moved in and all."

"They might end up with blood on the sofa," his uncle answered. "Which would be an improvement."

Another tenant, backing out of the opposite carport, glared at them while maneuvering around the van. Lucky waved in a friendly manner, and the man tilted his head in grudging acknowledgment.

"Out of curiosity, how many bathrooms does this house have?" Rod inquired, eyeing the towels.

"Three and a half," said Zora.

"For how many people?"

"Five." Lucky jumped down from the van.

"That's not bad, but you'll have a traffic jam if you work the same hours." Rod adjusted his fedora to block the sunlight.

Anya sighed. "I'd have killed for that many bathrooms when I was growing up. We had two for nine people."

"One of our bathrooms is in my suite downstairs," Lucky said. "You're welcome to use it whenever you want."

"Thanks." She gave the nurse a vague smile.

Jack tried not to scowl. "Why don't we bring down the rest of the furniture?"

"Sounds like a plan." Anya gave Jack a vague smile, too.

Half an hour later his muscles were throbbing, but he would have rather worked to the point of collapse than admit defeat.

Fortunately, he was in the right place when Anya, approaching the parking lot with a box marked *Dishes,* halted abruptly, the color draining from her face.

"Are you okay?" Jack rushed to relieve her of the box but had to dodge a near-collision with Lucky.

"I've got it." The male nurse snatched the container from Anya's shaky grasp.

Zora approached, struggling antlike with a crate much too large for her. "Anya? Are you sick?"

"Go on," her roommate told her. "I'm fine."

"Well, okay." Zora staggered toward the truck. Lucky ignored her.

"Sit down." Jack took Anya's elbow. "I'm speaking as a doctor."

"Yes, a nurse couldn't possibly figure out what she should do." Lucky sent him a poisonous glare and carted off the dishes.

"I can manage." All the same, Anya leaned on Jack as he escorted her to a wrought-iron bench bordered by flowering bushes.

From around the corner, Rod appeared, carrying a toilet plunger and a pack of bath tissue. "Doing my bit," he announced, waving the lightweight items in the air and strolling on his way.

Jack gladly refocused his attention on Anya. How vulnerable she looked, sitting there twisting the hem of that huge T-shirt. "Can I get you some water?"

"No, thanks. I just drank half a glass." She sucked in a breath, as if gathering strength from the fragrance of the flowers. Despite the cool air, she must have overheated from her exertion.

To distract her, Jack said, "I've been meaning to tell you how terrific you were with Tiffany." They hadn't had a chance to talk privately since Thursday.

"How'd things work out for her?"

His niece's freckled face popped into his head. He'd been thinking about Tiff a lot these past few days. "When her parents learned she was safe, they were relieved for about thirty seconds before they became furious."

"Understandable, I suppose," Anya said. "They must have been worried sick."

"Helen said they blistered the phone. She refused to let them talk to Tiffany until they calmed down."

"Good for her." Anya tucked a wedge of dark hair behind her ear. She'd lost her clip, he noticed. "Did they drive up?"

"They flew into Orange County in their private jet." John Wayne Airport, the closest to Safe Harbor, accommodated both commercial and private aircraft.

"That's a short hop." Anya swallowed, still struggling with whatever was bothering her.

"Twenty minutes in the air, I gather." Judging by how tense she'd become when he'd just sat beside her, touching her wouldn't be welcomed, so Jack folded his arms and went on talking. "However, with all the arrangements, it took them about two hours, roughly the same as if they drove. But that wouldn't have satisfied Vince's sense of importance. That gave us time to order pizza and play a round of Monopoly."

"Who won?" Anya asked.

"Rod." Jack smiled at the memory of his uncle battling for turf with Tiffany, both of them relishing each small victory and flourishing every Get Out of Jail Free card. "He's a tough customer."

"He didn't cut a twelve-year-old any slack?"

"Kids can't deal with life if parents pave every step of their path," the anesthesiologist responded, sauntering back from the truck.

"I don't imagine her parents are making *her* life easy," Anya said.

"A reasonable point." He stepped aside for Lucky and Zora to file by. "However, there's a difference between berating a child, as they do, and teaching her that concentration and strategy pay off."

Hoping his uncle would move on so he could have Anya to himself again, Jack narrowed his eyes. "Yes, Monopoly is an excellent metaphor for life."

"Also, I like to win." With a grin, Rod departed.

"You didn't run into the parents, did you?" Anya's cheeks had regained some of their healthy pink color. "Considering the legal issues, that would have been awkward."

"We aren't suicidal," Jack assured her. "Helen asked Portia to phone when she landed, so we knew when to clear out."

"Then how do you know what happened when they got there?"

"Helen called." Rod had said the older woman had been near tears on the phone.

"Was it bad?"

"Vince stormed into the house and called Tiff a spoiled brat." Although Jack had never met the man in person, he'd seen pictures. Vince came across as large and intimidating, even in a headshot.

"He sounds awful." Anya's dark eyes smoldered. "What a bully."

"Tiff's not easily cowed." Jack was proud of his niece. "She had to work hard at appearing contrite, according to Helen. Then she took your advice and cried to her mom about how much she'd missed her grandmother. That it was cruel to deprive an old lady of her grandchildren. Also, she mentioned something about spiderwebs and dust."

"Did it work?"

"Helen thinks her daughter was swayed, but there's no telling what Vince will decide." Jack's aunt had always struck him as a strong person—maybe a little too strong, in view of the way she'd treated Rod—but she seemed unwilling or unable to stand up to her second husband. "Even if he agrees, they might choose to fly Helen to San Diego rather than letting Tiff and Amber come here."

"Let's hope not." It was Rod, toting a small reading lamp. "The girls need a break before those people crush their spirits."

"Tiffany doesn't strike me as crushable," Anya said. "But if she runs away again, she might end up who knows where."

Jack had no intention of allowing that to happen. "I made it very clear that if she can't reach Rod or Helen, I'd meet her anywhere, anytime."

Her hand fluttered to his arm. "You really care about her. That's so sweet."

He fought down the instinct to gather her close. "Of course."

Rod cleared his throat, but apparently reconsidered whatever he'd been about to say and vanished toward the parking lot. For once, he'd picked up on the vibes around him and showed a trace of sensitivity. *And I'm sure I'll hear about it later.*

Anya lifted her hand. "Sorry."

"Nothing to be sorry about," Jack told her.

"Listen." In the dappled sunlight, she raised her face to his. The soft light emphasized the velvet texture of her skin and the fullness of her lips. "We should meet for coffee. Or tea. Or juice."

Finally, she was ready to move past this tough patch in their relationship. "Any beverage will do." Encouraged that she'd taken this step of her own volition, Jack cupped her hands in his. "Now that you're moving to Karen's house, we won't be running into each other outside of work. I'd like to remedy that. I miss you."

She swayed closer, then slid her hands free and scooted back. If he'd been paying attention to their surroundings, he'd have heard the footsteps, too. Jack would gladly have kicked Lucky and Zora, except that might have made them drop the TV they were carrying.

Agonizing seconds passed. When they were alone again, he asked, "What day is good for you?"

"For what?"

"Drinks."

"Oh, that." Anya studied him as if seeking the answer to an unasked question. "Just suppose…what if Tiffany and her sister had to move away somewhere that you and Rod would never see them? I mean, if it was best for them. Like, witness protection."

What a bizarre idea. "There are no circumstances under which my nieces would not need their father," Jack responded vehemently.

"Oh."

She seemed to shrink away.

What was that about? Surely she knew his anger wasn't directed at her. "I could meet you tomorrow afternoon when you get off." Jack worked an overnight shift on Sundays in labor and delivery, so he had Mondays free. Well, free aside from sleeping.

Rod bustled past on the walkway, whistling and keeping his gaze trained ahead. He didn't have to be so obvious about ignoring them, but it was better than if he'd stopped to gab.

"No, the whole thing is a bad idea." Anya stood up. "We work together. Let's keep it professional."

"Wait a minute." She was the one who'd proposed to meet for a drink. "Is this a game?"

"I beg your pardon?"

Jack brushed off his slacks as he stood. "I realize you weren't feeling well…"

"Probably low blood pressure," she said.

"Regardless, that's no excuse for jerking me around." He'd interrupted his breakfast plans and overtaxed his muscles, which would now probably hurt like hell during the long night ahead. That was all fine—she hadn't requested his assistance, and he didn't begrudge a few aches and pains—but it was unfair to suggest they meet for coffee and then behave as if he had pressured her. "If you'd rather I kept my distance, fine. But don't issue invitations you don't mean."

"I didn't…it wasn't like that." A familiar pucker appeared between her eyes.

Jack nearly softened. She had an astonishing ability to stir his protective instincts. But no one had appointed him her guardian. She had plenty of friends, and if she'd rather drink coffee or simply hang out with the other nurses, male or female, that was her business.

"I'm glad you're feeling better," he told her. "If it's low blood pressure, you should eat something."

"Crackers." She swallowed. "I think we packed them. But that's okay. Karen and Melissa promised to fix sandwiches."

Lucky strode by. "The first of many meals. I don't suppose you've seen the updated kitchen? It's impressive."

"No." Jack was sure he had a much better idea of how to make the most of a kitchen than Lucky did.

"And all that space!" the man crowed. "Once we settle in, it will be a fantastic party house."

"Knock yourself out." Jack had endured enough veiled taunts for one day. Also, he realized, the apartment must be nearly empty by now. "I'll let you folks finish on your own. Enjoy your sandwiches."

"Thanks for the help," said Anya.

"Don't mention it."

He'd reached the parking lot before he remembered that the van still blocked their cars. Then he spotted Rod's distinctive fedora. His uncle was facing a statuesque lady in formfitting green slacks and a halter top. Golden-brown hair floated around a determined face as she waved.

"Hi," Jack called. What was the Realtor's name? Della? Danielle? It always reminded him of old-fashioned countertops. Formica. No, that wasn't right.

"Danica was just mentioning she had a couple of very lonely apple pies," Rod informed him.

"There's more than I can eat," Danica confirmed. "It's my mother's closely guarded recipe. Homemade crusts, too."

"With whipped cream, they'll be better than waffles," Rod said. "There is whipped cream, isn't there?"

He noticed a mischievous glint in her eye, hinting that the whipped cream might be put to all sorts of creative uses. "Absolutely. And espresso."

He'd struck out with Anya, so why not? "Sounds wonderful," Jack said. "Very kind of you."

"My pleasure."

The real estate agent linked one arm through Rod's and the other through his as if laying claim to them both. That didn't last long, though, since it was impossible to climb the exterior steps in that formation. As they were separating, he caught Anya's expression from behind the truck.

She looked…hurt. Or was he kidding himself?

Much as Jack enjoyed her company, he was done behaving like a teenager with a crush. If she chose to retreat from

what they'd shared and return to acting strictly professionally he respected that.

Besides, he was starving.

Chapter Five

Empty of furnishings, the apartment had a pathetic air, Anya thought as she took a last look around. Matted patches of carpet revealed the shapes of their sofa and chairs. But after the management had the place professionally cleaned, those marks would vanish, leaving no sign of the two women who had spent a year within these walls.

When she'd agreed to pair up with Zora, Anya had been happy to bid farewell to the motel suite she'd been living in since her arrival from Colorado. Anya had found a sympathetic soul in her roommate, who'd been licking the wounds of her husband's betrayal. The women had formed a team as they popped corn, shared movie nights and, playing on their names, joked about being experts on everything from A to Z.

Now that transitional period of their lives was ending. Maybe that explained Anya's rush of nostalgia. Also, she would no longer enjoy the awareness that just around the corner of the next building dwelled a guy with a devilish grin and the most skillful hands she'd ever encountered, in *or* out of an operating room.

She hadn't meant to drive him to that rapacious woman who flaunted her surgically enhanced breasts at every opportunity. Right now, they must be sitting at that woman's table with their legs bumping underneath. Anya hoped Rod was bumping his legs in there, too.

And she still had to break the news of her pregnancy to Jack. That comment about his nieces needing their father, no matter what the circumstances, didn't bode well for gaining his consent to adoption. Yet surely he wouldn't raise a baby by himself. And he couldn't force Anya to take on a role for which she was completely unprepared.

Their child deserved better. Surely he'd see that eventually, but she dreaded the confrontation. His attitude only reinforced her belief that she should entrust the task of informing him to someone else.

After checking her bedroom for overlooked objects, Anya peeked into the bathroom. The medicine cabinet was empty, no leftover shampoo in the tub...oh, wait. There on the windowsill sat the remarkably robust African violet. Far from withering away, it was thriving. Perhaps, as she'd read on the internet, it really did prefer humidity and filtered light.

She'd intended to toss it in the trash, but it would be cruel to kill a blossoming plant. Lowering it, Anya admired the dark fuzzy leaves and tiny purple flowers. "You deserve another chance, no matter who gave you to me," she murmured as she exited the bathroom. "It isn't your fault Jack knocked me up."

A gasp from the kitchen was followed within milliseconds by a crash. Dismayed to realize she'd been overheard, Anya stared at a shocked Zora as she rushed into the kitchen.

Freckles stood out against her roommate's face. "He what? You're what?"

"Forget you heard that," Anya commanded, despite the futility of such a request.

"See what you made me do!" Zora transferred her distress to the shattered millefiori vase, its delicate colors and swirling, kaleidoscope-like neck reduced to shards on the kitchen floor.

"I thought you gave that away." The beautiful vase had been an anniversary gift from the treacherous Andrew, who'd bought it on a business trip to Italy.

"Like you said, there's no sense blaming an object just because a jerk gave it to you." Zora scraped up the broken pieces with paper towels.

"You have to get over him," Anya told her.

"He's still my husband," her friend retorted. A few months ago, Zora had gone so far as to throw a divorce party in the hospital cafeteria, proclaiming how happy she was to be free. But clearly she was neither happy nor, technically, free.

Anya refused to act as an enabler. "Andrew hasn't signed the final papers only because you haven't forced him to. He enjoys keeping you dangling. It's a power trip."

"Maybe he hasn't signed them because he still has feelings for me." Zora dumped the shards into a plastic trash bag.

Lucky stomped through the front door, which they'd propped open. "Did I hear what I think I heard? You're hanging on to that cheater? You're an idiot."

Zora shot him an unladylike gesture. Anya wished Lucky would quit meddling in their business. Just because he'd overheard their conversation didn't mean he had the right to pass judgment. Besides, whereas Anya's criticisms were prompted by concern for her friend's well-being, his motive was less charitable.

Most of the hospital staff had forgiven Zora for her husband-stealing once nurse Stacy Layne had happily remarried. But Lucky had taken the situation to heart because Stacy had married his beloved boss; therefore, he resented any and all harm that had ever been done to her.

"Let's lock up, okay?" Anya said. "Melissa and Karen must be wondering if we had an accident on the drive over."

"Just double-checking the premises." Finding nothing further to remove, Lucky marched out. Their arrangement was for him to drive the rented van while the women transported personal and fragile items in their cars.

"I'll return the keys to the manager," Anya offered brightly, eager to escape.

Zora blocked the doorway. "We haven't discussed your pregnancy."

"We'll talk about it later."

"When did this happen? *How* did this happen?"

"New Year's Eve, and in the usual way." There—she'd

answered the questions. Quickly, Anya added, "Not a word to anyone."

"You can't expect to hide it for long."

"That's not your problem. And I'm hungry. You shouldn't make a pregnant woman go without food."

Scowling, Zora went out. Still holding the African violet, Anya locked up and took both sets of keys to the manager.

I should have held my tongue. Well, Zora would have found out sooner or later. So would everybody else, Anya conceded. At least about her pregnancy. Not necessarily about the father.

As for Jack, she'd figure out a way to handle this promptly and efficiently. Unlike Zora, she didn't plan to drag out the paper-signing until the bitter end.

Carefully, Anya wedged the plant into a cup holder in her front seat. Stroking its furry leaves quelled the nausea rising again in her stomach, just as Jack's scent had soothed her earlier. Something about male pheromones and lime had a therapeutic effect on her morning sickness.

Wondering where she'd find the right spot for the little plant, she headed for her new home.

"It was the jasmine," Zora said. "Or maybe the honeysuckle."

"No, we had stuffy noses," Anya corrected her as they stood in front of Karen's house.

The two-story stucco home, freshly painted white with blue trim, glowed in the afternoon sunlight. Most of the other structures on Pelican Lane had been removed over the years, reportedly bought up and razed by supporters of the adjacent marsh. Isolation only added to the place's dignified beauty.

Trellised roses and bougainvillea, along with other flowering plants, tumbled across the yard that wrapped from the front lawn to the back of the house. What a luxurious spot— if only it didn't smell like rotten eggs. Maybe the perfumed flora or the lingering paint smell had disguised the stink a few weeks ago when they'd first considered Karen's offer, but Anya would put her money on their head colds.

Beyond the house and off to their right, toward the Pacific, stretched a green and brown expanse where saltwater and freshwater met. In the estuary, birds nested, nature lovers in sturdy shoes hiked the dirt paths and coyotes prowled, while plants and mollusks decomposed. And reeked.

The African violet quivered in the breeze, as if in sympathy with the dying vegetation. Anya had decided to carry it inside immediately because harsh light through her windshield might damage it.

"Paula doesn't like it here," she told Zora.

"Who?"

Anya indicated the plant. "African violet's proper name is Saintpaulia, after the German baron who took credit for discovering them in Tanzania." She'd checked out the subject online.

"I'll bet the natives didn't think he discovered them," Zora muttered.

"I'm sure you're right."

"Anyway, why did you name your plant?" her friend asked.

"Because it has personality."

"No, it just has memories of Jack. Speaking of which, does he know about this?"

"Oh, look. Here comes Lucky." Anya wasn't making that up. He'd parked the van in the gravel driveway, blocking the unpaved turnaround where they'd left their car. He had to take it back to the rental place tonight, so it would be gone before anyone needed to leave.

"We can unload your stuff later," he called on approach. "Let's eat."

"Okay." Anya fell into step alongside Zora, ignoring a skeptical expression from her friend that warned this conversation was only on hold.

Despite the foul smell, Anya hadn't lost her appetite. Quite the contrary. Pregnancy had carried her to new realms of hunger.

As the wide front porch creaked beneath their feet, Karen

opened the front door. Wearing a long woven skirt and top, she had a relaxed air. "The gang's all here! Come on in."

Anya wiped her shoes on the doormat before entering. Even so, she was glad they didn't traipse through the living room, with its striped sofa and polished curio cabinet, or into the formal dining room. She'd hate to mess up the newly vacuumed carpets.

Instead, they veered left around the staircase and traversed the rumpled family room. Near a pair of sliding glass patio doors, a comfortably chipped table was set with a sandwich platter.

"Finally!" Melissa, dark blond hair loose around her shoulders, set down a fruit salad. "Karen and I almost started without you."

Where to put Paula? Anya set the plant in an empty spot on the floor, away from the traffic pattern. "It's only till I finish lunch," she told it and went to wash her hands.

Then, taking a paper plate from a stack, Anya joined the others, grateful for the healthy selection of food. When she came up for air, she surveyed the circle of new housemates: tanned Lucky, devouring his second sandwich; Karen, blooming with good cheer now that she'd rented out all her rooms; Melissa, who'd piled her plate with fruit, and Zora, sitting as far from Lucky as possible.

It occurred to her that, in this house, she'd be progressing through the formative months of her baby's gestational life. Instead of a family, she'd be relying for support on a group of people who were—except for Zora—casual acquaintances. How would they react when they learned of Anya's pregnancy?

A longing to burrow into Jack's arms and rely on his powerful paternal instincts twisted through her. He'd take care of her, wouldn't he? *And then he'd assume he's the boss of me. I'd be stuck raising a kid and trying to please a guy and chewing my fingernails to the quick like I used to.*

No, she wouldn't because Anya had a choice now, unlike when she'd been growing up. She'd been the fourth child in the family. Her sister Ruth, older by nine years, had been tired of helping supervise their twin brothers and, when Anya was born, had openly resented the newcomer. Anya had spent her toddler and preschool years tagging along after her parents as they worked in their feed store. Naturally, there'd been chores, from collecting chicken eggs in the morning to sweeping the floor after dinner, but they hadn't been burdensome.

At age five, those relatively carefree years had ended when her mother had given birth to triplets. Although the older siblings occasionally babysat, everyone assumed that Anya would pitch in with diaper duty and clean-up. And as arthritis sapped her mother's mobility, more and more of the care of her three little sisters fell to Anya.

Everyone had worked hard, so she hadn't complained. Maybe she should have been more cantankerous, like Ruth, who'd argued a lot with their parents and married at nineteen. Or quicker to shrug off domestic duties, like her two brothers, although they *had* assisted Dad in the feed store. But, sensitive to the deepening lines on her father's face and to her mother's silent pain, Anya had carried on.

She'd expected the pressures to ease when she entered college and the triplets threw themselves into high-school activities. However, the family had figured Anya, as a nursing student, was the natural person to assist their increasingly disabled mother and to babysit Ruth's growing brood when difficult pregnancies sidelined her. The few occasions when Anya had spoken up, her family had simply dismissed her complaints. The more she tried to distance herself, the bigger the guilt trips they laid on her.

Though there'd been sweet moments, too. When she received her nursing degree, the triplets—juniors in high school at the time—had thrown her a surprise party. It had been their version of the now-abandoned "capping" ceremony in which nurses used to receive their white caps. Because modern nurses don't wear caps, the girls had bought an array of funny hats for the whole family to wear while they cut the cake and sang silly songs.

But as her career progressed, so did Anya's desire for independence. She developed a passion for surgical nursing, and it was frustrating to be summoned home for one thing after another on top of the hours she put in doing her family's housework and supervising her mom's home medical care. The last straw was when Anya was forced to trade shifts for an "emergency" at home, losing a chance to assist at a major transplant operation. She'd arrived home to learn that the urgent situation was that her dad needed her brother to do stock inventory and so he couldn't drive Molly to physical therapy.

Mom had apologized profusely, but it wasn't her fault. The rest of the family had taken Anya for granted, refusing to change *their* schedules or recognize that Anya's work was just as important as theirs. She'd realized they never would, and the only way to have her own life was to move away. In frustration, she'd signed up for a nursing registry and moved to California. Later, she'd learned of an opening at Safe Harbor and she'd leaped at the chance to apply.

Most of her family still didn't understand why she'd left, although she'd explained herself frankly as recently as last Christmas. The holiday had been a miserable series of criticisms and nags for her to move back. Her mom, who might have intervened, had been under the weather while adjusting to new medication and hadn't spoken up.

She kept hoping her father and siblings would finally grasp why she'd left and why she had to stay away. It hurt that they didn't.

Yes, she was better off leaving her family out of this pregnancy and sticking with her new friends.

"Later today I'd like us to draft some ground rules," Karen said, breaking into Anya's thoughts. "Establishing guidelines should make this house-sharing experience run smoother."

"What kind of ground rules?" Lucky asked.

"All sorts of things. For instance, how we'll handle cooking—whether we do our own or if we each cook for a week on and then have a month off." Melissa's smooth reply indicated she'd prepared for this discussion. Although she was a decade younger than Karen, they'd become close friends.

"We should set a schedule for cleaning, too, so no one gets stuck with more than their fair share," Karen said. "What other issues concern you guys?"

"How we divide up community expenses," Lucky said.

"And what temperature we keep the thermostat." Zora always seemed to be cold, even in summer.

"Privacy," Anya said.

"Entertaining—who, when, how loud and how many," Melissa put in.

"Great!" Karen responded. "We'll hold a roundtable meeting as soon as you guys unload your truck."

Anya wasn't sure she liked the sound of that. Her experience with group discussions in her family had been, *Let Anya do it*. "If there's conflict, how do we decide?" she asked.

"We vote on it," Karen replied.

That sounded ominous to Anya. "You mean, the majority always rules?"

Her tension must have been evident to Zora, who asked, "What if there's a chore somebody really hates?"

From across the table, Lucky grimaced. "Opting out of bathroom duty, are you?"

Zora blinked. "What?"

"She was asking because of me," Anya told him. "My family tended to dump the nasty stuff on me."

"Nobody gets dumped on." Karen's narrowed eyes sent Lucky a back-off message. *"Nobody."*

Zora and Anya both folded their arms and added their stares to Karen's.

"Message received." Lucky scooted away from the table. "Let's get to work."

All five of them carried in furniture and other possessions. By evening, Anya was worn out but determined not to show it, especially to Zora. Her hovering was already making Lucky curious.

Through her weariness, Anya struggled to concentrate as,

over a dinner of pizza and salad, they put together a cleaning schedule. Regarding kitchen duty, Karen proposed they take turns as chef, each planning meals, shopping and cooking for a week.

"It's a lot of work, but then we get a month's break," she said. "Also, the cook doesn't have to clean up."

"Is it okay for the cook to buy takeout?" Lucky asked.

"As long as it's not pizza every night," Karen said. "Okay, everyone?" Heads bobbed.

"It's important that we choose healthy foods," Melissa qualified. "Plenty of fruits and vegetables, organic if possible."

"Right. Actually, I'd prefer that we eat vegetarian." Lucky reached for his third slice of olive-and-pineapple pizza.

"That could get boring," Zora said.

"You'd be surprised how many types of cheese there are," he told her. "And I'm willing to include fish."

Anya stirred from her near-stupor. "No soft cheeses and no sushi." Catching the curious looks from around the table, she wished she could recall her words. Too late.

"Surely you aren't…?" Melissa broke off.

"She isn't what?" Lucky asked.

"That's what they tell pregnant women to avoid," Karen filled in.

So much for keeping my secret. "Huh," Anya said.

Her three tormentors turned to Zora, who sent a pleading glance at Anya. Which only had the effect of confirming their suspicion.

"This is an interesting development," Lucky remarked.

"And nobody's business." That wasn't precisely true, though, Anya supposed, because her pregnancy was likely to affect everyone. "It was an accident and I'm giving it up for adoption once the father signs the waiver."

"And who is—" Lucky broke off as, from both sides, Melissa and Karen kicked him. "Ouch."

"That's wonderful of you, to carry the baby for someone else," Karen said. "So many couples are desperate to have children. We wish our fertility program could help them all, but it can't."

"You shouldn't do any cleaning duties that involve chemicals," Melissa insisted.

"Everything's composed of chemicals." Anya had no intention of shirking her fair share of the responsibilities. "But we don't use anything toxic, do we?"

"If we do, I'll handle it," Lucky said. "And at the risk of getting kicked again, I think the father should pitch in. Which brings up the question of who that might be…"

Zora, who rarely flared at him on her own behalf, leaped into action for Anya's sake. "Give it a rest! If Anya wants to reveal the father's identity, that's her decision."

With a duck of his head, Lucky yielded the point but not happily.

"To return to our topic, we definitely shouldn't use toxic chemicals. If I get pregnant…" Melissa exchanged glances with Karen.

"Oh, now, what's this?" Lucky appeared torn between curiosity and disapproval. What right did he have to be so judgmental? Anya wondered. "I hadn't heard mention of a boyfriend."

"I've been considering artificial insemination," Melissa hurried on before he could raise further questions. "Anyway, until then, I'm willing to do extra for Anya's sake."

Zora and Karen spoke almost in unison. "Me, too."

Anya raised her hands. "Stop. This isn't your problem."

"It isn't a problem at all," Karen told her. "It's a privilege."

Tears pricked Anya's eyes. "Thank you." But it wasn't only their kindness that affected her. It was the longing to see the same tender expression on the one face that wasn't here.

She had to tell him about the pregnancy. But if Jack reacted with this kind of loving concern and urged her to keep the baby, what if she wasn't able to stand against him? On the other hand, if she saw condemnation in his face, she'd be so angry she might say something she'd regret.

It was all too much, and right now, Anya's eyes threatened to drift shut.

"You're drooping," Lucky said. "You should rest."

"She should choose for herself when to rest," Zora shot back.

"You ladies are tough customers." Rising, Lucky collected their paper plates. After today, they'd agreed to use ceramic dishes for the sake of the environment, but tonight, everyone was too tired to wash. "I'd better watch my step."

Speaking of that, his foot was dangerously near the African violet, which Anya had forgotten until now. Guiltily, she bent down and snatched Paula to safety. "I'll take this upstairs."

"I'll come with you." Zora stood.

Lucky regarded her dubiously. "It takes two people to carry a tiny little plant?"

"Huh," said Anya.

Lucky grinned. "I think that means I should butt out. By the way, I forgot to say congratulations."

"Thanks," she muttered, making her way around the table.

"I mean it." He spoke in earnest. "Having a baby grow inside you is amazing. It's an experience we guys miss out on."

"If he says that when you go into labor, I'll smack him for you," Zora said.

"No picking on the lone male in the household," he countered. "You women are touchy."

"Maybe yes, maybe no," Melissa said.

Karen collected the leftover pizza. "There are five leftover slices, one for each of us. We can all count. If any one of us comes up short, the thief will be sniffed out, drawn and quartered."

Everyone nodded. Living together might actually be fun, Anya thought as she carried Paula upstairs.

When she entered her cozy corner room, her gaze went to the window, which had a splendid view of the marsh and farther out to the ocean. The winter sunset sent a pale gold sheen over the misty marshland, and as she peered out, a pelican swooped low.

Zora followed her gaze. "Looks like that pelican caught something."

"Judging by the lumps in his pouch, he's collected a lot of somethings." Anya cradled the plant as if to protect it from the distant pelican. "I think she'll be happy on this little table. It catches a lot of light." She positioned the plant, moving aside her e-book reader.

"Getting back to Jack…" Zora began.

"Must we?"

Her friend persevered. "You mentioned having him sign a waiver. What if he refuses to let you give up the baby?"

Anya squared her shoulders. "He can't force me to raise a child, and I doubt he's prepared to be a single father. What other choice is there?"

"Well, remember to stand your ground." Plopping onto the cushioned window seat, Zora slid off her shoes. "Men talk a good story, and then they leave you to pick up the pieces."

"Jack's not like that." She hadn't meant to spring to his defense, but she *did* respect Jack's integrity.

"You think so?" Zora rubbed one foot. "He has quite a reputation as a ladies' man."

Although Anya had heard that, in her observation it was more a case of women flirting and Jack merely being polite in return. With a pang, she remembered that real estate agent, Danica, hanging on his arm and sauntering up to her apartment with him. "Maybe he deserves it and maybe he doesn't."

"How'd it happen?"

No sense dodging again. She'd have to fill in the details eventually. "As you guessed, it was after he drove me home New Year's Eve."

"That's it?" Zora's eyes widened.

What was she expecting, a tale of seduction and intrigue? "This isn't a complicated story."

"I mean, you only did it once?" her friend clarified.

"It happens. Not everybody suffers from infertility," Anya pointed out.

Zora took a different tack. "New Year's Eve—he took advantage of you when you were drunk."

"I only had two drinks, and the attraction was mutual. Plus, I assured him I was on the Pill, which was true." Anya explained about the St. John's wort. "So I'm at least as much to blame as he is."

"Taking a silly herb doesn't make it your fault," Zora said loyally.

"It's not his fault either." Anya preferred to focus on her most pressing problem, though. "I dread telling him."

"You think he'll get mad?"

That reaction might fit Zora's soon-to-be ex-husband but not Jack. "Exactly the opposite. He loves kids with a passion." Anya paced around the room, too agitated to stand still. "What if in a weak moment I back down? I have to stand strong on adoption. One chink in my armor and I'd be boxed into a responsibility I'm not ready for."

Zora began massaging her other foot. "You should let Edmond give him the waiver."

"Who's Edmond?"

"My lawyer," Zora said. "Talk to him. He could present the whole thing to Jack from a guy's perspective."

Zora was right: a man could explain in practical terms what all this meant. And having the lawyer handle it reduced the risk of Anya caving in.

All the same, she had doubts. Breaking such important news via a third party might infuriate Jack.

"Edmond's not some old codger who'll treat me like a fallen woman, is he?"

"No, he's young and good-looking." Her friend smiled. "And he's Melissa's ex-husband. But she still recommends him as an attorney. And since he doesn't want kids himself, you should have his sympathy."

In view of Melissa's powerful desire for children, Anya understood why they were divorced. Still, he must be a skilled lawyer if she *and* Zora spoke well of him, and Anya would need an attorney to handle the adoption anyway. Might as well start now. "I'll call him tomorrow for an appointment."

"Great." Zora slid her feet into her shoes. "Go for it."

"I will." With that weight off her mind, Anya opened one of the boxes that lined the walls and set to work unpacking.

Chapter Six

Friday was a long day for Jack. He'd arrived early for surgery, then took a break for a late lunch and had barely retreated to an on-call room for a nap when he was summoned to Labor and Delivery. With an unexpectedly large number of women laboring at once, all hands were needed.

After delivering five babies, he arrived late for his patient appointments at his shared third-floor office suite and had to remind himself to slow down and give each woman the attention she deserved. But when his last scheduled patient of the day failed to arrive, relief washed through him. He phoned Rod to ask for a ride; his uncle's aging car was in the shop yet again and Rod was borrowing Jack's car.

Jack thought of the less-than-exciting weekend ahead. Patient appointments on Saturday followed by an open calendar. Well, Danica *had* invited him to join her and a group of friends for a movie Saturday night, which might be a good way to meet new people. However, it would be unfair to encourage Danica's interest while Anya's dark, skeptical eyes haunted Jack's dreams.

He'd kept his word about leaving Anya alone. When they saw each other in the O.R., she acted politely distant, and so did he.

He wasn't sure how much longer he could keep that up, though. He'd noticed she'd gone pale several times during surgery. She'd always rallied and performed her duties flawlessly, but it worried him. When he'd asked her about it between surgeries, she'd said she'd stayed up late yakking with her new housemates.

They must be having a great time, Jack thought with a touch of bitterness. Certainly he didn't wish for her to be unhappy. Well, maybe a little unhappy. He wanted her to miss him and be keenly aware that he was honoring their agreement to remain at arm's length.

He was frustrated and more than a little disappointed that she didn't seem to feel either of those things.

Rod poked his head in the staff entrance to the suite. "Ready?"

"More than." Jack gave a farewell nod to the nurse.

Ned Norwalk, RN, a blond fellow noted for his surfing prowess, glanced up anxiously from the phone. "Dr. Ryder? I'm glad you haven't left. Your patient was waiting in the wrong office. She's on her way up from the second floor now."

Rod rolled his eyes.

"How did that happen?" Jack asked.

The nurse set down the receiver. "Apparently she got confused between you and Zack Sargent. Then she forgot to check in, so they didn't realize they had our patient in their waiting room."

"Yes, Ryder and Sargent sound exactly alike, don't they?" Jack grumbled.

"It's more the Zack and Jack part," said his uncle. "Rhymes with Frick and Frack. Did you know they were a team of comic Swiss ice skaters?"

Jack ignored his uncle's riff. "You'll wait for me, right?"

Rod waggled his eyebrows. "Sure. I have some great new apps on my cell."

"Now you're playing games?" His uncle used to scorn that sort of activity.

"Just the ones for preteens." Rod hadn't given up hope of renewing contact with his daughters, although they'd heard nothing from Tiffany in the week since her surprise visit.

When Rod had called Helen, she'd declined to nag or pry

information out of her granddaughter. "Give Tiffany a little credit. She and Amber will figure something out."

After having his hopes raised, Rod wasn't about to back off completely. Instead, he was apparently channeling his energies into getting up to speed on the world of preteens.

"Have fun," Jack told him.

"I'll be in the waiting room." He sauntered off.

The patient arrived. While Ned prepped her, Jack performed breathing exercises to calm his annoyance at her delayed arrival. Every patient deserved his best.

He studied her medical records. In her early sixties, the woman had been in excellent condition during her recent annual checkup, aside from normal symptoms of menopause. She'd declined to take hormones because of concerns about cancer risks.

In the examining room, he found a trim, alert woman, her champagne-blond hair carefully styled. "It's my hot flashes," she told him. "They've started keeping me awake at night, and I practically have to carry a fan around with me. Isn't there anything you can recommend other than hormones?"

"Let's talk about dietary changes." Jack mentioned avoiding caffeine, spicy foods and alcohol, as well as stress, hot showers and hot tubs, and intense exercise. As they talked, he noted that she showed no confusion, so perhaps the office mix-up had been a simple mistake rather than a sign of the brain fog sometimes referred to as mentalpause.

"You might try soy products," he added. "Some women find them helpful."

"One of my friends recommended an herb." She consulted her notebook. "Black cohosh?"

"It has been associated with cases of liver damage, so I don't recommend it." To present more options, Jack added, "There are no studies that prove acupuncture helps, but some women like it. And on the plus side, it probably can't do any harm."

She jotted down his recommendations. "Okay. I think I'll start by cutting out the spicy Indian and Chinese food."

"You eat those a lot?"

"Three or four times a week."

Hoping that would help, Jack said goodbye to the woman and returned to the waiting room, empty save for his uncle. "Now you understand why I chose anesthesiology," Rod said, sticking his phone in his pocket. "Regular hours and limited patient contact."

"But you miss the highs," Jack pointed out. Performing surgery and delivering babies provided a thrill that never faded. He'd also learned that simple discussions, such as the one he'd just had with his patient, could result in major quality-of-life improvements.

Hot curries and Chinese food three to four times a week? He suspected that might give *him* hot flashes.

"Highs tend to be followed by lows," his uncle advised.

"It's worth it."

"Not to me."

The outer door opened. No other doctors were on duty at this hour, so somebody must be lost, Jack thought, an impression reinforced when a man in a tailored suit entered. In his early thirties, he might be a pharmaceutical rep, promoting his company's products. "Can I help you?"

"Is one of you Dr. Jack Ryder?" The fellow pushed up his glasses.

"Are you a process server?" Rod demanded. He'd been hit with a ridiculous number of summonses during his legal battles with Portia.

The man blinked. "Not exactly."

That wasn't promising. Might as well get it over with. "I'm Jack Ryder."

The man extended his hand. "Edmond Everhart, family attorney."

Reluctantly, Jack shook it. "What's this about?"

The man glanced at Rod. "Is there somewhere we can talk privately?"

Rod tipped back his fedora. "I'm his uncle and I'm staying."

Jack appreciated the support. "What's this about?" he repeated.

A thin line forming on his forehead, Everhart plucked a sheet of paper from his briefcase. "My client asked me to give this to you to sign."

That sounded ominous. "Someone's suing me?"

"No." The man's frown deepened. "She didn't discuss this with you?"

"Who?" Jack asked impatiently. "Discuss what?"

"Miss Meeks," the fellow clarified, casting a glance toward the unoccupied reception desk. "Do you have a private office? This is a very personal matter."

Rod, who had little tolerance for dithering, snatched the paper from Edmond's hand and read the heading aloud. "Waiver of parental rights." He studied Jack askance. "Do you know anything about this?"

Unbelievable. "She's pregnant? And she breaks the news with a waiver?" Taking the document, Jack confirmed that it was, indeed, a form to sign away his parental rights. "Is this how the matter is customarily handled?"

The lawyer shook his head. "No. I had the impression you were already informed."

"Obviously not." Jack stood there stiffly, fitting the pieces together. Anya's upset stomach last Sunday and her pallor during surgery—now he understood the cause. But if she was carrying his baby, why push him away? And why send a stranger with this odd request? "I don't understand why she wants me to sign this."

"Miss Meeks has requested I arrange an adoption for her child-to-be." Edmond spoke with a touch of embarrassment, and no wonder. Anya had put him in an awkward position. "When she requested I deliver this form, I assumed you'd agreed to sign it."

It wasn't like Anya to lie. However, her tendency to speak tersely meant that her words might easily be taken the wrong way, especially if she wanted them to be.

While Jack was considering that, Rod filled the silence.

"I'm surprised a lawyer would bring this in person. Isn't that what process servers are for?"

Edmond chose his words carefully. "Some of my clients seem vulnerable. I like to be sure matters are handled with tact."

Vulnerable—yes, that fit Anya. It was hardly an excuse, though. "She's been pretty damn tactless, if you ask me," he muttered.

"No kidding," Rod seconded. "It's harsh, sending a lawyer to inform my nephew that he's going to be a father. Then there's my own trauma in learning, without preamble, that I'm about to be a great-uncle. Don't I have any rights?"

"I'm afraid not." Edmond didn't crack a smile at the absurd question. To Jack, he said, "Miss Meeks strikes me as a reticent person. Perhaps she finds you intimidating."

"I don't see why. But she *has* been avoiding me." For the sake of accuracy, Jack amended that to, "Outside work. She's a scrub nurse—a surgical nurse."

A smile touched the attorney's face. "I know what a scrub nurse is. My ex-wife works in the medical field." He cleared his throat. "I recommend that you and Miss Meeks review this matter face-to-face. I can mediate if you like."

"Are you sure that you *are* the father?" Rod asked Jack. To Edmond, he said, "I had a situation where I supported my children for years before discovering I wasn't their genetic father. And then—well, no sense getting into *that* mess."

Anya had claimed to be on the Pill, Jack recalled. Not that it was infallible and not that he would blame her for a pregnancy that resulted from their mutual involvement, regardless of what contraception she did or didn't use.

But if he signed that document without a DNA test and some other fellow was the real father, it would be a mess. Although Jack doubted there was another man, Anya *had* been evasive lately. "Let's conduct a DNA test before we proceed, just to confirm."

The attorney took this in coolly. "I'm not the doctor here,

but since the baby hasn't been born yet, doesn't that require an invasive procedure?"

"Not anymore," Rod said. "Just snip, snip, snip."

"Excuse me?"

With a quelling glare at his uncle, Jack explained, "He means it's no longer necessary to perform an amniocentesis or chorionic villus sampling on a pregnant woman." Both procedures required inserting a needle into the mother and carried a small risk of miscarriage, infection or amniotic fluid leakage. "An SNP microarray procedure can be done with a simple blood test on the mother as early as the ninth week. Hence, the term *snipping*."

"What's SNP stand for, exactly?" Edmond asked.

"You don't want to know," Rod said.

"Humor me."

"Single nucleotide polymorphism," Jack answered.

"I see." Refocusing, the attorney went on, "I suppose a DNA test isn't too much to ask, then."

Anya might not agree, Jack supposed. Well, she'd decided to give up their baby without informing him, and he had a stake in this, too. Okay, she *had* informed him via Edmond, but he suspected that was only due to a legal requirement. And if there was even the smallest chance this might not be his baby, he couldn't in good conscience sign those papers.

"Can we hire you to serve her with a demand for a DNA test?" Rod asked.

"You'll have to find another attorney." Edmond spread his hands apologetically. "I can't represent you both."

"But you can mediate for us both?" Jack challenged.

"I would recommend you bring your own attorney to any negotiations. Or a quiet conversation might be appropriate, depending on your relationship with Miss Meeks." The lawyer tilted his head sympathetically. "I'll admit, if I were you, I'd be mad about the way this information was presented, too."

Information? That was a rather impersonal way to refer

to the stunning news that Jack was going to be a father. But that was probably typical lawyer-speak.

"Try royally ticked off," Rod responded. "I'd like to tell Miss Meeks precisely what I think of her so-called reticence."

"Excuse me." From his full height, Jack peered down a few inches at his uncle. "Whose baby is this?"

"Family's family." Rod stood his ground.

"Leave Anya alone. Got it?" Jack might be furious with her, but he'd tolerate no interference. To the attorney, he said, "Thanks for stopping by."

"Sorry the news came as a surprise." As they shook hands, Edmond studied him with concern. "May I make a personal observation?"

"Knock yourself out."

"People don't always act rationally when it comes to having children," Edmond said. "I recommend communicating, listening and weighing all aspects before choosing a course of action."

"Duly noted," Jack said.

"Have a good evening." With a nod to his uncle, who didn't bother to extend a hand, Edmond exited.

Belatedly, it occurred to Jack that Ned might have overheard the discussion. However, a check of the suite showed that the nurse had departed. Also, health care workers were accustomed to keeping anything they learned at the office strictly confidential. He hoped that applied to private conversations of physicians as well as patients.

As Jack turned off the lights and locked up, his brain raced. Anya was pregnant. She was carrying a child, their child. Didn't she understand how much this mattered to him?

It would be unfair to equate her conduct with his former aunt's duplicity. But he also had the dubious example set by his mother, who viewed the world strictly in terms of herself and her selfish wishes, despite her devotion to charity work.

Case in point, when Jack had asked her to find a project where they could spend a summer together providing medical care to impoverished women and children, she'd sent him a list of websites. Then off she'd gone on her latest cause, raising funds to buy whistles so women in Haiti could summon help when attacked.

Yes, Mamie Ryder did a lot of good. But only in ways that suited her.

Rod was waiting by the side exit. "You and Anya had sex. When and where did *that* happen?"

Jack switched off the hall light. "Boundaries," he reminded his uncle.

"Don't dodge the question."

"None of your business." That seemed plain enough.

"Must have been New Year's Eve." Rod strolled beside him toward the elevators. "That would put her pregnancy at about seven weeks. Hmm. Looks like I'll be an uncle by the end of September."

"Great-uncle," Jack amended.

"I am, aren't I?"

"Rod," he began in a warning tone.

His uncle pressed the down button. "Okay. I'll shut up." About two seconds later, he said, "One more thing."

Jack narrowed his eyes.

"If you don't sign the paper and she insists on adoption, what then?" Rod asked.

"How do you feel about turning the living room into a nursery?" Jack retorted. When the elevator door opened, he stepped inside, grateful there was another person in the elevator to stifle the conversation.

He appreciated that his uncle, apparently lost in thought, barely spoke the rest of the way home. Jack hadn't meant to propose they raise the baby themselves; how could they? Yet, how could he give his child away?

Chapter Seven

Feet propped on the worn coffee table in the den, Anya skimmed her email on her phone. Her favorite department store was having a sale—how frustrating since she'd soon be shopping at The Baby Bump instead.

Beside her, Zora swore under her breath at the square she was crocheting, or trying to crochet, from a baby blanket pattern. "I keep messing this up. I wish I could call Betsy. She's the expert."

"I don't need a baby blanket," Anya reminded her.

"Who said it's for you?" her friend muttered. "It's for Harper." Nurse Harper Gladstone and her husband were expecting twins via a surrogate in June.

Lucky peered at them both from his laptop. Although the table was ostensibly part of the kitchen, it bordered the family room. "Speaking of Betsy, how're you getting along with your ex-mother-in-law, anyway? Or should I say, almost ex-mother-in-law?"

Safe Harbor Nursing Supervisor Betsy Raditch was, in Anya's opinion, much too nice to be the mother of the faithless Andrew. "Why do you care?"

"Zora can answer for herself," he said.

"Why do you care?" Zora echoed.

Their housemate grinned. "You guys are like a brick wall. I can't make a dent."

"That's the idea." Anya missed their old living room, where she and Zora had been able to relax without male intrusion. Also, she was too restless tonight to concentrate on her own task, reading a book.

Edmond Everhart had promised to present the waiver to Jack by the end of the week. She hadn't heard any explosions or seen flames rising from the central part of town, but neither had Edmond called or messaged to say Mission Accomplished.

Had Edmond put it off? He seemed trustworthy, although Melissa refused to discuss her ex-husband in a personal manner, which implied that he'd sinned in some major and irredeemable way. Still, Anya felt a twinge of guilt that she'd let him assume that she'd already informed Jack of the pregnancy. Although she hadn't lied, she hadn't corrected his obvious mistaken impression either.

Lucky flexed his shoulders. On his right bicep, exposed by his sleeveless T-shirt, a colorful dragon writhed. "It's Friday night. Let's throw a party."

"At the last minute?" Zora sniffed.

"Lame," Anya told him.

"We should plan a housewarming, at least," he returned, unruffled.

"Bring it up on Sunday," Zora said. All five housemates had agreed to hold weekly meetings to coordinate schedules and nip any problems in the bud.

"Fine. But you guys are way too buttoned-up," Lucky said. "Live a little."

"I thought you got enough of that lifestyle with your old roommates." Anya had heard him complain more than once about his party-hearty pals.

"They were noisy slobs," he said. "And inconsiderate when I was trying to concentrate on my thesis." He'd almost completed work on a master's degree in medical administration.

"If your thesis is so important, why are you talking to us?" Zora asked.

"I'm taking a break."

The doorbell rang. "Who could that be at eight o'clock on a Friday night?" Zora dismissed her own question when she added, "Maybe a friend of Karen's." Karen, whose longtime friends occasionally dropped by unannounced, was attending a play at South Coast Repertory with Melissa.

"I'll get it." Lucky pushed back his chair.

But Anya had a pretty good idea who it might be. "Stay there," she commanded and hurried to the front hall.

When she opened the door, there towered Jack, dark hair mussed and green eyes as hard as emeralds.

The first time she'd seen him, she'd had to catch her breath. Then she'd found out she'd been chosen to assist this brilliant surgeon with movie-star looks, and a tremor had gone through Anya's knees. In the year since then, he'd grown more handsome, more confident and more terrifying, especially when he was angry, like now.

The impulse to apologize nearly wrenched a "sorry" from her lips. She bit down so hard her teeth hurt. Okay, he had good reason to be mad, but ultimately, there was no debate. He had to sign the waiver.

She ought to warn him that they had an audience within earshot. But Anya couldn't force out the words. Guilty twinges about sending Edmond in her stead, and about taking St. John's wort, quivered through her. Or possibly that was morning-and-evening sickness.

He was waiting for her to speak first. Finally, she managed to say, "I gather you met Edmond."

"I can't believe you did that." When Jack glared, his body seemed to grow to mammoth size, like a genie released from a bottle. "How do you think I felt when a *lawyer* informed me I was going to be a father? Oh, and here, sign away your rights on the dotted line while we're at it."

"You don't have any rights. It's a legal dodge dreamed up by male legislators to oppress women." Anya had no idea if that was true—it might have been a court ruling. But the point was the same.

"You think I'd dismiss having a child that lightly?" he demanded.

"Think about the alternative," she retorted. "Have you

ever raised a baby? I helped raise three of them. They stole my adolescence. That was enough."

"I didn't realize it was such a burden." Her anecdotes about her sisters, which she'd shared in bits and pieces during their operating room discussions, had often been humorous.

"They're sweethearts," Anya conceded. "But when they were little, I used to cry myself to sleep thinking about the stacks of diapers and the endless chores around the house."

Jack's manner softened slightly. "I can imagine that colored your assumptions rather darkly. But you're not an adolescent and we aren't discussing your sisters."

"To me, adoption is the only reasonable choice," she told him.

"We're having a child," he replied quietly. "This is not something you just throw away."

Providing a child with an adoring family hardly constituted throwing it away. But that wasn't the point. "What's your assumption—that I'll raise it because you say so?" Anya asked. "That I'll be a robot you can order around for the next twenty years?" She'd lived through that experience already. Once was enough.

"Of course not." Jack shifted uncomfortably. "How about inviting me in?"

Because there was nothing to be gained by rudeness, she moved aside. As he entered, Jack peered around and gravitated to the now-empty living room. Good. All the same, their voices could carry.

"I should warn you…" she began.

He took up a stance in front of the curio cabinet. "I won't sign the waiver until I'm sure the baby is mine."

His statement drove all other considerations from Anya's mind. "You think I sleep around?"

"I didn't mean that." Jack stuck his hands in his pockets. "But I'd like confirmation."

"Don't be ridiculous."

"It's a simple blood test," he said.

"You have incredible nerve!" Her earlier hesitation evaporated in the face of this insult.

"Then my consent will have to wait until after the baby's born so we can test it on its own." His level tone proved just as maddening as his outrageous demand.

"I can't wait that long. I need to choose an adoptive family who'll pay my bills." The attorney had explained that it was customary for the adopting parents to pay expenses related to the pregnancy, such as medical care, maternity clothing and other necessities.

"I'll pay your bills," Jack told her.

"I don't want your money!" Accepting his support would put her completely at his mercy.

Even though his hands were in his pockets, she could see them form into fists. "Why do you refuse to acknowledge that I have a stake in this pregnancy?"

"Because any stake you have is nothing compared to…" Anya broke off because her stomach was in full rebellion. *Please don't let me throw up in Karen's living room.* Losing her balance, she grabbed an end table, an unfortunate choice. The thing wobbled and then tipped, sending her and a lamp crashing to the floor.

"Anya!" Jack rushed to catch her, too late to prevent a painful bump on her hip. Still, his strong arms prevented any further tumbling.

Had she broken Karen's lamp? Mercifully, it appeared intact on the carpet.

Footsteps thudded. Around the corner rushed Zora and Lucky, colliding by the stairs. "Back off, you big oaf!" Darting under his arm, Zora hurried forward.

Lucky stayed in place, surveying the scene. "I guess this answers the question of who the dad is."

Jack's lip curled. "You told them you were pregnant before you told me?"

"It slipped out." Anya wiggled free from his grasp. Her stomach had subsided, thank goodness, but her temper hadn't. "You see what I have to go through? My tummy hurts, my feet hurt and I can't imagine how I'll feel when I'm as big as this house."

Zora helped her up, with Jack taking the other side and assisting her to the couch. "Men have it easy," her friend added.

"He wants me to take a DNA test," Anya said.

"She hired a lawyer to break the news to me," Jack defended himself to their audience of two.

"Pretty cold," Lucky agreed from across the room. "Seriously, Anya, a lawyer?"

"I can't believe you're taking his side." Zora straightened the table while Jack gingerly lifted the lamp. "Or maybe I should expect that. After all, guys stick together, don't they?"

"There are no sides," Jack said. "I'm here to help Anya, not hurt her. But getting back to our topic, how else can I declare legally that I'm the father? I'm not her husband or even her steady boyfriend. If I sign those papers without proof that I'm the father, I could be guilty of defrauding the adoptive parents. If some other guy shows up later and claims paternity, it would be a painful mess."

Judging by Lucky's nods, that argument must make sense from a male perspective. Anya was insulted all over again. However, much as she resented Jack's attitude, the alternative—waiting until she gave birth before choosing adoptive parents—was unacceptable. "If I take a DNA test, you'll relinquish your rights?"

That stopped him briefly. "I'll consider it."

"Not good enough."

"Once the baby's born, he can get a court order for the test," Lucky reminded her.

"What kind of judge would let him stick a needle in a helpless baby?" Zora flared.

"All newborns have a few drops taken from their heels to screen for serious medical conditions," Jack informed her. "It's no big deal."

The discussion swirled around Anya as if she weren't there or weren't the primary person carrying this baby. It reminded her unhappily of her family's behavior at Christmas as they discussed why she ought to move back to Colorado.

Suddenly queasy again, she gripped the arm of the couch. No one had bothered to ask if she'd like a cup of tea or anything else.

That gave her an idea.

FRUSTRATED, JACK wondered how to penetrate the guard Anya had raised around herself. He'd stated his case, including his willingness to support her. Now he had to deal with her roommate fluttering around, raising objections. Thank goodness the male nurse had grasped his point. The guy was improving on closer acquaintance.

Jack's request was perfectly rational, and Anya would realize that if she weren't so—well, not irrational but far from completely objective. Pregnancy hormones were well known to affect moods.

Stop thinking like a doctor, and pay attention. What was it that lawyer had recommended? Oh, yes, communicating, listening and weighing all aspects.

Focusing on Anya, Jack saw that she'd gone pale again and was hanging on to the arm of the couch. "You obviously feel lousy," he said. "Should I get a basin?"

Her chin came up. Although he wished she were less stubborn, he admired her spirit.

"Ice cream," she told him. "Lucky ate the last of it earlier."

"There was only one scoop," protested her housemate from his post by the stairs.

"Two scoops. The one in your bowl and the one you ate standing over the sink," Zora corrected. "Lucky should go out for more."

"Jack can do it." Resolve strengthened Anya's words. "If I have to go through this, you shouldn't get off scot-free. It's only fair that you share some of the burden."

"You mean earn the right to a DNA test?" he asked drily.

"I wouldn't exactly put it that way," Anya said, "but you should be willing to help out."

"I can make grocery runs." He nodded. "What else?"

"Foot massages would be nice." She regarded him as if testing the waters.

That might be fun. "I'm happy to." And after the stories she'd told him about the work she'd done for her sisters and mother, Jack supposed it was about time someone—namely, him—did the same for her. "Sure, bring it on. Whatever you need."

"My favorite flavor is butterscotch," Lucky said.

"Chocolate," Zora put in.

"Take a hike," Anya told them both. "It's vanilla with caramel ripples."

"Hold on." Jack had no intention of becoming the household puppet. "I'm helping Anya and only Anya. But how long before you take the blood test?"

"You're the doctor," she said. "How soon is it feasible?"

That would be at about nine weeks. "Rough estimate, two weeks from now. Do we have a deal?"

"Maybe." To the others, she said, "This is between Jack and me, guys."

With a shrug, Lucky retreated. Zora wrinkled her nose, but she, too, departed.

Sitting beside Anya and taking her hands in his, Jack found them unexpectedly warm. Blood volume increased during pregnancy by as much as 50 percent, but mostly in the later stages.

You're thinking like a doctor again.

"Let's agree on terms," he said.

"Terms?"

No sense risking a misunderstanding. "If I do as you ask, do you promise to take the test as soon as your OB approves?"

"Yes. And then you promise to sign the paper," she countered.

Jack's chest squeezed. He remembered Tiffany and Amber as toddlers, running to him with hugs and butterfly kisses, playing horse by climbing onto his back and tumbling off with shrieks of glee.

But that wasn't the same as being a single father. Parenthood was a commitment that should take priority over everything else. How could Jack meet the child's emotional and practical needs while building his medical practice and paying off educational loans? It would be different if Anya were willing to participate, but alone, how could he provide the kind of loving, attentive home this little one deserved? As much as it hurt, he couldn't.

"If you're still absolutely determined to seek adoption at that time, I'll sign."

"Define *absolutely.*"

Her response startled a chuckle from him. "You missed your calling. You should have been a lawyer."

"Don't change the subject." She left her hands in his.

"You have to be willing to discuss the issue frankly," Jack said. "No avoidance."

"That's my survival strategy," she protested. "Duck and run."

"Like hiring an attorney to break the news to me."

She flushed. "Sorry about that."

"So you agree to be straight with me about adoption? If your feelings change, I have a right to know."

Slowly, Anya nodded. "Okay, after we get the results of the DNA test, I'll think it over carefully. But if you fail your part and don't take care of me to my satisfaction, you'll sign after two weeks *without* a DNA test. Because if you won't even inconvenience yourself that much, you have no business insisting I raise a child."

"*Help* raise a child."

"Mothers do two-thirds of the work even under the best of circumstances."

"It depends on the father, but let's stay on topic." Although tempted to demand an objective standard for judging his cooperation, Jack had to admit that would be difficult. And he didn't believe Anya intended to cheat him. He'd already insulted her enough by requiring a DNA test to confirm his paternity. However, he still had to be clear about this bargain they were striking. "I'll let you decide whether I've kept my part of the bargain, but your demands have to be reasonable."

"Define…"

"…*reasonable,*" he finished for her. "No jerking me around."

"Such as?" she demanded.

"No phoning in the middle of the night for something minor like rubbing your feet, unless you allow me to move in with you." Jack hadn't been angling for any such thing, but now that he thought about it…

"That won't be necessary," she said quickly. "What else?"

"No interrupting my work unless it's an emergency."

"Of course not." Anya regarded him indignantly. "I'd never interfere with patient care. Even if I keel over during surgery, you keep at it. Somebody else can cart me off."

"We'll see." Jack hoped nothing like that would happen. "Have we covered everything?"

"I guess so." Anya released a long breath.

He transferred her right hand into his and shook it. "Done. Jack Ryder agrees to approximately two weeks of catering to Anya Meeks's pregnancy-related needs. In return for which she agrees to take a DNA test."

"And then he agrees to sign the relinquishment."

"If she's still set on adoption," he concluded. "Can we stop referring to ourselves in the third person now?"

She chuckled. "This is a funny bargain."

It felt strange to Jack, too—but rather pleasant. "As long as we're both satisfied, I deem these negotiations successful."

"You actually listened to me," she said with a touch of wonder.

"That surprises you?" He hadn't meant to ride roughshod over her in the past.

"It's not what I'm used to." She tilted her head. "What now?"

"Vanilla," he said, rising.

"With caramel ripples. Better get extra," she warned. "My roommates are a hungry lot."

"Anything else you need at the store?" Jack asked. "Fresh vegetables? Yogurt? Milk?"

A few minutes later, shopping list in hand, he decamped. Darkness had fallen over the marsh, punctuated by chirps and whirring noises above the thrum of the ocean. A sea breeze had eased the rotten egg smell, and a pale winter moon hung low in the sky.

Jack's instincts warned that by agreeing to sign the waiver, he was embarking on a path that would affect him for the rest of his life. Until now, in many ways, he'd been in control of his destiny, or he'd imagined he was.

Not anymore.

The idea of losing his child, knowing those special moments and precious photos would belong to another family, nearly made him rush inside to retract his offer. Yet these days, birth parents weren't necessarily kept in total ignorance of their child's well-being. The right parents could notify him and Anya about the baby's health and progress. He'd know for certain that his child was loved and happy.

A lump formed in Jack's throat. He'd never expected to face such a difficult situation. And not only in regard to the baby.

The sight of Anya stumbling, flailing in vain for a grip and falling, had wrenched at him. She was in this vulnerable state partly because of his actions.

Fortunately, there was an upside to their pact. Although he couldn't be here every minute to catch her, their agreement meant he didn't have to keep his distance either.

His spirits rising, Jack set out for the market.

Chapter Eight

"I should never have let you go to that house alone." Rod, his gray-laced brown hair sticking out wildly, stalked around the apartment living room. "You've been railroaded."

"Brush your hair," Jack told him.

"What?" Patting the top of his head, the older man stopped pacing. Earlier, he'd taken Danica out for brunch while wearing his fedora. Now, he smoothed his disheveled mop, though it was a lost cause. "Don't change the subject."

"I wasn't trying to." Stretched out on the sofa, Jack used his phone to order underwear and socks from his favorite on-line retailer. The old stuff had become frayed, and you never knew who might see it.

"You made this unholy concession Friday night and you're only breaking the news to me on Sunday afternoon—that means you're embarrassed about it," Rod declared. "Didn't you learn anything from my mistakes?"

"I have enough trouble learning from my own mistakes," Jack replied. "As for why I'm just telling you now, I was working Saturday and by the time you got back from feeding the animals"—his uncle volunteered at the Oahu Lane Shelter—"I wasn't in the mood to discuss it."

"Because you knew I'd hit the roof."

"That, and you smelled like a barnyard."

"Barnyards smell healthy," retorted his uncle.

"And you say this based on your vast farming experience?" As far as Jack was aware, the closest his uncle had come to a barnyard was a visit to a petting zoo when his daughters were young.

Rod leaned in the kitchen doorway. "You promised her you'd waive your paternal rights. That's huge. You should consult a lawyer. You also should have consulted me."

They'd already been over this, so Jack cut to the chase. "Anya might rethink her decision to give the baby away. If she doesn't, I have no idea what it would take to be a single dad to an infant. Neither do you, for that matter."

"They don't play video games?" Rod asked waggishly.

"Not that I've heard."

"However, I doubt they run away from home either," his uncle said.

Jack saw no point in arguing with such nonsense. "Can we move on, please?"

"To what?"

"Almost anything."

As his uncle fell silent, his smile disappeared. Jack was startled to notice new lines around Rod's mouth and eyes. As his closest friend and relative as well as his roommate, Rod had become a fixture in Jack's life—and like any fixture, he rarely drew close inspection. Now, Jack took a second look at his thin, graying uncle.

Forty might not be old, but the years weighed on Rod. Perhaps the sudden reconnection with Tiffany—followed by ten days of agonizing silence—had reawakened old sorrows. He also seemed unduly upset by the discovery that Jack might lose a chance to be a father.

If only the guy had a girlfriend, he'd be a lot happier. Jack loved his uncle, but Rod needed more than him. Anger flared at Portia, who'd not only robbed her husband of his family but who'd soured him on women in general. Since his divorce, Rod had shied away from all but the most casual relationships.

The older man had apparently held his tongue as long as he could bear to because he returned to his previous theme.

"At the very minimum, as that Edmond fellow recommended, you ought to hire your own lawyer."

Jack shook his head. "That risks turning this into a battle."

"There's nothing wrong with protecting your rights." Rod's phone sounded. "Now who could that be? Probably another salesman for solar panels."

In Jack's hand, his phone also beeped. "I hope this isn't a citywide emergency." He checked the readout. "Nope, it's Anya."

Rod had vanished into the kitchen. Good.

"Hey," Jack said into his phone. "What can I do for you?"

"You don't have to be at Labor and Delivery until 8:00 p.m., right?" she said.

"Yup. And I'm ready for action." He'd been almost disappointed at the lack of a request yesterday.

"We're having our weekly house conference at four," Anya said. "It was supposed to be after dinner, but it got moved up. Anyway, I forgot I'd promised to bring a snack, and I'm kind of tired. I wondered if you were willing to run out to the store again."

This was exactly the kind of thing Jack had volunteered for. "Glad to. What kind of snacks did you have in mind?"

"Chips and dip will be fine."

"No problem." It was almost three now. Jack had plenty of time to swing by the Suncrest Market.

"You can just drop the stuff off," Anya added.

Eager to get rid of him, was she? He'd see about that. "Sure."

As they ended the call, Jack was already figuring out a healthier alternative to chips and dip. He might not be able to raise his child, but he could provide a healthy start for him or her. Celery sticks with cheese or peanut butter, perhaps. Or fruit would be excellent.

"Good news!" Rod reappeared, grinning. "That was Helen. The girls are arriving next weekend for a three-day visit."

"Great." It was too early in the year for spring break, Jack noted. "What's the occasion?"

"A week from Monday is Presidents' Day, and there's no school. The kids've been nagging hard, I gather, and their parents caved." Rubbing his palms together, Rod added, "Helen liked my idea that they volunteer at the animal shelter on Saturday."

"Where they'll run into you," Jack said.

"Purely by chance," his uncle tossed off blithely. "I'll bet we can think of other ways for them to stumble across me, too."

"You bet—as soon as I get back." Sticking his phone in his pocket, Jack explained about the errand.

"Just one sec." From the hat tree that held his assortment of toppers, Rod selected a gray fedora.

"You're coming with me?" That might not be the best idea, in light of Rod's attitude.

The older man tipped his hat by way of an answer.

"No digs at Anya," Jack ordered.

"I'll be on my best behavior," his uncle answered easily.

Jack didn't find that statement reassuring. "Exactly what constitutes your best behavior?"

"I'm there for your protection," his uncle said. "In case you haven't noticed, it's not safe for you to be alone with those people."

"We work with those people," Jack reminded him.

"Different context." Rod pocketed his keys from the side table. "What's on the menu?"

"Celery and...hmm." An idea occurred to Jack that might let him stick around for the house conference. He'd love to hear what those folks were up to.

It was worth a try.

ANYA'S HOUSEMATES STARTED wandering into the den at a quarter to four. From the kitchen, Karen called out that there was hot apple cider with cinnamon sticks. "Help yourselves."

"Jack should be here any minute." Anya felt a little guilty about passing her responsibility to him, even though he deserved it after his ridiculous demand for a DNA test.

"Let's get started," Lucky said once they'd filled their mugs with steaming, aromatic cider. "We're all here, and we can take a break when the food arrives."

Their first item was a disagreement about the kitchen. Karen and Melissa preferred that all dirty plates, cups and tableware be placed immediately in the dishwasher. Zora and Anya were accustomed to accumulating items in the sink between meals.

"It's more efficient than having to open the dishwasher a dozen times a day," Zora said.

"Except someone else might need to use the sink," Melissa pointed out. "I had to put away your coffee cups this morning so I could bake muffins."

Anya had enjoyed the blueberry muffin Melissa had shared with her. "I guess that's reasonable."

Zora shrugged. "Okay. It isn't a big deal to me."

Lucky had stayed out of this one, Anya was glad to see. She'd been concerned that he might try to boss the women around, but it appeared he'd learned better. Or perhaps he simply didn't care about this particular matter.

"Next item." Karen tapped her list. "Do we each stock our own toilet paper, or should we purchase it in bulk? And what about paper towels? We can't very well have separate rolls for each of us."

Before anyone could answer, the doorbell rang. Anya rose quickly. "That should be for me."

As soon as she opened the door, a green T-shirt stretched across Jack's muscular chest dominated her field of vision. Next, she noticed the well-filled grocery sacks he carried on each side, while, behind him, Rod Vintner's arms encircled a third bag.

She stepped out of their path. "You didn't have to buy out the store."

"I figured this late in the day, we might as well bring dinner." Jack moved past her into the family room. "Don't let me interrupt," she heard him announce. "We brought cold cuts and bread for sandwiches. I'll set these out in the kitchen."

Anya found herself face-to-face with Rod. His flicker of reproach vanished so fast she wondered if she'd misinterpreted it.

"Tiffany and Amber are visiting next weekend," he said in a mild tone. "I'm sure your suggestion helped. Thanks."

"I'd love to see them." From the way he lingered in the entryway, she sensed he had more to say. "What?"

His gaze dropped to her abdomen. "Congratulations." The curl of his lip indicated she *hadn't* mistaken his reaction to her.

"Don't start on me," Anya warned.

Rod gave a jerk of surprise. "What did I say?"

"It's what you were thinking." No doubt this man who'd lost all rights to his daughters held a strong opinion about the future of his great-niece or nephew.

"Now you're a mind reader?" The man feigned innocence about as effectively as a toddler with chocolate smeared on his face and a plundered cookie jar behind him.

"Yes," Anya said. "Watch it."

At the hospital, he might be a lordly doctor. Well, semi-lordly; anesthesiologists didn't have the same cachet as surgeons. But in *her* house, he'd better behave like a good guest.

After a tense moment, Rod yielded. "My nephew would agree."

"He's a wise man."

She rejoined her housemates in the den. After greeting the small assembly, Rod trailed Jack into the kitchen.

Anya sneaked a glance at Lucky, half expecting him to complain about the intruders. Instead, he leaned back with a satisfied air. *Oh, right.* It was his week to cook, and they were relieving him of the duty.

The roommates returned to the topic of paper goods, agreeing it would be sensible to pool their money and buy in bulk. Karen promised to set up a kitty to which they would all contribute each month.

During the discussion, Anya remained keenly aware of Jack's quiet presence as he set a series of platters—breads, cheeses, sliced meats—on the table. He'd gone to a lot of trouble.

The others wrapped up the meeting quickly, no doubt enticed by the sight and smell of food. Rod seemed to take pride in arranging a stack of pastries pyramid-style on a plate. "No meal is complete without dessert," he informed the residents as they poured in from the den.

Anya decided against reminding Jack he was supposed to drop off the snacks and then depart. That would be ungracious. Besides, her housemates were clearly relishing the treat.

From a cabinet, Karen took a stack of plates. "There's plenty of apple cider left if you doctors would like some."

"I've seen you at the hospital but we haven't been formally introduced," Rod said to Karen. "I'm Rod Vintner."

She smiled. "Karen Wiggins. I've seen you, too." Her pleased expression hinted at an attraction.

Rod beamed right back at her. "You do such interesting things with your hair. I liked the dark color with the pink stripe, but this reddish-blond is nice, too."

"It's called strawberry." She stood in the middle of the kitchen, unaware that everyone else was waiting for her to set down the plates.

"Why don't we eat in the dining room?" Melissa asked. "The table's larger."

Her words stirred Karen into action. "Great idea."

"I'll bring the silverware." Lucky lifted the entire organizer from a drawer.

"We can use the kitchen table as a serving buffet," Zora added.

Everyone pitched in. Jack gravitated to Anya's side. "I get why you moved here. It's like being part of a big family."

No, because they aren't ordering me around. "It's better than a family," she said softly. "We respect each other."

"Don't families do that?" Jack murmured. "Good ones do, surely."

"I suppose." Because no one appeared to be listening at

the moment, she added, "Jack, this whole setup—I wasn't expecting you to bring dinner."

"The surprise is half the fun." He snagged a plate from the pile Karen had set down. "Can I fill this for you?"

It felt weird, having someone offer to wait on her. Weird, but nice. Too nice. "Thanks, but I'm not an invalid."

"Understood." Jack handed her the plate and stood back to let her serve herself. Both he and his uncle were in good spirits. They might not have been invited, but she was glad now that they'd joined the group for dinner.

In the dining room, Karen opened the curtains. Late-afternoon sunlight played over the backyard—the brick patio, the lawn and the plot of cool-weather vegetables. Around the perimeter, bougainvillea, honeysuckle and climbing roses obscured the fence with a wealth of pink and orange blossoms. Beyond them stretched the marsh with its subtle shadings of brown and gold.

"It's beautiful here." Rod gazed out admiringly. "There's only one drawback."

"The smell?" Karen said.

He tilted his head in agreement. "You must get used to it."

"Yes. I grew up here," she said. "And I'm grateful for this full house so I can afford to stay."

The seven of them took seats around the oak table, which Melissa and Zora had set with place mats. Jack wound up between Lucky and Melissa, which should have pleased Anya, but she missed him. She was wedged between Rod and Karen, who talked over and around her.

That felt familiar.

A smile played across Jack's face as he observed his uncle and Karen. Anya shared his pleasure at seeing sparks ignite between the couple.

She'd moved here to put distance between her and Jack. It didn't seem to be working out that way.

At the moment, though, she was rather enjoying the warm feelings she had when he was near and the sound of Jack's laughter at a remark of Lucky's. Her cheese-mustard-and-sprouts sandwich was delicious, too. A woman could get used to being coddled.

During a pause in the conversation, Rod remarked, "You folks ought to throw a housewarming party."

On Anya's other side, Karen said, "What a great idea!"

"I was going to propose that at the meeting," Lucky said. "Thanks for reminding me."

They settled on a barbecue next Saturday afternoon, with each of the residents preparing a dish and guests bringing desserts. For entertainment, they would play croquet on the lawn and set up board games in the den and living room.

"My daughters will be here from San Diego," Rod told Karen. "As long as they're in town, is it all right to invite them and their grandmother?"

"Of course!" She looked as delighted as if he'd offered to bring the cast of her favorite TV show. "How old are they?"

"Ten and twelve," Rod said.

Anya figured they'd enjoy the party more if they had a role to play. "They could dress up as waitresses—wear frilly aprons and serve hors d'oeuvres."

"How adorable," Zora said.

"Anya's good with kids," Lucky noted. "She could supervise the hostess brigade."

"She's *great* with kids," Jack affirmed. "Tiffany's crazy about her."

Their praise flowed over Anya like perfumed lotion. And being around girls that age would be more like play than work. "Sure, I can do that."

"Who else shall we invite?" Karen asked. "Let's make a list."

After they'd drawn up the names of coworkers and friends they wanted to invite, Rod asked Karen for a tour of the house. "This is my dream home," he added.

"I'd be happy to show you around."

Lucky cleared his throat. "Not to rely on stereotypes about rich doctors, but I would have assumed you'd have a place of your own by now."

"Long story." Rod helped Karen from her chair. "I'll tell you while we walk, if that's okay." He'd cut Lucky out of the explanation, which served the guy right, in Anya's opinion.

Lucky accepted the situation with good grace. "Since it was my turn to cook and you guys saved me the trouble, I'll clean up."

"I can help," Zora said. When the others stared at her in surprise, she added, "He's always accusing me of shirking my share of the work. I'm just proving him wrong."

"I do not," Lucky protested as he arose.

"Yes, you have, several times," Anya told him.

"Really?"

"I'll help, too," Melissa said. "It's dangerous to leave you two alone. There might soon be chalk-marked bodies on the kitchen floor."

Rod and Karen sauntered into the living room. Jack followed, so Anya went along, too.

"That's quite a collection." Rod examined the colorful plates in the curio cabinet, each bearing the design of a different geographic location. "You must love to travel."

"Most of these belonged to my mother, from when she was younger." Karen's voice thinned. "I did love to travel with her, but my ex-husband broke most of my plates that I bought on our trips."

"That's awful!" Anya had heard that her friend was divorced, but she didn't know any of the details.

"He was a nasty— Well, I'd rather not use an ugly word." Karen hugged herself, a movement that emphasized her slender figure.

"I'm sorry." Rod touched her shoulder lightly. "I didn't mean to bring up bad memories."

Karen moved toward the stairs. "We've been divorced for ten years. It's old news."

"My wife left me six years ago," Rod told her as they climbed, his voice drifting back to Anya. "She was a nasty piece of business herself."

"He isn't exaggerating," Jack said from beside her. "I can vouch for that."

Anya poked him in the ribs. When he swung toward her questioningly, she indicated the older couple, who'd reached the second-floor landing. "They could use some privacy," she murmured.

He gave her a conspiratorial wink.

While Rod and Karen ambled left toward the master suite, Anya detained Jack in the wide upstairs hall. "That's Safe Harbor in the 1930s." She indicated a sepia-toned photo of bare bluffs overlooking a harbor smaller than its present formation, with a scattering of vacation cottages where shops, a hotel and restaurants now stood. "Karen says it was dredged and enlarged later."

His gaze dropped to the purple couch from Anya and Zora's apartment. "I'm glad to see you guys were able to haul that sofa up here in one piece."

"If you notice any blistered paint, it's from Lucky's cursing." Keenly aware of being alone with him, Anya fought the impulse to draw closer to his warmth. Chattering more than usual to fill the void, she said, "He doesn't even use it, since his room's downstairs."

"Being on this floor with three other women must be like living in a dorm," Jack mused.

It isn't all women right now. Ignoring her mental digression, she said, "I never lived on campus. I'll bet it's fun."

"It is. Almost everyone lives on campus at Vanderbilt."

He'd mentioned before how much he'd enjoyed the excellent premed and medical training in Nashville. However, there was one question he hadn't answered. "Why did you decide to become a doctor?" Anya asked. "Was it Rod's influence?"

"Partly. If not for him, I'm not sure I'd have believed it was possible. But that wasn't the main reason." Jack's expression grew thoughtful. "My mother told me once that my dad had longed to be a doctor but couldn't afford medical school. He turned to firefighting instead as another way to help people. He died after re-entering a burning apartment building to find an elderly woman who was still missing. The roof collapsed on him."

Anya touched his arm. "What a terrible loss."

"That's the risk firefighters accept."

"What happened to the woman?"

Jack shook his head ruefully. "Turned out she wasn't even there."

She searched for a more pleasant subject. "Why'd you go so far away to medical school? I mean, being a California resident, it would have been cheaper to go to a UC campus, and they're world-class."

"I wanted to experience a different part of the country and a different climate." Jack stroked the back of her hand, which still rested on his arm. "Since I won a partial scholarship, the cost was comparable to in-state tuition, and Vanderbilt has an outstanding program."

"Lucky you." His caress quivered through her. "I'd hoped to pursue a master's degree to become a nurse practitioner." In rural communities and inner-city areas that lacked doctors, nurse practitioners often provided vital primary care to infants, children, adults and the elderly, which had originally been her plan. "But without a grant, I had to stop at my RN."

"Why'd you decide to become a scrub nurse?" He watched her with keen interest. Not just making idle conversation, Anya realized.

Being the center of his attention felt wonderful; it showed that she mattered to him. "I got a job at a hospital and started helping in the O.R. The more surgeries I assisted with, the more I loved it. I developed my skills on the job."

"So you found your true calling more or less by chance," Jack said. "Maybe not getting a grant was a lucky break."

Anya laughed. "I never thought of it that way."

He indicated the three bedroom doorways. "Which one's yours?"

"Back corner."

"I'll bet it has a great view."

Taking the hint, she led him into the room. "Ignore the

mess, okay?" She'd left a stack of clean laundry on the bed to be folded.

"You consider this a mess? I like what you've done with the room. It's nice." Hardly high praise, but then, her plain, inexpensive furnishings didn't merit compliments.

She found Jack's nearness even more enticing in these intimate quarters. Everything about him appealed to her, from the chest-hugging T-shirt to the light in his green eyes.

Longing shimmered through Anya. As a diversion, she hurried to the window. "It's especially pretty at sunset."

"It sure is." Jack came to stand close to her, not quite touching, and the air heated between them. His arm circled her waist, drawing her close.

Anya relaxed against him. Jack turned her toward him and touched his lips to hers, and the longing that rushed through her underscored how much she'd missed him.

Pleasure tingled through Anya as she stroked his thick dark hair. New Year's Eve hadn't been a tipsy aberration. She'd longed for him from the moment they met. And now she longed for more.

As they eased away from the window, they bumped into a small table. Wrenched from her reverie, Anya grabbed the small plant rocking on its drip plate. "Oh, no!"

Jack barely glanced at the African violet. "No harm done. It was nearly dead anyway."

"That's what's so awful." She stared in dismay at Paula. Robust and blooming a week ago, the plant now drooped in its pot. "I can't believe it's in such bad shape. I didn't even notice."

"You said you expected to kill it," he reminded her, his cheek against her hair.

Anya tried to figure out what she'd done wrong. "I must have overwatered it. I was afraid it would dry out, away from the bathroom."

"It'll recover."

"Are you kidding? It's a goner." Guilt flooded Anya as she fingered a wilted leaf. If she couldn't care for a plant, how could anyone expect her to raise a child? Not that she planned to. "I hope it isn't suffering."

Jack released her with a sigh. "I'm sorry the plant is so upsetting. I should have given you a silk one."

"Would you throw her away for me?" She couldn't bear to dump poor little Paula in the trash.

"No problem." Lifting the plant and drip pan, he bore them from the room and she followed.

Belatedly, Anya reflected that she'd spoiled their tender moment. But that was just as well. What if someone had walked in on them? Worse, what if someone *hadn't* walked in on them?

In the hall, Rod and Karen were talking earnestly on the couch. They broke off as Anya and Jack approached. "Good tour?" Rod asked Jack.

"The best."

His uncle studied the plant. "You have quite an effect on growing things."

"One scowl and it withered away," Jack said cheerfully.

As they descended the stairs, Anya heard Karen and Rod's conversation shift to next weekend's housewarming party. Karen was bubbling with enthusiasm about meeting Rod's daughters, and he had a new lilt to his voice.

If she hadn't insisted that Jack wait on her, he and Rod wouldn't have been here tonight, Anya thought. For Karen's sake, she was glad they'd come. But talking about her dreams and witnessing Jack's sadness about his father had made her even more vulnerable to him. She'd nearly welcomed him into her bed all over again.

If not for the baby, she'd love to spend more time with Jack. But she remembered she'd too often acquiesced to her family even as an inner voice warned that it was a mistake. She had to listen to that voice this time. She wasn't ready to be a mother. Her spirit rebelled at the prospect of taking on the responsibilities—the fears, the worries, the inadequacies—she'd only recently escaped. And with that frame of mind, she'd be a poor mother anyway.

As she reached the ground floor ahead of Jack, Anya's hand drifted to her abdomen. Startled, she snatched it away.

She couldn't do anything about work or next weekend's party, but aside from that, she would stop requesting Jack's assistance. The less time they spent alone together, the safer she'd be.

Chapter Nine

Jack hefted his tray and surveyed the nearly full hospital cafeteria. Tables outside on the patio, warmed by heat lamps in the brisk February afternoon, sat empty. Inside, he spotted several tables occupied by his fellow surgeons and other specialists, including Rod.

So he couldn't claim that there was nowhere else to sit, but then, he didn't require an excuse. *Just march over there and plunk yourself down.*

Aware that he was breaching an unwritten rule of cafeteria etiquette, he navigated the maze of tables to join Anya and three of her housemates. "Hope this chair isn't taken," he said and sat beside her.

Whatever she'd been discussing with Lucky, Melissa and Karen, the conversation died. No sign of Zora. Probably had an ultrasound to perform.

From his tray, Jack handed Anya a small salad. "That's yours."

"I didn't ask for anything," she said rather ungraciously.

It was Thursday and she hadn't made a single request since last weekend. "It's my job to take care of you. You should eat more vegetables."

Melissa nodded wordlessly. He'd scored points with someone.

"Well, thanks." Anya poked a cherry tomato with her fork. "How'd you know I like ranch dressing?"

"Who doesn't?" Jack responded.

"I had you figured wrong," Lucky observed.

"Oh?" While Jack wasn't keen on conversing with the fellow, he could hardly avoid it. Especially because he'd invited himself to their table.

"I took you for a stuck-up talks-only-to-God surgeon," the tattooed nurse responded.

Jack didn't bother to ask what he'd done to deserve such an assessment. "I condescend to mingle with the masses occasionally."

Karen brushed crumbs from her blouse. "You have to drop this reverse snobbery if you plan to be an administrator, Lucky."

"Is that your goal?" Jack tackled his teriyaki chicken with an appetite stoked by a long morning in the O.R.

"He's earning a master's in administration," Melissa explained.

"I graduate this summer."

Lucky's air of pride was deserved, Jack acknowledged. "Then what?"

"Then I hope a suitable position opens up here at Safe Harbor."

"Otherwise he might have to move," Karen noted.

"Good luck." *Enough about him.* Jack turned to Anya. "While we're on the subject of Saturday's housewarming party…"

"We aren't." She started eating the salad.

"Give Jack a break," Karen said.

Had Karen always been a sympathetic soul or only since her new friendship with Rod? In any case, Jack appreciated the support.

Anya waved her fork. "You're right. Jack, what were you about to say?"

He dredged up the excuse for barging in he'd decided on earlier. "That was a great idea you had about the girls acting as servers, Anya. I heard the thrift store rents costumes, so I swung by there and reserved two cute waitress outfits. I can pick them up tomorrow."

Anya's nose scrunched. "Might be awkward."

"Why?"

"Didn't Rod tell you?" Karen asked. "Our boss, Jan, and her husband are bringing their daughters, too."

"They're nine and ten," Melissa put in.

Jack adjusted his plans in a flash. "I'll rent extra costumes. They had more, and as for the sizes, it shouldn't matter if they're a bit loose."

"Especially if there are apron strings we can tighten," Karen said.

"I'll make sure of it."

"You'd be a great dad," Melissa said. Catching the dismay on Anya's face, Melissa raised her hands apologetically. "I just find Jack's attitude refreshing. My ex-husband hated the idea of parenthood. I wasn't keen on it, either, at first, but working in the fertility field, being around babies, I developed this intense desire. More than a desire—a conviction that having children is why I was put on this earth."

"And he didn't stand by you?" Jack found it hard to imagine a man abandoning his wife on such a fundamental level.

"He went out and had a vasectomy without telling me." Melissa's classic features tightened into an angry mask.

Abruptly, Jack made the connection: the attorney who'd brought the waiver to him was Edmond Everhart—same last name. He'd seemed a decent enough guy, but to Melissa, an action like that must have been tantamount to a betrayal. And once a person betrayed your trust, Jack didn't see how they could regain it.

"When I was in my twenties, I'd have liked to have been a mother," Karen said wistfully. "Then my ex's drinking got out of control. Even if you divorce, children bring all kinds of legal and emotional ties to the other person. I couldn't bear being yoked to that man for life."

"Wow, this is a heavy discussion," Lucky said.

"Does it make you uncomfortable?" Jack teased.

"What are you, a psychologist?"

"He sounds like one sometimes," Anya said. "In a good way."

Jack chuckled, surprised by her response. "Glad you think so."

"Well, you deserve a compliment now and then." She indicated her empty salad plate. "It was kind of you to bring this."

"Uh-oh, better watch out for knives in your back, Anya." Melissa indicated a nearby table where a couple of young nurses were glaring in their direction.

"What's their problem?" Jack asked.

"You didn't see them eyeing you and toying with their hair?" Karen asked. "I was afraid that leggy one was going to trip you when you walked by her."

Jack frowned. Why would a nurse trip him?

"She means they were flirting." Lucky blew out his frustration. "Man, the rest of us guys kill ourselves trying to get that kind of response, and you don't even notice."

"I have more important things on my mind."

Lucky turned to Melissa. "Speaking of more important things, what's on Saturday's menu?"

"It's my week to cook, which puts me in charge of the meal planning," she explained to Jack. "We're barbecuing burgers and hot dogs. Veggie burgers, too, for Lucky. You guys are fixing the side dishes."

"Pasta salad," Karen volunteered.

"Fruit." Anya left it at that.

"Green salad." Lucky gazed around the table. "We're short one person. What's Zora bringing?"

"Something," Anya said.

Jack laughed. Now that he was growing accustomed to her terseness, he rather liked it. Especially when it came at someone else's expense.

A clatter of dishes signified the departure of the nurses at the other table. One rolled her eyes at him, as if questioning his judgment. The leggy one pointedly ignored him.

He hoped none of them were invited to the party. It would be a lot more fun without their ridiculous tactics.

Too bad he couldn't get the same kind of attention from the one person he really wanted to receive it from.

"THEY'RE SO CUTE!"

"How darling!"

"I want to put it on right now!"

Four little girls swirled around Anya in the den, holding up lacy white aprons and caps, shiny black under dresses and frilly white socks. Tiffany, the oldest, seemed as entranced by the notion of playing dress-up as did her ten-year-old sister, Amber. With their red braids and freckles, the two were a matched set, save for height.

No such hesitancy came from stepsisters Kimmie and Berry Sargent. They looked nothing alike—nine-year-old Kimmie had elfin features, whereas Berry was tall for her ten years, with a smooth dark complexion inherited from her late mother. Anya had heard that Berry's stepfather, Zack Sargent, had been raising her as a single dad when he re-encountered his first love, Jan, and they'd blended their families.

The girlish chatter reminded Anya of the special moments when her triplet sisters used to rush to her with their joys and concerns. Supervising them hadn't been *all* hard work and feeling trapped. She was proud to think of them graduating from college this spring. Could they really be that old?

"My friend showed me how to carry a tray like a real waitress," said Berry, the tallest of the young group. "You hold it to the side with your hand open underneath. Oh, she said to load the heavy stuff in the middle so it doesn't tip."

The other girls looked impressed, all except for Kimmie, who was hopping up and down with excitement. "Where can we change?"

"In my room," Anya said. "Berry, after we change, I'd love for you to show us all how to carry the trays."

"Me, too?" teased Jack, who'd arrived in a black vest and slacks and a crisp white shirt. The man could easily pass for the maître d' at a five-star restaurant, where that devilish grin would net him plenty of tips. If the surgery business ever dried up, at least he had a fallback, Anya mused.

She straightened his rakish bow tie. "There you go."

"Thanks." His gaze caught hers for a shimmering moment.

"We love the clothes, Uncle Jack," Tiffany said.

"I'm glad." He beamed at his nieces.

Anya draped her waitress outfit over her arm. She hadn't expected him to bring one for her, too, but was glad he'd thought of it. "Girls! Follow me upstairs, and hold on to the railing. No shoving."

They snaked through the crowded house, the girls dodging under grownups' arms and bumping their elbows. It was a miracle they didn't leave a trail of spilled drinks.

In Anya's room, the girls dived into their outfits. Their high spirits were infectious; even quiet Amber giggled when Kimmie tied her apron around her head so it flowed down the back, saying, "Don't you guys just love this cool hat?"

Seeing Tiffany about to follow suit, Anya waggled her hand for attention. "Aprons around the waist, please. Hats on heads. Socks on feet." Her no-nonsense tone did the trick.

As she donned her black dress and apron, Anya saw that she'd left her laptop sitting on the low table, open to her social media page. She was about to click it off when she noticed her grandmother's stern, beloved face on the screen. Grandma Meeks had never been the cuddly, brownie-baking type of grandmother, but it had been she who'd recognized Anya's aptitude for nursing.

"It's not all bedpans and massages," she'd declared when her granddaughter initially dismissed the suggestion. "In my day, nursing was considered a challenging career, and it still is. And you can save lives while you're at it. Can't beat that!"

Her grandmother's enthusiasm had inspired Anya to volunteer at a nearby hospital. She'd been surprised how much she enjoyed the setting, and after talking to some of the nurses, she'd realized Grandma had been right. Then she had the idea to become a nurse practitioner and run her own practice, which had excited her even more. In retrospect, it would probably have been a tougher path than she'd imagined, but at the time, the prospect of gaining her independence while filling an important medical need had fired her with purpose.

But as Jack had pointed out, it had all worked out in the end.

While the girls finished dressing, she read the post on the site. It was from her sister Ruth. Grandma Rachel would be celebrating her 80th birthday in April. The whole Meeks family was invited—or rather, commanded—to gather in their Colorado town for a big blowout.

A string of responses bore the names of Anya's siblings, aunts, uncles and cousins. Many offered suggestions and hardly anyone had demurred. It would be a shame to miss this event, Anya conceded, but she'd been planning to avoid her family until next Christmas because she didn't want them to know about the pregnancy. Now what was she going to do?

Downstairs, she found Jack in the kitchen, arranging hors d'oeuvres on trays that Karen had produced. "Young ladies!" he commanded the four little waitresses, who quit poking each other. "Who wants to serve outdoors?"

"What if someone hits us with a croquet ball?" Berry asked.

Jack peered out the window. "I don't see anyone playing right now. As for the badminton game, those plastic shuttlecocks wouldn't hurt a fly."

"Berry and I can go outside," Kimmie said. "That's more fun and we don't mind the smell."

"Speak for yourself!" Kimmie's sister scrunched her face.

"Put a drop of perfume on your upper lip," Tiffany advised.

"I'd rather stay in."

"I'd rather be outside," Amber piped up.

Hearing the girls' preferences, Anya took charge. "Here's how we're doing it. Berry, you show everyone how to carry a tray. Then you and Tiffany can stay in the house because you're taller and it'll be easier for you to avoid smacking into everybody. Amber and Kimmie, you'll be the outdoor team."

Heads nodded. Soon they were balancing the trays, following Berry's example.

After they marched out to perform their duties, Jack gave Anya a thumbs-up. "I'm impressed. You had them all figured out."

"It's best to pair them by age, anyway," Anya told him. "This way they can make new friends. And it's important to take what they want into consideration."

He lounged against the counter, his gaze lingering on her until heat rushed through her body. "You make a sexy waitress."

"And you're a smashing head waiter." Her fingers itched to loosen that tie and undo the buttons on his starched shirt.

He was moving toward her when a small throat clearing from the corner drew their gazes to Helen Pepper, who'd been dozing on a chair. Jack paused, and Anya eased away.

"You're both wonderful with children," Helen said as if she hadn't noticed the vibrations between them. "Today you've brought the sparkle back to Amber's face. She's been much too quiet since she arrived."

"Anya's the one who understands kids," Jack told her.

"It's self-defense." Anya took a chair across from the older woman rather than talk down at her. "I practically raised my three younger sisters after my mom became disabled. But as for my maternal instincts, they're pathetic. I even managed to kill an African violet."

Helen chuckled. "They're delicate plants. I murdered an entire bed of begonias and that practically requires a blow torch."

"Overwatering?" Anya asked.

"Taking a vacation and forgetting to arrange for any watering at all." With an indulgent air, Helen patted Anya's hand. "Don't worry. You would never mistreat a child, even by accident. You're a natural mother."

Anya was eager to skip that subject. "Can I get you something to eat or drink?"

"Those little sandwiches look delicious."

Jack presented a platter with a low bow. "At your service, madam."

"You're so handsome—all the girls must adore you." She patted his cheek before selecting a couple of sandwiches. "But take my advice and stick with Anya."

"I agree," he said. "There's no one like her."

A spurt of joy caught Anya by surprise. Did Jack really want her for who she was, rather than just because she was pregnant with his child? At unguarded moments, he still had the power to melt her with his tenderness and sensitivity, and as for this buzz tingling through her...

Embarrassed, she realized Helen was observing her reaction. "I'd better go check on my waitstaff."

"I'll come with you." Jack set the platter aside.

To Anya's relief, Rod popped in to speak to Helen about the girls, distracting Jack. Rod had a store of questions, which the older woman seemed more than willing to answer.

Anya lingered with the trio just long enough to confirm what Tiffany had said during her previous visit—that the girls were unhappy but not suffering from physical abuse. Then she slipped away to check on her outdoor team.

The smell from the marsh didn't bother her today thanks to the appetizing scents wafting from the barbecue where Melissa was grilling burgers. The aromatic smoke also mitigated the queasiness that occurred whenever Anya went more than an hour without eating.

Or without inhaling Jack's aftershave lotion. No, it must be something about male pheromones, she corrected herself.

The crack of a mallet against a wooden ball warned Anya to move off the lawn or risk having her ankles smacked by a croquet ball. She stepped into the drift of the game's onlookers, where the girls were circulating.

Anya was glad to see that Kimmie's bouncy manner had rubbed off on Amber, who laughed readily at her new friend's antics. The girl deserved a family that brought out her happy side, Anya thought.

Though things might be getting a little *too* high-spirited, Anya realized as Kimmie tripped over a rough patch of lawn and was forced to put a hand down to break her fall. The remaining hors d'oeuvres on her tray went flying.

"I'm sorry." Kimmie was crestfallen.

"Don't worry about it," she soothed the girl. Anya took both their trays, while other guests disposed of the dropped food in a nearby trash can. "Dinner will be ready soon. You guys go have fun."

With a squeal of glee, Kimmie led Amber on a dash into the house. How cute they were, Anya mused.

An image of a little girl with dark hair and green eyes toddling across a lawn flashed through her mind. *My daughter. Jack's daughter.*

This little person was growing inside her right now. Anya's chest tightened. A sweet moment, a baby kiss, the feel of chubby arms around her neck—those were precious, but, she reminded herself sharply, a real mother had to be prepared for the sleepless nights, the anxieties and irritations, the loss of privacy, the weight of unending chores and that sense that your best was never good enough.

If more women had Anya's experiences growing up, world population growth would cease to be a problem, she mused as she toted the trays through the sliding doors into the den. And adoption would be far more common.

Pausing to let her eyes adjust to the dimness, Anya noticed Zora in a corner, holding up a square of mangled crocheting. Betsy Raditch, short caramel-brown hair fluffed around her head and half-glasses perched on her nose, examined Zora's work and made a comment that Anya couldn't hear. Her friend mouthed a grateful thank-you for the advice.

Anya had always liked the nursing director, who brought calm efficiency to her job. She always seemed approachable despite a long list of duties.

Too bad the woman had, in a sense, lost two daughters-in-law, Stacy and Zora, of whom she'd grown fond. Now Andrew had announced his engagement to a woman he'd met on a business trip to Hong Kong. Maybe three times would be the charm, but Anya doubted it.

"I can't imagine why he hasn't signed those divorce papers." Anya heard Betsy's words through a lull in the ambient chatter. "It's unfair for him to keep you dangling like this."

"Maybe he's changed his mind about marrying that, that... woman." Zora's voice trembled. Anya hoped her friend wasn't clinging to the absurd notion that Andrew still had feelings for her. The man cared about nobody but himself.

"I have no idea what my son is thinking," Betsy said. "He's got too much of his father in him, but I shouldn't be talking about that."

And I shouldn't be eavesdropping. Anya scurried off before anyone caught her.

As she entered the kitchen, she halted, her path to the counter blocked by Lucky's muscular shape. He was removing a bowl of salad from the fridge, too intent on his task to notice her.

Beyond him, Jack remained clustered with his uncle, Karen and Helen. "I've done everything I can think of," Jack was saying. "Why can't she see the obvious? You were right, Helen. She's a natural mother. She'd be perfect with this baby."

Resentment flamed through Anya. Never mind that she was eavesdropping again; anybody could overhear Jack discussing her future as if she was common property and he had the right to make decisions for her.

Lucky closed the refrigerator door. His eye roll made it clear he hadn't missed what was being said, nor her infuriated expression. "I'll get out of the line of fire."

Ignoring him, Anya dumped the trays into the sink with a clatter. When Jack looked up, she didn't bother to hide her scowl.

"Anya." He paled. "Sorry. That was tactless. But..."

"You made a promise to sign away your rights." Having

to confront him in front of Rod and Helen and Karen added to her fury.

"Only if you're still as determined…" he began.

"I'll take the DNA test next week. The lab will need a specimen from you, too." Though he probably knew that, being an ob-gyn. "Once I've kept my part of the bargain, a deal is a deal."

Without waiting for a response, she stalked out of the kitchen.

Chapter Ten

By the following Friday, the entire hospital staff knew about Anya's pregnancy and Jack's paternity, a situation for which Jack blamed himself. Sitting with her in the cafeteria, although he'd only done it once, had attracted plenty of attention, and his big mouth at the party hadn't helped either.

Everywhere he went, conversations stopped, then resumed behind his back. And his uncle's moodiness about the girls' departure prevented him from running interference with his usual acid rejoinders. Not that he'd been around much anyway.

In Jack's opinion, it was a good thing Rod had taken to spending his spare time with Karen. She had far more patience than Jack to listen to Rod's concerns about Tiffany and Amber and his frustration that he couldn't count on future visits.

Despite Anya's annoyance with Jack over his comments at the party, she had kept her share of the bargain. They had both submitted blood samples, with the DNA results due next week. By mutual consent, they would receive the news together at Adrienne Cavill-Hunter's office. Having an objective third party would hopefully help them figure out their next step.

Anya gave no indication that she'd changed her mind about adoption, not that they'd had much chance to discuss the matter. Before the party, Jack could have sworn she was mellowing toward him, and observing her shepherding the flock of little girls had been a treat. If only he'd clamped down on his opinions and avoided that painful moment in Karen's kitchen, maybe she'd have begun to see for herself how wonderful she was with children.

Sensitive to the undercurrents, the nursing supervisor had taken to assigning other staff to assist at Jack's operations. He supposed that was wise. But he missed Anya's tart comments and rare, endearing smiles.

The closer they came to learning the DNA results, the more powerfully he felt drawn to babies. He gazed in fascination at the tiny people he helped bring into the world. Their arrival had always been a miracle, but now he understood how his patients could love a child from the moment of conception, putting its well-being first even when complications endangered their own lives.

And the day of reckoning was fast approaching. How could Jack go back on his word—yet how could he sign away his rights to an infant he already loved?

The questions plagued him even into surgery, though once he got under way, he was able to focus on the procedure. Today, his scrub nurse was the always-reliable Erica Benford Vaughn, who usually assisted Dr. Tartikoff. Short and deft, she was quick to anticipate Jack's needs as he performed a laparoscopic myomectomy. This microsurgical operation removed uterine fibroids—noncancerous tumors that could cause significant pain—while preserving the patient's uterus for future childbearing.

Jack loved working with the Da Vinci robotic system. Seated at a console with a 3D high-definition camera providing an on-screen view inside the patient's body, he manipulated the master controls. The system transmitted each careful movement to the tiny instruments with precision, allowing him to operate with the smallest possible impact on the patient.

Despite the equipment's invaluable aid, the surgery still depended primarily on the surgeon's skill as well as that of his support team. He stayed alert for any complications.

As always, the surgery involved the assistance of numerous other staff, but Jack paid little attention to the conversational remarks swirling around him, mostly concerning the staff members' young children and their fun-but-sometimes-maddening extracurricular activities.

Erica, while focusing on Jack's requirements, shared insights about her lively year-old son, who'd begun refusing to use his high chair. "Jordan would rather stand on a regular chair, which means spilling food everywhere. He's driving Lock crazy." Lock was her husband, a private investigator.

"He isn't driving *you* crazy?" Rod asked from nearby, where he was monitoring the patient's vital signs on his equipment.

"Oh, I sit back and enjoy the show." She chuckled. "Lock was so keen on being a dad that after I got pregnant, he was ready to raise Jordan by himself if I refused to marry him. As if he had any idea how hard it would be!"

"It wasn't a planned pregnancy?" Jack wouldn't normally ask such a personal question, but she'd raised the topic herself.

"Definitely not. Initially, I insisted on adoption." She cut him an embarrassed glance, which meant she'd heard about his situation.

"Your husband must have had experience with children," commented the circulating nurse. "Had he taken care of a younger sibling?"

"Not at all." Erica double-checked her tray, where she'd readied the tools to attach to the robot's arms. "He was kicked around foster homes until he finally landed in a good one. His younger foster brother helped whip him into shape, from the way they tell the story."

"So why would he want to be a single dad?" That didn't sound logical to Jack. Surely the man had grasped what a major challenge he'd be facing.

"His birth mom entrusted him to the wrong adoptive couple," Erica explained. "They got hooked on drugs, which is how he ended up in foster care. That's why Lock has such a low opinion of adoption."

The circulating nurse bristled. "I'm sorry for him, but that's unfair. My husband and I adopted *our* children, and we love those little guys more than anything."

"I'm sure that's more typical," Erica agreed.

Jack fell silent, concentrating on his work. In the back of his mind, though, her comments presented a tantalizing possibility. *Could* he raise the child himself? He'd dismissed the idea previously, assuming it was unrealistic.

He had a tendency toward perfectionism. That was essential for a surgeon, but it had drawbacks in relationships and especially in parenting.

The idea jolted him. Had he been demanding too much of himself? Maybe he *could* succeed as a single dad. Kids needed a lot of love and careful supervision, and he would certainly provide those.

"If you and Lock hadn't married, would he have raised Jordan alone?" Jack asked Erica.

"I doubt it," she said. "Not after I insisted he go through some hands-on training."

"How did he do that?" If there was a boot camp for daddies, Jack might give it a try.

"I arranged for us to babysit Dr. Tartikoff's twins." Her words glimmered with amusement. "Two little tykes at once. It was very demanding. That convinced Lock he couldn't raise a child without backup, especially considering his odd hours as an investigator."

"Then you fell in love and decided being a mom isn't so terrible?" the circulating nurse teased.

"That was part of it. Also, we both had to face up to some personal issues." Erica didn't specify what those were.

Her words echoed in Jack's mind. He, too, worked occasional odd shifts, but most of them were regularly scheduled. Although he knew childcare was no simple matter, several women on the staff juggled medical careers with single parenthood. Plus, if he required emergency help, Rod had experience with diapers and that sort of thing.

He'd probably be willing to fill in, especially once he fell in love with the baby.

So it might be possible for him and Rod to create a loving home that met a child's needs. Jack would never want his little one to grow up as lonely as he had been. But plenty of single mothers raised children successfully despite busy work schedules and financial pressures. And he had the most important quality: a heart full of love for his child.

Before he suggested any such thing, however, Jack would need to learn more about single fatherhood—talk to other parents, do research on the web—and draw up a plan to persuade Anya to give him custody. Or, if upon further investigation he found he wouldn't be able to give the child what he or she needed, then he had no business urging Anya to be a single mom either.

ANYA DIDN'T UNDERSTAND why she'd been so distracted—next week's meeting with Dr. Cavill-Hunter was unlikely to bring any revelations. She knew Jack was the father of her baby, so the only question the DNA test would answer was the baby's gender. And ultimately, that changed nothing.

Jack had promised to sign the papers. So why did she have this nagging worry that he might spring a surprise on her? Surely he wouldn't go back on his word.

Sitting at the breakfast table, she set down the Sunday entertainment section of the *Orange County Register* and stared out the glass doors at the misty March morning. The fog lay so thick, she could barely see past the fence that marked the border of Karen's yard.

Only Zora remained at the table, sharing her box of cereal but saying very little. Anya had no idea where everyone else had disappeared to or why her friend was acting so subdued. Zora had been preoccupied since the party, and Anya realized with regret that she'd failed to ask why her friend was so downcast. *Just because I have problems doesn't mean I should ignore Zora's.*

"You going to tell me what's the matter?" she asked.

Zora's head jerked up. "Why do you assume anything's wrong?"

It wasn't like her to dodge a question. "First, you aren't talking a mile a minute." Usually, her friend's chattiness provided a pleasant counterpoint to Anya's reticence. "Second, if you pull on your hair any harder, you'll yank it out by the roots."

Zora stopped twisting a strand around her finger. "I thought I'd have heard from Andrew by now."

"About what?" *Don't be dense.* "You prodded him about signing the divorce papers?" Perhaps Betsy's comment had borne fruit.

"I stopped by his house Monday." Zora folded her arms defensively.

"And?" Anya prompted.

"That woman wasn't there." Her friend's tight jaw emphasized the thin planes of her face. "She flew back to Hong Kong."

What difference did that make? "That's where her family lives, isn't it? She might be preparing for her wedding."

"She can't be!" Zora exclaimed. "He doesn't love her, not the way he loves me."

As a rule, Anya allowed people to indulge their delusions, but Zora was in desperate need of a reality check. "And you believed him when he swore he never loved *Stacy* the way he loved *you*."

"Maybe he didn't." Zora fiddled with her napkin. "Don't forget, I knew him before she did. We were inseparable all through high school. I never understood why he dumped me."

"That's not exactly an indication of true love," Anya noted dryly.

"He was young and confused," her friend answered. "When he met Stacy in college, he had a crush on her for a while, that's all."

"Awhile?" The couple had been married for several years, from what Anya had heard.

"A couple of years. Then we ran into each other at our high school reunion and—well, you've heard the story."

"He sold you a bill of goods and you fell for it." Anya winced at the harshness of her analysis, but it was far kinder than Andrew was likely to be. "Zora, he cheated on Stacy and he cheated on you. That's the kind of person he is. He's not capable of loving anyone but himself."

She stopped on seeing angry denial on her friend's face. Anya had to admit, she only knew Andrew by reputation. No, that wasn't true; she also knew him by the pain he'd caused Zora far too often this past year.

"You're wrong!" Despite Zora's defiance, a hint of uncertainty trembled in her voice.

A light tap from a nearby doorway reminded Anya that Lucky's room lay on the far side of the wall. He poked his head out. "Sorry to intrude, but I couldn't help overhearing."

Zora slammed the table, rattling the dishes. Thankfully both cereal bowls were empty. "Don't you start on me, too!"

He raised his hands in protest. Shirtless, Lucky was quite a sight. On his right shoulder, a cartoon woman in skimpy armor wielded a sword that extended along his arm. On his left side wriggled a colorful dragon. "Wouldn't dream of it. I just wondered if you noticed the envelope Andrew dropped off for you last night."

"What envelope?" Zora peered around.

In the den, Lucky scooped up a manila envelope from the coffee table. "I heard someone at the door, but by the time I got there, he was already pulling away from the curb. Maybe I should have left it at your place on the table, but I figured it might get soiled." He handed it to Zora.

She swallowed hard, staring at her name handwritten on the front.

"You ought to know…" Lucky grimaced. "There was a woman in the car with him."

Anya didn't ask what the woman looked like. It scarcely mattered whether his fiancée had returned or whether he'd picked up someone new. "Thanks. Now go away," she told Lucky.

"Yes, ma'am." He ducked out. No argument. The guy was making impressive progress in adapting to his roommates.

Why was Zora staring at the packet as if it contained an order for her execution? "It's the divorce papers," Anya guessed.

"It can't be."

"Why not?"

Her friend shot a glance at Lucky's door. Although he'd closed it, their voices carried, as they'd just learned. "Upstairs."

After clearing the table, the women went to Zora's room, which faced the street. Despite the foggy morning, the glare was intense due to the western exposure.

While Zora tilted the blinds, Anya perched on her friend's floral bedspread. The room was about the same size as Anya's but had more feminine décor, including a ruffled bed skirt and dainty pink throw pillows.

Breathing fast, Zora opened the envelope and drew out the papers. Despite having waited months for this, she stared at the signature white-faced.

"Sit," Anya ordered.

Her friend collapsed onto a chair. "I can't believe it."

"Why not?" Anya repeated her earlier question.

"Because we…" Tears started down Zora's cheeks.

Anya mentally cursed Andrew. "You had sex."

"He said he'd made a mistake, leaving me." Her friend's hands clenched in her lap. Anya leaned forward and plucked the papers from her grasp. While she doubted a few wrinkles would invalidate them, the last thing Zora needed was to have to get them signed again. "He told me he missed me terribly."

Anya laid the papers atop the bureau. "And you believed him."

"I must be really stupid." Zora's gaze pleaded for understanding.

"He took advantage of you." *Again.* "That's the kind of

jerk he is." *And speaking of stupidity...* "You used contraception, right?"

Zora's blank expression gave her the answer. "I never thought about it."

"You're an ultrasound technician," Anya pointed out. "You spend all day showing people their unborn babies, and pregnancy never occurred to you? I'm not trying to be mean. I goofed, too, but…"

"But you were on birth control pills and I'm not," Zora finished. "Well, that was Monday, so it's too late for me to use a morning-after pill."

"You're not late already, are you?"

"No." Zora blew her nose into a tissue. "I'm sure I'm not pregnant. We tried for a whole year to have a baby and it didn't work."

"There. You're safe." Anya was relieved for her friend.

Judging by the fact that Zora was shredding the tissue, though, *she* wasn't relieved. "On the other hand, my stomach's bothering me."

Uh-oh. "Bothering you how?"

"Churning." Her friend stared at her in dismay. "Not only in the mornings, though. That means it's from tension, right?"

Their gazes met. "Or not."

They shared a silent moment of dread. Then Zora asked, "How early do those pregnancy tests work?"

"We might be able to get results this soon." Despite choosing not to test herself, Anya had read the label on one of the kits at a drugstore. "They work as early as seven days past ovulation."

"I don't track my ovulation."

"When's your period due?" Anya asked.

"Like, yesterday." Wistfully, Zora said, "Betsy would love to have a grandchild."

"You mean you'd keep it?" Anya couldn't imagine that, not only because of her own feelings toward motherhood but even more because of her friend's messy relationship with her ex-husband. "How do you suppose Andrew would react?"

A sodden tissue hit the wastebasket. Zora snatched another. "He won't bring me ice cream and cute costumes, I can tell you that."

There was no comparison between Andrew and Jack. Appreciation flooded Anya for the kind, caring guy she'd chosen. *Except you didn't choose him, and this is way off topic.* "You aren't still fantasizing that Andrew loves you, are you?"

A deep sigh. "I guess not." Zora perked up a little. "If I keep the baby, he'll have to pay support. That's fair, right?"

"And you'll be tied to that creep for life. He'll keep you dangling, paying late and playing other games, just like he did with the divorce papers." Hoping Zora would abandon this crazy line of thought, Anya added, "Not to mention how much the baby would remind you of him."

Her friend wrapped her arms around herself. "Don't tell me you haven't imagined your baby resembling Jack. He *is* handsome."

"We aren't talking about me."

"But he'd take care of you," Zora persisted. "Jack's like the prince in a fairy tale."

"Get real!" Anya's idea of happily-ever-after did *not* involve being locked in a castle, wearing glass slippers that hurt her feet and curtseying every time his Highness entered the throne room. "Back to *you*."

"If I want to keep my baby, that's my business," her friend said.

Anya saw no sense in arguing. "Okay. Besides, your period will start, and that will be that."

"I want to know *now*." Determination transformed her friend from weepy to demanding.

"As in, this very instant?"

"Yes."

Might as well get it over with. "I'll drive you to the drugstore," Anya said.

Less than an hour later, they were back in the bedroom, side by side on the bed, staring at a pink stick. Not faint pink either. Bold and definite.

"Oh, pickles," Zora muttered.

"Pickles?" Anya would have chosen a stronger word.

"I can't use bad language where the baby might hear."

Anya started to laugh. Zora glared, and then she, too, dissolved into giggles. They fell into each other's arms, laughing until they cried.

"Don't take this the wrong way, but I'm kind of glad we're in this together." Her friend sniffled.

"Me, too." From the day they'd met, they'd been in sync with each other—not that Anya had anticipated anything like this. "You have to tell Andrew."

"I'll send him an email." A faint smile broke through. "And copy it to his mother."

"We should warn his fiancée so she understands what kind of man he is," Anya said.

Zora shrugged. "He'll give her a snow job and she'll buy it like I did. Besides, she'll find out sooner or later."

"Before the wedding would be helpful."

"I'll let Betsy break the news."

Now that they knew for sure—or almost sure—that her friend was pregnant, Anya hoped Zora would think carefully what was involved in raising a child alone, with or without financial support. "Just to get the facts, you should talk to your attorney about adoption."

Zora shook her head. "This may be the only baby I'll ever have. I want a little person to love."

Would Anya ever have another child? She hadn't considered her pregnancy in that light.

Still, it was one thing to long for a baby, as Zora apparently did. For Anya to hang on to her child simply because this might be her only shot at motherhood would be far more selfish than relinquishing it.

Yet later, alone in her room, she wondered what it would be like to stay on in the house after the babies were born. She'd been picturing having fun with Zora the way they always had, dancing and catching the latest movies and sampling ethnic food at Orange County's many street fairs.

Instead, there'd be a little person toddling about, cute and demanding and requiring all Zora's attention. How was Anya going to handle watching another baby grow and flourish after giving up her own child?

Chapter Eleven

She wasn't meeting his gaze. Shifting uncomfortably on the waiting room couch, Jack studied the tumble of dark hair that masked Anya's face.

When he'd entered a few minutes ago, she'd already been sitting there, glaring at her phone. If she'd seen him out of her peripheral vision, she gave no sign. Surely she couldn't be angry already; she hadn't heard what he had to say. What was so infuriating?

The nurse had called in another patient ahead of them, leaving them alone. At 6:30 p.m. on a Tuesday, the medical building was nearly empty, and no one was at the reception desk.

Jack decided not to waste this chance to speak to Anya. He'd been anticipating her arguments for days, educating himself about childcare options, talking to staff members both single and married about their biggest parenting challenges and winning Rod's support, however tentative. If they could get a running start on the issues, they might avoid a painful argument in front of Adrienne.

Not that Jack figured he had much chance of escaping Anya's wrath. He *had* promised to sign the waiver.

Moving closer, he noticed that, at this angle, her little nose seemed to have wrinkled in disgust. "If it's that bad, why are you reading it?"

"Excuse me?" Anya glanced up, eyes startled, full lips parted.

He restrained the urge to brush back the sweep of her hair. She hadn't assisted him in the operating room for a week, which might have been good for his concentration but left him feeling hollow. "You look ready to smash that thing."

"It's not the phone. It's my sister Ruth." She held up the device, displaying a social media site. He couldn't read the post, but the accompanying photo showed a woman slightly older than Anya with sterner features on a similar heart-shaped face.

"What's this dragon done?" Jack asked.

Her faint answering smile faded quickly. "The whole family's gathering in Colorado for my grandma's 80th birthday in April. Ruth arbitrarily assigned me to supervise all the babies and children."

Anya might be suited to the job, given her skill with youngsters, but it was unfair to drop such a big job on her without her consent. Another objection also occurred to Jack. "How does she expect you to arrange all that when you're out of state?"

"Oh, she's decided I should arrive a few days early." Anya scowled at the screen. "And all my cousins have started weighing in with their head counts. So far there are four infants, six toddlers and I've lost count of the school-age kids."

"Why can't they watch their own children?"

"Because Ruth's a control freak." Anya heaved a frustrated sigh. "But if I get into a squabble with her, she'll lay a guilt trip on me in front of everyone. Plus, my cousins will feel entitled to debate this, as if I were their property."

Much as Jack would have liked to produce a simple solution, he didn't have one. Besides, his job was to defend and protect Anya, not mediate a family dispute. "That's too heavy a burden for you, especially in your condition."

"They don't know about my pregnancy and I'm not sure I'm going to tell them." She closed down the website. "Ruth's pregnant, too, with her fifth child. I can't expect any sympathy from her."

Jack took her hand. "Whatever you decide, let me know how I can help."

"I'll have to miss Grandma's birthday party." Sadness shaded her gaze. "It's too stressful."

"Don't you want to be there? Turning eighty is a big deal." Having lost his grandparents when he was young, Jack envied her chance to attend such an event and connect with relatives. But then, Anya couldn't enjoy the occasion if she was buried in babies.

"I'll plan a trip to see Grandma later, when we can spend more time together." Unhappily, Anya added, "It'll have to be after the baby's born."

"Won't your sister raise a storm over your decision not to attend?"

"I won't announce it for as long as possible." Anya stuck the phone in her purse.

She'd mentioned that avoidance was her survival tactic. Jack was beginning to understand why. "That'll give her even more ammunition to fire in your direction," he warned.

"By now, Ruth ought to realize she can't boss me around," Anya replied. "If she's surprised by the consequences, that's her problem."

The nurse, a short woman with thick glasses, opened the door to the inner sanctum. "Dr. Ryder? Miss Meeks?"

They both rose. Instead of an examining room, though, the nurse escorted them to a small office with *Adrienne Cavill-Hunter, M.D.* on the door. "The doctor will be right with you."

"Thanks." Jack held a chair for Anya.

As she slid into it, he noted that her snug T-shirt revealed a still-flat stomach and well-defined breasts enlarged by pregnancy hormones. His body sprang to alert, remembering the feel of them beneath his lips… *Quit staring. And quit thinking about that.*

While they waited, Anya studied a wall chart depicting the stages of embryonic growth. Jack didn't need a reminder that, at ten weeks of development, their baby was about an inch and a half long. This week marked the end of the embryonic period, after which the term *fetus* was used.

It amazed him that the little creature was already becoming the distinctive individual who might live into the next century. He wished he knew exactly when personality manifested itself. Maybe genetics and epigenetics were already kicking in with whatever talents or traits would distinguish this wonderful child.

Jack wished Anya shared his sense of delight. From long habit, she'd schooled her expressive face into a mask. Anger stirred in him at the family members whose tactics had trained her to hide her emotions.

After a light tap, Adrienne breezed into the office, a white coat open over her tweed slacks and tailored blouse. She shook both their hands, then produced printouts. "These are for your files, but I'd suggest not reading them until we review a few details."

Anya set the papers in her lap. "Such as what?"

"Let's start with your reason for taking the DNA test. The probability that Jack—Dr. Ryder—is the father," Adrienne said.

"Yes?" Although he'd more or less taken the answer for granted, Jack felt a tremor of suspense.

"It is 99.9 percent likely."

His muscles relaxed. This was his baby. Unlike with his uncle's kids, there remained no risk of confusion or deception.

"You don't have to tell me," came Anya's tart response. "As far as I'm concerned, it's 100 percent. He's the one who questioned it."

Jack ducked his head in embarrassment. "I didn't mean it that way. But it seemed important to eliminate any doubt."

Adrienne maintained an air of professional detachment. "This test also reveals the gender of the baby. That's why I suggested you delay looking at the results, in case you prefer not to know."

Eager as he was to find out, Jack was willing to wait until he was alone if necessary. "Anya?"

She fingered the paper. "Go ahead. What is it?"

"It's a girl." Adrienne waited for their reactions.

"Oh." That was all Anya said. No indication if that made any difference.

Jack hadn't cared about the gender, but now the child in his mind came into even sharper focus: a little girl with brown hair and expressive eyes. No one would force her to hold herself back, to guard against emotional manipulation. She'd grow up with parents—*a* parent—who loved her and encouraged her to be herself.

It was still possible she'd be raised by strangers, but he hoped not. If only he could persuade Anya to stop distancing herself from the situation. "You're allowed to have feelings," he told her.

She folded the paper. "I do have feelings."

"So do I." *Here goes.* "I realize I promised to waive my parental rights—"

She gripped her purse. "Don't you dare go back on your word!"

Jack made what he hoped was a conciliatory gesture. "I have an alternate proposal."

Leaning against her desk, Adrienne folded her arms. She didn't bother to hide her curiosity, but Jack was sure he could count on her impartiality.

Anya swallowed. "I'm listening."

It was impossible to tell whether anger seethed beneath the surface. Still, having anticipated an immediate fight, Jack appreciated the opportunity to present his case. "I acknowledge that you aren't prepared to raise a child, with or without my help."

She cleared her throat. "That's right."

"So I'll raise the baby myself." Fingering the notes crammed in his pocket—the mere touch seemed to jog his memory—Jack outlined his plan: daycare at the hospital's child center, a licensed private sitter during his overnight shift in labor and delivery and off-hours backup provided by

Rod. "I don't underestimate the challenges, but lots of single parents cope, and I will, too."

"I can recommend a licensed sitter that my husband and I trust with our little boy," Adrienne said. "However, I strongly advise counseling. This is a major decision."

"I hate counselors," Anya said. "They make you confront things."

"You can have as much or as little involvement as you like, Anya," Jack said. "If you want to make things official, you can sign a waiver of parental rights."

"I should point out that you can't waive your financial obligation to the child," Adrienne warned her patient. "A lawyer can give you the whole picture."

"Your attorney, Edmond, seems reliable," Jack agreed. For some reason, he trusted the fellow.

Anya's shoulders hunched. What did that mean, he wondered.

"There's no need to decide now," Adrienne said. "The baby isn't due for over six months."

"I want this settled." Anya regarded Jack sternly. "What if something happens to you? With an adoptive family, she'd have two parents."

"Adoptive couples aren't immune to issues like divorce, illness and death," he reminded her. "And I'll appoint a guardian, just in case."

"Your uncle?" she asked dubiously.

"He's willing, and he has parenting experience." Jack returned to the main issue. "Honey, I love this baby. Maybe that sounds crazy because she isn't born yet, and I wasn't expecting to be a father, but I love her."

"An adoption means a clean break," Anya said slowly. "If you raised her, you'd still see me as backup."

"I promise I won't."

"What if she gets sick?" she challenged. "What if Rod isn't around when you need him? I'd be mommy on call."

"That's not true."

"How can you be sure?" She didn't sound argumentative; she appeared almost regretful, in truth.

Jack struggled to marshal his arguments. But what if she was right?

"This decision deserves more consideration," Adrienne repeated. "You don't have to resolve it now."

Her presence, initially helpful, was beginning to chafe on Jack. "If you have a patient waiting, you can go."

"I allowed extra time for this consult," the doctor assured him. "I'm fine."

Too bad. Jack could see Anya's uncertainty, but if they delayed this conversation, her default position—just say no and run for cover—would kick in.

To him, the fact that she hadn't immediately rejected his plan indicated that her determination to give the baby up had softened. All the same, Jack respected her right to say no.

And her objections had merit. How *could* he be sure he'd keep her out of the picture while raising their daughter? There was no way to try things out in advance. Or was there?

The last time they'd had a serious disagreement, Anya had put him to a test of sorts to earn the right to have her take the DNA test. Jack hadn't minded shopping and handling other chores; he wished she'd requested more, in fact. Although he couldn't prove that he'd keep his end of this new bargain, a good-faith attempt might reassure her. And it'd be a learning experience for him, too.

He dove in. "Let me prove that I won't lean on you. That I can handle extra pressure at home and not give in to frustration or dump my problems on you."

"How?"

"A few weeks ago, you gave me a challenge," he reminded her. "Let's agree on another one. I'll cook for your entire household for two weeks. That includes shopping and paying for the food."

Adrienne blinked. "That's quite an offer."

"I don't see what difference it would make," Anya said doggedly.

"Some nights I'll be tired and cranky, and I'll have to field the demands of a bunch of people." As he spoke, Jack reflected that he wasn't sure *how* he'd deal with the sometimes irritating group of housemates. But if he couldn't, maybe he wasn't cut out for single fatherhood. "It'll be a test for my own information as well as yours."

She seemed to be weighing his offer. "Why two weeks?"

"Two weeks from now is the earliest we can schedule an ultrasound, right?" He looked to Adrienne for confirmation.

"That's correct, doctor," she said.

Jack plowed onward. "At that time, maybe the best course of action will be clear to both of us." He didn't believe he'd change his mind. But when Jack had asked for Rod's cooperation, his uncle had pointed out that being a parent was harder than most people expected.

The nurse knocked, then looked in. "Doctor? The next patient is prepped."

Jack got to his feet. "Thanks, Adrienne. You've been great." And she had, despite his internal carping.

"Good luck to both of you," she said. "Since it's after hours, Eva will have to get back to you about scheduling the ultrasound."

"It's okay if Zora does it," Anya told the nurse. "If that simplifies the scheduling."

Eva nodded. "Okay."

Was Anya agreeing to his proposal? Jack wondered as he accompanied her out through the waiting room. Or was she saving her refusal for when they were alone?

ANYA'S HEART CONTRACTED. She was carrying a little girl like Tiffany or Amber or like Anya's two-year-old niece, Kiki, a sensitive child who seemed lost among her three siblings. After Christmas dinner, Kiki had nestled in her aunt's lap, content to watch the world go by from the safety of Anya's arms.

What a sweetheart. But Anya hadn't missed the exhaustion on Ruth's face by the end of the day, when she and her husband shepherded their children home. Cuddling a toddler for a few hours shouldn't be mistaken for a taste of motherhood.

As for Jack's plan to embrace single fatherhood, it reeked of good intentions that would only go awry. So why hadn't she put her foot down back there?

He promised to relinquish his rights. Keeping his word was a matter of honor.

As the elevator discharged them into the lobby, Anya admitted that there'd been an escape clause in his earlier promise. His words were engraved in her memory: *If you're still absolutely determined to seek adoption, I'll sign.*

Each day, she became more keenly aware of the baby taking shape inside her. Plus, now that Zora was planning to raise *her* child—although she still hadn't broken the news to the father—Anya was troubled by the prospect of having to live with an ever-present reminder of the baby she'd given up.

Jack had promised she could have as much or as little involvement in raising the baby as she liked. Of course, she preferred zero, but that meant she'd have to avoid Jack because seeing him would mean seeing their daughter, too.

It was hard, struggling through a thicket of possibilities. Also, in the short term, Jack's offer to cook for the house was tempting.

Zora's cooking duties started on Sunday, with Anya's the following week. They could both use a break.

Adoption. Adoption. Adoption.

But why did she have to repeat that mantra if she truly believed in it?

You only get to make this decision once. Then you'll bear the consequences for the rest of your life.

Yet Jack's nearness had the oddest way of calming Anya. The thought of having him around the kitchen was almost irresistible.

Surely by the date of the ultrasound, she'd have a clearer idea of what course to choose. *You're procrastinating.* Well, so what?

In the parking garage, Jack accompanied Anya to her car.

Even beneath the meager lighting, his earnest, vulnerable expression pierced her defenses.

"You deserve a shot," Anya said.

"Really?"

"Better grab the chance before I rethink this."

Joy blazed from his eyes. "Thank you."

"That's all it is—a shot," she cautioned.

"I understand."

They stood close enough for her to feel the ripple of energy he generated, a force that drew everything nearby into his aura. The first time she'd experienced it, in the operating suite before their first surgery, she'd known he was dangerous.

Too bad she'd ignored that on New Year's Eve.

"You can start on Sunday," she went on. "I'll tell the others. Actually, you should come to our meeting that afternoon. They'll want to give you their food preferences."

"Great!" Jack grinned like a schoolboy given a new video game. "Since I won't know what to shop for that night, how should I plan dinner?"

"You can order pizza and a salad." Recalling Lucky's requirements, she added, "Be sure there's a vegetarian one. Pineapple and mushrooms are fine."

"Done."

It was on the tip of her tongue to repeat that she wasn't agreeing to let him raise the baby. But he already knew that. "See you."

Jack waited until she drove off. Watching over her. Ah, that sense of safety.

She'd better not get used to it, Anya told herself sternly. When she thwarted him again in two weeks, he might never forgive her.

THE WOMAN CONFOUNDED him. Anya seemed as stubbornly independent as ever, so Jack had no idea why she'd said yes to letting him cook.

As he took the stairs down to the doctors' parking section on the ground level, he reflected that he'd put himself in a position to be pushed around by her housemates. Let them bring it on. It would be good training because from what he'd heard, toddlers could out-demand and out-harass anybody.

Already, menus flashed through Jack's mind. The vegetarian dishes posed an interesting challenge. It was also an opportunity to provide healthy meals for his little girl.

His daughter. The garage lights blurred beneath a sheen of moisture. Jack could have sworn he saw rainbows from the corners of his eyes.

Sunday couldn't arrive soon enough.

Chapter Twelve

Monday night's menu:

*Green salad with tomatoes, apples and cheddar cheese
Lentils and bulgur wheat with walnuts
and chopped apricots
Fresh-baked pita bread
Hummus
Apple pie*

Jack had Mondays off after working an overnight shift, so he spent much of the afternoon planning and shopping for the week's meals. He arrived at the house around 4:30 p.m., letting himself inside with a key that Karen had loaned him for his tenure as household chef.

After posting the menu, he cast an appreciative glance through the window at the flower-filled yard and the wetlands beyond. Yesterday had marked the start of Daylight Savings Time, bringing lingering daylight to the mid-March afternoon. The sunshine set the grays and greens aglow and picked out brilliant spots of red and yellow wildflowers. Just beyond the fence, a large raccoon paused to stare back at him, bold and unafraid.

Now, down to work. Hungry people would soon be arriving.

Yesterday, after serving pizza and interviewing the residents about their food preferences, Jack had explored the kitchen, inventorying the spices and cooking gear. Today, he assembled bowls, pots, utensils and ingredients on the counter.

Pleased at being in control of his environment, Jack set to work. He'd considered making a splash tonight by fixing salmon—until he calculated the cost of buying enough for six people. Given the high cost of groceries, he had to be realistic, especially considering he might soon have to equip his apartment for child-rearing.

He'd hit on a less costly entrée involving lentils and a cracked whole-wheat grain. He'd bought the ingredients at the Little Persia Mart, along with fresh-baked pita bread and hummus redolent of garlic, olive oil and chickpeas.

Half an hour later, with preparations well under way, he heard a car pull into the driveway. The first to enter his new domain was Karen, who'd changed her hair from strawberry blond to black with a silver streak in front. She was wearing a black top with silver threads and a long charcoal skirt that suited her new color scheme.

"Find everything okay?" she asked.

Jack gave her a thumb's up. "Perfect."

She retrieved a fruit drink from the refrigerator. "The kitchen's a bit squirrelly. I never liked having to angle around to get into the pantry, but I couldn't change the entire floor plan."

"Doesn't bother me. The new appliances put our apartment to shame." Jack particularly admired the range, with two high-intensity burners, a pair of medium burners and a simmer at the back. "Who sets the table?"

"I will tonight," she said. "We'll eat in the dining room while you're here. That other table's too small."

"Good idea." Jack resumed chopping an onion.

Standing by the fridge, Karen read the menu. "How do you fix the lentil dish?"

Jack indicated the recipe he'd set up in a plastic holder. "It's all right there. I'm doubling it."

"You might want to triple it," she said. "We're big eaters."

Jack performed a fast calculation. "I should have enough ingredients."

"That's a good sign for the future. Parents have to be flexible." She lifted her drink can in salute.

"Indeed they do."

While she carried china and tableware into the dining room, Jack put the wrapped pita in the oven to warm. Next he began frying the onions, and as they cooked he washed the romaine lettuce, drying it in a salad spinner. A few minutes later, Lucky wandered in to observe, having changed from his nurse's uniform into a muscle T-shirt and weather-defying shorts.

Either the guy overheated easily or he was emphasizing his masculinity in the face of this male intruder into his domain. However, Jack detected no hostility as Lucky watched him dice.

"Where'd you learn to cook like that?" his companion asked.

"High school." Thank goodness boys no longer drew sneers for taking cooking classes, at least in California.

"I appreciate the vegetarian menu." Lucky coughed, as if it hurt to thank Jack for anything.

Quit projecting onto the guy. You two could be allies here.
"My pleasure."

From the den came the musical sound of Anya's voice. Even without being able to distinguish the words, Jack could instantly peg her mood: a little tired but upbeat. And fairly energetic, considering her condition and that she'd worked all day.

He'd been glad to find her in his operating room on Friday, but that had been three days ago and he hadn't caught even a glimpse of her since. Jack kept his face averted, not wanting Lucky to see how eager he was for the sight of her.

He needn't have worried. Muttering something about a snack, Lucky darted into the pantry.

The women were moving this way. "You should tell your sister where to get off," Zora was commenting.

"You'd think she'd notice I haven't agreed to her plan," Anya grumbled.

"Your cousins seem to already assume you have." Zora stopped at the entrance to the kitchen. "Oh! Jack. I forgot you'd be here."

Anya, shorter and rounder, steered her friend aside so she could enter. "Smells fantastic."

"Menu's on the fridge." Jack chopped apples into bite-size squares.

The friends took side-by-side positions as they read the menu. "Why do you put apples in the salad?" Zora asked.

"Because tomatoes have no flavor this time of year, although I toss in a few for the lycopene," Jack said.

"What's that?" Zora asked.

"It's a nutrient in red fruits and vegetables," Anya told her.

Jack nodded. "Helps prevent DNA damage, cancer and heart disease."

"All that?" Zora responded. "Aren't you afraid they'll put doctors out of business?"

"Not quite yet," he said.

Anya drifted to peer over his shoulder. The smell of disinfectant that clung to scrub nurses faded beneath her appealing blend of femininity and flowers. "Enough talk about diseases. It bothers my stomach."

"Me, too." Zora headed for the pantry. "A few raisins won't spoil our dinner, right?"

"Brace for impact," Jack murmured to Anya.

"What?" When she turned toward him, their faces were so close that he brushed a kiss over her lips. She blinked in surprise.

"Sorry." But he wasn't.

Zora's squawk must have echoed through the entire house. "You rat! How dare you hide in here and spy on us."

"Hey! Cool it." Lucky dodged out. Seizing a broom from inside the pantry, Zora swept at his heels as if shooing vermin.

"What were you doing in the pantry?" Anya demanded.

"Eavesdropping," Zora declared as she stuck the broom back in the closet.

"Organizing the supplies for Jack." Lucky folded his arms, a position that made his muscles bulge.

"Is that right, Jack?" Anya asked.

He chopped the last of the dried apricots into a bowl. "Leave me out of it."

Facing Lucky, the women planted hands on hips, mirroring each other's body language. "No one's buying it," Zora said. "You're a snoop."

"Believe whatever you want. I have better things to do." The male nurse fled with what dignity he could muster.

Jack tried not to be self-conscious about performing for an audience as he continued cooking. He liked having Anya there but wasn't so keen about Zora's presence until she said, "I sure admire what you're doing."

"Don't encourage him." Anya softened her words with a smile. "But this *is* a treat."

"For me, too." Jack handed her the salad bowl and gave Zora a serving plate piled with pita. "Mind putting these on the table?"

"Sure."

Zora left, but Anya hung back. "Why would this be a treat for you? Or were you just being polite?"

Stirring the nuts and apricots into the lentil dish, Jack gave her a serious answer. "I grew up without a family. This is fun."

"And I grew up with too much family." She sighed. "Too bad we couldn't have averaged it out."

"I hope your experience hasn't poisoned you forever." Jack didn't mean to lecture her. Still, this seemed like a chance to reach out. "Just because your sister tries to push you around…"

The doorbell rang. "Wonder who that is," Anya said, scooting out.

Avoidance. Well, what had he expected?

AWARE THAT ZORA was wrestling with the issue of how, when and what to tell others—including her ex-husband—about her pregnancy, Anya empathized with her friend. And understood Zora's envy of Jack's support.

So far he'd done well, choosing a menu that even Lucky approved of. And as Jack worked smoothly in the kitchen, his blue-checked apron emphasized his strong build and easy comfort with his own body.

Definitely comfortable in his body. Ambling into the living room to find out who'd rung the bell, Anya still felt a thrill of electricity, remembering the tenderness of Jack's stolen kiss. But despite her hunger for more, the intimate contact didn't augur well for his promise to leave her out of the child-rearing process.

Or for her ability to stand her ground.

Karen reached the door first, admitting Rod. He'd trimmed his graying hair and foregone the usual hat. "Thanks for inviting me," he told his hostess and gave Anya a friendly nod.

Anya wasn't sure where she stood at the moment with Rod's mercurial personality. Because he was a guest in the house and presumably on his best behavior around Karen, Anya supposed they'd get along well enough.

Jack peered out of the dining room, a bottle of salad dressing in one hand and a container of hummus in the other. "You invited him? No wonder you suggested I triple the recipe."

"It didn't seem fair to leave your uncle home alone," Karen replied cheerfully.

"Yes, I might get into all sorts of trouble." Rod gave her shoulders a squeeze that almost amounted to a hug.

Jack rolled his eyes. "Like an overgrown kid."

"That's right," said his uncle. "I'm here at my most infantile to test your parenting skills."

"Enjoy it while you can," Jack answered. "You'll have to grow up fast once—if—junior comes to live with us."

"Junior?" Anya asked.

"Junior-ette." In the dining room, Jack waited until the

others were settled before taking the empty chair across from Anya.

"No footsy under the table," Rod warned.

"You're in a good mood," Jack said to his uncle as he passed the butter to Karen.

"I just found out the girls are coming back next week for spring vacation." Rod explained that he'd received an email from Tiffany. "Apparently they've been so cooperative since visiting their grandmother that their parents agreed to let them do it again."

"That's wonderful news," Karen said.

"Okay if I bring them to dinner next weekend?" Rod asked. "Especially since Jack's cooking."

"And paying for it," Lucky put in.

Heads bobbed agreement. "We can add a card table for extra places," Karen said.

"Invite their grandmother, too. I'm prepared to be flexible," Jack said.

I'm not agreeing to anything, no matter how flexible you are. But as the words echoed in Anya's mind, she was glad she hadn't spoken them aloud because she'd have blushed. Jack *was* flexible in all sorts of ways that didn't bear dwelling on.

"You don't think this is a little too easy?" asked Melissa, who'd been quiet until now. "I mean, allowing the girls to return so soon when their parents have been completely rigid until now?"

Rod's smile faded. "You may be right."

"I hope their folks aren't suspicious." Karen plucked half a pita from the napkin-wrapped stack.

"They could create a lot of trouble if they are," Rod said ruefully.

Speculation flowed as to what Portia and Vince might be planning. "We'll have to be careful," Jack said. "If they learn that Helen's in league with you, that'll be the end of it."

"And Vince won't be satisfied with a discreet win," Rod said. "He's a heavy-handed bully."

Anya imagined jack-booted security troops raiding the
house and yanking the girls from the dinner table. She'd been
watching too many of Lucky's macho TV programs.

"We might need a backup plan for the girls' activities,"
Karen said.

"If Vince realizes I'm involved, I doubt we'd be able to
fool him." Rod passed the salad to Melissa. "Although I appreciate the input, this discussion is making me grouchy.
Let's change the subject."

The table fell quiet. Melissa clicked her tongue, which
drew everyone's attention. "If you guys don't mind, I could
use an objective opinion about something. Especially with
Jack here."

"What's Jack got to do with it?" Anya asked.

"It's his profession." Melissa traced a slim finger over her
misty water glass. "I'm facing a major decision. I have to give
my answer soon and if I make the wrong choice, it will affect the rest of my life."

That aroused Anya's curiosity. Maybe Jack's presence *was*
a good thing for her housemates, beyond his cooking talents.

"I'll help if I can," he said.

Melissa's hands fluttered gracefully. "I've been considering having a baby on my own because…well, never mind the
background. But to deliberately bring a child into the world
without a father, that troubles me. Now an opportunity has
come up at work."

"Not mentioning any identities," Karen reminded her.

"Of course not." Like doctors and nurses, they respected
patient confidentiality.

"Go on," Jack urged.

A woman in the fertility program had delivered healthy
triplets after undergoing in vitro fertilization, Melissa explained. The patient and her husband had frozen three more
embryos but decided they couldn't handle more children.
Also, after a difficult pregnancy, the mother's health might
be compromised if she tried again.

"They're wonderful people, and their babies are darling,"

she said. "I'd mentioned that I was considering artificial insemination. The mom asked... Well, she offered to let me have their embryos—on the condition that I use all of them. She's eager to have this resolved. If I don't implant them soon, she might choose someone else."

"Three embryos?" Zora crossed her arms as if shielding her abdomen. "Seriously?"

"You should discuss this with your doctor," Jack told Melissa.

"I have. Dr. Sargent says if I choose to go ahead, he's fine with it." Melissa pulled back her long, honey-blond hair and re-clipped it with her barrette. "I wish this weren't so sudden, but I have to give them an answer. Also, I'll need to start taking medications right away to go through the procedure this cycle."

That *was* soon. "It isn't right for them to pressure you," Anya said.

"But it's a miraculous offer. Still, having triplets could be overwhelming in a lot of ways." Melissa regarded Jack as if he possessed magical insight. "How likely is it that they'd all take?"

"Frozen embryo transfers at Safe Harbor have about a fifty percent success rate," he said. "I'm sure Zack Sargent went over that with you."

"Yes, but he tends to be gung ho about the egg donor program," she replied frankly. "I want an objective opinion."

All eyes fixed on Jack.

Anya wondered if he could be truly objective, considering his desire to raise junior-ette.

"It's unlikely that all three embryos will implant," he said thoughtfully. "However, since you can't discount the possibility, you'd better be prepared. You should consider your physical condition, your motivation and your support system, and whether they're able to handle three children at once."

"Support system is fine," Karen announced.

"I'm grateful for my friends, and I'm in good physical

shape." Melissa swallowed. "As for raising three little guys, well, I'd be lucky if that happened."

"They might be born early," Jack warned. "What if there are complications?"

"If she obsesses about everything that can go wrong, she'll never have kids," Lucky countered.

"That doesn't mean she shouldn't consider all the risks," Zora argued. "I remember when one of the nurses provided eggs for a surrogate. She went through a grueling regimen, with all kinds of hormones. There were some serious dangers, too."

"A frozen embryo transfer is much less stressful than an egg donation," Jack responded. "It takes less medication to prepare the uterine lining than to stimulate the ovaries." He glanced quickly at Anya. "I'm not sure this is the best topic for dinner-table conversation, though."

"That's okay. I'm finished eating," she said.

"There," Lucky announced triumphantly. "As I said, there's no reason to obsess about dangers."

"What about the risk of having triplets?" Zora returned Lucky's frown and doubled it. "*Somebody* has to remind her of the down side."

"And *somebody* has done that plenty," he snapped.

Rod waggled his eyebrows. "Shall we have fisticuffs for our postprandial entertainment? I'll referee."

Karen chuckled.

"Thanks for your input, Jack," Melissa said. "And you too, Zora. You're right. It's important to consider all sides."

"Speaking of sides, what's for dessert?" Rod rounded his eyes at his nephew.

"That was probably the most tortured segue I've ever heard," Jack answered. "In case you guys hadn't guessed, my uncle will bend a conversation like a pretzel to get to dessert."

"What *is* for dessert?" Lucky asked.

"Yes, Jack, what's for dessert?" Karen teased.

"If you guys can't read a menu, you don't deserve any apple pie." Jack pushed his chair back.

"I'll clear!" That was Lucky.

"I'll serve!" Karen added.

"Where's the pie?" Rod, of course.

Grinning at the surge of responses, Jack said, "In the fridge," and nearly got trampled by the herd stampeding past him into the kitchen.

Anya followed more slowly with a couple of serving dishes. Jack's debut as household chef had been a triumph. Too much of a triumph, in her opinion.

She hadn't considered that this test might bring him closer to her housemates. Already they were looking to him for advice, accepting him as an arbiter of sorts. Although she couldn't help being proud of him, what would it be like if he was raising their baby?

She'd have a hard enough time staying away from Jack and the child on her own. Now her friends were becoming his friends, too.

She'd left Colorado to preserve her freedom. Come September and the baby's delivery, would she have to leave Safe Harbor, too?

Chapter Thirteen

Jack's surgeries ran longer than expected on Friday morning. Because he saw patients in the afternoon, he decided to skip lunch rather than postpone appointments. "Also, that would make me late for fixing dinner," he remarked as he washed up, speaking as much to himself as to his uncle.

"Unacceptable, since we might have guests," Rod responded, though his recent upbeat attitude was blunted by uncertainty. The girls were expected to arrive today, but Helen hadn't been sure when or whether they'd be flying, taking the train or traveling by car.

"I was planning on them joining us tomorrow night," Jack said.

"Why not both meals?"

That meant making larger dishes, with a possible extra supermarket run. Rod had eaten with the household all week, which had increased Jack's work, but ultimately he approved. He was glad to see his uncle's friendship with Karen blossoming. And Jack hadn't been entirely comfortable with abandoning his uncle at dinnertime for two weeks.

So far, the meals had gone smoothly, aside from Zora's dismay on Tuesday when he'd fixed asparagus, which she hated. There'd also been a touch of awkwardness last night when he preheated the oven for lasagna and discovered belatedly that it was filled with soiled plates and cups, now burning hot.

Flustered, Zora and Anya had admitted hiding their breakfast dishes in the oven because they'd been running late and hadn't had time to empty the dishwasher. "It's a house rule," Anya had informed him. "We can't leave stuff on the counter."

"We didn't think about you using the oven," Zora had added.

"You should have looked inside before you turned it on." Anya had crossed her arms. "Imagine what a toddler might have put in there."

Jack had agreed and resignedly used pot holders to empty the oven.

But now, as he removed his surgical gloves, he realized that he was far less concerned about kitchen mishaps than about Anya's stubbornness in holding him at arm's length. Although his primary goal in serving as cook was to prove his readiness to be a dad, he'd hoped the experience might draw them closer.

He could have sworn she also longed to be closer. Those sideways glances, the teasing tension between them and, more important, the moments when they simply talked. They'd discovered they shared a fondness for nature documentaries on TV, especially those featuring birds, although neither had ever owned a pet bird.

"I'd rather watch them in the wild," Anya had said. "I think there are birds nesting in Karen's bushes and maybe out in the estuary."

He'd loaned her his binoculars so she could sit on the patio, put up her feet and bird-watch. After dinner one night, they'd sat outside, taking turns observing the birds and occasionally looking up details on their phones. They'd agreed that a hummingbird might be nesting in one of the honeysuckle bushes, especially because when Jack approached for a closer look, it had dive-bombed him with a sharp noise that warned him to retreat. He did, to Anya's amusement.

Yet when he'd suggested they bird-watch again last night, she'd declined and made a vague reference to having plans with Zora—pulling back, just when he'd hoped the barriers between them were falling.

Jack brought himself up sharply. Anya was honest about her approach to emotional attachments: when things got tough, cut and run. Much as he longed for her to stay in his life, as a resource for the baby and for other, very personal reasons, he'd better remember that in the end, she'd leave. She might not even give him warning. She still hadn't informed her sister about skipping their grandmother's birthday party next month. Unless Ruth had picked up the signs—which surely she ought to—she was in for an unpleasant last-minute shift in arrangements.

So far, Anya was running true to form. Only a fool would assume she'd change.

"Since you're feeding me dinner, I suppose I could bring lunch to your office this afternoon," Rod commented as they sauntered out of the operating suite.

"Tuna melt," Jack said.

"Kind of late for the cafeteria to fix a hot sandwich."

"Cold tuna on rye will be fine."

"Done."

On the main floor, Jack let his uncle precede him out of the elevator but nearly ran into the slightly shorter man when he stopped suddenly. "Hey!"

Rod didn't answer. He'd gone rigid.

Near the entrance to the fertility support services suite, a cluster of familiar figures caught Jack's eye. Hospital administrator Mark Rayburn, M.D., distinguished by his thick, black hair and the build of a former high school football player, dominated the group. Karen stood out, too, with her black-and-white coiffure. But it was their companions who'd surely riveted Rod's attention.

Vince Adams lacked Mark's height, but he stood out anyway. Maybe it was his aggressive stance—feet planted apart, head up and nostrils slightly flared—or the pin-striped dark suit that looked as if it had cost thousands of dollars.

Beside him, lean and fashionable in a hot-pink designer dress and jacket, Portia stood poised in her high heels. She must be about thirty-eight now, Jack figured, but already her unlined forehead and cheeks hinted at Botox injections. The bright red hair that Tiff had inherited had been tinted auburn and woven with strands of gold and honey-brown.

He'd seen photos of the pair in a magazine, portrayed as a beautiful power couple. To Jack, they seemed hard, with an underlying cruelty that flickered like hellfire through the cracks in their veneer. But that was because he'd witnessed how they'd manipulated the legal system.

Rod had no gift for disguising his emotions. Even from behind, his taut body language told Jack he was glowering.

"Hang in there," he murmured to his uncle.

Judging by her uneasy expression, Portia had spotted them. So had Karen, although she betrayed only a flicker of recognition.

When Vince turned, triumph distorted his features. He not only loved winning, but he also enjoyed grinding his opponent's face into the dirt. Obviously, he and his wife had become suspicious about the girls' behavior, which accounted for their visit to Safe Harbor. But why were they at the hospital?

The administrator didn't miss the tense, silent interchange. A furrow between the eyebrows was all the sign he gave, however, that it concerned him.

"If it isn't Dr. Vintner." Vince just couldn't let the moment pass, could he? "Good to see you again." His sneering tone converted the pleasantry into an insult.

"The pleasure's all yours," Rod growled.

"I didn't realize you were acquainted with members of my staff, Mr. Adams," Mark said.

"Rod is my ex-husband." Portia blinked as if startled. "Jack? I had no idea you were back in Safe Harbor."

"Hello, Aunt Portia." Jack strained for civility. "I've been here for two years now."

"Jack's a fine surgeon," Mark said. "The head of our fertility program, Dr. Owen Tartikoff, brought him on board."

"Does Jack work with Dr. Rattigan?" Vince addressed his question to the administrator.

Cole Rattigan, Lucky's boss, was a world-renowned specialist in male fertility. Did Vince, who reputedly was unable to father children, plan to consult him?

"I'm an ob-gyn," Jack said.

"I take it that means no." Vince kept his eyes on the administrator. "Now, what about those cutting-edge labs you mentioned?"

"They're on the next floor down," Mark said. "Karen, thanks for reviewing our egg donor program."

"Glad to do it. Nice meeting you, Mr. and Mrs. Adams." Karen shook their hands, then tossed off a quick, "Doctors," with a nod to Jack and Rod, before vanishing into her suite.

Since Rod remained frozen between the visitors and the elevators, Jack touched his arm to interrupt his fixation. "You owe me a sandwich."

Rod was vibrating with unspoken rage. But after a moment, he took a few steps to the side, no doubt in deference to the administrator.

As the trio passed, Mark kept up a running narration to the visitors. "Our original plan called for acquiring the dental building across the plaza. When it fell into protracted bankruptcy proceedings, we had to improvise. That's why our fertility offices are scattered across several floors. We installed the laboratories in our basement."

"Doesn't a basement mean problems with dampness and mold?" Vince swaggered by as if Rod weren't there. Portia spared a thoughtful glance for Jack.

"We've installed advanced HEPA filtration systems." The administrator pressed the down button. "The temperatures and sterility are strictly regulated. I'll let Alec Denny, our director of laboratories, provide the details."

To Jack's relief, the elevator arrived, and he was able to lead his uncle away at last. "That was a shock," he said once the others were out of hearing range.

Rod moved stiffly. "They're here to spy on me."

"Surely they wouldn't waste Dr. Rayburn's time to do that," Jack said.

"Oh, but they love to gloat." Unhappily his uncle added, "This means no more time with my daughters."

"Not for a while," Jack agreed.

Rod rolled his shoulders, fighting the tension. "Don't you have patients waiting?"

"Yes, actually. See you later. Tuna on rye." As he headed for the adjacent office building, Jack was glad they'd be having dinner with Karen. She might have insights to share.

As for Tiff and Amber, he hated missing a chance to see them. But they were aware now that Rod and Jack loved them.

Vince and Portia couldn't keep them apart forever.

"THEY'VE RENTED A beach house a few miles from here, on the Balboa Peninsula," Karen said that night over a serving of Jack's peanut butter pasta. "Portia seemed genuinely worried about how much her mother misses her granddaughters."

"Worried or guilty?" Rod asked dourly.

Even with seven of them around the table, Anya was keenly aware of the girls' absence. She'd been looking forward to seeing them tonight or tomorrow, or both. Having grown up in a family of nine, sometimes she missed the joyous babble, the give-and-take of a group where interactions crisscrossed like global airline traffic lines on a grid.

"It does reduce the risk that Tiff will run away again," Jack ventured, although the situation had clearly put a damper on his mood, too.

"Why were they at the hospital?" Anya asked. "Dr. Rayburn doesn't give tours to the general public."

"They were dropping hints about some type of endowment," Karen said.

"It's a ruse to spy on me," Rod replied angrily.

"Maybe Vince just wants to move to the head of the line for a consult with Cole Rattigan," Jack said. "I understand he books up months in advance."

"Oh, he tries to work in any patient who's in urgent need." Lucky plucked a second dinner roll from a basket. "Of course, if they *had* come to the office, I couldn't mention it."

"Is that a no-they-didn't or are you obfuscating?" Zora asked.

"Is he doing what?" In contrast to the generally downbeat mood, Melissa sounded amused. Her spirits had lifted since she'd begun receiving injections of estrogen and progesterone in preparation for receiving the embryos.

"Confusing the issue," Zora translated.

"No one's confused about anything except your weird word choice," Lucky batted back.

"I thought you two had stopped picking on each other. Just spare the rest of us, okay?" Karen promptly returned to the subject of the day. "When Portia mentioned her daughters, I suggested they might enjoy volunteering at the hospital. I said our program encourages an interest in science."

"How'd that go over?" Jack asked.

"She seemed interested."

"And Vince?"

"Not so much."

"It'll never happen." Agitated, Rod glared across the table at Anya. "I don't understand why people fail to appreciate parenthood when it falls in their lap."

"Excuse me?" Jack asked.

Anya was grateful for the sharp response. Her pregnancy was none of his uncle's business.

"You heard me." For whatever reason, Rod continued to target his anger at her. "Why are you forcing my nephew to prove himself over and over? Just sign that waiver you considered such a minor detail when the shoe was on the other foot."

"Butt out," Anya said, summing up her position.

Around the table, the others regarded Rod with varying degrees of disapproval. Lucky's face tightened, Melissa stopped smiling, Zora frowned and even Karen looked distressed.

"You're a fine one to talk," Jack put in. "When I proposed bringing the baby to live with us, you brought up every obstacle in the book."

"I had to be sure you meant it," retorted his uncle. "Obviously, you did. And to keep your own mother ignorant of it—"

"What are you talking about?" Storm clouds darkened Jack's eyes.

"You hadn't told Mamie you're going to be a father."

"My absentee mom who didn't even stick around to raise me?" he snapped. "Why should I?"

"She's older now, and she has regrets."

"Where is this coming from?" Jack regarded his uncle sternly. "I thought you and your sister communicated by exchanging Christmas cards."

"I gave her a call to catch up on things," Rod said. "You should talk to her more often yourself."

Although pleased to no longer be the object of Rod's tirade, Anya resented his criticism of Jack. Honestly, just because the man was upset didn't give him the right to scattershot his anger at everyone else.

"Wait a minute." Jack's jaw pushed forward belligerently. "You called to catch up, or to tell her Anya's pregnant? That takes one hell of a nerve!"

"After what happened today…" Rod seemed, for the first time, to notice the negative reactions from the others. Stubbornly, he persisted. "It struck me that Mamie might never have another chance to be a grandmother. She deserves to be in the loop."

"No," Jack said. "She doesn't."

"Well, too late." His uncle swallowed. "We hadn't been in touch for a while, so I called her."

Fury radiated from Jack. "This is Anya's and my concern. Not yours, and not my mother's."

"It is now." Rod cleared his throat. "She was deciding whether to attend a conference in LA next week and this tipped the scale."

Next week? That was when they'd scheduled the ultrasound, Anya recalled. Just what they needed, another form of pressure at a key moment. How typical of families—even from far away, they had a gift for meddling.

"Call her back and tell her she's not welcome," Jack snapped.

"You call her," Rod said.

"I want her as far from Anya and me as possible."

To the best of Anya's knowledge, Jack had never openly rejected his mother before. "Are you sure?" she asked him. "I mean, she's your mom, so of course I'll leave it up to you."

He gave her a nod of acknowledgment, then resumed glaring at his uncle. "Why can't you grasp the fact that my mother doesn't give a damn?"

"If she's so indifferent, what's the big deal if she stops by?" Rod asked with an attempt at his usual flippancy.

"The big deal is that I should have the right to break the news to her when and if I want to." Jack's hand tightened around his fork. "If we choose to put this baby up for adoption, there's no reason for her to know. Ever."

"You're wrong." Rod straightened, regrouping. "She does care, more than you think."

A flicker of uncertainty pierced Jack's fury. "She said that?"

"I heard it in her voice."

Noting the conflict in Jack's expression, Anya wished she were sitting close enough to touch his arm and offer silent comfort. *Stay out of it, you idiot,* she warned herself.

"I'll talk to her," Jack said tightly.

"And tell her not to come?" his uncle queried.

"And tell her whatever I damn please." Jack stood up. "There's ice cream in the freezer."

"On my way." Lucky hurried out, escaping the tension.

"I'll help." Melissa rose gracefully, and the others began clearing the table.

"Anya?" Jack swung toward her. "A moment alone?"

"Sure." She'd hated saying no to him about the bird-watching last night. They'd had fun, peering into the twilight, listening to the chirps and trying to identify the various species. And tonight, he'd defended her to his uncle. As if they were in this together. Which, until the baby's birth, she supposed they were.

Conscious of the others watching—despite their attempts

to pretend otherwise—she kept her gaze straight ahead and her pace moderate as they climbed the stairs. Once on the second floor, they hurried to her room. The sunset cast a scarlet glow across the bed and bookcase. Anya switched on the lamp. "Shoot."

Jack paced the floor.

Funny how a man's presence changed everything, emphasizing the smallness of the room and filling the air with subtle allure that reminded Anya that she'd tossed her comforter over invitingly rumpled sheets.

Stop, now. That's how you got into this mess.

He halted. "I apologize for my uncle's behavior."

She waved away the apology. "Not your fault."

"Would you mind…" He broke off.

To her, the glitter in his eyes spoke of old wounds reopened—and old hopes springing to life. "Meeting your mom?" Anya guessed.

"Or even…" Jack hesitated again, uncharacteristically. Then he said, "If she does care, it shouldn't be in an abstract sense. I need to be sure."

She hazarded a guess. "You want to invite her to the ultrasound. That's quite a switch." Moments before, he'd been prepared to boot her all the way back to whatever third world country she was currently aiding.

"It hit me all of a sudden, but I didn't want to mention it in front of my uncle," Jack explained. "What do you think?"

Having his mother present might be like tossing a lighted match onto dried-out California underbrush during fire season. Yet it meant a lot to Jack, and thus far, he'd been willing to meet Anya halfway.

But if his mother *did* take a stand against her, what then? Though Mamie wasn't likely to volunteer to help raise her granddaughter, considering she'd ducked out on her own son. And she'd have to possess incredible chutzpah to pressure another woman to take on the duties she herself had shirked.

And so far, Jack had respected Anya's feelings. It was time to trust him.

With the sense of taking a dive off a cliff, Anya said, "Okay."

He waited, as if expecting more. Then he noted, "I'm not even sure she'll be able to come. I suppose it depends on her conference schedule."

It would be inconvenient but not impossible to change the sonogram appointment. Anya saw no need to bring that up yet, though. "Whatever."

Jack ran his hands over her shoulders, massaging them lightly. "Will I ever figure you out?"

"I hope not." In her view, keeping him off-balance promoted equal power in the relationship. But right now, she was content to relax and enjoy the magic sensations his fingers inspired. "You could do more of that."

"Happy to comply, ma'am," he responded with a heart-stopping smile.

Anya leaned closer. His chest materialized beneath her cheek. "Mmm."

Strong arms closed around her, and she nestled there. Would it really be so bad if, together, they...?

Stop right there. She'd already taken a step in his direction, figuratively speaking, by agreeing to allow his mother to come to the ultrasound. That meant, she conceded, that if Mamie unexpectedly offered her son the nurturing he'd been denied all these years, Anya could hardly refuse to give him—them—the baby.

That might mean having to leave Safe Harbor afterward for her own emotional safety. Freedom could be a lonely place, but for now, they'd reached a welcome accord.

All the same, she ducked away before their embrace could lead to more.

Chapter Fourteen

On Saturday, Jack reported that Mamie had cheerfully agreed to attend next Thursday's ultrasound, scheduled for 7:30 p.m. at Dr. Cavill-Hunter's office. "She seemed upbeat about the whole situation," Jack said as he set out the ingredients for his planned dinner of angel-hair pasta with wine and onions.

"She isn't upset that Rod broke the news about the baby, rather than you?" Anya asked.

She felt a little guilty that Jack had spent more than he intended on these large meals, and was glad he'd decided to fix a low-cost entrée tonight. His explanation that the alcohol in the wine would evaporate during cooking hadn't been necessary, but she appreciated it.

"I'm not sure it's sunk in that she's about to become a grandmother." He placed the cutting board on the stove top to chop onions, turning on the fan to draw off eye-burning fumes.

"Every woman reacts differently, I guess." Anya was slicing tomatoes on a second cutting board. She'd volunteered to assist, having discovered that conversations with Jack flowed more naturally when they worked side by side. Perhaps due to their shared experiences in the O.R., they moved easily around each other without colliding.

"What about *your* mother?" Jack scraped the onions into a large pot and set to dicing garlic cloves. "You've hardly mentioned her."

With a start, Anya admitted she hadn't thought about how

her mother might react to the baby. Molly Meeks's name suited her retiring personality. Even before arthritis had sidelined her, she'd been almost a background player in the household, relying first on Ruth to help raise her second and third children and then on Anya to supervise the triplets.

"Mom's always been overshadowed by my grandma—my father's mother," she said. "Not that Grandma was underfoot. She lived around the corner from us and values her independence. But on important issues, her views tended to prevail."

"She's the one who's turning eighty next month?"

"That's her." Anya hoped he'd refrain from inquiring about the gathering. It *was* awkward that she hadn't responded yet. But Ruth had stopped tallying childcare requests on social media, and although that didn't amount to an acknowledgment that Anya might not show up, it implied her sister might be facing reality.

Or preparing another line of attack. Anya sighed.

"If you're tired, you should sit down." Jack moved his cutting board to the counter. "I can finish the salad."

"No, I just…" *Don't want to discuss my family issues.* "You're being wonderful," she said.

He flashed a grin. "I am, aren't I?"

The meal turned out to be another of his triumphs, though she couldn't get the conversation about their mothers out of her head. She had enough issues from her own family. Was she prepared to take on his issues, too?

The next few days passed quickly. Mamie planned to arrive in Los Angeles on Wednesday for her conference. On Thursday, Rod was going to collect her from her hotel at 4:00 p.m. and bring her to the house so she could enjoy dinner with everyone and meet Anya prior to the sonogram.

But on Thursday morning, everything changed. A disgruntled Jack caught Anya in the hallway of the hospital.

"Can we reschedule the ultrasound?" It turned out his mom had to attend a press conference early that evening for her Haitian charity, he explained. "She apologized profusely and swears she can come Friday afternoon."

"I'm not sure. It was hard to make arrangements for a weekday evening, let alone a Friday." Because of Dr. Cavill-Hunter's overnight shifts in labor and delivery, her office hours didn't start until 6:00 p.m.

"Mamie can't attend in the evening. Her flight's at 7:30 p.m., and she has to be at the airport an hour and a half early." As usual, Jack referred to his mother by her first name.

It struck Anya that Mamie would be missing tonight's dinner, too, on which Jack had spent a small fortune. He'd bought steaks and was planning on making twice-baked potatoes stuffed with cheese. But that was less important than the sonogram.

"I don't suppose my doctor *has* to be there," Anya conceded. "And it will be easier to find a tech to work during the day."

"Adrienne can review the results with us later." His gaze locked onto Anya's.

"Let me see what I can set up. I'm just sorry she'll miss your delicious cooking." Anya hoped he didn't think she was criticizing his mother.

Jack shrugged. "Mamie has a tendency to play the drama queen. But it sounds like this is an important press conference. There are major potential donors in the L.A. area."

"It's a worthy cause," Anya agreed, although she only vaguely recalled the nature of the project—something about providing security for Haitian women living in tent encampments. "We'll figure out the ultrasound."

That proved more difficult than expected. Dr. Tartikoff had scheduled a complex surgery for early Friday afternoon and was relying on Jack to assist. The sometimes crusty head of the fertility program, on learning of the circumstances, promised to free Jack by 3:30 p.m., but that was the best he could do.

Locating an ultrasound tech presented further problems. Zora had back-to-back assignments and another tech was out with the flu. It would be unfair to bump a patient who'd had her session planned weeks in advance.

"I'm sorry," Zora told Anya over lunch. "I'm disappointed I'm going to miss out on meeting the famous Mamie Ryder, too." Rod had been regaling the dinner table all week with tales of his sister's colorful exploits around the world.

"I'll fill you in," Anya responded distractedly. Her main concern was that the ultrasound might not take place this week at all. She was trying not to dwell on the implications of meeting Jack's mother.

"I'll do it myself," Jack said a short time later when she informed him she couldn't find a tech. She'd spotted him in the busy corridor just outside the cafeteria. "Performing sonograms was part of my training."

"Aren't you a little rusty?" she asked.

He steered her out of the path of a gurney being pushed by a volunteer. "You mean like performing an operation with a rusty knife?"

"Ouch!"

Jack laughed. "I assure you, I'm competent. And it isn't an invasive procedure, so I can't very well cause harm."

Anya thought of a plus. "Also, you get to show off for your mother."

"She *is* proud of my accomplishments," he assured her. "Mamie's seen me operate, via remote camera. She found it fascinating."

It was good to hear him speaking well of his mother. In fact, this past week, he'd spoken up during Rod's tales, adding a few flattering details about Mamie. Squelching an uneasy sense that he and his mother might soon join forces against her, Anya said, "I'll line up an examining room, then."

"Thanks." Jack traced a finger across her cheek.

She stepped back, surprised at the tender gesture given in full public view. "Have you forgotten how bad the gossips are around here?"

"You mean they'll be shocked that two people having a baby together show signs of affection?" he teased.

She chuckled. "You never know."

On Friday, despite Anya's efforts to train her mind away

from the upcoming procedure, she became increasingly nervous as 3:30 p.m. approached. She'd lined up a room and made sure ultrasound equipment would be available. And, she reminded herself, she already knew the baby's gender. So what was the big deal?

Yet she dropped her purse twice in the nurses' locker room and arrived at Dr. Cavill-Hunter's office on the second floor of the medical building before recalling that the sonogram was to take place on the third floor where Jack shared quarters with Dr. Tartikoff.

It was 3:25 p.m. Afraid she might be keeping him and his mother waiting, Anya took the stairs up a floor rather than wait for the elevator. As she climbed, she noticed how tightly her jeans were fitting, a reminder she'd soon have to buy maternity clothes. By twelve weeks, some women were already ballooning. Anya had made a point of eating moderately, hoping to delay displaying her condition to the world as long as possible.

She wouldn't be able to hide it much longer, though. Not that many people weren't already aware of her situation anyway.

Anya put her shoulder to the heavy third-floor door. She'd barely wedged it open and was shimmying through when the phone rang in her pocket.

Another change of plans? She plucked it out.

Ruth.

Oh, great timing. Irritably, Anya sent the call to voice mail, but she was so nervous she must've tapped the wrong spot. "Anya?" came her sister's voice. "Hello?"

If she cut off the call now, Ruth would take offense. And with good reason.

Anya put the phone to her ear. "I'm here. Listen, this is a bad time."

"I'd hoped you'd be off work by now."

She *was* off work, but Anya couldn't explain to her sister what she was really doing. "Uh, I am. But there's a meeting."

"You haven't responded about the birthday party." Barely

pausing for breath, Ruth pressed on, "Everyone's counting on you. Grandma would be heartbroken if you aren't here. You're her favorite grandchild."

"Don't be ridiculous." Including cousins, the third-generation count reached well into the double digits.

"It's obvious to everyone but you." Ruth must have prepared to go on this offensive before she placed the call. "You'll be arriving a few days early, as we agreed, right?"

"We didn't agree." Tensely, Anya wondered if her voice carried into the nearby offices. "I'm not in a place where I can talk."

"Are you coming or not?"

She nearly responded in the negative. But why should she let Ruth's bossiness prevent her from honoring her grandmother? She'd learned over the past few weeks that her duck-and-run philosophy could cheat her out of some very happy moments. Instead, she decided to address the real problem. "I'm not running a day care center. People can watch their own children."

"Selfish as always!" Her sister's ragged voice rose to a shrill note. She sounded tired and resentful—and was aiming it all at Anya. "Everyone's pitching in, although most of the work falls on me, as usual."

"You live there," Anya pointed out. "Besides—"

"It isn't my fault you chose to move to California," Ruth went on. "I've got four kids and I'm carrying another."

"Somebody else can take up the slack." Although Ruth might be the oldest of the cousins, that shouldn't obligate her to run every family gathering.

"That's what I'm trying to do," her sister snapped. "I'm delegating. And your job is supervising the children."

"I appreciate how hard you're working." Guiltily, Anya conceded that she hadn't given her sister enough credit for bringing everyone together. "It isn't fair for everyone to assume you'll organize the whole party. But parents can make their own babysitting arrangements. I wouldn't expect someone else to take care of my child, if I had one."

"But you don't. You're too busy living it up, being single and hanging out at the beach." Now, where had Ruth picked up that idea? "You're letting everyone down—as always."

Anya badly wanted out of this conversation. Not to mention that her watch was edging past 3:30 p.m. "We each make our own choices."

"If that's how you feel, just stay home!" The call went dead.

Ruth had hung up on her? Despite the temptation to call back, Anya turned off her phone. Discussion tabled until whenever. But she was glad she'd stood up for herself.

She let herself into the waiting room. Several women looked up from their magazines. At the receptionist station, she spotted nurse Ned Norwalk.

"Come on in." He indicated the interior door.

A patient frowned in her direction. Because Anya had changed out of her uniform, the woman might have assumed she was jumping the line to see the doctor.

Must be my day to tick people off.

Anya hurried to the designated room. Inside, she found Jack alone with the portable ultrasound equipment plugged in and ready for action.

His white coat was much more flattering than operating scrubs, and no ugly cap covered his thick dark hair. Half his patients probably had crushes on him, Anya reflected. Well, so had she, until…

Actually, she still did. But that was irrelevant.

"I'd have been here sooner, but my sister called at the worst possible moment." She kicked off her shoes.

"I can't wait to hear all about it." Jack raised an eyebrow. "Would you like me to leave the room while you change?"

That seemed silly, Anya thought as she picked up the hospital gown set out for her. "Just turn your back."

"As my lady wishes."

After he swung to face the door, she shed her clothes and put on the gown. "Where's your mom?"

"Rod called. They'll be here any minute."

That raised another potential problem. "About your uncle…"

Jack squared his shoulders. "You'd rather he wasn't here."

"Right."

"I don't like the way he treats you either. You don't want him here, so he won't be."

Anya tied the gown in front, a fruitless task because it gaped open. Who had designed these things, a Peeping Tom?

"Ready." She sat on the edge of the examining table.

Jack came alongside her. From this position, he towered over her, yet the gentleness of his expression soothed her. Stretching out, Anya quivered at the realization that he was about to touch her bare abdomen and run his hands over her.

As a doctor. But also as a father.

"We should start. My mother has a tight timetable." He picked up the scanning paddle, which reminded Anya of a computer mouse. "I'm out of practice, so it may take me a while to find the right angle."

She leaned back, her head slightly elevated by the table. "You can take pictures, too, right?"

"Yes! Don't let me forget. First baby pictures." Gently, Jack spread gel on her stomach. "It's a little chilly. Sorry."

Anya scarcely noticed. She was too keenly aware of his large hand stroking the gel across her abdomen. "No problem."

"At this point, the tech would normally explain that the paddle emits very high frequency sound waves, above the range of human hearing," he said. "That's where we get the word *sound* in ultrasound."

"And they bounce off structures inside me to produce an image," she finished. Sonography was used in many types of medical diagnosis, as Anya was well aware.

"Structures," he repeated as he laid the paddle on her tummy. "Otherwise known as the baby." His intake of breath belied his clinical tone.

On the monitor, gray tones shifted and seethed. For all Anya could tell, the darker shapes might be her kidneys or her bladder—oops, better not think about that, with the device pressing down right there.

Then she saw, unmistakably, a tiny backbone visible through the fetus's nearly translucent skin. The paddle moved, and into view came a beating heart, the rhythm faster than an adult's. As Jack adjusted the paddle, she discerned the shape of a curled baby, from its head to its rump, arms and legs moving.

"She's wiggling," she said, astonished even though she should have expected this. "A lot. I can't feel her yet."

"That's because she's only about two inches long. She has plenty of room for gymnastics." On the equipment, Jack flipped a switch and the rushing, thumping sound of a heartbeat engulfed the room.

A glow filled Anya, a miraculous sense of the person inside her—those fingers and toes already formed. Tiny eyes stared about almost as if the baby could see her parents.

Jack drew in a ragged breath. "This is unbelievable. I've watched a lot of ultrasounds and delivered a lot of babies. But this is different. It's our daughter."

Pulling her gaze from the screen, Anya noticed tears misting his eyes. He became blurry until she blinked and cleared her own tears.

She'd been fighting this connection for months, and now it nearly overwhelmed her. When the baby twitched, Anya could have sworn she made out a tiny nose shaped like her own.

She'd never understood how women could swear that once they held their baby, they almost immediately forgot the anguish of childbearing. Now, though, she teetered on the edge of forgetting the pain, not of childbearing but of child-rearing.

Endless piles of diapers, uncounted bottles to warm, cries in the night driving sleep to oblivion as each baby woke up her sisters. But Anya wasn't carrying triplets as her mother had. This was a single small girl.

Jack swallowed. "Look at her. She's really there, Anya. Our daughter."

Your daughter. She meant to say that aloud, but the words caught in her throat.

She's my daughter, too.

The door flew open. Startled, Anya realized she'd forgotten they were expecting company.

With a swish of fabric, a flood of exotic perfume and a flash of color, a dark-haired woman swept into the room. Tall and slim, she had spiky short hair and sharp eyes. Brilliant blocks of red, yellow and green marked her long halter dress.

As Jack switched off the Doppler sound of the baby's heartbeat, Anya stared at the apparition who'd just joined them.

"I'm here! We can start now." Her gleaming smile encompassed them both in the greeting.

Mamie Ryder had arrived.

Chapter Fifteen

Jack's first response, to his astonishment, was irritation. Did his mother have to arrive *now*?

This was his and Anya's private moment, their first meeting with their daughter. He'd seen Anya's resistance melting and her heart opening. Couldn't Mamie have given them a few more minutes?

Grudgingly, he bit down on his reaction. "Mamie," he greeted her—even when he was small, she'd preferred he use her name because "Mommy" made her feel old. "I'd give you a hug, but..." He lifted the paddle.

"Don't let me interrupt," she sang out. "Sorry I'm late. We hit a ridiculous amount of traffic."

"Not that much," Rod observed, entering behind her, his fedora slightly askew as if he'd run from the parking garage. "We were late leaving the hotel."

"All that packing." Mamie smiled at Anya. "This must be the new mommy. Hi. I'm Mamie."

"Nice to meet you." True to form, Anya wasted no words.

When her attention flicked to Rod, Jack recalled his promise. He zeroed in on his uncle. "Thanks for driving and for waiting outside."

Rod's mouth opened and promptly shut. "It *is* a bit crowded in here. I'll be out there playing with my phone."

That had been easy. Perhaps chauffeuring Mamie had proved trying. Jack spared no sympathy for his uncle, considering that it had been Rod's idea to invite her.

All the same, he appreciated that his mother had made the trip to Southern California.

Despite being in her early fifties, she struck him as ageless. Only twenty-one when he was born, she'd been a youthful mom, full of energy and vitality. In absentia, Mamie might inspire disappointment or even resentment, but in person, she was a force of nature.

Jack indicated the screen. "There she is. Our little girl."

Setting down her shopping bag, Mamie advanced toward the monitor. "My goodness." She frowned. "Are you sure it's a girl?"

"Yes," he said.

"Then what's that?" She indicated something poking from between the baby's legs.

"It's the umbilical cord." He moved the paddle to show a better angle.

"Oh. I see!" She searched for another comment. "Have you picked a name?"

"No." Jack doubted that Junior-ette qualified.

"My mother's name was Lenore," Mamie reminded him. "It's beautiful, isn't it?"

"It is." Jack became aware of Anya taking in this scene with a puzzled expression. He, too, was wondering when his mother would show the sense of wonder he and Anya had felt when they first glimpsed their child.

She will. Give her time.

"What was your pregnancy like?" Anya asked. "With Jack, I mean."

"In what respect?"

Anya rephrased the question. "Was it complicated? Or did it go smoothly?"

Mamie blinked. "I'm afraid I've forgotten. Honestly, my late husband was much more excited than I was."

Jolted, Jack stood there numbly. Did his mother have any idea what she'd just revealed?

"Well, you did a good job." Anya deserved credit for filling the pause before it could lengthen uncomfortably.

"Oh, I'm very proud of my son." Mamie's smile lacked warmth, as if she were reciting a line she'd rehearsed.

To Jack, this encounter was both disconcerting and disconnected. His mother had traveled thousands of miles for this, yet her fidgety body language implied an eagerness to leave.

Achingly, he realized he'd hoped for much more—that, as a mature adult, he could finally perceive the deep well of love that he'd missed when he was younger. At some level, he'd believed his mother's drive and dedication had torn her away from him but that the delight of meeting her granddaughter would reveal how much she cared.

He should have known better. Anger flared at himself for being gullible.

Mamie cleared her throat. "Do you have a nanny lined up?"

Anya gave a start. "No, we aren't…not yet."

"Don't wait till the last minute. I hear good nannies are hard to find," his mother advised.

"Thanks for the tip." Was Anya being ironic? Jack couldn't tell. And he had to rely on her, of all people, to keep the conversational ball rolling while he collected his thoughts. To his gratitude, she did. "That's a gorgeous dress."

Mamie whirled, showing off the striking design. "It's from Haiti, of course. So are the sandals." She lifted her feet to reveal strappy shoes that, to Jack, appeared to have soles shaped from recycled tires. "I only buy clothes made by the poor. They're so desperate! You should see the conditions they live under. As a mother, your heart would break for their children."

"I'm sure it would," Anya agreed.

"That reminds me. I brought a gift for the baby." From her shopping bag she pulled a large, angular metal construction. It was a lizard with a blue head and tail, orange legs and a green and yellow pattern on its body. "I'd have wrapped it, but they'd never have let it through airport security."

Anya waved her hand. "Just more paper to put in the recycle bin."

"Exactly!" Mamie beamed. "It's made out of old oil drums. Isn't it gorgeous? Look at the artistry. It's a gecko, by the way."

"Very cheerful," Anya said. "It'll be stunning on the wall."

That was diplomatic of her, considering that she planned to give up the baby. He'd relayed that to his mother when he'd phoned to discuss her visit, but apparently the information hadn't sunk in. Or she'd chosen to ignore it. The conversation had been a little strained, as if she were trying to say the right things but wasn't sure what those were. Jack had tried to be encouraging, despite his qualms.

"I suppose it is a bit large to put in the crib." Mamie held the gecko at arm's length, studying it. "You might hang it overhead, though, to stimulate Lenore's imagination."

With those sharp edges and possibly toxic paints? Clearly his mother hadn't wrapped her head around the idea of a baby. But she'd meant well.

"Jack, how about some screen shots of, uh, Lenore?" Anya prompted. "I'll bet your mother would like to take one with her."

"Sure."

"I'll show them off to my friends in Haiti." Returning the sculpture to the bag, Mamie rubbed her hands together. "They're thrilled that I'm going to be a grandmother."

As Jack adjusted the paddle and clicked to save a picture, he processed the fact that Mamie had spread the word about her grandchild despite his warning that they were considering putting her up for adoption. If Mamie were a doting grandma, it might be understandable, but he had the troubling sense that the baby appealed to her primarily as a way to show off to her friends.

Don't be judgmental. But he was still trying to absorb the statement that she hadn't been thrilled about her own pregnancy, about having him.

As he worked, Anya asked about the press conference, and Mamie waxed eloquent. "We must attract more businesses to revitalize the economy. Did you know Haiti is the poorest country in the Western Hemisphere? Unemployment is sixty to eighty percent. Just a few years ago, the island was devastated by an earthquake. Two years later, half a million people were still living in tents."

She cited shocking statistics about diseases and further damage from a hurricane. Passion blazed from Mamie's face.

Jack felt guilty. The work she was doing mattered to a lot of people. Still, she was the only mother he'd ever have. And today she'd reopened a wound that ran soul-deep.

With a knock, Rod returned to tell them that it was time to leave for the airport. Jack was sure that news came as a relief to everyone.

When Rod and Mamie were gone, the room suddenly felt peaceful. "Huh," Anya said.

After switching off the machine, Jack wiped the gel from her stomach. "My mother's an original, isn't she?"

"Are you okay?" She watched him sympathetically.

He nearly answered with an automatic yes, but that wasn't true. "I felt like we were actors in a stage play," he said as he helped Anya sit up. "Everything about that scene with my mother rang false. What did I miss? Am I that out of touch?"

Outside in the hallway, voices murmured as Ned escorted a patient past. "We should go somewhere else," Anya said.

"Good idea." Jack's phone hummed in his pocket. "Excuse me." Plucking it out, he read an unfamiliar number. Cautiously, he answered. "Dr. Ryder."

"Jack? Are you still at the hospital?" It was a man's voice.

"Right next door," he said.

"It's Zack Sargent. Thank goodness I caught you."

Jack was glad to deal with a professional matter. "What's up?"

"I'm scheduled to perform an embryo transplant but I must have caught my daughter's stomach flu because I just threw up." Zack *did* sound shaky. "I can't expose the patient to this. The embryos are already thawed. Owen thought you might still be on the premises."

"Yes. I'd be happy to step in." A potential conflict occurred to Jack. "Who's the patient?"

"It's Melissa Everhart," Zack told him. "I know you're acquainted with her personally but I've cleared it with her."

"In that case, how quickly do you need me there?" Given that the embryos were thawed, it was important to proceed at once, but Jack hoped he could spend a few minutes with Anya first, to clarify his feelings about Mamie.

"She's prepped now."

After getting the details about where to report, Jack signed off.

"Emergency?" asked Anya, who'd dressed while he was talking.

Although Melissa would no doubt fill her in later, that was the patient's choice. So Jack merely said, "I'm afraid so. But I'd like to meet you later." Another problem occurred to him. "And I still have to shop for dinner. I suppose I could throw together some kind of pasta dish."

"I could do the shopping," Anya said. "What's on the menu?"

"I was going to spring for salmon if my mother decided to delay her flight." What an optimistic idiot he'd been to imagine her doing such a thing. "I have a favorite recipe I got from a medical school colleague."

"Tell me what to buy." Anya raised a finger. "Wait. There's no reason for you to cook for my housemates tonight. We could eat at your place."

"Great idea." And that would make the salmon more affordable, too. "Save the bill and I'll pay you back. No arguments." From memory, Jack listed the ingredients for the meal and gave her a key from his ring. "I don't want you standing outside with the groceries."

"I'll be alone in your apartment?" She grinned mischievously. "Could I leave a rubber spider in Rod's bed?"

"How will you know which room's his?"

Her eyebrows shot up. "Honestly. You guys do smell different."

"Too much information." He assumed she was kidding about the spider anyway.

"I'll put the equipment away." She indicated the rolling cart beneath the sonograph machine, which Ned Norwalk had fetched earlier from a hall closet.

"Thanks. See you soon."

Heading out, Jack fixed his mind on the procedure ahead, reviewing the necessary steps. No surgery was required; for the patient, an embryo transfer felt much like a Pap smear.

The procedure involved the use of ultrasound to aid his manipulation of the catheter loaded with the embryos. The angle of the catheter was vital, both for the patient's safety and for proper placement.

Before he knew it, he was climbing the stairs to the second floor. For now, everything that had happened—seeing his daughter, encountering his mother, striving to understand his mixed emotions—could remain safely tucked away.

HOLDING THE GROCERY sack in one arm, Anya let herself into Jack's apartment. From outside, she lifted Mamie's gift bag and set it beneath a small table, atop which she placed the key.

Despite having lived around the corner from Jack for a year, she'd never ventured into his apartment until now. The living room was about the same size as the one she and Zora had shared, although the kitchen and hallway layouts were flipped. The place smelled of lemon oil and cleanser—a cleaning service must have visited recently—and the furniture included a cherrywood entertainment center and a tan curved sofa. Because Anya had expected a pair of bachelors on tight budgets to buy minimalist gear, she wondered if Rod's ex-wife had left these behind.

She was laying out her purchases on the kitchen counter when she heard the front door swing open. Instantly she recognized Jack's footsteps.

"Hi." His mood seemed upbeat as he regarded her. Performing the procedure—something to do with fertilization, she gathered—must have invigorated him. "Find everything okay?"

"I hope I got the right kind of apricot preserves." Anya indicated the jar. "And I bought the refrigerated horseradish. I think it's stronger than the other kind."

"Sounds perfect." He whipped a pair of aprons from a drawer, brushing past her with a rush of lime scent mixed with disinfectant. "You mind fixing the salad?"

"My specialty."

The kitchen was organized with surgical precision, with none of the messy jumbles that Anya recalled from the few other bachelor pads she'd visited over the years. As they cooked side by side, they kept the conversation light, instinctively delaying the emotional topics that thrummed beneath the surface.

Jack reported that the procedure had gone smoothly without providing details. And Anya explained that she'd texted Karen, who'd assured her the household could assemble dinner from the leftovers cramming the fridge.

"Cooking for everybody was a big job. You were astonishing," she told Jack as she sliced tomatoes.

"I've enjoyed it."

Now that she'd raised the topic, Anya braced for him to mention the reason for his cooking. She could hardly refuse him custody of the baby after all this. That meant she'd have to leave Safe Harbor, and him, and her friends, unless she planned to be intimately involved in raising her child. At the prospect, the light seemed to drain from the room. What a bleak prospect: losing this family of friends and especially Jack. How was she going to bear that? Thinking about a future without him was much too painful.

"Did you buy a plastic spider?"

"What?" The question jerked Anya back to the moment.

"For Rod's bed."

Grateful for the interruption, she arrayed the tomatoes around the salad bowl. "On further reflection, it struck me as childish."

"We're talking about my uncle here," Jack teased. "I have my own score to settle with that rogue. Although maybe driving my mom is punishment enough."

"The Friday night traffic coming back from LAX must be awful." She hoped Rod wouldn't arrive until after their meal.

"He called to say he'll eat dinner in L.A. to miss the worst of it." Jack gazed down at the baking dish. "I'm supposed to marinate the fish in lime juice for a couple of hours. But it should taste fantastic anyway. Too bad I don't have Myrna's number so I can ask her."

"Myrna?"

"Fellow med student." With a half smile, he added, "I assure you, she's happily married and not at all interested in me."

"Doesn't matter. If this salmon is as good as you say, I can forgive you anything."

And it was. The fish melted in Anya's mouth. With crusty French bread and salad, the meal proved memorable. Jack served it on his best china, a flowered set that he confirmed had once belonged to his aunt.

Anya nearly blurted that they had to give up the baby because she couldn't bear to move away from him. Only she kept picturing Junior-ette as she'd appeared on the sonograph screen, tumbling happily in the utter safety of...

Of me. Her mom.

"I could use your help." Jack set down his fork, and Anya realized that she wasn't the only one in anguish.

Yanked from her reverie, she took a deep breath. "You want to talk about it now?"

"You heard what my mother said." A muscle worked in Jack's jaw. "She never wanted me."

"She didn't say that, exactly."

"She might as well have." He scowled. "My whole childhood, I blamed myself for her absence. I was too much trouble, too hard to take care of. Now I find out I never had a chance."

"She does care about you, on some level," Anya noted. "Why else did she come today?"

"Because Rod shamed her into it." Bitterness darkened his words. "When I was a kid, she used to blow into town with an armload of presents, charming everyone. I adored her and always thought someday we'd be close. Now I know we never will."

"What she said today hurt you." Overwhelming as Anya's family could be, she'd never had reason to doubt their love.

"I'm not just hurt, I'm angry." His hands clenched into fists. "I've been a damn fool for clinging to her all these years when she barely makes a show of doing the right thing. Her only reaction to the ultrasound was to wonder if the baby was a boy after all. And that sculpture she brought—how could any sane person consider putting it in a crib?"

From her seat around the corner of the table, Anya cupped one of his fists with her hand. "I think she was genuinely trying to behave the way she should. But her instincts were all wrong."

"What do you mean?"

She wasn't sure how she understood this, but it was the only way her impressions of Mamie made sense. "Some people are tone deaf or color blind. And others have a hard time sensing emotions and gauging reactions. It's like she had to rehearse, and she kept watching us for clues about how she should act."

"She had to fake being a grandmother?" Jack's forehead furrowed.

"Something like that," Anya said. "I'm not excusing her because it's unfair that you had to grow up the way you did. I'm guessing your grandparents weren't real champs in the hugs and kisses department either."

"You're right about that." His wrist turned and his hand clasped hers. "How could she *not* experience how miraculous it was to see the baby?"

"How can some people bliss out on a symphony that others find boring?" Anya mused. "There are women who just don't have the maternal instinct, no matter how hard they try to fit into others' expectations."

He went very still. "Are you talking about yourself and our baby?"

Tell the truth, Anya. "No." Tears filled her eyes. "No, she is the most wonderful thing I've ever seen."

Warmth and tenderness blazed as he lifted her hand and kissed it. "For me, too."

Today they'd shared the most intimate connection of Anya's life, even more than when they'd conceived the baby. And she longed to be closer still.

When Jack pulled her up into a hug, she tossed her napkin on the table and tilted her face for a kiss. A long, loving kiss that blossomed through her entire body.

This time, as they made their way to his bedroom, she didn't pretend it was a momentary indulgence or anything less than the chance to claim Jack as she'd been yearning to do all along.

And never mind the consequences.

Chapter Sixteen

To Jack, Anya had always been beautiful. Tonight, in the room that too often echoed with solitude, she was radiant.

Touching her aroused him at every level. She held their baby inside this exquisite, velvety body; in her parted lips and questioning gaze he read an openness he'd never sensed in her before. And she understood him, understood his life, had just solved a fundamental mystery and identified an issue he hadn't even grasped until today.

Treasuring her sweet natural scent, he eased off her shirt and jeans. No need for words; she never seemed to have much use for them, and for once, neither did he. Brushing her hair back from her heart-shaped face, he trailed kisses across her full mouth and ran his thumbs down her swelling breasts.

Her eager groan hardened him. When she pulled down his jeans, Jack aided her eagerly. Then he collected her onto his lap, sitting on the edge of the bed, drawing her hips down against his hardness and entering her slowly.

As they merged, he gasped from the intensity. The self-protective instincts he'd honed over a lifetime dissolved. Anya of the silent watchfulness, Anya of distances, Anya of sudden, unpredictable moods—he loved her. Wildly, despite the risk, despite the way she'd always retreated when he needed her. Now they were one.

Jack shifted his hips, and Anya eased up and down along his shaft, her dark hair screening them with a private cloud.

What a joy to run his palms down her back and trace the swell of her derriere.

Ecstasy seized him. After a brief, vain struggle to resist, he let the thrill take him. He luxuriated in Anya's moaning as they veered fast, faster, into a zone of brilliant light. Colors exploded; heat flooded him.

After an eon of pleasure, Jack wrapped his arms around Anya. "Let's stay here forever."

She laughed softly and rested her cheek against his neck. "Okay."

"Or we could wait until we catch a second wind."

"Okay."

A chuckle welled up in him. "You're agreeable tonight."

Her palm caressed his cheek, rough with a day's growth of beard. "Don't take this personally, but you're the sexiest man I've ever met."

"Why can't I take it personally?"

"It might go to your head," she whispered in his ear and rubbed her soft core against him.

"And that's a problem?" He could scarcely breathe as she reawakened his senses.

"The other nurses already fall at your feet."

"Who cares about them?" he answered, struggling to concentrate on what he was saying. But it was a lost cause because the rest of him had become supercharged.

"That was fast," Anya murmured.

"Let's not waste it." He lifted her until she slid onto him again. Then Jack rolled Anya onto the sheets. When her legs wrapped around him, he lost himself in her. The sensation of belonging was so intense, it filled him again and again, just as his body filled hers.

His climax came like the roll of a heated ocean, wave after wave beneath a fiery, liquid sky. No horizon, no limits, only a glorious shared blaze.

In an aftermath like a summer sunset, Jack held Anya among the tangled sheets. "I love you." He let the words linger for only a second before he said, "Did I mention that I love you?"

"Twice."

"As many times as we made love," he teased.

She nuzzled him without speaking. She hadn't responded that she loved him, too, but then, Anya wasn't the type to blurt something like that out on impulse.

While she was thinking it over, Jack decided to go for broke. "Marry me," he said.

GROWING UP, Anya had instinctively censored her own wishes and interests, her mind echoing with her father's imagined disapproval. So her dream—and increasingly urgent need—had become to truly be herself, independent and free of intrusive criticism and judgment.

Now, her love for Jack nearly smothered that need. Oh, how she yearned to shout "Yes!" and transform into the bride doll atop the wedding cake. To lie beside him every night, to share the precious moments as their baby grew, to talk earnestly and to sit silently, always and forever.

A fine fantasy. Reality had a nasty way of intruding, though.

And now she had to choose: take what her heart wanted or insist on what her soul demanded. How could she give Jack up, especially now that he'd trusted her with his future? After the emotional desertion Jack had suffered from his mother, after the betrayal he'd seen devastate his uncle, he was still willing to reach out to her.

"Anya?" Jack propped himself on one elbow. Half covered by a sheet, the man was spectacular. Rather than the bulked-up build of a jock, he had a solid, well-muscled strength coupled with the delicate skills of a surgeon.

She had to stop thinking such things. Or did she?

"I love you, too." Anya took a shaky breath.

A relieved smile curved his mouth. "Was that so difficult?"

"Huh."

"I guess that's a yes." His forefinger tapped the tip of her nose. "Now say yes to the other part."

Marry me. "I can't," she said miserably.

His muscles stiffened. "Can't or won't?"

"Marriage is too big a step." Did they have to go that far, involving the rest of the world in their private business? Maybe they could meet in the middle. "I have an alternate proposal."

Skepticism warred with hope in his expression. "Shoot."

"Let's live together." That wasn't the same, Anya knew, but she forged on. "Plenty of people do." And if they weren't married, he'd have no right to assume he owned her. Not that Jack acted bossy now, but marriage changed people. A nurse she'd worked with in Denver had been deliriously happy after her honeymoon, only to be stunned at how demanding her bridegroom soon became about her cooking, her spending habits and her occasional girls' nights out.

"Live together for how long?" Jack asked warily.

She hadn't considered that. "To raise the baby."

"Twenty years?" His tone was dubious.

"That sounds about right."

"What if we decide to have a second child?"

Anya clapped her hands against the sides of her head. "Honestly, Jack!"

"It wasn't a joke. You're refusing to commit to me or to a family," he accused.

"I refuse to be boxed into a role," she countered. "Taken for granted. Assigned to childcare for the duration."

Sitting up against the headboard, Jack blew out a frustrated breath, then folded his arms. Was he angry? She couldn't tell.

"I *am* willing to make a commitment." Anya sat up, too. "Only not the formal, public kind. I love you, Jack. I'll never love anybody else." She was growing teary again, darn it. "But you're a powerful guy, the lord of the operating room. You might get full of yourself. Don't argue. You'll start taking for granted that you're my boss at home, too. And I can't bear that."

He studied her. "Marriage scares you."

"You could say that." She bit her lip before adding, "Does it have to be all or nothing?"

"You know my family history."

Yes, she did. And he knew hers. "Marriage is no guarantee of permanence."

"Hmm." The cryptic response was maddening. *Like the cryptic responses I usually make.*

"I'll communicate better, I promise," she volunteered.

He still didn't answer. Anya leaned back. He'd allowed her to think things over, and she had to do the same.

A BEAUTIFUL ANYA strolling down the aisle in a white dress, the moment when he slid the ring onto her finger, the celebration with their friends and family—all recorded to enjoy when they were old. Such things mattered. Most of all, Jack craved the vow to always be there for each other. How could he accept anything less?

Glancing at her sweet little face—knowing how stubborn she could be, but also how funny and warm—his heart squeezed. He loved her. She loved him, too. Anya had said so straight out, and she never babbled easy words.

It all boiled down to trust, Jack reflected. And whether this was a risk worth taking.

Would she stick with him? If they faced serious medical issues or a financial crisis, would the absence of marriage vows make a difference? He suspected it might. But he understood, too, what a wedding represented to Anya.

They each had to trust the other. In the meantime, they both had to give a little, too. "Okay," he said.

Her eyes widened. "Seriously?"

"On one condition."

Now *her* arms folded, making them a matched set. "What's that?"

"Relationships hit rough patches—it's inevitable," Jack pointed out. "I have to be sure you won't run for the hills when that happens."

"I promise," she said.

"Prove it."

She looked startled. "How?"

"Face up to your family." As her jaw dropped, he added, "I'll go with you, if you want."

She averted her gaze. "It's next weekend."

"So?" He'd clear his schedule. If any of his patients couldn't wait, Zack Sargent owed him a favor, and he suspected Owen Tartikoff would fill in, too, when he heard the reason.

"They'll all be there—my parents, my siblings, my cousins," Anya said. "We should wait for a better occasion."

"Not good enough." He hated to push her. If she balked, they'd be back to square one. But their confused instincts—his to mistrust, hers to duck tough issues—were the greatest enemy to their future. "You're stronger than you think, Anya, but you have to believe that, or every time we argue, I'll wonder if I'm going to come home to an empty house."

"I wouldn't do that!"

"Are you sure?"

She swallowed. "Jack…"

He touched her hair, wondering what he'd do if she refused. "Hmm?"

She appeared to be thinking hard. "I'm not ready to answer you."

"As you mentioned, the gathering's next weekend, and I'll have to cancel appointments," he reminded her.

"Give me twenty-four hours," she said.

They were both getting a lot of practice at compromising, Jack mused. "Done."

Her smile flashed, lighting up the room. Then she snuggled closer, and he was grateful for this truce, however long it lasted.

ANYA HAD LEFT by the time Rod came home. Jack refrained from mentioning her visit, although his uncle couldn't miss the smell of his cooking and probably picked up other clues. The man was like a bloodhound.

Jack had no tolerance for his uncle's prodding. His nerves were strung taut because his future was being decided inside Anya's unpredictable brain.

Rod stuck a chunk of French bread into the toaster oven. "I've missed having leftovers."

"I thought you ate dinner." Jack loitered in the kitchen doorway.

"I grabbed a quick burger." His uncle finger combed his hair.

"At the airport?"

"Nearby," Rod explained. "Mamie didn't want me to park, so I dropped her and her luggage at the curb. I presume she got off okay."

"I'm sure she's fine. She's a seasoned traveler." Jack never worried about his mother.

Rod laced his fingers on the table. "I owe you an apology."

"For inviting her?"

He gave an embarrassed nod. "I figured this would be a watershed moment for my sister. Instead, she kept chattering about how great you looked, how nice Anya is and the marvels of modern technology. The woman saw her first grandchild in action and she didn't have a word to say about it. Oh, except for asking what I thought about naming her Lenore."

Jack chuckled. "What did you say?"

"I said that's your and Anya's decision." Rod regarded him with a puzzled frown. "You don't seem upset."

"About what?" Mamie was the last thing on Jack's mind.

"She owes you something," his uncle said. "An apology for dumping you on our parents like a pet poodle. Now that it's her turn to be a grandmother, she ought to act like one."

"And you even missed the best part," Jack replied. "She told Anya she scarcely remembers being pregnant with me, that my father was much more excited about it than she was."

Rod smacked his forehead. "Jack, I'm sorry."

"Since you're the only relative I can rely on, I forgive you."

A groan greeted this response. "You couldn't rely on me this time. I let you down. I overestimated my sister."

Jack shrugged. "Just because a person becomes a biological parent doesn't mean she has nurturing instincts." He recalled Anya's insight. "Just as some people are tone deaf or color blind, others can't handle intimacy."

The toaster bell rang. Rod plucked out the hot bread. "That's borderline profound. Is this Anya's influence?"

"Yes."

"I underestimated your girlfriend. On average, I came out even." His uncle spread butter thickly. "Mind fetching that jar of preserves you hide in the lettuce bin?"

"I didn't think you ever opened the lettuce bin."

"Only when I'm searching for where you hide the preserves," Rod said.

Yielding to the inevitable, Jack went to oblige.

WHEN ANYA GOT home, she found her housemates in the den, sharing a bottle of sparkling apple juice. If they noticed her tangled hair—she'd misplaced the brush she usually kept in her purse—they had the tact not to comment.

"Big day!" Melissa announced. "I don't suppose Jack said anything to you about it."

Said anything about what? So much had happened that Anya couldn't sort through it all. "Jack doesn't discuss his patients with me, if that's what you mean."

"Melissa was implanted," Karen said. "With three embryos."

"Congratulations." Anya remembered the earlier dinner-table discussion. "Isn't Zack Sargent your doctor?"

"Stricken with a sudden illness." Lucky angled back the recliner, which he was hogging, as usual. "Stomach flu, I hear."

Was there any gossip too minor to escape his radar? Anya wondered.

"I'm on pins and needles!" Ordinarily the calmest mem-

ber of the household, Melissa fidgeted on the sofa. "I have
to wait another week before I can take a pregnancy test."

"I'm thinking positive. We'll have a house full of babies."
Karen grinned at the prospect.

Not if I move in with Jack. Anya hadn't considered how
that would affect her housemates or Rod. She certainly didn't
intend to share a small apartment with *him*. Well, she'd deal
with those issues later.

"It's very unlikely the embryos will all attach," Melissa
reminded Karen.

"I'm sure at least one will," her friend said. "And there'll
be two infants, anyway."

"I thought Anya was giving hers up," Lucky said.

"I didn't mean…" Karen halted guiltily. She must have
found out about Zora, and hadn't meant to let it slip.

"Who else is pregnant?" Lucky demanded, and immediately answered his own question. "There's only two possibilities, and if it were you, you'd be crowing from the rooftop."

Sitting at the table apart from the others, Zora stared
moodily into her glass of juice. "Just shut up about it."

"Who's the dad?" He broke off as the other women glared
at him. "Yeah, I know, none of my business. Oh, please tell
me it wasn't break-up sex."

Melissa steered the conversation away from Zora. "I'd be
due in December," she said. "Anya, you mentioned September, and, Zora—"

"November," Zora muttered.

"If it's a multiple birth, mine are likely to come early," Melissa said. "In any event, it would be nice to set up a nursery.
Lucky, you might have to move out." She chuckled.

"First positive thing I've heard all day." Zora barely
cracked a smile, though. Something must have upset her,
beyond the revelation about her pregnancy.

"I think I'll go upstairs." Anya didn't have to fake a yawn.
"Zora, you look tired, too."

Her friend mirrored her yawn. "Yeah, I'll go up, too."

On the second floor, Anya said, "My room."

But Zora turned away. "I need to sleep."

"It's way too early." Anya caught her arm. "Come on. Don't keep whatever it is bottled up inside."

A sigh. "I suppose not."

In Anya's room, they settled on the window seat. Through the glass, she noted the darkening sky over the estuary, with stars appearing between the deep-blue-on-blue clouds. During her two months in this house, she'd grown to love this view.

"Did you tell Andrew about the baby?" Anya prodded.

"No." Zora stared blearily at her hands. "I never got the chance. He..." She broke off.

"What did he do?"

"He got married in Las Vegas last weekend," she choked out. "Betsy told me today. She waited till the end of the day because she knew how upset I'd be."

"Did you mention that she's going to be a grandmother?" Anya asked.

Zora shook her head.

"You *are* going to tell him about the baby, right?" Before her friend could answer, Anya added, "It's not like Betsy won't notice you're pregnant."

"Her first loyalty is to her son, not me," Zora said miserably. "Oh, I don't want to talk about this anymore. What about *your* day?" Gray eyes bored into hers. "What happened at the ultrasound? Did you meet Jack's mother? And what were you doing for the past few hours?"

"It's complicated."

"Start anywhere."

Anya sketched the day's events. In retrospect, Mamie had been rather funny, except for her unhappy effect on Jack. As for the salmon dinner, she hoped he'd fix it again for her, soon. And the rest...she was still figuring that out. "If we move in together, his cooking will be a big plus." Along with a lot of other things.

"You guys are together." Zora swallowed. "I should be glad for you. I *am* glad for you."

"I'll still be here for you." Anya clasped her friend's hands. "And I haven't agreed to go to Colorado. Seriously, this whole business is kind of crazy. I'm not a mom. Just because my body betrayed me…"

"Are you out of your mind?" Zora's thin face became more animated than it had been all evening. "You must be the stupidest person I ever met."

Anya dropped her hands and scooted back a few inches, which was all the space she had. "Thanks a lot."

"Shut up and listen." Zora drew herself up. Even sitting down, she was taller than Zora. "That man's in love with you. And you adore him, although the idea scares you half to death."

"All the way to death." Quickly Anya corrected, "It isn't love that scares me. It's marriage."

"It's relationships, with or without a license," her friend insisted. "If I had a guy like Jack begging to marry me, I'd jump at the chance."

"There are strings attached," Anya said. "If I go to Colorado, it'll be like Christmas all over again. My whole family trying to reorganize my life, laying guilt trips on me."

"And if you don't go?" Zora pressed.

Anya's gaze fell on the end table, where an empty space reminded her of the African violet that had once lived there. "I can't keep a plant alive.… I'm afraid I'll be like his mother, with all the wrong instincts." Now that she'd opened up, more truths spilled out. "Sometimes I hated my little sisters. I'd never have harmed them, but the weight of the responsibility was horrible. Every day, diapers and more diapers. Waking up all night, hearing their cries, and never being sure what was wrong or if I could help—I just wanted to run as far and as fast as I could."

"What your parents did was unfair." Zora seemed to have gained strength as she listened. "You shouldn't have had to shoulder so much of their responsibilities. But, Anya, you're only having one baby, not three. Plus most mothers get cranky with their kids once in a while. And you'll have Jack to help."

"I wish he wasn't insisting I go to my grandmother's birthday party. They plan to stick me with supervising the kids without even asking me if that's okay." She'd hardly have a free minute to spend with her grandma or anyone else.

"Jack's right. You have to stop seeing yourself as this helpless teenager backed against a wall by your big bossy family," came the response.

"If I refuse, it'll be a nonstop battle."

"You're an adult and you're having a baby—just stand up to them," Zora reproved. "Besides, you'll have Jack on your side. Do you have any idea how lucky you are? If Andrew were a tenth the man that Jack is, I'd be in heaven."

Tears sparkled against Zora's cheeks. She'd spoken from the heart. Most people would agree with her, too, including Jack.

But Zora and Jack had missed the point. *And so have I.*

With that realization, Anya suddenly knew what she had to do.

Chapter Seventeen

Having once attended a medical conference in Denver, Jack wasn't daunted by its large airport, and he easily navigated the hour-long drive to Anya's hometown using the computer system in their rental car. But as they left the main route and bumped along a narrow road on the final leg of their journey, he was keenly aware that they were traveling not only into a different landscape but also into the past. *Her* past.

For him, this high grassland with its mountainous backdrop brought no memories, merely a faint headache due to the altitude, over a mile above sea level. He turned on the car's heater against the cold, crisp late afternoon air—another change from Southern California. Having been warned that April might bring almost anything, he was grateful that the forecast contained no snowstorms.

What did all this signify to Anya? It was impossible to discern from her stone-wall expression.

A week ago, she'd informed him of her decision. "I need to find out exactly what I want from my life," Anya had told him. "Do I want my family involved? Do I want to be a mother? I love you, but people who love each other can't always live together. What I realized is that the person I most need to confront is myself."

She'd sent a message to her sister to say they'd be arriving today, Saturday. Since then, Anya hadn't mentioned her family.

Although Jack found her announcement unsettling, he

knew it was important that she face her issues and reach a conclusion. Once she resolved this, there should be no more question of her disappearing when things got tough.

By tomorrow night, he'd have his answer. He hoped it would be one that made them both happy.

"You're giving her too much power," Rod had argued when he heard about their bargain.

Jack had disagreed. "I'm keeping our daughter, regardless of whether Anya chooses to stay in the picture. But I love her, and we can't build a future unless she's ready to commit whole-heartedly. Don't forget that it was me who insisted on this trip."

"You may regret it," his uncle had muttered over their take-out fried chicken dinner. Since Jack had finished his cooking stint, he'd indulged in fast food most evenings. But while he enjoyed the freedom from a rigid schedule, he missed the give-and-take around the dinner table. Mostly, he missed Anya.

"She's taking the bull by the horns," he'd told Rod. "Considering her usual operating method, this is an improvement."

"Remains to be seen," Rod had said, but he'd kept his peace after that.

Anya's hometown, when they reached it, had an Old West design, including the weathered wooden facade of the tack and feed store Anya pointed out, which her parents owned. "If you want any cowboy boots or a hat, you can buy that there," she said.

"I wonder how Rod would look in a Stetson."

"Weird."

"In other words, his normal self," Jack joked.

"He should stick with fedoras," she mused. "They've grown on me."

Past the commercial district, the car rolled onto a road bordered by homes set far back on lots large enough to accommodate horse corrals. Following Anya's directions, Jack turned left at the next intersection.

He felt a quiver of unease. They'd brought sleeping bags,

since the only motel in the area was fully booked. Anya had explained that guests would camp out where they could, mostly in her parents' and grandmother's houses. It was the "mostly" that bothered him. Sleeping in a chicken coop or barn wasn't his idea of fun.

It's only for one night, so no complaints. He'd hate to come across as a spoiled city boy.

Another turn, and he spotted the address on the mailbox. A sprawling ranch house was half-hidden behind a cluster of RVs parked along a wide driveway. "Looks like most of the gang's here already."

Anya gripped the armrest. "They're probably out back, barbecuing."

Rolling down a window, he inhaled the delicious scent of grilling. "Hope there's enough for us."

"I should have brought a dish. I don't know why I didn't think of it." Anxiety laced her words.

"How exactly would you have carried a casserole through airport security?" He piloted the compact car between the larger vehicles. "Surely they don't expect that."

"I have no idea what they expect," Anya admitted. "I haven't been reading their texts or any other messages."

Jack had believed the point of this exercise was to break her habit of avoidance. She obviously saw that in relative terms. Or rather, in terms that excluded her relatives. "I'll bet they loved that."

"I guess we'll find out."

He parked close to the house on a patch of gravel. "You did mention you were bringing me, right?"

"I said me and a guest."

"That's it?" Jack groaned aloud. "Anya!"

She cupped her hand over his on the car seat. "I'm sorry. I'm already stressing out. If I'd had to argue with Ruth ten times a day, I'd be a wreck."

He had to admit, he understood the logic of her approach. Nevertheless, "This is a good way to drive other people crazy."

"I won't do that to you." She tightened her grip on his hand. "I promise, Jack. The difference is that you listen to me, and they don't."

"Glad to hear there's a difference."

She loosened her grip. "Might as well get this over with. Leave the suitcases."

"You think we might be heading back to Denver tonight?"

"It's a possibility," she told him, and got out of the car.

APPREHENSION FILLED ANYA. For heaven's sake, this was only her family, yet the arguments from last Christmas rang in her memory. She was letting everyone down, her father had said. She ought to grow up and stop playing truant, Ruth had snapped. Even Grandma hadn't showed her usual enthusiasm for Anya's nursing career.

"I counted on you to be around in my old age," she'd said, and turned to hug one of her great grandchildren before Anya could reply.

Her younger sisters had been so busy texting their friends and sharing inside jokes about college that Anya hadn't really had a conversation with any of them. In retrospect, she supposed they'd been deliberately ducking the quarrels. *Following my example.*

She squared her shoulders and rang the bell. That felt odd, since she'd grown up in this house, but in many respects, she was a stranger.

As was the little girl who opened the door. About four, she had an open, freckled face. "Hi," she announced. "Which one are you?"

Behind her trailed other youngsters, including a familiar two-year-old with dark blond hair. "Kiki," Anya said. "Remember me?"

"Aunt Anya!" The tot raced into Anya's arms as she and Jack entered the hall.

"I'm Belle," said the girl who'd opened the door, and Anya finally placed her as the daughter of her older brother Benjie. Or possibly Bart. Since they were identical twins who'd each had two children, it was hard to keep track of which was which.

The floor creaked beneath an onrush of feet, and Anya looked up to see a swarm of people. Ruth stood out, appearing reserved but relieved, too. The triplets were giggling—honestly, at twenty-one, the girls should be past that—and there were Bart and Benjie and a host of cousins and husbands and wives. They parted before Anya's father, his leathered face a study in mixed emotions.

"I was afraid we'd chased you away for good," he said, then halted as he took in her maternity top. "What's this? Or perhaps I should say, who's this?" His gaze moved to the man at her side.

"Dad, this is Jack Ryder." Anya let the circumstances speak for themselves.

Her father thrust out his hand. "Hello. I'm Raymond Meeks, Anya's dad."

"It's an honor to meet you, sir." Jack shook his hand firmly.

In the introductions that followed, Anya sensed the unasked questions—about her pregnancy, her relationship to Jack, her decision to attend. She let them go unanswered, for now. Mostly, she appreciated the outpouring of welcome.

"Everybody's been on my case since they found out I didn't get your consent about the child care," Ruth admitted as they made their way through the house to the large rear deck, where heat lamps had been turned on to take the edge off the chill. "I guess it was a heavy load to dump on one person."

"How did you decide to handle it?" Anya ventured, her defenses ready to spring up if Ruth took that as an opening.

"We hired a couple of teenagers," her sister said. "They're playing games in the den." Fixing her gaze on Kiki, she commanded, "Off you go."

After a last dazzling smile at her aunt Anya, the toddler obeyed. "What a doll." Although she'd have liked to cuddle her niece longer, Anya was pleased about the sitters. She also sympathized with her sister's advanced state of pregnancy.

"Organizing all this must have been hard for you, especially now. I forgot—when are you due?"

"Next month," Ruth said. "And you?"

"September."

"Are you and Jack…"

Anya didn't hear the rest of the question, because she'd just spotted her mother sitting by the food-laden table. Sitting in a regular chair, from which Molly arose with only a trace of stiffness. "Mom! When did this happen?"

Her mother beamed. "Oh, I still use the wheelchair sometimes, but my new medication is working wonders. Goodness, look at you!"

Another round of hugs followed. Anya was full of questions, which Molly answered gladly. The doctor had started her on a new type of drug called biologics, combined with an older drug. The results had exceeded expectations.

Since Jack was handling the large crowd smoothly, shaking hands and introducing himself, Anya turned her attention to the older woman waiting quietly at the side of the deck. Grandma Rachel's stern expression reawakened Anya's doubts.

You came here to face up to your family. Don't chicken out.

She stooped to embrace her grandmother. "Happy birthday."

When they separated, tears sparkled on Grandma's lashes. "I was afraid you'd stay in California."

"I nearly did," Anya admitted. "I posted my pictures in the family album, though." In lieu of gifts, her grandmother had requested that everyone upload favorite pictures on a website for all to enjoy. One of the cousins had volunteered to incorporate them into a scrapbook later.

"We laid quite a guilt trip on you at Christmas." With a nod at Jack, currently surrounded by Anya's brothers and cousins, Grandma asked, "Who's your young man?"

Anya took a seat beside her. "Jack."

"That's it? He only has a first name?"

"Dr. Jack Ryder," she said.

"A doctor. That's nice." Grandma tapped Anya's left hand. "No ring?"

"He asked," she replied. "I'm deciding."

Catching their glances, Jack approached. "This must be the birthday girl." When he flashed his killer smile, Grandma beamed.

Anya introduced them, and they shook hands, Jack careful not to squeeze the old woman's frail bones. "You're quite the catch," her grandmother said, to Anya's embarrassment.

"So is your granddaughter," he answered.

Grandma slanted an admiring gaze at him. "You're a smart young man."

"And a lucky one."

Inside Anya, anxieties melted. While she didn't entirely trust this sense of emotional safety around her relatives, it was lovely for however long it lasted.

Ruth's husband, Bryce, called out that he'd grilled the last of the hamburgers, and everyone gathered for a blessing over the food. Once Anya's dad finished giving thanks, they lined up to fill their plates. The children and their sitters went first, then retreated to the den. The adults filed into the dining room, where a series of tables covered with cloths extended into the living room.

Anya was wedged between Jack and her younger sister Sarah. She listened with interest as Jack chatted with Bryce about the feed store, where her brother-in-law was assistant manager and the heir apparent when their father retired in a few years. Then Anya turned to Sarah, eager to learn more about the girls' upcoming graduation.

All three triplets were earning RN degrees at the University of Colorado. Until now, Anya had figured that was Grandma's influence.

But Sarah said, "We went into nursing to be like you. It's so exciting that you're a scrub nurse. Do you and Jack operate together?"

"He operates. I assist." In response to more questions,

Anya filled in the blanks. "He earned his M.D. and did his residency in obstetrics at Vanderbilt."

"How'd he end up in Safe Harbor?"

"It's my hometown," Jack said from her other side.

Anya couldn't resist bragging a little. "He was selected for a surgical fellowship by the head of our fertility program, Dr. Owen Tartikoff."

"Wow!" Sarah ruffled her short hair, a few shades lighter than Anya's. Her coloring was darker than that of the other two triplets, who were identical. Sarah, born at the same time but conceived from a different egg, was their fraternal sister. "That's impressive."

"Some people think so," Jack responded lightly. "But Anya keeps me humble."

"She's amazing, isn't she?" Sarah said. "She's my role model."

Across the table, Ruth dropped her fork with a clatter. *Oh, here it comes.* Anya set down a forkful of potato salad.

Blithely, Sandi—another of the triplets—asked, "Why did you move so far away, Anya? There's a world-class hospital in Denver."

"So she could have fun, fun, fun in California." Ruth's statement dripped with resentment.

"Hon…" The endearment from Bryce carried a warning note. Bryce was a good man, although his long hours left her sister with much of the hard work raising their four—soon to be five—children, as well as tending their vegetable garden, chickens and dairy goat.

"I'd like to have fun, fun, fun in California," Sarah said wistfully.

"Sounds good to me," said the third triplet, Andi.

Since Ruth appeared about to ignite, Anya hurried to correct their impression. "That's not why I left. I did it so I could be myself."

From the head of the table, her father joined the conversation. "You could be yourself right here just fine."

"Seriously?" After years of trying to be diplomatic, Anya

had had enough. "I could hardly hear myself think. Everyone had expectations of me. Sometimes they fit, like when Grandma encouraged me to become a nurse. Other times, they were simply slots for me to fill."

"We all have obligations," Ruth snapped. "You ran out on yours."

Around them, the conversation dimmed. Under the table, Jack's hand cradled hers. Having him on her side allowed her to catch her breath and weigh her response.

In the past, she'd have retreated into angry silence, or snapped that it wasn't her fault Ruth had chosen to marry at nineteen, drop out of college and bear one child after another. Instead, she replied calmly, "I met my obligations and then some."

"You have to be kidding!" Ruth flared.

Their mother spoke up then with more force than she'd mustered in years. "Anya spent her high school and college years looking after me and the triplets. They should have been my responsibility, but I could barely take care of myself. She worked incredibly hard."

Ruth cleared her throat. "I don't remember it that way."

"You were married and out of the house by then, so you didn't see it."

"I was right here," Anya's father joined in. "It didn't seem to me she had it so tough."

Molly turned to her husband. "Ray, you were working from dawn to dusk at the store. So you may not have noticed that she took over the grocery shopping, the cleaning, even scheduling my doctor visits, all while attending college and commuting an hour each way."

"The younger girls pitched in," he said stubbornly.

"Yes, the triplets helped with meals, but they didn't take over many of the other chores until after Anya left. We also hired a cleaning service and our two wonderful daughters-in-law volunteered to drive me to appointments. Anya used to do all of that herself."

Anya blinked back tears. If she hadn't been afraid of shaking the table and everyone's dinners, she'd have run around to embrace her mom. "I knew that you needed me, Mom. But once the girls were old enough to handle things, I was ready to leave."

Her father cleared his throat. "I guess I was a little hard on you."

Anya wasn't going to let him off so easily. "A little? All you noticed were my screwups."

"I wasn't that bad, was I?"

"You were always picking on her," Benjie said. "Honestly, Dad, I even told you a few times to lay off."

He had? No one had mentioned that to Anya.

"I'd forgotten that," their father admitted.

"It was like Anya couldn't do anything right," Bart chimed in. "You were always comparing her to how Ruth used to do things."

That was true, but she hadn't been aware that her brothers had noticed it, too.

"Well, Ruth did a great job," said their father, his forehead wrinkling.

"And moved out the minute I got the chance," Ruth admitted, adding, "Luckily, I fell in love with the right man. Didn't I, Bryce?"

"You did. And other than that, I'm staying out of this conversation," said her husband.

Raymond Meeks's shoulders sagged. "Girls, I'm sorry. Maybe I've been too hard. And, Anya, I was on your case at Christmas because your mom was having trouble adjusting to her new medication, and on some level I blamed you."

"Well, I didn't," Molly said. "Anya, you deserve to lead your own life. I'm proud of you."

"So am I." Her father regarded Anya. "I've been worried about your mom, and a little guilty for being gone a lot. Maybe that's why I magnified every mistake you made. Thank you for everything you've done."

"That goes double for me," her mother said.

A murmur of appreciation ran around the table. A rush

of joy filled Anya. In spite of their missteps and misunder-
standings, her family loved her.

"We've missed you." Sarah touched her shoulder. "You
gave us the best advice about classes and professors."

"And our boyfriends," noted Sandi.

"Those were *my* boyfriends you kept stealing," teased
Andi.

"That's because I'm cuter," said her identical sister.

Everyone chuckled, including Ruth. Anya was glad she
hadn't lashed out or withdrawn, as she would have before
Jack. If she had, this discussion might not have happened.

"Besides, if she hadn't moved to California, she'd never
have met me," Jack commented. "And we wouldn't be having our daughter."

That changed the subject quite effectively, as Jack no doubt
intended. From along the table, questions flew: "You know
what sex it is already?" "What will you name her?"

The answer came instinctively to Anya. "Rachel." She
heard the murmur of approval and saw the sparkle of pleasure on her grandmother's face. Afraid she might have presumed too much, she amended that to, "Rachel Lenore," and
glanced at Jack for confirmation.

"Isn't that a beautiful name?" he said. "It's for both our
grandmothers."

"The best present you could have given me." Grandma
smiled. "And your sister's naming her new boy after your
grandfather, Harold."

Ruth took a breath. "I suppose it's all worked out for the
best."

"Too bad you had to give up your life in high school for
us," Sarah noted, while the other triplets nodded.

Anya waved away the apology. "I only have one regret."

Everyone waited.

"If I'd been able to join the botany club, I might not have
killed the African violet Jack gave me."

Amid a ripple of laughter, a child scampered in to ask
about dessert.

"I almost forgot about the birthday cake!" Benjie's wife leaped to her feet. "I'll light the candles."

"I'll dish out the ice cream," volunteered Bart's wife. "Who wants vanilla and who wants chocolate?"

Others hurried to clear the table, insisting that the older generation and the pregnant women relax. "That feels odd," Ruth admitted, while Sarah carted off her plate.

"I'm glad you hired the sitters," Anya told her.

"Me, too." Ruth's mouth twisted in irony. "Honestly, I wasn't thinking straight. There's no way you could have supervised all those little ones and spent time with the rest of us."

"We're used to believing Anya is a superwoman," her mother said.

"Or just my annoying younger sister." Ruth cringed. "Which I hadn't realized I was doing, until now."

The rest of the family returned, along with all but the youngest children. Someone dimmed the lights, allowing the candles—two large ones spelling out 8-0—to shimmer atop the sheet cake.

As Anya surveyed the beloved group and joined them in singing the birthday song, joy swelled inside her. How lucky she was to be part of this family, and most of all to share this moment with Jack. Yes, she knew she could stand on her own now, but she also realized they were stronger together.

And a lot happier.

THEY SLEPT THAT night on Grandma's foldout couch, with a single sleeping bag spread out beneath them and the other serving as a cover. Exhausted from the long day, plus a touch of jet lag and the effect of altitude, Anya expected to fall asleep instantly.

Instead, her brain replayed her experiences at dinner. Her younger sisters' admiration...Molly's unexpected rise to her defense, showing Anya's father and Ruth how limited their perspective had been...Jack's steady presence, bolstering her confidence. The world had shifted. She could be herself now, wherever she was.

In the dimness of Grandma's living room, she inhaled the scent of lemon oil from the antique armoire. Against the wall, moonlight showed dark rectangles that she remembered were old family photographs of her great grandparents and great-aunts and uncles, of the town in the horse-and-buggy days, of people and places long gone yet still living in their descendants.

Her hand drifted to her abdomen. Rachel Lenore would come here for holidays, discovering her cousins and her roots. What a marvelous sense of connection she would have, just like Anya had.

Beside her, Jack stirred. "Do you still want to live with me?" he murmured.

It seemed an odd question. "Of course."

He heaved a sigh, then rolled away from her.

Had she said something wrong? Puzzled, Anya tried to figure it out. But before she could, sleep stole over her.

Chapter Eighteen

On Sunday, Anya bubbled with high spirits. Although Jack had the nagging suspicion he'd outsmarted himself, he enjoyed seeing her happy and reconciled with her family.

In the morning, children tumbled underfoot until the sitters came, and the noise level rose further as more relatives arrived, including newcomers who hadn't been able to attend last night. Jack took charge of the row of waffle-making equipment, producing piles of deliciously browned waffles while the triplets stirred batches of mix. People ate in shifts, scattered around the house. It was a big jovial party, and by midday, when he and Anya left for the airport, he could identify almost all the adults and quite a few of the tots.

What a great experience—and what a pleasure to relax in the quiet car as they drove to Denver. Anya seemed to share his enjoyment, both with her family and without them. All his life, Jack had longed to be part of a group like this, and the Meekses had exceeded his expectations. Yet he also understood, at the gut level, why Anya craved distance, as well.

He'd insisted on her confronting them, and she'd done so. Now he had to keep his word, even though the prospect of raising their daughter when he and Anya weren't married troubled him. It was too easy for people to throw away a relationship under the pressure of an illness or injury, a financial setback, problems with a child or a temporary divergence in their interests. Despite the high percentage of marriages that broke up, at least the steps leading to a divorce forced the couple to face the seriousness of what they were doing and encouraged them to seek counseling.

Jack yearned for the commitment. Old-fashioned though it might be, he longed to have Anya as his wife and to be introduced as her husband. Their rings would tell the world that they belonged to each other.

But although Anya had resolved some of her issues, she apparently hadn't changed her mind.

The next few days in California, they barely had a chance to talk, let alone decide where or when to move in together. At the hospital, Anya cast Jack the occasional quizzical glance, as if trying to gauge his thoughts. He couldn't reassure her while his mood remained restive.

The following Saturday, her housemates invited him and Rod for dinner. "It's our turn to cook for you," Karen told Jack when she stopped by his table in the cafeteria.

"Need any help?" He missed being the master chef, although not every day.

"We'll be fine. Maybe Rod can pitch in," she said.

"Uh-oh." His uncle's culinary catastrophes were notorious. "I hope you'll put him in charge of arranging pickles and olives on a relish tray."

"That bad, huh?" She grinned.

"Worse."

"Guess I'll pass on suggesting he help cook."

On Saturday, Jack assisted with an overflow in Labor and Delivery, performing two emergency Caesarian sections. Afterward, he had to wait for Rod to pick him up, since his uncle's car was once again on the fritz. They arrived at Karen's house a few minutes past six.

The days were already lengthening, and he spotted flocks of birds circling. He wondered whether they were in the midst of a northward migration or if they'd be nesting here.

"Is it me, or has the smell improved?" his uncle asked as they strolled along the driveway.

Jack inhaled. "I can say with confidence that your smell hasn't improved."

"It should have. I borrowed *your* deodorant."

"Now I know what to buy you for Christmas."

When they reached the porch, Melissa swung open the door, abandoning her usual reserve. "I'm pregnant!"

"Congratulations." Jack shook her hand. "This is terrific news." He was glad he'd been able to contribute to this joyful result.

"*That's* how you congratulate her?" Rod gave the woman a hug. "That's the proper response."

"As one of her physicians, I prefer to behave like a professional."

"Since when did you start sending out your shirts to be stuffed?" his uncle retorted.

Jack ignored the gibe.

"I can't wait to find out how many babies I'm carrying." Melissa ushered them inside. "Three more weeks and we can do an ultrasound, right?"

"Correct," Jack said. A sonogram was usually performed five weeks after an embryo transfer, both to determine how many had implanted and to ensure the pregnancy was progressing normally. Of course, she was Zack Sargent's patient, so Sargent would be supervising her care from now on, rather than Jack.

Inside, Karen was setting out roast chicken, potatoes, steamed vegetables and a small brownish loaf that she explained was a vegetarian turkey substitute called tofurkey. Anya appeared with a bowl of salad.

Hurrying to her side, Jack said in a low voice, "Sorry I couldn't come early. I was hoping to talk privately."

She blinked. "Oh. About that….." She frowned at Lucky, who hovered nearby. Jack could almost have sworn the man's ears were quivering. "Later, okay?"

Reluctantly, Jack nodded.

As they took seats at the table, he noticed that Zora didn't seem to share the general high spirits. Anya had mentioned during the trip that her friend was pregnant by her ex-husband, who'd just remarried. What a jerk.

From a sideboard, Karen fetched wineglasses. "Let's toast our houseful of pregnancies."

Lucky appeared from the kitchen with a bottle of grape juice. "Good thing I have my quarters downstairs," he said as he poured. "Gives me a break from the supercharged estrogen level."

"I doubt you're in any danger from our hormones," Melissa said. "Is he, Jack?"

"Cole Rattigan is the expert about male hormone levels," he said. "But I doubt it."

They raised their glasses of juice. "May all the pregnancies in this household be safe and healthy," Karen said. "May the babies grow up secure and loved."

"Hear, hear!" Rod glugged down his juice in a single show-off gulp. He promptly choked, spluttering and coughing while Karen pounded him on the back.

"Serves you right," Lucky said.

"That's mean." Zora frowned at him.

"Was it?" The male nurse shrugged. "Sorry, Rod."

Jack's uncle started to answer, wheezed painfully and sipped water. He recovered well enough, though, to take second helpings of the food.

The discussion moved from Melissa's big news to the latest recommendations for maternal nutrition, and then to the name Anya and Jack had chosen for their daughter. Everyone agreed that honoring both grandmothers was inspired.

"Speaking of daughters." Rod cleared his throat. "Tiffany emailed me today—they'll be spending part of the summer here."

"Are they staying with their grandmother?" Karen asked.

He grimaced. "No such luck. Their mother will be riding herd on them at the beach cottage. Vince plans to visit when his schedule allows."

"Which means they'll be under lock and key." Jack ached for his uncle. Despite Rod's breezy manner, the situation must be torture. "Karen, any chance the girls will volunteer at the hospital as you suggested?"

"That would be fun." Anya sparkled with enthusiasm. "They're such cuties."

"I don't know." Their hostess set down her fork. "I've heard—though this is very preliminary—that Mr. and Mrs. Adams might be interested in sponsoring male fertility research. Naturally, the hospital would love that."

"Which means the Adamses will be spending a lot of time here," Jack observed.

"And I'd be persona non grata if I screw it up." His uncle scowled.

"Dr. Rattigan must be thrilled." Lucky dug into his tofurkey, which nobody else was eating. "It could be a good thing for me, too. If the program expands, there might be a new administrative position."

"Perfect timing for you," Melissa said. "You could stay at Safe Harbor *and* use your new masters degree."

"This is all speculation," Karen said sternly. "I want the girls to volunteer at the hospital, too, but Rod's right. We can't risk antagonizing a major donor."

Being rich shouldn't give Vince the freedom to strut around the hospital like a peacock, taunting the man he'd ripped off. However, Jack understood the realities. "We'll figure something out."

"The girls enjoyed helping out at the animal shelter," Anya reminded them.

Rod sat up straighter. "That's a good idea. I'll run it by Helen."

One way or another, Jack reflected, having the girls nearby would open up possibilities. Also, a major expansion of the men's fertility program might lead to the hospital acquiring the empty dental building, bringing additional space for a range of uses. *Including offices for newer doctors like me.* Obnoxious as they might find Vince Adams, his potential involvement with Safe Harbor Medical wasn't entirely a bad thing.

Dinner ended with a pecan pie from the Cake Castle bakery. Jack was considering how he might steer Anya away from the others when she said, "Excuse me. Jack and I have a few things to discuss. See you guys later."

Startled, he accompanied her upstairs. "Thanks. I was wondering how to handle that diplomatically."

"Oh, was I diplomatic?"

Jack chuckled. Then, at the risk of tripping on the steps—or of being observed from below—he circled her waist with his arm. "I missed you the past couple of days."

"Me, too." Mischievously, Anya kissed his cheek, then pulled him toward her bedroom. "I have something to show you."

He tried to keep his mind off the fact that they hadn't made love since before the trip to Denver. "I'm sure I'll like it, whatever it is."

"You will." She underscored her reply by closing the door behind them.

Alone, finally, Jack caught her and planted a kiss firmly on her mouth. Mmm. Pecan pie and Anya. His favorites.

She melted into him. Jack forgot everything but her, and the bed, and her softness. Anya apparently did, too, until they bumped the table as they crossed the room. "Oh!" She wriggled free. "Seriously, we need to talk."

"How about we talk later?" He was breathing hard.

She sighed. "With all those people downstairs straining to hear?"

"Ignore them."

"Including Rod? He already doesn't like me," Anya said.

"He's coming around."

"Does he know we're planning to live together?" she asked.

Jack had to admit that he hadn't told his uncle yet. "I figured I'd wait until we have more definite arrangements."

"We could rent a new apartment." She grinned. "Or keep yours and kick your uncle out."

"I can't do that!" However, neither could he expect Anya to share a place with Rod. And once the baby arrived, they'd need both bedrooms. "Unless he has a better place to move. Like here."

"That would solve two problems," Anya said.

"What's the other one?"

"Karen needs the rent."

Enough about his uncle. They had more important topics to discuss. "What did you want to show me?"

Anya smiled. "This." From a small table, she lifted an African violet. "I named her Paula the Second."

That was it? "A plant?"

She turned the purple-flowered plant lovingly in her hands. "It's a leap of faith, to prove to myself that I can nurture something without killing it."

"You can do a lot more than that." Jack gave up trying to avoid pressuring her. "Damn it, Anya, I love you. You're going to be a wonderful mother. I want us to spend our lives together."

To his annoyance, she merely handed him the pot. "Take a closer look."

He spared a quick glance at the deep green fuzzy leaves. "It's very pretty. One of these days we'll be able to buy our own home with a greenhouse window. You can grow all the African violets your heart desires."

"They're non-toxic," she said cheerfully. "Safe to have around children."

"Wonderful." Why had he fallen for the one woman in the world who could drive him to the edge of madness? "We can plant an entire vegetable garden. Anya…"

"Look harder."

Gritting his teeth, Jack stared at the violet again. From the soil jutted a shiny piece of paper, which he'd assumed held care directions.

Plucking it free and gently blowing a few crumbs of soil into the pot, he unrolled it and studied the glossy pictures of jewelry. "Rings." His throat clamped shut.

"We can pick them out together," Anya said. "That is, assuming your proposal still stands."

"Yes." He swallowed, and took a deep breath. "You enjoy keeping me on edge, don't you?"

"Not deliberately." She reached for him. "I've been in awe of you since the day we met."

Setting the plant on the table, Jack drew her into his arms. "You could have fooled me."

The face that lifted to his was open and vulnerable. "If I'd let on, I'd have been just another of those nurses who follow you around like puppy dogs."

Jack didn't know whether to laugh or growl. Instead, he tightened his hold on her. "You planned the whole thing?"

"Just the opposite," Anya admitted. "I kept you at bay for my own safety."

"And now?"

"I love you too much," she said raggedly.

"Really?" He could hardly believe it.

"You overwhelmed my good judgment." She buried her face in his chest. "Promise not to take advantage."

Grinning, Jack moved back a step, pulling her with him. "I plan to take advantage every chance I get."

"Don't push your luck."

"Let's see how it goes," he said, and lowered her onto the bed.

As THEY LAY contentedly side by side, Anya's head was still spinning. Marrying Jack and trusting him meant no more guarding her emotions. They'd be sharing their home, their hearts and their baby. Or babies. Always and forever.

It wasn't as if she had a choice. Last Sunday as he'd fixed waffles for her family, he'd been the calm center of a swirl of people. Watching him, she'd tumbled off a cliff—or finally recognized that she'd been in free fall for a long time.

He was Anya's other half. A very different, masculine other half—they wouldn't always see eye to eye. There'd be disagreements and difficult choices. Sometimes they might hurt each other without meaning to. But he wasn't sitting in judgment on her, and she was strong enough to set him straight if he ever tried.

They belonged together. All week at the hospital, she'd barely restrained herself from shouting to the world that he was hers.

Burrowing into him, inhaling his wonderful scent, Anya released the last of her self-protective fear. She didn't need it anymore.

Love had taken its place.

* * * * *

HER SECRET, HIS BABY

BY
TANYA MICHAELS

Three-time RITA® Award nominee **Tanya Michaels** writes about what she knows—community, family and lasting love! Her books, praised for their poignancy and humor, have received honors such as a Booksellers' Best Bet Award, a Maggie Award of Excellence and multiple readers' choice awards. She was also a 2010 *RT Book Reviews* nominee for Career Achievement in Category Romance. Tanya is an active member of Romance Writers of America and a frequent public speaker, presenting workshops to educate and encourage aspiring writers. She lives outside Atlanta with her very supportive husband, two highly imaginative children and a household of quirky pets, including a cat who thinks she's a dog and a bichon frise who thinks she's the center of the universe.

Dedicated with gratitude to Barbara Dunlop—
wonderful author, friend and dinner companion.

Chapter One

Never in her twenty-five years had Arden Cade done anything so rash. *What was I thinking?* Although she usually woke in gradual, disoriented stages, this morning she was instantly alert, hoping to discover the previous night had been a dream—a vivid, thoroughly sensual dream.

But there was no disputing the muscular arm across her midsection or the lingering satisfaction in her body.

Physically, she was more relaxed than she'd been in nearly a year, her loose limbs at odds with her racing thoughts. Her first impulse was to bolt from the bed, putting distance between herself and the still-sleeping cowboy. She hesitated, not wanting to wake Garrett before she'd had a chance to gather her composure. Besides, his body heat and the steady rumble of his breathing were soothing. Beckoning. It was so tempting to snuggle closer beneath the sheets and—

Don't you learn?

Cuddling into his heat was what had landed her in this situation. But she'd been cold for so long. She'd needed to feel something other than suffocating grief. If only yesterday hadn't been the ninth of March.... What the hell had made her think scheduling a photography job would keep her too busy to mourn?

Memories of the night before flooded her—the despair that had gaped like a chasm, the encounter with a charming stranger, the reckless bliss she'd found in his arms.

"If you don't mind my saying so, ma'am, people usually look happier at wedding receptions." The man's teasing tone was deep and rich, unexpectedly warming her.

She had to tilt her head to meet his clear gray eyes. Knowing her clients deserved better than a photographer who depressed the guests, she struggled for a light tone as she gestured toward the crowded dance floor. "I was feeling sorry for myself because I'm not out there," she lied. "I love to dance."

A slow grin stole over his face, making him even more attractive. As the younger sister of two ridiculously good-looking brothers, Arden didn't impress easily, but this man made her pulse quicken.

"I'd be happy to oblige," he offered. "I realize you're working, but I have some pull with the groom. Hugh was my best friend in high school."

His casual words pierced her. Arden had kept the same best friend from preschool into adulthood, rejoicing three and a half years ago when the sister of her heart married Arden's oldest brother and became her sister-in-law. This was the first March 9—Natalie's birthday—since the car accident that had killed Natalie and her toddler son, the first March 9 in over two decades Arden hadn't spent with her friend.

"Rain check," she'd managed to respond, abandoning the stranger to snap shots of the twirling flower girl.

After the reception ended, Arden should have gone home, but facing her dark, empty apartment seemed unbearable. She packed her equipment, then sat in the hotel bar while ice melted in her untouched whiskey. Time passed with excruciating slowness.

Then Garrett Frost walked in, his earlier suit replaced with a casual button-down shirt and a pair of dark jeans that somehow made him even more devastatingly handsome.

"I'd offer to buy you a drink, but..." He raised one jet-black eyebrow at the liquor she was clearly ignoring.

"Guess I wasn't thirsty, after all."

Their gazes locked, and she wished she had a camera in hand to capture his mesmerizing eyes. He's beautiful. *Sculpted cheekbones, full mouth—*

"If you're gonna look at me like that," he'd drawled softly, "it's only fair you tell me your name."

"Arden. Arden Cade."

He extended his hand. "You still want that dance, Arden Cade?"

She'd accepted. Sometimes what a woman needed most in the world was to be held....

"Mornin'." Tinged with sleep, Garrett's voice now was every bit as compelling as it had been last night—when he'd breathed her name as he slid into her.

Arden! Focus! Last night's impulsiveness was one thing. She'd been emotionally raw, had needed to feel alive in some primal way. But she couldn't rationalize a repeat performance. She'd had only two sexual partners before, and they'd both been serious boyfriends.

She scrambled for the edge of the bed, trying to secure the sheet around her as she moved. "Yes, it is. Morning, I mean. Time for me to go."

"Don't hurry on my account." He lay back on his pillow, grinning at her in utter contentment. His appeal was more than physical good looks. She was drawn to his easy confidence, how comfortable he seemed in his own skin.

"Checkout's not 'til noon," he continued. "Thought I might order us an obscenely large breakfast from room service. I'm starvin'."

So was she, Arden realized. After months of being numb, of having no appetite whatsoever, the hunger felt both foreign and exhilarating. "I could eat," she blurted.

"Good. I'm gonna hop in the shower, then we can look at the menu. I'll only be a minute. Unless you want to join me?" He gave her another of those lazy smiles that left her dizzy. Garrett made love the way he smiled. Completely and thoroughly, in seemingly no rush.

"N-no." She ducked her head so that her long dark hair curtained her face. It was probably bad manners to look appalled at the thought of being naked with a man who had rocked your world mere hours ago. "I'll, uh, wait."

He sauntered across the room nude, and Arden resisted the urge to sneak a final glance. Not that her resistance held for long. He was male perfection.

And he'd been exactly what she'd needed last night. As unplanned and perhaps unwise as her actions had been, she had to admit she felt…lighter. She could almost hear Natalie's mischievous voice in her head. *Damn, girl, you really know how to celebrate a birthday.*

Arden squeezed her eyes shut. *I miss you, Nat.* That ache might never go away, but it was time Arden stopped letting it drag her down like a malevolent anchor. Natalie would have hated how listless she'd become.

The sound of the shower in the adjoining bathroom pulled Arden from her reverie. Garrett had claimed he'd be back in a minute. What was she going to say to him? All she really knew about him was that his family owned a cattle ranch several hours south of Cielo Peak and that he'd come to town for the Connors' wedding. She didn't know how to be glib about what they'd shared, and she didn't want to burden him with a heavy emotional explanation about the losses she and her brothers had endured. Wouldn't the simplest solution be to leave now, without an awkward goodbye?

She zipped her wrinkled dress, trying not to think about how she'd look to anyone she passed in the lobby. Cielo Peak attracted plenty of tourists, especially during the Colorado ski season, but there were fewer than fifteen hundred year-round citizens. The Cades were well known in the community; gossip about Arden hooking up with a guest at an event she covered would not enhance her professional reputation.

Her hand was already on the door when she stopped abruptly, recalling how Garrett had touched her the night before, his maddening tenderness. He'd made her nearly mindless with desire, and it had been the first time in months the pain had receded. Among her many conflicted feelings this morning was gratitude. He would never truly understand how much he'd given

her, but she didn't want him to think she regretted being
with him.

She grabbed the pen and notepad that bore the hotel
logo and scribbled a quick note. It wasn't much, but it
helped ease her conscience.

Garrett, thank you for last night. It was...

A barrage of words filled her mind, none of them
adequate. Suddenly, the water stopped in the bathroom.
Adrenaline coursed through her. She crossed out the
last two words and wrote simply *I'll never forget you.*

Chapter Two

Six months later

Justin Cade shuddered at the brochures on the kitchen table. "I will paint nursery walls, I will assemble the crib, I might be wheedled into a few hours of babysitting once the peanut is born, but no way in hell am I attending birth classes with you." Then he flashed his trademark grin, a mischievous gleam in his blue-green eyes. "Unless you think there will be a lot of single women attending?"

Arden ignored the question. He'd already proven he wasn't comfortable dating a single mom. Justin, the middle Cade sibling, had raised casual dating to an art form and steered clear of women with complicated lives. The ski patrolman didn't like being stuck in a relationship any more than he liked being stuck indoors.

Thank God he's a more dependable brother than he is a boyfriend. "I didn't pull out the brochures to show you, dummy. I'm going to ask Layla to be my labor coach. She's coming over for dinner in a couple of hours."

Back in June, when the "first trimester" nausea Arden had thought would disappear actually intensified, she'd hired a temporary assistant to keep up with the administrative side of the studio. High school Spanish teacher Layla Green had been happy to make some extra money over the summer. The women's friendship continued to grow even though Layla had quit to prepare for the new school year.

"Layla, huh?" Justin crossed the small kitchen to pour another glass of iced tea. He frequently joked that the desert theme of her red-and-yellow kitchen made him extra thirsty. "She's good people. Cute, too."

"Hey! We've talked about this. You are not allowed to date my friends. Your one-hit-wonder approach to relationships would make things awkward for everyone. I was even a bit nervous when Natalie…" She trailed off, the memories bittersweet.

The sharp sting of missing her best friend had lessened over time. As Arden progressed through the trimesters, she found herself thinking of Natalie as a kind of guardian angel for her and the unborn baby. After losing so many loved ones in her life, it seemed cosmically fitting that Arden had conceived on Nat's birthday.

"You wondered if it would hurt your friendship when Natalie and Colin first started dating?" Justin asked. "To be honest, I thought the age difference would be a problem, that they wouldn't have enough in common for it to be long-lasting. But she made him damn happy."

While Arden was finally healing after the deaths of her sister-in-law and young nephew, Colin had withdrawn further. Not only had he taken a sabbatical from his job as a large-animal vet, but he'd also recently announced that he was putting his house up for sale.

She leaned an elbow on the table, propping her chin on her fist. "I'm really worried about him."

"Colin will be okay." But the way Justin avoided her gaze proved he was equally concerned. "He's always okay. He's the one who holds us together."

Their mother had died the winter Arden was in kindergarten, their father a few years later. Although a maiden aunt had come to live with them, it had been Colin who had essentially raised his younger brother and sister. He'd been so strong. But this most recent shattering loss—burying his wife and child? It seemed as if something inside him had broken beyond repair.

Justin dropped down next to Arden's chair, squeezing her shoulder. "He *will* be okay. Maybe selling the house will help him let go, give him a chance to move forward with his life."

Arden placed her hands over her distended abdomen. "Do you think this makes it harder, my having a baby? I'm sure it reminds him of Danny." Her voice caught on her nephew's name. He'd been a wide-eyed, soft-spoken toddler with an unexpectedly raucous belly laugh. His deep laugh had caused double takes in public, usually eliciting chuckles in response.

"If you're happy about Peanut, then we are happy for you," Justin said firmly. "But if you want to offer Colin some kind of distraction, I'm sure he'd be eager to track down the jerk who knocked you—"

"Justin!"

"The jerk responsible for your being in a blessed family way."

"He wasn't a jerk. He was..." A gift. Even after six months, she vividly recalled Garrett's ability to make her temporarily forget everything else in the world, the power of his touch.

Justin recoiled with a grimace. "Seeing that look on my little sister's face is disturbing as hell. You sure you won't tell us who he is so we can punch his lights out?"

"He doesn't live anywhere near here." Thank God. Most of the locals hadn't been brazen enough to ask outright who the father was, but the mystery had caused whispers behind her back. Some of the teachers in the district had begged Layla for information, but Arden—who'd shared only the vaguest details—had sworn her to secrecy. The first time Arden had encountered Hugh Connor in town after her pregnancy began to show, she'd held her breath, wondering if Garrett had ever mentioned their night together to his friend. But Hugh had merely asked for a business card because he planned to recommend her to a business colleague looking for a good photographer.

Meanwhile, Garrett lived in a different region of the state, on a ranch he'd told her had been in his family for generations. He had deep roots there. Maybe even a girlfriend by now. Arden didn't plan to repay the kindness he'd done her by upending his existence. They'd used birth control during their night together, and the news that it had failed would most likely be an unwelcome shock.

It had taken her weeks to process the news that she was expecting, but she knew firsthand that life was precious. She chose to see conceiving this baby as a miracle. *Her* miracle.

Garrett Frost held his parents in the highest regard. An only child, he worked alongside his father running the Double F Ranch and was impressed with the man's drive and integrity. Garrett's mother, the one who'd spent many afternoons giving him advice in their kitchen while she baked, had always been wise and articulate. So why, today, had Caroline Frost lost the ability to string together a coherent sentence? Ever since the restaurant hostess had seated Garrett and Caroline at a small booth, she'd been spluttering disjointed, half-finished thoughts.

"Breathe, Momma." He took the breadbasket out of her hand. As jittery as she was, she was about to send the rolls flying to the floor. He gave her a cajoling smile. "You wanna tell me why you're as nervous as a kitten in a dog pound?"

Her gray eyes clouded with worry. "You've always hated surprises," she muttered. "Not that it's your fault if you take this badly! Anyone would…. I don't— Lord, I've messed this up before I even started. But I don't know how to make it better. Easier to hear."

Okay. Now *he* was nervous. Garrett waved away the approaching waitress. Something was very wrong. He doubted his mom wanted an audience for whatever she needed to explain. Although, if she had something personal and difficult to tell him, why had she suggested going to a restaurant?

They could have easily had a conversation in his parents' main house or in the luxurious cabin Garrett had built on the back forty. The most logical explanation for her dragging him this far from home was so they could speak freely without any risk of his father overhearing. Was something wrong with him? Long, arduous days of ranch work could take a toll, and Brandon wasn't getting any younger. But his father was direct to a fault. If there was bad news to be delivered, he would have told Garrett himself, not delegated the job to someone else.

"Momma, is everything all right with you?" he asked slowly. "Is there some irregular test result or something I should know about?"

"With me? I'm fit as a fiddle." But she'd gone completely pale.

"Oh, God. Then it *is* Dad?"

Caroline did something he hadn't witnessed since the day of his high school graduation. She burst into tears. "No. And y-yes. Your father's quite ill. B-but it's not wh-wh-what you think." Taking deep gulping breaths, she clutched the edge of the table in a visible effort to regain her composure. "I'm so sorry. Brandon isn't your father."

GARRETT PUNCHED UP the volume on the music in his truck, but it was pointless. Not even the loudest rock and roll could drown out his tumultuous thoughts. He pounded his fist on the steering wheel, rage rising in him like a dark tide. Tangible enough to drown him.

For the first day after his mother's avalanche of revelations, he'd been too numb to feel anything. Once emotion rushed in, he'd realized he had to get away from the ranch. Away from her. She'd had thirty years to tell the truth but had never said a word—not to him and not to the man he'd always believed was his father. Now she'd made Garrett an unwilling accomplice in keeping her adulterous secret. "I swear it was only the one time," she'd sobbed. "A lifetime ago. Confessing my sins to Brandon might ease my conscience, but why wound him like that?"

Her single indiscretion had been with a longtime family friend, recently hospitalized Will Harlow. Complications from Will's diabetes had irreparably damaged his kidneys. Though his condition was currently stable, renal failure was inevitable. Without a kidney transplant, his prognosis was grim. Caroline insisted they couldn't tell Brandon now. "If Will died with animosity between them, your father would never forgive himself!"

How had Brandon remained oblivious to the truth for all these years? He was an intuitive man. Certainly perceptive enough that he would notice the awful tension between his wife and son. So Garrett impulsively announced that he was spending Labor Day weekend with Hugh Connor.

"I don't know exactly when I'll be back," Garrett had warned his dad. "With calving season behind us and time before we need to make winter preparations, can you spare me?"

Brandon had readily agreed that he and their hired hands could cover everything, adding that Garrett didn't seem himself and maybe a week of R & R was just what the doctor ordered. Garrett's sole motivation had been escape; he hadn't consciously chosen Cielo Peak as his destination. Had he named the town because he knew it wouldn't sound suspicious, his visiting an old friend?

Or was he lured by the heated memories of a glorious night spent with Arden Cade?

Their encounter had left such an impression it was haunting. She appeared in his dreams at random intervals. He'd developed a fondness for brunettes and had caught himself unintentionally comparing a date to her. Over the summer, while packing for an annual weekend with some cousins, he'd discovered Arden's note stuck to the lining of his suitcase. *I'll never forget you.* Was that sentiment invitation enough to look her up while he was in town?

She was a beautiful woman, and over six months had passed. Even if she still resided in Cielo Peak, there was likely a man in her life. Unless, like Garrett, she was between relationships? Maybe he could casually broach the subject with Hugh.

When Garrett had phoned his friend, it had been to ask for suggestions of a not-too-touristy rental cabin that wouldn't already be booked for the holiday weekend. He hadn't actually planned to stay with Hugh and Darcy, who were practically newlyweds. Learning of his mom's infidelity had soured Garrett's opinion of wedded bliss, and he doubted he'd be great company. But Hugh was stubborn. Besides, Garrett secretly questioned whether too much time alone with his thoughts was healthy. After all, he was having trouble surviving just the drive, battered by emotional debris from Caroline's bombshell.

He fiddled with the radio dials again, trading his MP3 playlist for a radio station. A twangy singer with a guitar droned on about his misfortunes. *You think* you *have problems, pal?*

Garrett faced not only bitter disillusionment about the woman who raised him and unwilling participation in her long-term deception, but also a monumental medical decision.

Despite Caroline's emphatic vows that her fling with Will was an isolated event, that they didn't harbor any romantic feelings for each other, the man had never fallen in love with anyone else. He'd remained a bachelor with no children. Garrett was his best hope for a close match and voluntary organ donation, which would drastically shorten the wait.

"I know you need to think about this," his mother had told him. "No one wants you to rush a decision." But they both knew Will didn't have forever.

If Garrett agreed, would he feel as if he were betraying his father? If he said no, was it the same as sentencing a man to die?

He was mired in anger and pain and confusion. Little wonder, then, that his mind kept turning to that night he'd shared with Arden, the perfect satisfaction he'd experienced. Right now, it was difficult to imagine he'd ever feel that purely happy again.

Chapter Three

Arden sighed wistfully at the seafood counter. "I miss shrimp."

"Throw some in." Justin indicated the grocery cart he was pushing for her. "How about this? I'll pay if you'll cook." Even with the holiday sales price, it was a generous offer. Since ski season hadn't started, he was scraping by on a reduced off-season salary working for a local ambulance service.

After a moment of letting herself be tempted, she shook her head. "Nah, I've read warnings that pregnant women should avoid shellfish. Skipping them completely might be overreacting, but I really want to do this right, you know?"

She rarely missed her mom, having been so young when Rebecca Cade died, but she sure could use a woman who'd experienced the wonder and worry of impending motherhood. Her only living aunt who'd had children was well over sixty, her memories of pregnancy and childbirth hazy and outdated. Arden hesitated to take advice from a woman who'd chain-smoked and enjoyed cocktail hour through all three trimesters. Cousin Rick never had seemed quite right in the head.

Arden changed the subject, eyeing her brother curiously. "You know, you've been hanging around an awful lot lately. Does this sudden fascination with helping me have anything to do with missing Elisabeth?" Though Justin's relationships never lasted long, Arden thought she'd sensed genuine regret after his most recent breakup—and not only because he missed the job as hiking guide and first-aid administrator at the lodge Elisabeth's family owned.

"What? No. I barely think about her. *You're* the one who keeps bringing her up!"

I am? Arden wracked her brain, trying to recall the last time she'd mentioned Elisabeth Donnelly.

"I'm giving up my Sunday afternoon because you shouldn't be lifting things," he added virtuously. "What would you have done if I hadn't been here to grab the pallet of bottled water?"

"Um, asked any one of the numerous stock boys for assistance?"

He shoved a hand through his dark brown hair. "Humor me, okay? I have two siblings I care the world about, and one of them, I don't have a clue how to help."

So he was overcompensating by lending a hand with her menial errands? That she could believe.

"Besides," Justin drawled, "being such a good brother makes me look all sensitive and whatever to any single ladies we encounter. Major attraction points."

On behalf of women everywhere, she socked him in the shoulder. "You go to the freezer section and get us an enormous tub of vanilla ice cream. I'll grab caramel and chocolate syrup."

"And some straw—"

"Of course strawberry syrup for you," she added.

There was no accounting for taste. "Then we'll need bananas. Meet me in produce, okay? I'll make chef salads for dinner and sundaes for dessert."

He turned to go, then hesitated. "Should we invite Colin to join us? Granted, he's not exactly Mr. Fun these days, but…"

"I'll call him," Arden promised. "But you know he'll probably decline. Again."

"If the situation were reversed, he wouldn't give up on either of us. Maybe it would help if you pick up some of those minimarshmallows for the sundaes. He's a sucker for those."

"Minimarshmallows?" she echoed skeptically. "That's our plan?"

Justin shrugged. "Hey, we all have our weaknesses."

GARRETT WHEELED THE shopping cart into the produce section, absently navigating as he consulted Darcy's grocery list. He'd asked her to let him do the supermarket run as a way to pay the Connors back for room and board. It was more diplomatic than saying he needed a break from the doting couple.

Conversation between Garrett and Hugh had been uncharacteristically stilted. Garrett wanted to confide in his friend but hadn't quite worked up the courage. It felt disloyal to tell anyone what Caroline had done, and it rocked Garrett's sense of identity to admit Brandon wasn't his father. He'd never said the words aloud, and they were harder than he'd expected.

The other potential topic of discussion Garrett wrestled with was Arden Cade. He'd started to ask about her half a dozen times, but stopped himself. After their in-

timate night together, she'd left without saying goodbye. That seemed like a strong indicator that she wasn't
expecting to see him again.

Blinking, Garrett whipped his head around in a double take. A dark-haired woman in his peripheral vision
had triggered his notice. *You're pitiful.* Just because
he'd been thinking of Arden, now random shoppers
looked like her?

Or, maybe… Could it actually *be* Arden? The long
fall of shiny brown hair was familiar. He could recall
its silky texture between his fingers. Given the crappy
week he was having, had fate decided it owed him a
favor? He hadn't figured out a casual way to look her
up, but he couldn't be blamed for a chance encounter.

Steering toward her, he asked hopefully, "Arden?"

"Yes?" She smiled over her shoulder but froze in recognition, his name on her lips so soft he saw it rather
than heard it. "Garrett."

He couldn't believe she was here—and even more
beautiful than he remembered. Her cheeks were rosy,
her aquamarine eyes bright and lively. He couldn't recall noticing a woman's skin before, but Arden's creamy
complexion beckoned him to touch her.

Garrett realized two things at once: he was staring,
and she didn't look happy to see him. Then he came
up alongside her, getting his first real look at her profile, and had a startling third revelation. Arden Cade
was pregnant.

It wasn't immediately obvious until one saw her stomach. She seemed to be carrying the baby completely in
front. From behind, other than the curve of her hips,

there hadn't been— Good Lord. He was ogling a pregnant woman.

He swallowed. "So. How've you been?" He punctuated his question with a wry glance at her abdomen. He knew nothing about pregnancy. His understanding was that women didn't show for a few weeks, although Arden was slim enough that perhaps it was more obvious on her than it would have been on someone else. He had no real sense of whether she was four months along or eight.

That was a sobering thought. Was there a chance she'd already been carrying when they'd made love? The possibility upset him beyond any rational justification.

"I, uh…" Her eyes cut to the side, as if she were seeking help. Or scoping exit routes. "It's good to see you."

Wow, are you a bad liar, sweetheart. "You're obviously busy." He gestured to the bananas she'd been perusing. "I won't keep you. I'm staying in town with the Connors for a few days, and when I saw you there, I thought I'd say hi."

The tension in her shoulders eased fractionally. "Hi." She managed a smile, but it didn't reach her eyes.

"Arden? Is there a problem here?" A broad-shouldered man approached, his tone possessive as he practically rammed his cart between Arden and Garrett. He was a tall son of a gun, even had an inch or two of height on Garrett.

"No problem, Justin. Except that I'm…feeling sick." Her progressively ashen color backed up her claim. She dropped the produce bag she'd been holding into the cart. "Get me home. I can come back later for anything we missed."

"Don't be ridiculous. *I'll* come back." When he glanced at her, Justin's features softened. But the glare he aimed at Garrett was flinty with suspicion.

Garrett's stomach dropped. He'd known there was a good chance Arden would be involved with someone. So why was his disappointment at being right so keenly bitter?

Wait a minute. His eyes narrowed, and he met Justin's unblinking stare. Those blue-green eyes were a lot like Arden's. And the thick brown hair they both shared? Arden's was streaked with honey and gold, while the man's was more like coffee grounds, but the resemblance was unmistakable.

A broad grin stretched across Garrett's face. "Is this your brother?"

"Damn right." The man took a step forward. "And *you* are...?"

"Justin, please." Arden's voice trembled. "I have to get out of here."

"Right. Sorry. Let's go."

With a hasty, departing wave from Arden, they were gone. Garrett stood there, bemused.

Had she truly been unhappy to see him, or did her not feeling well explain her behavior and the grimace she'd tried to cover? At first, he'd thought her skittish demeanor was due to the awkwardness of running into a fling while her significant other was nearby, but that wasn't the case. Maybe he'd misread the situation entirely.

But as he began piling groceries into the buggy, he

conjured her face again. He could have sworn the emotion he'd seen in her eyes was…fear. Why on earth would Arden be scared of him?

"GREAT DINNER," GARRETT complimented his hostess. Personally, he'd been too preoccupied to taste a bite of the meal, but Hugh had wolfed down his roast beef with gusto, so Garrett felt reasonably sure of his statement.

Darcy Connor, Hugh's pretty blonde wife, beamed from across the kitchen table. Her gregarious nature seemed at odds with the cliché image of a part-time librarian. "Lavish praise, doing the shopping for me—when word gets out about you, my single girlfriends are going to be lining up at the front door."

"Since you cooked, we can do the dishes," Hugh volunteered.

"Another time." She shooed them out of the kitchen. "Garrett just got here yesterday. You still have lots of catching up to do."

"Isn't she terrific?" Hugh asked adoringly as they relocated to the living room. He grabbed a television remote from the side pocket in his recliner, flipping through channels until he found a college football game. "If you'd told me when I was a freckled, fifteen-year-old comic book collector that I could get a woman like that to marry me…"

Garrett snorted. "You were also six feet tall and the team quarterback." His auburn-haired friend might well have freckles and an interest in superheroes, but he hadn't spent his teenage years lonely. "As I recall, you went to senior proms at three separate high schools."

Hugh grinned. "Did I? Before Darcy, it's all a blur.

What about you, man? You had a pretty active social life, too. I was surprised you didn't bring anyone to the wedding."

Boy, would that night have ended differently. A month prior to the wedding, he'd been dating a woman he'd planned to take to the ceremony, but they'd ended things when she got a job offer that took her to the east coast.

"Speaking of your wedding," Garrett said with studied nonchalance, "I never got to see how the photos turned out. Isn't there an album or something?"

"Darcy," he called to his wife, "you have a willing victim here. Garrett asked to see wedding pictures." Turning back to Garrett, he added, "Narrating our photos is one of her favorite hobbies, up there with bird-watching and snowboarding. I warn you, the collection is massive. There's the professional album our photographer put together, then the one Darcy crammed full of everything from wedding shower pics to the honeymoon."

"I remember the photographer," Garrett said. Understatement of the year—she was seared into his memory like a brand. "Arden, right?"

Hugh smirked. "Why, you looking for a photographer? Maybe planning to have some of those glamorized portraits done? You'd look pretty spiffy in a sequined cowboy hat."

"I think I ran into her at the grocery store earlier. The woman I saw was pregnant?"

"That's her, Arden Cade." Hugh clucked his tongue. "Poor kid. Being a single mom can't be easy under the best of circumstances, much less with gossips buzzing about the dad."

Garrett leaned forward on the couch. "Why? Who's the dad?"

"It's a big mystery. Far as anyone knew, she wasn't seeing anyone. Maybe it was a long-distance relationship with an out-of-town guy. People were shocked when she turned up pregnant and even more shocked those two brothers of hers didn't march the dude responsible into a shotgun wedding."

The fear he'd seen on Arden's face today flashed through his mind, and a completely insane thought struck him. *He* was an out-of-town guy. They'd used condoms, but those weren't effective one hundred percent of the time, were they? He'd heard stories.

"Out of…" His throat was so dry he had to try again. "Out of curiosity, do you know how far along she is?"

Hugh regarded him suspiciously but didn't challenge the bizarre question. "Hey, Darce? You have any idea how far along Arden is in her pregnancy?"

Darcy appeared in the doorway between rooms, drying her hands on a green-and-yellow-checkered towel. "Around six months, maybe? She said she's due the week of Thanksgiving."

Garrett's blood froze. *Six months.*

No, he was crazy to contemplate it. It was unfathomable that the woman who had been so open and expressive beneath him would keep a secret of this magnitude, cruelly excluding him. She knew he was friends with the Connors and could have found him easily. She could have called, emailed, sent a telegram—something! This was just his imagination running wild.

The unpleasant combination of newfound cynicism and sleepless nights had colored his judgment. The odds that Arden was pregnant by him… They'd used condoms, and they'd only been together one night.

Then again, Garrett himself was living proof that once was all it took.

"Layla, I am in trouble." Arden leaned back in the leather office chair, resenting the way it creaked. She hadn't gained *that* much weight. "Deep, deep trouble."

"Don't panic," her friend counseled over the phone. The words of wisdom were somewhat muffled around a bite of sandwich. In response to Arden's frantic text that morning, Layla was taking her lunch break in her car, away from the curious ears of students or fellow teachers.

"But he's here! Why is he here?"

"Um, didn't you say you met him because he was in town for a good friend's wedding? Makes sense that he'd occasionally visit said friend. The part I can't believe is that you saw him Sunday, yet waited until Tuesday to let me know."

"Because I spent yesterday in denial," Arden mumbled. She'd never been comfortable discussing her night with Garrett. It had felt so private, something meant only to be between them. Maybe if she'd known Layla back then, or if Natalie had still been alive… "Am I being punished for having a one-night stand? Am I a bad person?"

"Don't start pinning those scarlet *A*'s on your maternity clothes just yet. The fact that you'd only been with two men up until then is pretty solid evidence you're not a tramp."

"No, the fact that there had only been two previous lovers in my life is evidence that I have very large, very overprotective brothers," Arden said without rancor. Her brothers' local influence had probably helped prevent some impulsive mistakes in her teens. She nervously twisted the cord on the phone. "I think Justin suspects Garrett is the father. What if *Garrett* suspects as much?" So many emotions had rampaged through her when she'd seen him. She hadn't exactly maintained a poker face.

"Did he give you any reason to think that?"

"Not really. He was making small talk. I was busy freaking out."

"Then let's not borrow trouble," Layla advised. "Are you going to—"

"Oops, work beckons," Arden interrupted as the door to her studio swung open. "Maybe we can meet for dinner?"

"I don't know. I've got a stack of practice tests I have to grade so I can figure out how much my students forgot over the summer and plan accordingly. But give me a few hours to talk myself into it, and I'll text you later."

Arden disconnected, calling out, "Be with you in a second."

Over the summer, Layla had acted briefly as receptionist, but for the most part, Arden had always run a one-woman shop. She didn't get many random drop-ins. Customers usually called or emailed to schedule an appointment or, in the case of big events, to ask preliminary questions and do price comparisons.

Coming around the edge of her desk, she steadied herself with her hand. She was constantly readjusting to her ever-changing center of gravity.

"Hope I'm not interrupting your work." That smooth deep voice was exactly the same as it had been the first time he'd spoken to her, sending tremors through her body. Garrett Frost stood in the center of her reception area, cowboy hat in hand, an unreadable expression on his face.

Adrenaline surged, making her head swim. "Garrett." Her hands moved reflexively to cover the baby bump. That happened a lot lately when she was apprehensive.

He misinterpreted the protective gesture. "If you're trying to hide that you're expecting, it's a little late."

"I...I..." *Say something.* Preferably something intelligent. "Can I get you a cup of coffee?"

It wasn't until he shook his head that she realized she hadn't brewed any. She'd given it up during the pregnancy and hadn't been expecting clients for another few hours. Thank goodness he hadn't taken her up on the offer—her pride balked at the idea of making herself seem more ridiculous. She hadn't exactly been articulate at the grocery store.

"I'm sorry I was rude the other day," she said. "You took me by surprise. It was a shock, running in to you there."

"You weren't the only one stunned," he said pointedly. His gaze dropped before returning to her face.

"So, uh, how'd you find my office? Did your friend Hugh mention I was in this shopping center? I hope he and his wife are doing well." Her pulse was racing, and she heard her babbled words as though from a distance.

"Actually, I looked you up myself. Knowing your name and that you owned a photography studio was enough. It's not difficult to find someone, if you bother to look." His gray eyes were like thunderclouds. "If, for instance, a woman needed to locate a man, even one in a different town. I don't think there are many Garrett Frosts who are part owners of Colorado cattle ranches, but maybe I'm wrong. What do you think, Arden?"

She swallowed, knowing that his real question had nothing to do with addresses or phone books. He was asking if his suspicions were accurate, and she couldn't bring herself to answer. There was a huge difference between not tracking down a man to deliver life-altering news he probably didn't want to hear and actually lying to his face.

He took a step closer. "You seemed so startled to see me the other day. Terrified, as a matter of fact."

Feeling cornered, she took deep breaths, trying to lower her elevated blood pressure.

"Maybe I'm completely off base," he continued, "but extenuating circumstances have made me more distrustful than I used to be. If I'm wrong, you can laugh at me or indignantly cuss me out. But tell me the truth, Arden. Are you carrying my child?"

Chapter Four

Garrett had mentally rehearsed different ways this confrontation could play out—from her scoffing at his ludicrous accusation to her tearfully confessing all and begging his forgiveness. But he hadn't imagined her collapsing.

Her eyes rolled upward and she crumpled in on herself.

"Arden!"

He bolted toward her with just enough time to get his arms around her before she fell. What was he thinking, intimidating a pregnant woman? What if he'd caused harm to her or the baby? He lowered himself to the floor awkwardly, supporting her weight as he cradled her against his chest.

She blinked up at him, and it was such a relief to see those blue-green eyes open. At least she was conscious, although her chest rose and fell with alarmingly rapid exhalations. "G-Gar—"

"Shhh. Catch your breath first." He stroked her hair back from her pale face, feeling like an ogre. If he was right about the baby, then Arden owed him a major apology, but no matter how angry he was, he never would have deliberately hurt her.

She raised one shaky hand to press against her heart, her expression pained. "Water?"

He shrugged out of the lightweight denim jacket he'd been wearing, rolling it up as a makeshift pillow beneath her head. There was a water dispenser in the corner of the room, and he half filled a paper cup. "You have a history of fainting?" he asked. Maybe if this was something that happened routinely, he wouldn't feel like such a bastard.

"Only twice." She sipped her water, her words halting. "Overheated camping. Blacked out another time. When…I got bad news."

He wasn't sure whether this technically counted as fainting—had she lost consciousness completely? Was there a chance it would happen again when she was alone? "Should we get you to a doctor?"

She bit her lip, still struggling to breathe normally. "Probab— Probably overkill, but… The baby." Her eyes filled with tears, the palpable fear in her gaze knifing through him.

"Better safe than sorry." He helped her to her feet, noting her rocky balance.

"We have to lock up," she said. "Keys in my purse. Second desk drawer."

He got everything she asked for, then helped her out to the truck. She leaned against the seat, eyes closed. There was a lot they needed to say to each other, but it was challenge enough for her to give him rudimentary directions to the hospital.

The emergency room was fairly empty on a Tuesday afternoon. A mother sat in the far corner trying to coax a little girl to stop crying, and a burly man watched a daytime talk show with one eye while holding some kind of compress over the other. The blonde nurse working the admissions counter gasped softly when she spotted Garrett and Arden.

"Arden! You okay, hon?"

"Probably. I feel silly being here, but I think I fainted. Heart beating too fast, got dizzy…"

"Then you did the right thing by coming in." The blonde eyed Garrett with blatant curiosity but didn't ask who he was. "You two have a seat and fill out the forms on this clipboard. Oh, and this one for Obstetrics." She passed over a pale green sheet of paper.

Garrett caught sight of a long list of questions. None seemed as crucial as the one looming in his mind. *Who the hell is the father?*

"Need any help with those?" he offered.

"No!" Arden clutched the paperwork to her chest, not meeting his eyes. "I got it."

They sat down and she fumbled through her purse, retrieving her license and insurance card. Her hands were shaky as she muttered, "Damn, I hate hospitals."

He'd never thought much about them one way or the other. It occurred to him that Will Harlow could be in a hospital bed at this very moment, praying that his biological son agreed to give up a kidney.

Fury filled him, resentment at the secrets that had been kept. He struggled to keep his voice soft, nonthreatening. "Arden, you owe me an answer." At least here, if she became overwrought by his questioning, there were medical professionals twenty feet away.

"I know." She turned to him, the tears shimmering in her apologetic gaze an unmistakable reply. Still, he couldn't quite force himself to accept the truth until she added out loud, "It's you. You're the baby's father."

Garrett hadn't thought he could ever be more shocked than when he'd learned about his mother and Will. He'd been wrong. *I'm a dad?* If he hadn't retreated to Cielo Peak to cope with the last bombshell a lying woman had dropped on him, he never would have known.

He clenched his fists against his thighs. "What were you planning to tell the kid? Children should know who their fathers are!"

The clipboard trembled in her grasp. "To be honest, I hadn't thought that far ahead. I was already a couple of months pregnant by the time I realized what had happened, and the discovery was mind-blowing. I needed time to adjust."

He knew the feeling. But he was too angry to sympathize.

"Garrett, I—"

"Someone from Obstetrics is on the way down with a wheelchair." The blonde admissions nurse walked toward them. "They'll get you in a real room instead of one of these E.R. cubicles, probably put you on a fetal monitor for an hour or so to make sure the baby's not in distress. Ask you some questions, maybe take some blood, check for anemia. You want me to contact either of your brothers, hon?"

"No! The last thing Colin needs is another phone call from a hospital E.R.," Arden said adamantly. "And I figure calling Justin would be awkward for you."

"You mean because he dumped me?" the woman asked with a wry smile. She seemed more amused than heartbroken. "Don't worry, I knew what I was getting into with that one. It was fun while it lasted. Talking to him won't upset me, I promise. Would you like him to be here?"

"Not unless I'm going to need the ride." Arden slid a questioning glance in Garrett's direction. "Are you planning to stick around?"

He folded his arms over his chest, smiling for the nurse's benefit. "You couldn't get rid of me if you tried, sweetheart."

ARDEN STUDIED THE ceiling intently, as if the answers to her problems might magically be found in the speckled tiles overhead. She'd gained a momentary reprieve when Garrett stepped out of the room so she could change, but he'd be knocking on the door any second. She hadn't missed his smirk when she'd asked for the privacy—after all, he'd already seen her naked. That was how they'd landed in this mess.

"Not that I think you're making a mess of my life," she whispered guiltily, as if the baby had heard her tormented thoughts. Arden was plenty grateful for her child. She was just second-guessing her decision to raise the child alone, Garrett none the wiser. *But I am alone.* She and Garrett had no real history or future. How was she going to share the most precious thing in her life with a man she barely knew?

Instead of knocking, Garrett cracked the door open a quarter of an inch, calling out before entering. "You decent in there?"

In a thin piece of fabric that tied behind her and left most of her back exposed? Hardly. "Close enough, I guess."

He strolled into the room, filling it with his size. Having grown up with brothers, she normally found the presence of a strong man comfortingly familiar. But now trepidation rippled through her. Her brothers had never been as furious with her as Garrett seemed.

She expected him to interrogate her about the baby, but he surprised her. "That nurse downstairs—" he began.

"Sonja."

"She asked about your brothers. Not your parents?"

Arden kneaded the hospital blanket that covered her lap. "They're both dead. My brothers are pretty much all I have."

"Two of them, right? Colin and Justin?" At her nod, he continued. "Is this why Justin looked like he wanted to put his fist through my face at the grocery store— because I got you pregnant?"

"I think…" She averted her gaze. "I'm not sure what he picked up on between us, but I think he suspects you're the dad. He couldn't know for sure, though. I never told anyone who the father was."

"No kidding." Despite his soft tone, the biting sarcasm in his voice made her flinch.

"Garrett, I'm sorry. I—"

"Don't!" This time, he wasn't soft-spoken at all. Even he looked taken aback by the vehement outburst. He cleared his throat. "I've heard that particular phrase far more than any man should in one week. Enough already."

She frowned. Someone besides her had reason to apologize to him? Whoever it was should feel grateful to Arden—it was doubtful anyone else's transgression topped hers.

Garrett paced the room. Although he might have regained verbal control, forcing himself to *sound* calm, he couldn't mask the tension radiating from his body. "So is there a specific reason you hate hospitals? You mentioned Colin and emergency rooms. Did—"

"Knock, knock!" The cheerful voice preceded a gray-haired doctor poking his head inside the room. "I'm Dr. Wallace. I hear we're having some dizziness and tachycardia today?"

Why did doctors speak in plural like that, Arden wondered, as if using the royal we? "Does *tachycardia* mean my heart tried to pound through my chest?" she asked wearily.

"It's when your heart beats abnormally fast, yes. There are several reasons it can happen during pregnancy." Dr. Wallace went over the possibilities while looking at the vitals the nurse had collected. Then he checked the baby's heartbeat. "Just a precaution, of course. We have no reason to think anything's wrong with the little guy. Or gal."

Arden had grown accustomed to the use of fetal dopplers in her OB appointments and the reassuring *whoosh-whoosh* sound, but she'd forgotten this was Garrett's first time. He went completely still, the restless anger that had been palpable a few minutes ago fading into wonderment. His eyes widened.

"That's the heartbeat?" he asked reverently. "It's fast."

"Well within the standard range," Dr. Wallace assured them. But as Nurse Sonja had predicted, the doctor wanted to monitor Arden and the baby for some readings before letting them leave the hospital. He pushed Arden's gown up farther, the preliminary gel a cool tickle against her skin.

Although the sheet on the hospital bed kept her lower half covered, embarrassment heated her face. The last time Garrett had seen her unclothed, she'd looked a lot different than she did now.

When she was younger, Arden had stayed in shape by trying to keep up with her two athletic brothers. She'd been trim most of her life, and grief after Natalie's and Danny's deaths had robbed her of her appetite. Since her pregnancy had begun to show, she'd often felt awkward, but never fat—a growing baby was a healthy one. At the moment, however, vanity reared its head. Would Garrett be repulsed by her swollen body?

Why should you care if he is? Their night together had been amazing, but it had also been a one-time occurrence. It wasn't as if she wanted him to find her attractive. Even if she did, she suspected not contacting him about the baby had forever tarnished her in Garrett's eyes.

Within moments, the doctor had the sensors in place. "You try to relax, young lady, and I'll be back to check on you later. Meanwhile, I'll have the nurse bring you some water. It's important to stay hydrated."

All too soon, he was gone, leaving her and Garrett alone once more.

"You want to have a seat?" she offered. It was a small room, and the only chair would put him in uncomfortably close proximity to her. Yet almost anything seemed preferable to his earlier pacing. His taut strides made her think of caged predators.

He sat, but kept shifting position, obviously ill-at-ease. "Have you, um, had other problems during the pregnancy? Everything okay with you and the baby?"

"The doctors say everything's normal, even my being sick as a dog well into the second trimester." But she worried sometimes. It was frustrating to wake up with a sharp pain at three in the morning and have no one she could talk to about her fears. Early on, she'd posted a question to an online forum for soon-to-be-mothers. Despite a couple of helpful responses, the possibility of misinformation and the discovery that some people were far too willing to share horror stories had kept her from doing so again. "Apparently nausea can be a good sign that the baby's nice and strong. Plus, my being too sick to run the office alone led to hiring Layla, and she became a good friend. I…needed a friend."

Did Garrett hear the ache in her voice, the echo of solitude that had plagued her for so many months? What he'd said down in the emergency room was true. She *did* owe him answers. Starting with the night they'd met.

"My brother Colin married my best friend several years ago," she said haltingly. "Natalie and I had been best friends since kindergarten, the year my mom died. Colin's a great guy, but he's always had too much responsibility. He rarely laughed. Natalie changed that. She changed him. He doted on her and their baby boy. But then Nat and Danny were killed in a car accident."

Garrett watched her silently, obviously unsure what to do with this information but not interrupting.

"It destroyed Colin and devastated me. The day your

friend Hugh got married? That was Natalie's birthday, the first one I didn't get to spend with her as far back as I could remember. I was in a lot of pain that day. Meeting you was about the best thing that could happen to me. You were..." She broke off, assailed by memories that seemed excruciatingly intimate with him sitting only inches from her side. He'd been by turns tender and passionate, driving her need to such a sharp peak that there'd been no room in her for any other emotion.

On sheer impulse, she reached over and squeezed his hand. "Thank you."

He looked taken aback. "Uh, my pleasure."

"Having a baby was the furthest thing from my mind," she added. "At first I was too shocked to be scared or happy. But I've been around death, too much of it, and the idea of bringing a new life into the world... This may sound insane to you, but it almost felt like a goodbye present from Natalie. Some sort of cosmic full circle."

"And there wasn't room in that circle for anyone else?" He abandoned his chair in favor of resumed pacing.

Six months ago, he'd helped heal her hurting. The last thing in the world she wanted was to wound him. Another apology hovered on the tip of her tongue, but she recalled his hostile reaction to her previous attempt.

"I hardly knew anything about you," she reminded him. "I tried to imagine how my brother Justin would react if he discovered, completely out of the blue, that a near stranger was carrying his child. It was daunting. By the time the nausea and confusion subsided, months had passed. You could have had a serious girlfriend, plans for the future I would be ruining! Telling you seemed like too big a risk. After a lot of sleepless nights, I decided it would be best for my child to have no father than one who might resent it."

He stopped his pacing and stared her down. "So you were protecting both me and the baby by keeping the news to yourself?" His chuckle was like broken glass. "I wonder if all mothers have this gift for rationalizing dishonesty."

All mothers?

The slight knock at the door made them both jump, and a nurse entered with a pitcher of ice water and some plastic-wrapped cups. She drew up short, her smile fading as she registered the tension in the room.

"I hope I'm not interrupting," she said hesitantly. "Dr. Wallace asked me to bring some water."

Garrett nodded his head at her, making a visible effort not to appear intimidating. "Much appreciated, ma'am."

The nurse smiled at him before asking Arden, "Is there anything else you need?"

Yeah, a do-over button. Or, barring that, the words that would make Garrett understand what she'd been feeling, her belief that she was making the right decision for all three of them. What were the odds that the hospital stocked second chances and forgiveness alongside the antibiotics and lime Jell-O?

AFTER HER RELEASE from the hospital, Arden had tried to talk Garrett into driving her back to her car. "You can follow me home if you're worried about me," she'd proposed. But he'd categorically refused. Now, as she struggled to keep her eyes open, she found herself grateful for his inflexibility. If anyone had asked her a few hours ago, she would have sworn the day's events had left her too shaken to sleep for a week. But one of the periodic side effects of pregnancy was a full-body fatigue so encompassing it bordered on paralysis.

By the time Garrett pulled his truck into her driveway, the September sun was dipping below the horizon.

"This is it." She smothered a yawn. "Home sweet home." In terms of square footage, the cozy two-bedroom house was actually smaller than her former apartment. But once she'd learned she was pregnant, she'd wanted to own something, a place that was all hers. *Mine and the baby's.*

Besides, while walking up three flights of stairs every day might have been one of the lifestyle choices that helped keep her in shape, it would be more difficult to navigate while carrying boxes of diapers and an infant car seat. She'd traded all those steps for a neatly fenced-in postage stamp of a yard. Did it look sad and despondent to a rancher who was used to the open range, hundreds of acres of pastureland where cattle grazed beneath the Colorado sky? Based on Garrett's grudgingly solicitous manner, from not leaving her side at the hospital to not letting her get behind the wheel, she wouldn't be surprised if he insisted on walking her inside. Would he judge the meager surroundings inadequate for his child?

"This is a really good school district," she blurted.

He quirked an eyebrow at the spontaneous announcement.

Her face warmed. "Just thinking ahead." By five

years, plus or minus. Even though she might not be living here when it came time for the baby to go to kindergarten, she was doing her best to make all the right decisions.

She slanted a glance at Garrett's stony profile. Ironically, she may have already botched her biggest parenting decision thus far.

As he helped her down from the truck, she couldn't help noting that his hand was warm and calloused. How did a man with labor-roughened skin caress a woman with such silky gentleness? The way he'd touched her— *Whoa.* Where had that memory come from? She shook her head as if she could physically dislodge the mental image.

He frowned. "Everything okay? You look flushed."

"Pregnancy comes with a lot of weird side effects." Like hormones in hyperdrive. Mostly, those hormones had manifested themselves in very vivid, very detailed dreams that made her blush the next morning. One of the more anecdotal pregnancy books had mentioned the phenomenon, and the author advised women to enjoy the perk. But it was disquieting to experience that surge of lust in front of Garrett.

She yanked her hand out of his. When his expression grew even stormier, she tried to mitigate her action with a lame explanation. "I, ah, need to get my keys." As she unlocked the front door, her stomach emitted an embarrassing rumble. Hunger ran a close second to exhaustion.

"I'm starving," he commented. "Didn't get around to eating lunch today."

"Me neither."

"Let's get you situated and decide on a plan for food. Maybe I can whip up something for dinner."

"I don't know about that." She stepped inside, flashing a sheepish glance over her shoulder. "My grocery shopping got cut short the other day. The kitchen's not fully stocked."

Should she mention the nearby pizza place that delivered? Would she be able to sit through a meal in Garrett's presence, or would nerves keep her from eating? She appreciated how civil he was being, but the friction between them was as pointed as it had been when he strode into her office today. She was too drained to withstand much more.

Needing to get off her feet before she fell off them, she made a beeline for the ratty armchair she'd found at a rummage sale years ago. She'd had it steam-cleaned with the distant plan of someday reupholstering. Since she'd never gotten around to that part, the chair looked like blue-plaid hell, but it was inexplicably comfortable.

Garrett was slow to follow. After a moment, she realized he was examining the framed pictures on her wall.

"Did you take all of these?" he asked.

"Yes."

Portraits of Justin and Colin were scattered among a jumble of other subjects, from a black-and-white shot of a stone well to a close-up of a light purple dahlia bud in midbloom. There was a landscape photo taking up too much space; she'd squeezed it in to replace the family picture of Colin with his wife and son that had been exiled to temporary storage in her closet.

"You're very talented," Garrett said. "Darcy and

Hugh showed me their wedding album. They were thrilled with your work."

She swallowed, briefly closing her eyes. "Do they know about the baby?" Had Garrett told them about how she'd jumped into bed with him, shared his suspicions that this baby was his? Lord, what they must think of her. "I mean, of course they know I'm pregnant, I've seen them in town. But do they know...?"

"That I'm a daddy? How the hell could I have told them when *I* didn't even know?" he exploded. He began pacing, not that there was much more space here than he'd had in the hospital room. In a slightly calmer voice, he asked, "Does the idea of anyone knowing we were together bother you so much? I've never felt like a woman's dirty secret before."

"It's not like that," she said miserably. "It has nothing to do with you." She recalled the pitying looks her teachers had given her after her father died, the local news stories after Natalie's crash. She hated for anyone to have reason to talk about her and her family. But Garrett shouldn't be penalized for her hang-ups.

He rubbed his temple absently. "It's not as if your neighbors are gonna buy that the stork brought the baby. So who cares if they know it was me?"

"I'm handling this badly." She sighed. "I've never... I'm pretty inexperienced."

"You mean because you're a first-time mom?"

"Inexperienced with men. And, um, sex in general." At his startled look, she added, "I'd had sex before—just, infrequently. And only with long-term boyfriends I knew really, really well. I'm *not* ashamed of what happened between us. I'm just at a loss for… If I say 'I'm sorry' again, are you going to yell?"

His sudden grin was so unexpected and striking that it made her knees weak. *Thank God I'm already sitting.*

"No yelling," he promised.

"Thank you. I am sorry. I don't know what I'm doing." There were manuals and chat rooms, even documentary-style television shows that revolved around pregnancy and birth. But none of them had outlined the protocol for how to weather whispered rumors, or break the news to appalled, overprotective brothers or how to cope with the gorgeous one-night stand you'd never expected to see again.

His smile faded. "If you'd told me the truth, maybe we could have figured it out together. For the record, since you broached the subject today, there's no girl-friend, serious or otherwise."

The declaration warmed her far more than it should have. *Not because I'm interested in him romantically, but because I'd hate to complicate a third person's life with all of this.*

"Based on what Hugh said, can I safely assume there's no guy in the picture?" he asked.

She almost laughed at the suggestion that she was dating anyone. How many men fantasized about meeting a gal who barfed for months on end, then began steadily swelling to the size of a beluga? The hint of vulnerability that flickered in Garrett's gaze sobered her. Did he worry that someone else was poised to play the role of father to his child?

"No guy," she said softly. *Except you.*

His tense shoulders lowered the merest fraction of

an inch. There was relief and something less definable in his eyes. Possessiveness? Awareness sizzled through Arden, replacing her earlier lethargy with something more energetic. And far more complicated. Her voice caught in her throat.

Changing the subject, he clapped his palms together. "Point me in the direction of the kitchen. I'll check out the dinner options."

"I wasn't kidding about rations being low." She used the arms of the chair to hoist herself upward. "But I think we can manage salad and some grilled cheese sandwiches."

As someone who lived alone, she wasn't used to anyone else puttering around in her kitchen. Letting him wait on her would just be too weird. "Can I offer you something to drink? I don't have any sodas or beer, but there's lemonade or filtered water. I could brew some tea."

"Lemonade sounds great." He trailed her into the kitchen.

"I'll get glasses. Lemonade's in the fridge," she directed. "And there should be some fruit salad left."

He turned to the refrigerator but stopped when he caught sight of the sonogram photos secured with promotional magnets from the Donnelly ski lodge. The first picture was from so early in the pregnancy that the baby was a mere peanut-shaped blip; a circle the doctor had drawn in ink showed where the heart was. But the other pictures were from a recent appointment. It was easy to make out the baby's head and profile.

"So, um, that's the little guy. Figuratively speaking," she clarified. "I have no idea what the gender is. I've decided to be surprised." She'd had trouble explaining her decision to friends and family, but there had been enough ugly surprises in Arden's life. Why not revel in one that was wonderful? "I've been calling the baby Peanut since I'm not sure what pronoun to use."

Garrett traced his thumb lightly over the edge of a photo. "These are amazing. To have such a clear look at someone who's not even... I've looked at bovine sonograms, but this—"

"Did you just compare pictures of our unborn child to those of *cows?*" she interrupted with mock indignation. Reaching around him, she pulled butter and cheese from the refrigerator.

He shrugged. "Hey, it's the life I know. Sleep with a cowboy, you gotta expect the occasional livestock mention."

"Good to know. I'll keep that..." *In mind for next time.* The thoughtless words evaporated from her lips. Next time? With whom? Certainly not him.

For starters, her major lie of omission probably guaranteed there would never be anything tender between her and Garrett. That aside, romance of any kind had dropped completely off her list of priorities for the time being. She hoped that, eventually, she and Garrett could overcome the strain between them for their child's sake, and develop a smooth, cordial relationship. Romantic entanglement was a risk that didn't make sense. Long-distance dating was difficult under the best of circumstances, and if they braved a relationship, only to have it end badly... *I'll take 'Ways to Make an Awkward Situation Even Worse' for a thousand, Alex.*

No, definitely not worth the gamble.

Casting about for a neutral topic, she placed buttered bread in the skillet. Since he'd made the joke about live-stock, she decided that maybe his ranch was the saf-est subject.

"When you first told me what you do for a living," she began, "you sounded like you really love it. Do you think you would have eventually found your way into ranching even if you hadn't grown up surrounded by cattle and horses?"

He leaned against the kitchen counter, considering the question. "I honestly can't say. It's so much a part of who I am that I never gave any thought to another line of work. If I had to be cooped up inside an office like Hugh every day, I'd go stark raving mad. Running the Double F alongside my father... He's a hell of a man. I always wanted to be—" He broke off, his jaw clenched. Tension lined his rugged face.

Was there conflict between Garrett and his dad? Arden flipped the cheese sandwiches, backtracking quickly. "What about your mom?" Her voice was too shrill with forced cheer, and she struggled to sound natural. "Are the two of you close?"

"Not currently." He set the bowls of fruit salad on the table with a muted crash.

Strike two. "Any, uh, brothers? Sisters?"

"Only child."

She chuckled bleakly. "You with no siblings, me with no parents. It's like, between the two of us, we have enough puzzle pieces to make a whole family."

"A family." His expression darkened. "Maybe under different circumstances, we could have been. Maybe I would've known what it was like to teach my own son how to ride a horse, how to drive a tractor." He stared her down, so much pain in his steely gaze that it stopped her breath. "You know what? I'm not hungry, after all. Guess I'll head back into town."

Garrett, wait. At least eat something before you leave. She followed him, but her protests never made it any farther than her mind. She'd made a sufficiently disastrous mess of things for one night. Given his charged mood and her own emotional unpredictability, it was probably best to let him go.

He hesitated at the door, his look almost menacing. "I'll be in touch soon. Like it or not, we have a lot to discuss. I won't be a stranger in my child's life, Arden." With that, he left.

Possibly to do online research on Colorado family law and paternity rights. He'd looked furious. Was he enraged enough to challenge her for custody?

She pushed the horrible thought away. Garrett was a good man. Yes, she'd screwed up by not telling him of her own volition that he would be a father, but the baby wouldn't be here for another few months. She prayed that was enough time to somehow make this right.

Chapter Five

Garrett pulled over at the end of Arden's street and texted Hugh, asking if his friend could meet him in town. Fifteen minutes later, both men were parking their vehicles outside Hugh's favorite bar. The place didn't look like much—the lot was gravel rather than pavement and a couple of the light poles had burned-out bulbs—but Garrett had been here before and knew that the food was good and the drinks were reasonably priced.

"Thanks for joining me," Garrett said, his words brusque but sincere. "Feels like I've been asking you for a lot of favors lately. Hope I didn't interrupt you and Darcy's dinner."

"Nah, she's got book club at a friend's and isn't even home. For tonight, it's just us guys." Hugh squinted at him in the dim lighting. "So this might be a good time to finally tell me what brings you to town. Besides my obvious awesomeness."

Garrett had no idea where to begin. The astonishment over his mother's confession was still fresh, but now there was the tangle of Arden's deception, too. He felt battered by lies and weighty decisions he needed to make. "What would you do if Darcy ever lied to you?"

"What, you mean like about how expensive a pair of boots were?" Hugh asked.

"No. About something major."

Shaking his head, Hugh reached for the door to the bar. "She wouldn't do that."

Isn't that what Garrett had told himself twenty-four hours ago? That Arden Cade wasn't the kind of person who would hide her pregnancy from the baby's father? Lord, had he been wrong. But maybe he shouldn't be surprised. Apparently the closeness he'd felt between them during their night together had been merely superficial. An illusion. What did he really know about her?

That she's a talented photographer and a young woman who's lost too many people in her life, that she's scared but already loves this baby fiercely. He didn't want to empathize with her, but he couldn't help admiring how she'd dealt with the deaths of her best friend, her nephew and her parents. Even though he was avoiding his own mother right now, the thought of either of his folks dying one day turned his stomach and made his flesh clammy.

The men stepped inside and waited for the hostess to find them an available booth.

Amid the bar's many neon lights, the concern on Hugh's face was unmistakable. "I don't want to push, but, buddy, you look like you're gonna snap if you don't talk to someone."

It was a fair assessment. "Okay, but this conversation will require some time. And definitely some beer."

"CANNOT BELIEVE YOU'RE gonna be a daddy," Hugh slurred. It wasn't the first time he'd made the declaration. "I assumed it would be me before you. Since I'm, you know, actually married."

"Hey, I figured it would be you and Darcy first, too." Accepting reality was a cyclical process, one he'd been stuck repeating all day. It was like trying to unknot gnarled fishing line—each time he thought he was making progress, he'd have to start all over again.

"Have another glass," Hugh suggested sympathetically. He'd gone through more than half the pitcher while Garrett, now the designated driver, was busy spilling the story. Or at least an abbreviated version of it. He got through the upsetting news of his mom's affair, which had spawned this trip, to the secret of Arden's pregnancy. But he left aside the issue of Will needing a kidney transplant for now. It was too much for one night.

Garrett shook his head. "I don't think a second beer is really a long-term solution." Considering how Justin Cade had glowered at him the other day, maybe Arden's brothers would ultimately drop him off a steep cliff and eliminate the need for long-term plans. "Look, about Arden...I don't think she's really eager for people to know who the father is. The details—"

"Are her business. And yours," Hugh said firmly. "I won't keep secrets from my wife, but don't worry. Darcy and I won't spread any gossip."

"Y'all are the best," Garrett said, genuinely grateful. For the first time in days, he felt as if he could count on someone. Life had thrown him nothing but curveballs lately, and it was nice to be reminded that he had people in his corner. Hugh was as good a friend now as he'd always been in the past.

Garrett found himself nostalgic for the much simpler past. The present was full of perplexing psychological land mines. And he had no idea what to do about the future.

WHILE ARDEN UNLOCKED her studio early Wednesday morning, Justin impatiently shifted his weight behind her.

"Your secrecy is freaking me out," he complained. "First you were cagey about why you needed me to drive you to work this morning, now you won't tell me why you've called a family meeting."

The three siblings had long ago agreed that Cade family meetings were never to be called lightly and that attendance was mandatory.

Arden shot him a quelling look. "Of course I'll tell you—when the other part of the family gets here."

Justin went straight for the coffee supplies in the corner and began filling the pot with water. "You had a 'dizzy spell' yesterday and a friend drove you home," he commented. "Which friend? If it was Layla, you would've said so. I know there's something you're leaving out. You were a lousy liar as a kid, and you haven't improved with age."

She stood next to the coatrack, shrugging out of her jacket. "I got dizzy enough that I went to the hospital, okay? But I don't want Colin to know, so you'd better not mention it. He does *not* need any extra reason to worry that something will happen to me or the baby."

Justin was quick to agree. "My lips are sealed. Look, I'm as concerned about him going round the bend as you are. But you can tell *me* this stuff, okay? I'm too shallow to stay up nights obsessing over other people's safety."

The big faker. "No, you're not." The women he jilted might think of him as a heartless beast, but Arden knew there was more to him than that. Why was he so reluctant to let people see his caring side? "You've been a fantastic brother these past few months, and I don't know how I would have coped without you."

"Ah, is that what the family meeting's about?" he asked, spinning around a low-backed chair and straddling it. "Am I getting a medal for outstanding brothership? Is there a cash award involved? Because there's this new girl who works at the deli across from the ambulance station, and I would love to take her out for a night on the town."

Ignoring him, she booted up her computer for the day. Given Justin's flippant personality, he might be kidding about the girl at the deli. But if he was serious, she'd rather not know. His hit-and-run dating habits were too exasperating. She'd never seen him happier than he'd been with Elisabeth Donnelly. She understood that Elisabeth's life had changed drastically after being named guardian of a little girl, but she believed Justin had made a grave mistake walking away from the woman he loved. A gust of wind swept through the studio when the front door opened again, and her heart jumped to her throat. *Colin.* While she'd decided that this conversation with her brothers was necessary, she dreaded having to go through with it. Silly, really. Wasn't the hardest part telling them she was pregnant in the first place? Relatively speaking, explaining who the father was should be a piece of cake.

She watched her brothers exchange greetings. Colin's hello was terse, his voice a low rasp. He had his motorcycle helmet tucked under one arm, and his rich brown hair had grown shaggy, falling across his forehead. It almost covered his turquoise eyes, which resembled hard stone in more than just color. All in all, not someone you'd want to encounter in a dark alley.

It tugged at her heart that he tried, for her benefit, to smile. Even if it was a dismal failure. "Morning, Colin."

"You…look good. Glowing and all that."

"Thank you." She hugged him, trying not to be offended by how he stiffened at her embrace. The man who'd once cuddled her after nightmares and skinned knees could no longer bear to be touched.

He patted her on the back, then stepped away. "You haven't called a family meeting since you told us you were expecting. What's wrong?"

She heaved a sigh. "Didn't I say in the message, like ten times, that everything was okay and not to worry? That I just needed to talk to you guys?"

"Maybe this is when she tells us she's having twins," Justin mused.

"No." She led them to the table where she normally showed clients their photo selections, and they all took a seat. "This is when I tell you about the baby's father."

"About damn time." The playfulness vanished from Justin's gaze. "Tell me you've talked to him and that he's taking responsibility for what he did."

"What *he* did?" She rolled her eyes. "Where do you think I was in all this?"

Colin held up a hand, looking pale. "No details!"

She interlocked her fingers, trying not to fidget while

she searched for the right words. "I told you that you guys didn't know him—"

"Which I've always found suspect," Justin interjected. "We know pretty much everyone you know."

"Well, I didn't know him, either," she admitted. "He was an out-of-town guest at a wedding I shot. I'd only met him that night."

"You went to bed with a total stranger?" Colin roared. "And didn't have safe sex?"

Her face flamed, but she didn't get the chance to explain that they'd used protection.

"Do you have any idea how dangerous that was?" Justin demanded.

"Hey." She slammed her palms down on the table. "*No* yelling at the pregnant lady. It's not good for me or Peanut. We were careful. Or tried to be." She wagged her finger at Justin. "And you don't get to comment on my love life, you hypocrite. How many women have you slept with whose last names you didn't even know?"

He ground his teeth but didn't argue.

"I needed that night. It was Natalie's birthday, and I just—" She broke off, assessing her oldest brother. There was a time when his late wife's name made him flinch. Now he stared woodenly ahead. Difficult to tell whether that was progress.

She swallowed hard, picking up the thread of her story. "The next day, Garrett left town and went back to his regularly scheduled life. I was stunned to learn I was pregnant, but I saw it as a gift. Almost like…Natalie's gift to me. I didn't see him as part of the equation. Until he came to town for an unexpected visit."

"The guy from the grocery store!" Justin declared. "It's him, isn't it?"

She nodded. "He deduced that the baby is his, and he's justifiably *irritated*." The emphasis she put on the word kept it from being a laughable understatement.

Colin's scowl deepened. "What did he say? If he thinks he's going to upset *my* sister, I—"

"I do search and rescue," Justin said. "I know plenty of obscure places where no one would find his body."

"And you two boneheads don't understand why I wouldn't tell you who he was? Garrett isn't the one who messed up. He thought he was taking a few days in Cielo Peak for rest and relaxation, he wasn't expecting his life to get turned upside down. The thing is, I'm not sure how long he's staying and I need to…fix this. I don't want him hating me. Or suing me for custody. Or—"

"He threatened to take your baby?" Colin's voice was raw murder.

"No! That's an over-the-top, sleep-deprived worst-case scenario." The most recent of her 2:00 a.m. panic attacks, which ranged from concerns about genetic predispositions to wondering how difficult it would be to master the art of nursing. "Justin, if you're not on call tonight, I want to invite Garrett to dinner so you two can meet him."

"Absolutely," Justin said with relish. He and Colin exchanged bloodthirsty glances that detonated Arden's temper. A tsunami of conflicting emotions and pregnancy hormones crashed over her.

"Enough with the insane big-brother crap!" she thundered. "I don't need someone's knees broken. I need *support.* Mom's not here to hold my hand, to soothe my panic when I suddenly can't remember how long it's been since I felt the baby move. Nat was my best friend in the world, and she would've been supportive without judging me, but she's gone, too. After Thanksgiving, something between the size of a five-pound and ten-pound bag of potatoes is going to come *out of my body,* and then starts the *really* difficult stuff! I have to figure out how to raise a kid alone. Do I make enough money as a photographer? Even with Layla's generous offers of weekend and summer babysitting, how will I be able to take as many jobs? I've been terrified of screwing up, yet it seems like I already have. I kept Garrett in the dark, and I have no one but myself to blame if he detests me. One family dinner isn't going to make things right, but it's a start. You two are going to help me. You will come to my house for dinner, and *you will be nice!* Got it?"

Belatedly, Arden realized she was breathing hard. And standing. When had she shot out of her chair?

"Damn." Justin turned to Colin, lowering his voice to a stage whisper. "So much for *you* being the scariest Cade."

As SOMEONE WHO loved being outdoors, Garrett should be having more fun. The scenery was breathtaking, and the crisp bite to the early autumn air was a refreshing counterpoint to the bright sunshine. He knew Darcy had suggested this midmorning hike to keep him entertained while Hugh was at work, but Garrett spent a lot of hours with stoic ranch hands and equally nonverbal cows. He was unprepared for Darcy's nonstop, effervescent commentary.

"Don't you worry," Darcy had chirped on their drive to the trail's entrance. "Hugh told me everything, and I won't pester you with questions about you-know-who. We're going to get your mind off your problems!"

Evidently, her treatment for a troubled mind included two steps: fresh air and more information on birds than any normal human being could process in a lifetime. The summer day he'd first met Darcy, he'd commented on the finch tattoo across her shoulder blade and learned she loved birds. But he'd never known until now how much ornithological detail she could pack into a discussion.

Although, weren't discussions multisided? This fell more into the category of an academic lecture. Somehow, she'd worked her way around to the topic of orioles and their intricate nests, which she called "engineering marvels."

"They're really quite spectacular," she continued happily.

Garrett hoped his eyes didn't glaze over, or he might end up aimlessly walking off the mountain. He made a nominal effort to listen, but he was busy imagining an oriole hatchling hit with the news that his father was some other bird. *Actually, son, you know that cardinal a couple of trees over? I was going to tell you when you were old enough....*

The shock of Arden's pregnancy had temporarily eclipsed the reason Garrett had escaped to Cielo Peak in the first place. But now thoughts of Will Harlow were bubbling to the surface. Earlier, after navigating a particularly steep part of the trail, Darcy had become winded and asked to pause for water and a chance to catch her breath. She'd remarked that ranch work obviously kept Garrett in tip-top shape.

Garrett was beginning to realize that he often took his health for granted. He could climb mountains, gallop across a pasture on horseback or go for a spur-of-the-moment jog. *Or have really athletic sex with a woman you met at your friend's wedding reception.* Meanwhile, there was a man potentially dying whom Garrett might be able to save.

The funny thing was, if his mother had simply told him their old friend Will needed a kidney, Garrett probably would have agreed to be tested for compatibility. His driver's license already had him listed as a willing organ donor. But the way she'd gone about it… What would Garrett tell his dad? How long would recovery from surgery prevent working on the ranch?

It would be easier for Garrett if his dad knew the truth, if Brandon could give his understanding and approval of the decision.

"Oh! Warbler." Darcy's voice was a delighted whisper. She abandoned what she'd been saying and made her way up the path, reaching for her binoculars as she went. Garrett stayed where he was, drinking in the silence.

A few minutes later, she returned, holding her cell phone out toward him. "You should see these shots I—" The phone began playing an obnoxiously catchy pop song Garrett dreaded having stuck in his head for the rest of the day.

"Hello?" Darcy answered. Her eyes widened. "Arden!

This is a pleasant surprise. His number? I can do better than that. He's standing right here. Garrett, it's for you."

Knowing who it was ahead of time didn't stop him from experiencing an electric jolt at the sound of her voice.

"I'm so glad I caught you." Arden's tone was husky. With nerves, or something else? "I didn't have your cell number, so I thought maybe your friends could help me track you down. I hope you don't mind?"

Aware that Darcy was watching with avid curiosity, he bit back the retort that the only thing he minded was Arden *not* tracking him down months ago.

"No, I'm glad you called. Has, um, something else happened?" She'd seemed completely stable when he'd left her house last night, but what did he know about pregnancy?

"With the baby, you mean? We're both fine," she assured him. "It's just… I was up all night thinking. About us."

His heart did an odd somersault in his chest. It was uncomfortable yet not entirely unpleasant.

"Like you said, we have to decide how this is going to work," she said, "how involved you'll be. For better or worse, we're a part of each other's futures. I think we owe it to ourselves to get to know each other."

His undisciplined thoughts strayed to how intimately he knew her. Clearing his throat, he turned away from Darcy. "Sounds reasonable."

"I'd like you to meet my brothers," she added shyly. "They're a big part of my life."

That half of the proposition sounded a lot less appealing than the first part. "If I have to."

He could hear the grin in her voice. "They're not that bad. Once you get used to them. I know it's short notice, but do you already have dinner plans?"

"Nothing concrete." The Connors would understand his absence—and could point the police in the right direction if the Cade menfolk helped him disappear.

"Then how about my house, seven o'clock?"

"I'll be there." He disconnected, thinking how bizarre it was that, without having been on a single date, he and Arden had progressed to the meeting-the-family phase. But then, he supposed that wasn't as unusual as getting a woman pregnant without ever having dated.

"THAT IS NOT LASAGNA!" Arden slammed the oven door in frustration.

"It isn't?" Layla asked hesitantly.

"No, that is soup. I've made freaking lasagna soup." Arden covered her eyes with her hands and battled the urge to cry. Or swear. Or break plates. Any of the three might make her feel better, but none seemed like a productive use of her time with guests arriving in less than an hour.

"It smells wonderful," Layla assured her, coming closer to inspect the pan through the oven window.

"Thanks. But I screwed up. Normally I buy oven-ready lasagna noodles. You don't have to boil them first." Arden's words grew more rapid as she recounted her mistake. "You just add some water to the pan before baking, but the store was out of my preferred kind and I had to get regular noodles, only I was distracted so I added extra water even though I didn't need it, and it doesn't look as if the extra liquid is absorbing so now—"

"Breathe!" Layla gently squeezed Arden's shoulder. "In case you haven't heard, four out of five doctors are now saying oxygen is important."

Arden rolled her eyes, momentarily abandoning the pasta diatribe. "Oh, good. Make jokes."

The petite redhead grinned. "Well, it seemed like a better way to fix your hysteria than slapping you." She took a peek at the lasagna. "That's not too bad. Worst-case scenario, your sauce is slightly runnier than usual, but I bet it'll still taste great. You know your brothers will eat anything you serve them."

True. They'd been her test subjects in the early years, when she'd first been learning to cook. But Garrett...

"I wanted to impress him," she admitted. "At first, I looked up fancy recipes online, but that felt pretentious. I also considered a steak dinner, which I rejected because it seemed too on-the-nose for a cattle rancher." And those were only the food deliberations. She didn't want to admit how much thought she'd put into her appearance. After changing three times, she'd settled on a silky, oversize deep purple blouse with a pair of stretchy black leggings—her feminine pride had balked at pants with built-in maternity panels. Thankful that pregnancy was making her hair so full and shiny, she'd pulled it into a high ponytail.

"Honestly," Layla said, "I doubt Garrett will pay much attention to the food, not with everything else you've given him to think about. You yourself hardly ate for months, until the surprise wore off."

"You're confusing surprise with nausea. I couldn't

hold down a damn thing." But she understood her friend's point. No matter what she served, one dinner would not magically solve the problems she and Garrett faced. "Did I remember to thank you for stopping by? You're a lifesaver."

Layla had brought a loaf of fresh bread from the bakery to go with the lasagna and salad. She'd also lent a hand with setting the table and chopping vegetables, doing her cheerful best to keep Arden calm. A tall order, since the two brothers who'd never fully approved of any man in her life were about to meet the stranger who'd fathered her baby.

"I don't suppose you want to stay for dinner?" Arden asked a bit desperately.

"Can't. I have a PTA thing, remember? But I will call and check on you tonight. Partly because I care and partly because your life is way more engrossing than mine." An only child, Layla was always fascinated by stories of Arden's brothers. Now that Garrett had been added to the mix, Layla said talking to Arden was better than watching television.

They both stiffened when the doorbell rang. Arden glanced at the digital clock over the stove. "It's not even close to time! None of them should be here yet."

"Relax," Layla advised. "For all you know, it's the mailman dropping off a package."

But when Arden followed her friend to the foyer, they saw Garrett through the wedges of decorative glass that framed the front door. He was striking in head-to-toe black that started with his cowboy hat and stopped with his boots.

"Whoa," Layla whispered, her hushed voice filled with awe. "Is that him?"

"Yep."

"A man that virile can probably get a girl pregnant just by smiling at her. You didn't stand a chance."

Arden opened the door, trying to look welcoming instead of exasperated by his untimely arrival. "H-hi."

"I'm early," he said without preamble. "I thought maybe I could help. And that if I arrived before your brothers, I'd be less likely to walk into some kind of ambush."

Layla laughed, and Arden shot her a look.

"This is my friend, Layla Green. She dropped by to assist, too. Great minds thinking alike and all that." She moved out of the way, allowing Garrett to step inside and shake Layla's hand.

"Nice to meet you, ma'am."

Ever since Arden had seen him at the supermarket, she'd been assailed by trepidation, viewing him through the eyes of a woman with reason to avoid him. But seeing him now, through Layla's openly appreciative gaze, she remembered how she'd felt that first night, how drawn she'd been to the handsome wedding guest with his slow, beckoning grin and silvery eyes that made all kinds of mysterious promises. In his hotel room with her that night, he'd fulfilled every one of those unspoken promises.

Heat suffused Arden. Her body had been so hypersensitive lately that the idea of him touching her skin now—

"Arden?" Garrett's voice was strangled.

"Y-yes?" She guiltily met his gaze, wondering if her thoughts had been clear on her face for everyone to see.

"I should be going," Layla said brightly. "You kids… have fun." Her car keys jingled as she pulled them from her cardigan pocket, and she scampered out of the house.

Come back, Arden wanted to call after her. *Save me from myself.*

Garrett reached over and pushed the front door shut without ever taking his eyes off her, then slowly advanced toward her. With the wall at her back, she had nowhere to go. Not that she had the willpower to make an escape, anyway. "You have to promise me something, Arden."

Anything.

"Do *not* look at me like that in front of your brothers. They'll have me run out of town before dessert."

"I, ah…" She wished she could feign confusion. It was so undignified to be caught mentally undressing him. "Sorry. Pregnancy hormones are— Words fail me."

Seeming intrigued by her explanation, he raised his hand, brushing the back of his knuckles over her jaw. "You think it's because of the pregnancy?"

"Yes." That and his return to Cielo Peak. "S-something to do with increased blood flow. The books say it's perfectly normal." Like swollen hands. Or heartburn. But she couldn't find her voice to mention those less charged symptoms.

"I haven't been able to get you out of my head all day," he said hoarsely. "Maybe that's the real reason I'm here early. After you called this morning, I started with platonic intentions, trying to think about what happens once the baby comes. But the longer my thoughts lingered on you, the more I couldn't help remembering…"

Her lips parted. Oh, God. Was he going to kiss her?

If he didn't, did she possess the self-discipline *not* to kiss him?

Somewhere in the furthest reaches of her desire-fogged brain, a small voice reminded her that her brothers would be here eventually. The last thing she wanted was for them to walk into her house and catch her seducing Garrett.

She held up both her hands, theoretically to ward him off, but when her palms met the hard wall of his chest, need spiraled through her. "We can't do this now."

"Now?" His eyebrows rose, and he grinned down at her.

"Er…it's probably not a great idea for later, either, but— Can I get you a drink? I could use some ice water. You heard what Dr. Wallace said about staying hydrated." She tried to duck away nonchalantly, putting a safe distance between them, but given the current proportions of her body, it was difficult to move casually. She waddled toward the kitchen, suddenly neurotic about what she looked like from behind.

"Whatever's cooking smells delicious," he said.

"Fingers crossed. I'm, uh, not sure the sauce is going to be the consistency I wanted. Guess we can always order take-out," she joked wanly.

"After you, the woman carrying my child, slaved over a home-cooked meal? No, ma'am. I don't care what comes out of that oven, we're eating it. My momma raised me better…" His expression, which had matched the protective warmth in his voice, grew shuttered as he trailed off.

She recalled when she'd asked him the other day if he and his mother were close. He'd said "not currently." Were they fighting? Estranged? A pang of melancholy stabbed her. She hoped he didn't let some argument or difference of opinion deprive him of a relationship with his mother. Life was short.

"Garrett, this may be out of line, but—*oomf.*" She pressed a hand to her midsection, where her unborn child had taken up soccer. Or was possibly auditioning for the Rockettes.

"You okay?" Garrett was at her side in a heartbeat.

"Fine. The baby's just kicking."

How was it possible to look ecstatic and apprehensive at the same time? His gray eyes flickered with both emotions. "Can I… Would you mind if—"

Instead of waiting for him to finish floundering through the request, she took his hand and settled it over her tummy. Another dramatic jab occurred, and while the high-kick routine being performed among her internal organs wasn't exactly comfortable, she was glad the movements were forceful enough for Garrett to feel them.

He gazed at her with such reverence it was humbling. "We really did make a baby." He said it like a blessing rather than an accident, and she felt closer to him in that instant than she ever had to anyone else.

Her eyes welled. "We really did."

He grazed the side of her face with his thumb, wiping away a tear. Then he bent and kissed the spot.

"Garrett." It was a plea, and they both knew it. She

was already stretching up to meet him, anticipation sizzling through her veins. She inhaled his clean masculine scent, which triggered a cascade of sense memories from their night together. It had been six and a half months since this man had kissed her. If she had to wait another six and a half seconds, she'd spontaneously combust. His lips brushed over hers, barely making contact, more tease than touch, and a small sound of need escaped her. Then he kissed her for real, taking possession of her mouth.

Sensation shot through her, igniting every nerve ending in her body. Her skin tingled, her breasts ached, her nipples tightened. She met his tongue with her own, gripping his shoulder with one hand and plunging the other through his hair. She was dimly aware of his hat hitting the floor. He tightened his hold on her hips, tugging her closer. While her shape made it difficult for them to be as perfectly aligned as she would have liked, he was near enough for her to feel his erection. She moaned, shifting restlessly in her attempts to nestle against him.

Abruptly, Garrett straightened, his breathing ragged. "I heard a car door."

No, no, no. *Not now!* She could barely form a coherent thought.

He leaned down and bit her bottom lip. "Rain check, sweetheart."

She was still leaning against the wall trying to catch her breath when the front door opened. Justin called out, "Hey, sis. I see we already have company?"

In addition to putting his hat back on, Garrett had grabbed a dishtowel and a bowl from the rack next to the sink, making it look as if he'd been helping in the kitchen rather than ravishing her. Holding the towel casually in front of him, he extended his free hand. "We didn't formally meet the other day. I'm Garrett Frost."

Her brother hesitated, and Arden cleared her throat to remind him of his promise to behave. "Justin Cade." He turned to her. "I wasn't expecting anyone else to be here yet. Thought I'd show up a few minutes early and see if you needed any help."

"Garrett and Layla both had the same idea—you just missed her," Arden added innocently, as if she and Garrett had been chaperoned rather than making out in her kitchen.

"Well, I can take over where she left off. You don't need to be on your feet."

She knew from a lifetime of experience that arguing never stopped either of her brothers from fussing over her. "I'll sit, but get the lasagna out of the oven for me, okay? It's got enough problems without the edges burning."

"Problems?" Justin scoffed. "Your lasagna is kickass." He shot Garrett a suspicious glance, as if the cowboy were to blame for Arden's uncharacteristic lack of culinary confidence. Both men reached to pull a chair out for her at the same time, nearly colliding. Justin took a step back, his expression mulish. "Hell, Arden, you could drop it on the floor first, and I'd still eat it."

Was that supposed to be flattering?

Garrett squared his shoulders, rising to the challenge. "Same here. I already told her we'd be eating anything she served, no matter how bad it is."

Arden smacked her forehead with her palm. She'd

expected some blatant displays of testosterone tonight, but she wished they'd leave her food out of it. Nonetheless, she knew how tough her brothers could be on other males in her life, so she offered Garrett an encouraging smile. He responded with a wicked grin that made her think he was mentally replaying their kiss. She blushed, earning a frown from her brother. Justin stepped between them to place salad dressing on the table, jostling Garrett in the process.

Why had she thought this dinner would be a good idea?

In an attempt to keep the men occupied with something other than sizing each other up, she almost asked for a volunteer to slice the bread. Then she decided she didn't want either alpha male holding a knife until they'd decided to play nice. When she heard Colin's motorcycle roar into the driveway, she barely stifled a groan. *Oh, goody. Because he excels at lightening the mood.*

This should go well.

Chapter Six

Garrett had immediately recognized that Justin Cade didn't like him. Yet, compared to Colin, Justin was a welcoming ray of sunshine. Colin didn't even smile when he greeted his sister. He squeezed her shoulder in what was probably meant as an affectionate gesture, his aquamarine eyes scanning her face intently as if convincing himself she was well.

Then he turned his head toward Garrett, his voice wintry. "You must be the father."

The wrong one of us is named Frost.

"We've heard about you," Colin added, his expression just shy of a sneer.

Garrett would have bristled at the cold animosity if Arden hadn't told him about her brother's tragic past. Was it difficult for Colin, who'd lost his own child, to be around a man who'd so casually, inadvertently, stumbled into fatherhood? "I'm Garrett. Arden's told me a lot about you, too."

She smiled, her expression a little desperate. "Now that we're all here, we should eat! Hope everyone's good and hungry. I know I am!"

From the way Justin raised his eyebrows, Garrett guessed Arden wasn't typically this high-strung. "My sister's nervous." Justin leveled the words at Garrett like an accusation, holding him responsible for Arden's increased stress. Considering that Garrett's conversation with her yesterday had landed her in the hospital, perhaps Justin had a point.

"Not at all," Arden denied. "I'm not nervous, I'm starving. You know, eating for two now."

"You have any sisters, Frost?" Justin asked.

Garrett shook his head. "Only child." This information was met with a curled lip, as if not having siblings was a personal failing or meant he didn't value family. "My parents and I are very close." Except, of course, that his dad wasn't actually his father but didn't know it. And Garrett wasn't technically speaking to his mom.

Other than that, they were a tightly knit unit.

Arden shepherded everyone to the table. Her brothers sat at the two ends, and Garrett found himself with the best view in the house—directly across from Arden. He couldn't recall ever seeing anyone who blushed as easily as she did. Was it that increased blood flow she'd mentioned? Whatever the reason, her rosy cheeks made her look as if she'd just come in from the cold. Which made him want to cuddle her in front of a fireplace. And exchange more searing kisses. The memory of how she'd tasted left him hard and wanting.

It was a damned inconvenient feeling, seated as he was with her overprotective guardians on either side. And he still hadn't sorted out his emotional state. While part of him could understand why Arden hadn't come after him to tell him about the baby, he was still furious. A man had a right to know if he was a father. *Or if he wasn't.*

"Frost?" Justin's voice was sharp, and Garrett realized Arden's brother was trying to hand him the plate of bread slices.

"Thanks." He took a piece and passed the plate along to Colin.

Arden looked from Garrett to her eldest brother. "You two have a lot in common. Cows, sheep, horses. Colin is a large-animal veterinarian."

Garrett wondered if the aloof man was better with animals than people. "That so?" he asked, not sure where he was supposed to take conversation from here. He struggled to think whether any of the heifers in the Double F herd had demonstrated any symptoms he could ask about. In the Frost household, Caroline didn't stand for any discussion of parasites or erosive lesions at the dinner table, but desperate times called for desperate measures.

"Was," Colin said. "I was a large-animal vet, but I'm scaling back to more generalized services."

Arden froze with her fork halfway to her mouth. Her speared piece of lasagna fell to the plate with a gooey splat. "What do you mean, more generalized?"

"Traveling. Doing odd jobs on ranches. I've got plenty of contacts throughout the state." Colin shrugged, not meeting her eyes. "You knew I was making some changes."

"But I thought they'd be local changes—that you'd find somewhere else to live in Cielo Peak, maybe resume your practice someday." Agitated, she swiveled her head toward Justin. Was she checking to see if he'd known about this, or imploring him to intervene?

Although Justin took a more subtle, playful approach

in his response, he didn't seem any happier than his sister. "If you go on walkabout, who's gonna keep me and her out of trouble?"

Colin made a short, bleak noise that Garrett belatedly identified as a laugh. Or a mutated cousin of one, anyway. "It's been a long time since I was able to take care of anyone. I'll stay until the baby's born, but then…" He changed the subject, putting Garrett on the spot. "What about you? Will you be staying in Cielo Peak much longer, or heading back to your own ranch?"

Good question. "I haven't decided. I came here planning to stay a week, but I may have to extend that."

"Must not be very important on that ranch if they can spare you so easily," Justin said.

"Justin Alexander!" Arden sounded very much like a mom, making Garrett grin. "You will not be rude to my guest under my roof."

Instead of looking shamed, the man turned to Garrett. "Any chance I could persuade you to finish this conversation under my roof? A whole different set of rules apply there."

Garrett ignored him, focusing instead on Arden, who'd seemed so distraught over her brother's leaving. Over losing another person. "I can't stay in Cielo Peak indefinitely, but I'll figure out a way to be here for the birth," he said quietly. He could give a rat's ass what Justin or Colin thought of him, but he wanted Arden to know he wouldn't desert her.

She swallowed. "That could be hard to plan ahead. The doctors are estimating November thirtieth, but due dates are notoriously unreliable. Especially for first-time mothers."

Not to mention that having surgery to remove a kidney could seriously decrease Garrett's mobility. But those were details to be hashed out later, when he had more information. "I saw the brochures on your counter. Do you need a partner for those birth classes?"

She hesitated. "Technically, my friend Layla is signed up to go with me."

"And if she hadn't, I was going to," Justin said with a thin smile. "So we've got it covered."

"Oh, please!" Arden rounded on him. "Weren't your exact words last week *no way in hell?* I wouldn't let you come with me to scam on vulnerable women."

"I don't do anything of the sort," Justin protested. "I may not be looking for anything long-term, but *I* don't exploit women." He slanted Garrett a glance that made his fists curl.

Garrett hadn't exploited anyone. Hell, he was the wronged party here.

"I want to be involved," he told Arden stiffly. "This is my child, too." He wasn't sure yet how they would make the situation work from two different parts of the state, but being some faceless, distant entity in his own kid's life was not an option.

The brothers Cade exchanged significant looks. Apparently, neither of them appreciated his asserting paternal rights. Their hostility was beginning to goad Garrett past polite behavior.

Colin leaned forward, his body language aggressive. "I don't have much family left. Arden means the world to me. I hope you'll forgive my old-fashioned heavy-handedness when I say, you'd damn well better not hurt her."

How dare they act as if he was the bad guy? "I would never physically harm a woman, but you may have meant emotionally. Something along the lines of betraying her, maybe? Keeping secrets? Lying to her about the most important event of her life?" he snapped. "No, I wouldn't do *that* to anyone, either."

"Garrett." Arden's feather-soft voice was full of pain and remorse. All three men heard the tears quavering in her tone.

Justin was out of his chair in an instant. "You son of a—"

"No! He's right," Arden said. "I think Garrett and I should talk alone."

"Leave you alone with the jerk making you cry?" Justin demanded. "What kind of brother would do that?"

"The kind who is respecting his sister's wishes," Colin said wearily, getting to his feet. "We've met him, we know what he looks like. If we need to find him to kick his ass at some future date, we will."

This time Garrett held his tongue. He was too glad to see them go to take the bait. And he regretted his impulsive outburst. He hated to see Arden cry, and it wasn't in his nature to lash out at a pregnant woman. But the anger was a fresh wound. Had it only been yesterday that he learned the earth-shattering truth? His temper had been simmering, and Arden's brothers had provoked him past reason.

With the two men gone, silence permeated the room like a dense, chilly fog. *What now?* The night he'd met Arden Cade, everything between them had happened so naturally. He'd never felt so instantly connected to anyone else. This ironic reversal of fortunes would have been laughable if it weren't so maddening.

"I should apologize for my brothers," she began tentatively.

Garrett expelled a heavy breath. "No. You aren't responsible for their actions, only yours."

She began shredding her paper napkin into tiny pieces. "And that's the problem, isn't it? My actions. Or inaction."

"Yes," he said bluntly. There were a lot of things to like about Arden, but none of them erased her selfish decision. He wasn't sure he'd be able to completely forgive her. If he hadn't happened to be in the grocery store at that exact moment, she could have kept her secret indefinitely.

There would have been a child in the world who was *his* and he never would have known.

He would have missed birthdays and recitals and graduations. Illnesses, homework struggles, dating advice. Garrett had been raised to believe there was nothing more important than family and, at a time when he needed that anchor more than ever before, Arden would have taken his own flesh and blood from him.

She said she wanted what was best for her child. Had she really believed that raising the kid with no father, with unanswered questions and secrets, was better than letting Garrett be a part of their lives? The sting of that was indescribable.

"You must hate me." Her words were thick with self-recrimination.

"No. Whatever I feel for you...it's a lot more complex than that." It wasn't an easy admission. Understanding his reaction to her was difficult enough in his own mind, much less out loud. He began clearing dishes from the table.

"You don't have to do that."

"This is what I've been trying to tell you—I *want* to help. I want to be a decent father." And he didn't want to harden into this angry, unrecognizable version of himself. He wasn't sure how to forgive Arden. Or his mother. Or Will. But the alternative... He turned on the hot water. "I realize your brothers despise me, but I'm glad I met them. Colin was something of a wake-up call. I found something out last week that destroyed my view of the world. I've been very...bitter ever since. Cut off from the people in my life. Even though you love your brother, and vice versa, he's isolated. I don't want to be like that."

"He's damaged," she agreed, fighting a sob. "And God, I wish I knew how to help him."

Garrett rinsed the dishes wordlessly. The pat answer was that she had to give her brother time, but how did he know that would work? He'd never faced losses of such magnitude. How much time was enough?

He felt Arden watching him, wondered what she was thinking. That he'd ruined her family dinner, perhaps?

"This thing you found out," she asked, "was it about your mother?"

"Yes." Was he ready to share something so personal? *She's having your baby, it doesn't get much more personal than that.* He scrubbed a plate with escalating force. "My mother had an affair thirty-one years ago. My dad—Brandon Frost, the man I know as my dad—isn't really my father."

"That must have been hard. But it doesn't change the relationship you have with him. Does it?"

"Not in theory, but she still hasn't told him the truth. I don't know how to be around him, lying to his face day in and day out. The only reason she finally told me is because my biological father is dying." It was the first time he'd said the words aloud, and the severity of the situation struck him anew.

"Oh, Garrett. Do you know him?"

"He's a family friend. He spent a couple of Christmases with us here and there, sent me a check for way too much money as a high school graduation gift." Which made a lot more sense in retrospect. "He has diabetes, and his condition has messed up his kidneys. He needs a transplant. My mother told me about him because she wants me to consider giving him one of mine."

Arden's gasp was audible.

He shot her a grim smile over his shoulder. "See? You're not the only one with family drama."

WHILE GARRETT FINISHED with the dishes, Arden excused herself to the restroom. It was a lame attempt to get a few minutes by herself and collect her scattered composure. Was there a single emotion she hadn't experienced tonight? She sat on the edge of the bathtub, trying to find her balance. She'd been off-kilter since Garrett kissed her, unprepared for the enormity of her desire. The chemistry between them certainly hadn't dimmed over the months.

Once her brothers had arrived, she'd felt both gratitude for their concern and outrage at the way they'd treated Garrett. She'd gone through dismay and sympathy and shock. *And guilt.* The guilt was staggering.

In the past few days, she'd witnessed Garrett act with honor and periodic tenderness. Despite any hard feelings he harbored toward her, he was a gentleman, one willing to face up to his responsibilities. Embrace them, even. Maternal instinct told her he would make an excellent father. And she'd almost denied him that.

Her time with her own parents had been cut unforgivably short—what would she give for another day with her dad? Yet she would have sacrificed her child's time with Garrett.

"Arden?" There was a soft knock at the door. "I don't mean to intrude, but I was starting to worry."

Good hostesses didn't hide from their guests. "I'm fine." Physically. Mentally, she was a wreck. "Out in a minute."

Listening to his retreating footsteps, she closed her eyes and tried to relax by counting to ten and doing some meditative breathing. Deeming her efforts pointless, she gave up and joined Garrett in the living room.

"If I ever invite you to my house for a dinner party again, remind me that I suck at this, okay?"

"Oh, I've had worse evenings." He steepled his fingers beneath his chin. "There was a night I got salmonella poisoning at a county fair. And then there was that incident with a bull who'd been incorrectly tethered at an auction barn."

It was miraculous that, with all she'd put him through in the past twenty-four hours, *he* was trying to make *her* feel better. She sat next to him on the sofa, trying to ignore his now-familiar scent. "I wanted this to go differently. I wanted us to…" Her body tingled with the memory of his kiss. If only things between them could be as simple as finding sanctuary in each other's arms. "To be friends." She wanted to ask if that was possible but was afraid of his answer.

"I have an OB appointment Friday afternoon," she continued. "There's no sonogram or anything. The most interesting thing about the whole visit is that I have to drink a solution for the glucose screen beforehand but if you want to come…"

"I'd love to."

Feeling that she was offering too little, too late, she was driven by a need to include him in as many baby preparations as possible. "Would you be hopelessly bored going with me to shop for the nursery this weekend? For months, I didn't really buy any baby stuff because I was paranoid about something going wrong and too queasy to move. Then when I got my energy back, I was so focused on making up for lost time at work that I never got around to registering. I have portrait sessions at the studio all morning Saturday, and the high school hired me to take pictures at the homecoming ball Saturday night, but I'm free Sunday."

"Then it's a date. But after Sunday, I'll have to leave town. At least for a few days."

"To check on the ranch?"

"Yes." He looked away, the tension lining his face making her feel protective. She wanted to smooth his brow and soothe his troubles. "And to set up a couple of medical appointments of my own."

"Because of your fa— That man you told me about? You've decided to help him?"

"I don't even if know if I'm a good candidate," he said noncommittally. "Finding that out is probably step one. I don't know what will happen next."

His words resonated with her. Never knowing what came next was the story of her life.

ON THURSDAY, ARDEN met Layla for lunch at a barbecue place down the street from the school. Her friend had called the night before, as promised, but by the time Layla got home from her PTA event, Arden had been too drained to discuss her evening. But Layla had been off-campus for a meeting that morning and was free for lunch before her next class.

"So?" Layla pounced as soon as Arden walked into the restaurant. "I want to hear everything."

"Shouldn't we order our food first?" Arden asked. "You should eat before you get back to the school."

"This is my planning period." Layla rubbed her hands together. "I have almost an hour." But she waited patiently, allowing non-Garrett-related small talk while they walked to the register and placed their orders.

Arden struggled to hold up her end of the conversation. The second or third time she lost her train of thought, Layla frowned.

"Rough night, or is hunger sapping your mental energy? You don't seem yourself," her friend observed.

"It's been a…challenging morning." She'd love to vent about her earlier photo session from hell, but not with other townspeople in earshot. It was bad for business to publicly bash the clientele.

"You snag us a table," Layla directed. "I'll fill our cups."

Arden took the plastic tent marker with their number on it and sank into one of the only empty booths, right next to the window. The sunshine streaming through the glass made it seem like a much warmer day than it was. Unfortunately, the brightness only added to the discomfort in Arden's throbbing head. She massaged her temple with her thumb, hoping her afternoon clients weren't as difficult as this morning's.

She'd met with Mrs. Merriweather, a woman who wanted to surprise her husband with framed pictures of herself for his birthday. Normally, Arden tried several different backgrounds and cameras along with a variety of poses, so that the customer ultimately had plenty of options for purchase. But Mrs. Merriweather had argued about everything from the "unflattering" light to the way she was positioned. Early on in the process, she'd asked about Arden's own husband and when Arden answered that she was single, Mrs. Merriweather had glanced pointedly at Arden's stomach and sniffed in disdain.

By the time Arden left the studio for lunch, she was feeling a lot of pity for the unseen Mr. Merriweather.

"Here you go." Layla set a drink in front of her. "Food should be out soon. Sometimes getting a bite to eat helps when I have a headache."

"Thanks. I guess dealing with an opinionated client all morning was too much to take on top of not being able to sleep last night."

"Does it make you feel better to know you weren't alone?" Layla's smile was impish. "I couldn't sleep, either. The curiosity about how your dinner went was eating me alive!"

"Dinner was a fiasco. My brothers were complete asses." Annoyance flared again, but it was tempered with worry. "Colin's leaving town. I knew he was selling his place, but I thought he'd find something smaller, without so many memories. He's talking about looking for ranch work. It doesn't sound like he has a real plan, just some haphazard idea of jumping on his motorcycle and seeing where he ends up."

"Maybe that's what he needs," Layla said cautiously. "Grieving is a process everyone goes through differently."

"He told me he'll stick around 'til the baby's born. Garrett wants to be here for the birth, too. He's going with me to a doctor's appointment tomorrow."

"So you two are on friendly terms?"

Did wanting to tear his clothes off in her kitchen count as friendly? That had been the high point of the night, but there had been a lot of turmoil after that. "I've damaged his trust," she said somberly. "I don't know if it will be possible for us to ever be close. And the sexual awareness is confusing."

"Confusing? He's a hot cowboy. From where I sit, the sexual awareness makes total sense."

"That's not—" She paused when the waitress came over with a tray of food.

"Here you are, ladies. One pulled pork spud with a side salad, one sandwich plate. Enjoy!" Her smile dimmed suddenly, and Arden followed her gaze. Justin was walking toward their table.

After the waitress beat a speedy retreat, Arden rolled her eyes. "Don't tell me," she said to her approaching brother. "You dated her briefly."

He squirmed, not meeting her gaze. "It didn't end as amicably as I'd hoped. Hi, Layla. Mind if I take a seat?"

"Don't you dare!" Arden interrupted before her friend could reply. "I shouldn't even be speaking to you after that ridiculous, chest-beating macho display last night."

"I did not beat my chest," he countered. "The rest of it…may be accurate."

"Go find your own table. Better yet, find Garrett. And apologize."

"Returning to my classroom to conjugate verbs with sophomores is going to be really dull after this," Layla said to no one in particular.

"Sounds dull no matter when you do it." Justin hitched his thumbs in his front pockets, adopting a contrite expression. "Look, Arden, I'm not about to apologize to Frost. But if I did anything to upset you—"

"If?" she squeaked.

"I'll, uh, just let you two continue your lunch," he backtracked. "We'll talk later, sis."

As he shuffled off in search of a seat, Layla chortled. "It always cracks me up to see you put your brothers in their place. It's like watching a kitten scold a rottweiler."

"Kitten?" Arden echoed dubiously. "More like a hippo. I've never felt so ungainly." Part of the magic in Garrett's kiss last night was that, even while she hadn't been able to get as close as she'd wanted, with the baby wedged between them, he'd made her feel sexy as hell. She hadn't felt bulky or undesirable in the slightest.

"Penny for your thoughts."

"Nope." Arden doubted a penny was the going rate for adult pay-per-view, and that seemed to be the direction her mind was headed. Lusting after him was futile. She wasn't sure they could achieve friendship, much less anything more. But with her body chemistry all out of whack and the knowledge of just how good she and Garrett were together, it was difficult to keep her longing in check.

She rubbed her temple again, glad her afternoon was booked solid. It would keep her too busy to dwell on this unwise attraction or to worry about her oldest brother.

But, several hours later, as Arden's headache was evolving into a full-blown migraine, she felt less grateful for her afternoon lineup, especially Mrs. Tucker's twins. The three-year-old girls were...well, monsters. No other word was adequate.

When they were asleep, they were probably adorable.

Seeing them through the front window in their matching houndstooth dresses with brightly colored pockets, collars and belts, Arden had experienced a misguided instant when she thought they were cute. A fleeting notion. Before they were fully inside the studio, problems erupted. Odette, who didn't want to have her picture taken, had gone limp. Mrs. Tucker literally had to drag the child through the door. Meanwhile, the other twin, Georgette, was screaming that Odette had taken her purple crayon. The accusations were delivered at the highest possible decibel level and punctuated with flying fists. She pulsed with rage. Arden wondered if three-year-olds could have strokes.

"Could you watch her for just a moment?" the beleaguered Mrs. Tucker asked with a nod to Odette. "I'm going to take Georgie into the restroom to wipe her face and fix her hair before we get started." The little girl's red-and-yellow bow had been no match for her hurricane of temper.

As soon as Mrs. Tucker was out of sight, Odette lodged herself beneath a heavy train table Arden kept in the lobby for children. "No pick-sures!" the girl shrieked.

Arden's skull felt as if it were being squeezed in a vise. Her chest hurt, and the self-doubt that welled up within her was suffocating. What if her child was exactly like this? Would Arden know how to correct the situation lovingly, or would she overreact and set a bad example? Would she become like Mrs. Tucker, with her glazed eyes and resigned air of defeat?

By the time Mrs. Tucker wrestled both of her daughters in front of the backdrop, their dresses were askew, neither of them had hair bows anymore and Georgie's nose was running steadily.

"Um…" Arden peered through the camera and absently adjusted some settings, but nothing she did was going to make this a picture worth purchasing. "Would you rather do this on another day Mrs. Tucker? I'm flexible."

The woman gaped. "Are you *crazy?* Do you know what I had to go through just to get them here in the first place? I am not going through that again." She jabbed a finger at Arden's protruding abdomen, as implacable as the Ghost of Christmas Future pointing to the grave. "You'll understand soon enough."

Chapter Seven

"You don't look so good." Garrett regretted the words even as they were leaving his mouth. Why would he say something so stupid? He blamed a late night of researching organ donation until his eyes had crossed. Giving Arden a sheepish smile, he jerked his thumb over his shoulder, toward the lobby. "How about I step out, then come back in and start over?"

Her chuckle was wan. "Not necessary. I don't kick people out of my office for telling the truth."

His offer to pick her up for the OB appointment had been twofold—he was serious about them getting to know each other better, and it seemed silly to take more than one vehicle. But it also seemed lucky that he was here since she looked too tired to drive herself. He wouldn't be surprised if she fell asleep on the way to the doctor's office.

"Are you okay?" he asked. "No more fainting spells?"

"Nothing like that," she assured him, rising from her desk chair. "I just had a rough day at work yesterday, followed by the headache that wouldn't die. My medicinal options are limited now that I'm pregnant, and I was too uncomfortable to sleep."

"I wish you'd called me," he said, not sure why he

made the rash statement. What would have been accomplished by her calling? Chatting on the phone wouldn't have been fun for someone with a killer headache, and it wasn't as if he could have lullabied her to sleep. Garrett did not sing. The world was a better place for it.

Her expression mirrored his own incredulity. "You do?"

"Dumb, huh? I'd just like to feel useful. While I'm in town, feel free to phone day or night. If your heart starts racing too fast again or if you want someone to bring you pickles and ice cream." When she made a face at the silly cliché, he added, "Not literally. I meant, any craving you have that I could help satisfy."

Her eyes widened, and he reconsidered his words.

"Food cravings." Although, now that his mind had started down that path… Arden had confessed that one of her recent pregnancy symptoms was amplified desire. How would he respond if she called him in the middle of the night, her voice husky with need, and—

"W-we have to go." Her face was a brighter red than the scarlet mallow wildflowers that blossomed near the ranch every summer. "I already drank that sugar solution, and I need to reach the office at a certain time for the test to be valid."

"Right. After you." He almost felt guilty about his undisciplined lust, but he knew it was mutual. The way she'd kissed him a couple of days ago… *Dammit, Frost, pull yourself together.* This was a medical appointment, not a third date.

While they walked to his truck, he apologized for being distracted, hoping he could play it off as sleep deprivation rather than ill-timed sexual fantasizing. "As it happens, I didn't get much rest last night, either. I read living donor FAQs and articles about Colorado transplant centers into the wee hours." When he'd finally hit the pillow, terms like *laparoscopic* and *antigen match* had continued to swirl behind his eyelids.

"It must be daunting, the idea of going through such a physical ordeal."

He opened her door, shaking his head wryly. "Says the woman soon to have a baby?" A kidney was a lot smaller than an infant. And, *if* he went through with it, he'd get to be unconscious for the whole thing.

He was fastening his seat belt when he noticed Arden nibbling at her bottom lip, drawing his attention to her mouth. A man could get lost there.

"Something on your mind?" he prompted.

"Sort of. It's none of my business, though."

"We're becoming better acquainted, remember? I'm interested in your opinion."

"After I found out I was pregnant, I went on this information binge. I marked a bunch of sites on the internet, bought a stack of books, started DVRing this documentary-style show that follows expectant mothers. But none of those resources could give me what I really needed. Deep down, I wasn't looking for stats on fetal development and the most popular baby names, I was looking for peace of mind. Acceptance of the situation. It's commendable that you're doing your homework, preparing yourself with facts, but I don't think sites on renal transplants will give you the answers you're looking for."

He tightened his grip on the steering wheel. Could *anything* give him the peace of mind she mentioned?

He knew he had to talk to his mother, but whenever he mentally rehearsed the conversation, it spiraled into disjointed recriminations. They'd only communicated through texts since he'd arrived in Cielo Peak.

"You want to know the horrible truth?" he asked quietly. "A big part of me hopes I'm not a good match, because then the decision's out of my hands. I don't want to deal with these mixed emotions about my dad or Mom or Will. Cowardly, isn't it?"

"Human," she amended, blessing him with unconditional compassion. "You've had so much dumped on you in the past, what, week and a half? It's mind-boggling. Don't beat yourself up over needing time to process it. I've watched people deal with bad shocks before, and it can involve anything from going catatonic to drinking too much and picking bar fights. The way you're handling everything is…amazing."

"Thank you. And thank you for listening. I tried to tell Hugh about some of this, but couldn't quite put it all into words." Despite Wednesday's awkward silences, maybe Garrett's initial impression of her had been right, after all. "You're very easy to talk to."

She sniffled, diverting his gaze from the road as he checked on her.

"Did I say something wrong?" he asked in alarm.

"No. You made me think of Natalie. Her willingness to listen was one of my favorite things about her. There was nothing you couldn't tell her, and I miss that so much. It was major praise, hearing that someone saw a bit of that same quality in me." She fluttered her fingers in front of her eyes, as if that might stop her from getting weepy. He wasn't sure he followed the logic behind the action. "This is ridiculous. I'm crying at everything lately. I sobbed over a banner ad on a recipe site the other day."

He laughed, hoping she wasn't offended. It wasn't mocking laughter. The truth was, he found her sentimentality kind of adorable.

"Turn left up here," she instructed.

"So is the crying strictly a pregnancy thing?" he asked. "I mean, are you someone who normally needs a box of tissues during a sad movie, or is this just a hormone-based anomaly?"

"I'd love to say I'm usually tough, but I'm not. Pregnancy is magnifying everything about me. I've been known to cry at soup commercials. At least those are thirty seconds of actual story, with endearing characters. Banner ads are a new low! The sad-movie question is moot, though. I try to avoid them. What the heck's wrong with happy endings? We could use more of those in film and in real life."

Her wistful tone pierced him, making him want to shield her from any more sadness. She'd said *he* was amazing for coping? Honestly, this was the first time in his life he'd been tested. He'd always been healthy, had lived in a home with loving parents and had done perfectly well in school. He'd never loved anyone enough to propose, but he'd never been lonely or suffered through a traumatic breakup, either. Arden, on the other hand... She was only twenty-five, and she'd had to survive enough upheaval for two lifetimes.

"You need to get in the right lane before the next light," she said.

"Got it." He flipped on his blinker. "So, no sad movies. Comedies, then?"

"Actually, I'm a sucker for action movies. Possibly because I grew up in a house full of guys. I'll take the original *Die Hard* over the majority of chick flicks. And I like the action stuff with a science-fiction angle."

Arden kept navigating, but between directions, they exchanged DVD recommendations and got into a spirited debate over which sequel in a futuristic spy franchise was the worst. By the time he parked in front of the medical building, she was in much higher spirits than when he'd first arrived at her office. Her eyes sparkled with humor as she facetiously tried to convince him the hilariously bad '90s flop *Vengeance Before Breakfast* was the best movie of all time. Did she know how beautiful she was when she smiled liked that?

She stopped abruptly in the middle of her animated grenade-scene reenactment. "You're staring. You know I was kidding about it being a great movie, right?"

"Didn't mean to stare. I'm just glad to see you're feeling better. No more pinched look around your eyes, and you got your color back." Leaning toward her, he traced his finger up the slope of her cheek. Her skin was silky beneath his touch. *What are you doing?* He dropped his hand. "We should get inside."

A long interior hallway led them to her doctor's practice. Garrett opened the door for her, then hesitated, feeling unexpectedly like an invader in a foreign land. Surely it was normal for fathers-to-be to attend some of these appointments, but today, he was the only guy. Women of all ages, shapes and sizes sat beneath huge framed black-and-white photos. Some of the poster-size shots focused on a pregnant belly, others were of mommies cuddling newborns. The carpet was pale pink, and the chairs were cushioned in an assortment of pastel colors.

He was overwhelmed with a clawing need to run out and buy power tools. Or work on his truck.

Instead, he followed Arden to the check-in window, where she let the woman behind the counter know the exact time she'd ingested her test solution. The receptionist said someone would take her back momentarily to draw her blood, but then she'd have to return to the waiting room until an exam room was available.

"We're pretty busy today," the woman added unnecessarily.

They weren't able to find two unoccupied chairs next to each other, but a woman in her mid-fifties scooted over to make room for Garrett. He gave her a grateful smile.

"Sorry about the wait," Arden told him. "But at least I got to drink that syrupy stuff before we came. When Natalie was pregnant with Danny, she had to drink at the doctor's office, then wait a whole other hour after her appointment. I would have felt awful for making you sit here that long."

In spite of his earlier discomfort, he heard himself say, "There are worse ways to spend time than an extra hour with you." It should have been light, teasing, but it came out wrong. His voice was too sincere. The fact that he couldn't tear his gaze away from hers wasn't helping.

Her face flushed a soft, becoming pink.

The sight knocked loose a piece of trivia in his mind,

and he grunted in acknowledgement. "Huh. You blushed earlier, and it brought to mind a scarlet mallow. I just remembered the other name for that flower. Cowboy's delight." Disturbingly appropriate.

"Arden Cade?" A woman with a clipboard called Arden's name over the drone of conversations taking place.

"I'll be right back." Arden stood, slow to break eye contact. As if she didn't want to leave him. Not that it was much of a compliment that she'd rather stay with him than have a needle stuck in her arm.

The older woman who'd changed chairs for him struck up conversation. "First-time parents?"

He laughed. "Is it that obvious? She's read a bunch of books, but I don't have a clue what I'm doing."

"My husband was the same way. Don't think he'd ever held a baby until our first was born. He for darn sure had never changed a diaper. Parenting is all about on-the-job training. You'll do fine. Just love her and love the little one. Be patient with her for the rest of the pregnancy—it gets worse before it gets better. But the first time that infant's tiny fingers wrap around yours, you'll know it's all worth it."

He nodded weakly, even though he felt a little sick inside. On-the-job training? He might not have that opportunity. How were they going to handle custody? He would never challenge Arden's right to raise their child, but he didn't want his son or daughter to only see him on holidays and periodic weekends. Would she be willing to move? It would be a major life change—and she had her brothers to consider—but, in theory, she could take pictures anywhere. He couldn't very well bring one hundred head of cattle to an apartment in Cielo Peak.

He looked forward to teaching his son or daughter to ride horses, to show them around the ranch where he'd spent his entire life, the land that was in his blood. Loving his child would be easy. He was already half-smitten, and the birth was months away. But loving Arden? After what she'd done? The stranger meant well, but her counsel wasn't applicable in his situation.

To discourage further conversation, he grabbed a magazine off the nearby end table, opened to a random page and tried to look engrossed. His thoughts were racing, and he didn't even see the words printed in front of him. Nor did he notice Arden's return.

"Wow," she said, craning her head to see what he'd been reading. "I didn't know you were so interested in... the best remedies for hair-coloring disasters?"

"What?" He shut the magazine, and bold purple type on the cover caught his eye. "'Thirty-six ways to please him in bed?' Damn, are they overthinking that. You want to please a guy in bed, show up."

That startled a giggle out of her. She covered her hand with her mouth, as if embarrassed, and sat down. "Just show up? Sounds pretty passive."

"I don't remember you being the least bit passive, sweetheart."

She didn't blush or turn away. Those blue-green eyes locked on his as she tilted her body toward him and lowered her voice. "No, I wasn't, was I? As soon as you put your arms around me on that dance floor, I knew what I wanted and went for it."

Heat flooded him, shooting directly to his groin. Was kissing her in the middle of the reception area a bad idea?

Arden nibbled her bottom lip. "Can I ask you something?"

"Yes." *Whatever you want.* He'd give her the keys to his truck right now.

"Why me?" She spoke just above a whisper, and he had to get closer to catch every word. "That night...I'd never done anything like that before." She looked down, toying with a loose thread at the hem of her coat. "Is it normal for you? I have brothers. I know men have casual sex, I just…"

He was as charmed by her sudden shyness as he had been by her boldness a moment ago. "For the record, I don't think there was anything *casual* about what happened between us. I've never slept with anyone else that quickly."

"No?" she asked hopefully.

"My best friend had just gotten married. Happy as I am for him, it was odd to think he was settling down, buying a house, eventually having kids. Meanwhile, I'd broken up with a girlfriend a few weeks before and was feeling, not lonely, exactly, but restless? Then I saw you. And I forgot about everyone else. Even though it was Hugh's reception, I would have bailed in a heartbeat if you'd gone with me."

She peered at him through her lashes. "Professional photographers don't ditch the events they're working. Bad business. But it sure would've been tempting."

"Arden Cade?"

Her head jerked up guiltily, as if the nurse had caught them doing something illicit. "That's me." She turned to Garrett. "Okay, this is the part you can come back for. We'll probably get to hear the heartbeat again."

Plus, he got to remain in her company, which was far more enticing than it should have been.

ARDEN WAS FAMILIAR with the procedure by now. First, the nurse sent her to the restroom with a cup, then took her vitals—including weight. Face warm, Arden asked Garrett if he wouldn't mind waiting farther down the hall. He smirked but did as requested. Then the nurse showed them to room number three, sliding Arden's chart into the plastic file slot on the door.

Thankfully, for the visit she had today, Arden didn't need to disrobe, but she still felt oddly exposed atop the examination table.

Her doctor was Jason Mehta, an OB whose own wife happened to be expecting. Normally he was all smiles and full of anecdotes that put Arden at ease. But today, he entered the room looking troubled. He drew up short when he spotted Garrett; this was the first time she'd ever brought anyone with her.

"I am Dr. Mehta." He extended a hand. "Pleased to meet you."

"This is Garrett," Arden said. "He's the father. I thought he might like to listen to the baby's heartbeat, hear for himself that everything's going well?" Her nervousness made the last part come out as a question. Maybe Dr. Mehta was having a stressful day and his expression didn't have anything to do with her pregnancy.

His next words ruled out that optimistic thinking. "What did the nurse tell you about your blood pressure?"

"Nothing. She wrote it down on the paper but seemed

in a hurry to get me processed. You guys have a really full lineup today."

"She must have wished me to discuss it with you, so I could allay your concerns."

Arden straightened. "There's reason for concern?"

Garrett moved from his post by the door to her side, taking her hand. His thumb brushed back and forth over her hand. She appreciated the soothing gesture, but it couldn't completely prevent her alarm.

"Let's not panic," Dr. Mehta said. "Your blood pressure's never been a problem prior to this, and it was not abnormally high going into the pregnancy. Is it possible you've been under stress lately?"

A strangled laugh escaped her. "You could say that. Plus, I've barely slept the last two nights. Didn't I read somewhere that there's a correlation between lack of sleep and elevated blood pressure?"

"So this is probably an isolated occurrence." The doctor eyed her sternly. "You, young lady, need your rest. The blood pressure spike may well prove to be nothing of consequence, but this is after your twentieth week. I would not be doing my job if I didn't ask some follow-up questions. Any nausea lately?"

"Not in weeks." On the contrary, she'd been feeling pretty good. Especially when Garrett touched her, causing a giddy buzz of sensation. She darted a side-long glance in his direction. When he was this close, could he tell the effect he had on her?

"Any swelling?" When she glanced pointedly at her stomach, the doctor chuckled. "I meant in your extremities. What about headache?"

"She had a killer headache last night," Garrett blurted. "Why? Does that mean something?"

Dr. Mehta made a noncommittal noise, jotting notes on her chart. "Have you suffered blurred vision?"

"Well, yes, but I've had migraines in the past that frequently mess up my vision. I didn't think it was related to the baby."

"Hmmm. The good news is, there's been no protein in urine—at least, not more than the normal trace amounts."

Arden wanted to cover her face with her hands. She was more attracted to Garrett than any man in memory, and even if nothing was going to come of that, she'd rather he not be subjected to discussions about her bodily fluids. She snuck a peek at Garrett, who looked hyperalert, like a soldier at attention. As if he were memorizing everything Dr. Mehta said and avidly awaited instruction.

The doctor put a hand on her shoulder. "You are a healthy young woman. It's likely everything is fine. But you need to come back next week so we can check your blood pressure again and rule out preeclampsia. Meanwhile, to err on the side of caution, try to stay off your feet. I won't prescribe complete bed rest if you swear to me you'll take it easy."

She craned her neck to look up at Garrett. "Better cancel our nursery shopping trip for Sunday. That might be too much after a full day of work Saturday."

"What exactly does this day of work entail?" the doctor interrupted.

"I have a number of portrait sessions scheduled and

the big high school dance Saturday night. I'm the official photographer," she explained.

He scratched his chin. "And that would involve walking around and taking a bunch of candid shots in a noisy ballroom as well as being out late? Absolutely not. You should reschedule the other Saturday sessions, too. Unless you can promise me you'll be taking all the pictures from a chair without moving around much and that none of your clients are going to be demanding and in any way raise your blood pressure further."

She thought of Mrs. Merriweather and the Tucker twins. "Um…"

"That is what I thought."

"But…" Her eyes stung. "I'm a professional. I can't just flake out on everyone."

"Even professionals cancel when there is a medical necessity," Dr. Mehta said gently. "Arden, your baby needs you far more than the high school students do."

He was right. She knew he was right. But she'd already been worried about how the baby would affect her work *after* the birth. She was thrilled to become a mother, but babies weren't cheap. Photography was how she kept a roof over her head. She wasn't sure the high school administrators would be able to find anyone good on such short notice. If they did, would she be losing their future business to an unknown competitor?

She blinked rapidly, trying her damnedest not to cry in front of Garrett or the doctor. She was only able to half concentrate on the rest of what Dr. Mehta said during the visit. Thank goodness Garrett was there to help catch whatever she missed. Finally, the doctor left them, reminding her to make a follow-up appointment with the receptionist.

Garrett stepped to the edge of the table and pulled her against his chest for a comforting hug. It was exactly what she needed, but, unfortunately, she lost the battle with the tears she'd been struggling not to shed. The front of his shirt grew damp beneath her face.

"Y-you must think I'm s-so selfish, caring more about my j-job than—"

"Hush. I don't think that at all, sweetheart."

She sniffed. "I had to cut back while I was sick. Now that it's passed, I've been trying to take as many jobs as possible, to save up for—"

"Arden." He drew back so she could see his expression. "Don't worry about the money. I can help with that. What I can't do is keep this baby any safer. I know we haven't talked specifics yet—hell, this time last week, I didn't even know you were pregnant—but Peanut is my responsibility, too. No, not just responsibility. My *gift,* too."

She was dazed by his generous spirit. Not the financial generosity, but his emotional openness. Some men would be demanding a paternity test right about now to make sure the kid was even theirs before offering to pay a dime. She knew from his candor Wednesday night how angry Garrett was, yet he was at her side, hugging her. And when he talked about the baby, there was real caring in his voice.

Guilt seized her, raw and wrenching. This wasn't how parenthood should have begun for him. It should have been with someone he loved. She could easily imagine his joy at hearing the news for the first time.

He probably would've brought flowers for the woman, a big floppy teddy bear for the baby. He should have been there from day one, and she could never give that back to him.

She swallowed hard. "I need to go pay and set up that appointment. Heaven knows they need the room back."

"If you need another minute, they can wait," he said gruffly.

"I'm good." It was a lie, but one designed to put him at ease. She realized she was feeling as protective of him as he sounded about her.

They returned to the front of the building and arranged her next visit. She almost asked Garrett if he would come with her but bit her tongue. He'd mentioned that he would need to leave Cielo Peak. His entire life was elsewhere, and he had pressing concerns of his own. He couldn't drop everything to hold her hand.

Both of them were quiet on the ride back to her studio. Arden was dreading the phone calls she needed to make, rehearsing what she would say to the clients she was about to disappoint. "Rescheduling the individual sessions shouldn't be too bad," she mused aloud. "I can offer them a big discount for their inconvenience. It's losing the high school business that bothers me. All the future potential—yearbook photos, prom, graduation."

"I wish to God I knew the first thing about cameras. I'd go in your place," he vowed.

She smiled despite her sour mood. "You've already gone above and beyond the call of duty."

He snapped his fingers. "You mentioned yearbooks. Don't high schools usually have student staff, kids who take pictures for the yearbook and student newspaper?

Maybe several of them could cover the event for, I don't know, extra credit or something. I realize they'd be amateur pictures, but if the school uses more than one person, there could be a decent assortment of photos to choose from."

Plus, she wouldn't be handing a competitor her job on a silver platter. Bonus. "It's worth at least mentioning to the principal," she agreed. "Or maybe I could broach the suggestion with the journalism teacher first. I kind of know her a little, since Jus—"

"Let me guess. Your brother dated her?"

"You catch on quick."

"What is he, pathological?"

Truthfully, she couldn't tell if Justin was afraid of being alone or afraid of being with someone. Or both. But it seemed traitorous to discuss her brother's flaws with Garrett. "Anyway, I'll call the teacher when I get back to the studio. If I can get her jazzed up about your suggestion, she might help me convince the principal. Thank you—it's a really good idea."

"Wanna see if I can go two for two?" Garrett gave her a winning smile. "I have another great idea. Promise you'll hear me out before you answer?"

"Sure." She owed him that much.

"Come to the Double F with me."

"What?" It was the last thing she'd expected, an invitation to meet his family and see the homestead. Was he serious?

"Assuming that it's okay with your doctor, I can take you there for a long weekend. Maybe bring you back Tuesday. You're going to be miserable, canceling all your jobs this weekend, and I hate to think about you cooped up in your house, worried about that next appointment. Aren't fresh air and open spaces healthy? You'll come back rejuvenated with a suitably lowered blood pressure."

She laughed at his coaxing. "You know that for a fact?"

"I know I'll be worried about you the whole weekend if I can't check on you for myself," he admitted. "You have to see the place sometime. However we decide to manage this, our child *is* going to spend time there, right?"

"Yes." The word nearly got lodged at the back of her throat. There was no question that Garrett deserved time with the baby, but the thought of being separated even briefly stabbed right through her. For six months, this baby had been entirely hers. She already loved it more than anything in the world.

"You're too good a mother to let your kid stay somewhere you'd haven't already assessed," he said matter-of-factly. "So come with me now, before the baby's born and your schedule gets even more hectic. Who knows? Maybe you'll fall in love with the place."

Her worst fear—falling in love with yet one more thing she couldn't hold on to. One more thing that would break her heart.

NEITHER OF THE Connors was home when Garrett returned from dropping Arden off at work. He'd told her to call him when she was on the way home this evening so he could meet her at the house. "I'll help pack," he'd insisted. "You can supervise. From a comfy spot with your feet propped up and a glass of water in your hand." His tone had brooked no argument.

She'd groused some choice phrases about "high-handed males" but she'd agreed. After all, they both had the same goal—protecting the little one.

Using the spare key Darcy had lent him, Garrett let himself inside, thinking that it was probably best his hosts couldn't see him now. In spite of everything, he was grinning like an idiot. Knowing that Arden would be on his ranch, the land he'd loved since he was a boy, filled him with a sense of triumph and more joy than was strictly logical. As soon as he'd first wondered if she might one day agree to move, he'd been steadily consumed with a need to show her the Double F.

She was emotional right now, and he could imagine how a conversation where he asked her to uproot her entire life would go. It would simplify matters if she'd already grown fond of the area surrounding his home. Relocating might give their unorthodox family their only legitimate chance at bonding. Maybe he was getting ahead of himself, but it was invigorating to nurture some small spark of optimism in the pit of confusion his life had become.

Unfortunately, there was one thing he had to do before he took Arden to the ranch. He had to call his mom. So far, he'd responded to her texts but had managed to put off actually speaking to her. In every message she sent, he could feel her anxiety like a sunburn abrading his skin.

If he called the house now, his father would probably be outside, still working for the day. Assuming Caroline was home, she should be at liberty to talk. Should he practice what to say? Bitterness swamped him. He'd been raised on the propaganda that he and his parents could talk to each other about anything, yet now he had to rehearse just to endure a ten-minute phone call with his own mother?

Best to get this over with, then. Sitting at the Connors' kitchen table, he pulled his phone out of his pocket. He was up and pacing before the first ring had finished.

"Garrett? Oh, thank God." Her voice was full of maternal reproach. It made him crazy that, in spite of the position she'd put him in, *she* could make *him* feel guilty. "I've been worried sick!"

"It wasn't my intent to worry you by not calling," he said stiffly. "I told you I needed space. But I'll be coming home tomorrow, at least temporarily. If you talk to Will—" damn, those words were hard to say "—tell him that I've made a preliminary appointment consultation. My understanding is that's followed by up to a week in the hospital with testing to find out if I'm a good candidate. That's not to say I've decided one hundred percent to go through with the procedure even if I am, but—"

"It's a start. We're both so sorry to have to put you through—"

"Don't!" He didn't want to think about his mom and Will as a unified "we." The idea of the two of them, his *parents,* discussing him behind Brandon's back... His free hand clenched into a fist. Knowing he couldn't hurt granite, he took a swing at Darcy's countertop. It stung like a bitch, but left him feeling calmer. "There's something else I need to tell you. I'm bringing someone with me to the ranch. A woman named Arden Cade."

"Oh?" Beneath the expected surprise was a note of what sounded like disapproval.

"Is that a problem?" he asked defensively. He was a grown man with his own house on the acreage. He'd had overnight guests and weekend visitors over the years.

"Garrett, you're in a very tough place right now. Not quite yourself, and I don't want you doing anything drastic that you might regret later. I know a lot about regrets," she murmured. "Knee-jerk reactions to stress and jumping into—"

"I do not want your advice on relationships." He also didn't want to argue with her or listen to more apologies. "I'll text you before we hit the road. See you tomorrow."

He hung up the phone, angry with his own rudeness and her hypocrisy. He wasn't fourteen, looking for her wisdom on girls. How could she act as if their mother-son dynamic hadn't been irreparably altered?

If he hadn't gotten so ticked off, maybe he could have done a better job explaining his and Arden's situation. *Or not.* The righteous fury that had burned through him when he learned about his child was still there, boiling below the surface like lava, but other powerful feelings were developing, too. The instinct to shield her and the baby from all harm. The driving need to kiss her again. The appreciation for her inviting nature— when he wasn't actively angry with her, she was easier to talk to than almost anyone he knew.

The more time he spent with Arden Cade, the less he understood just what their situation was. Now they'd be together for three days in his one-bedroom home. Would he come out of this weekend with answers? Or just more questions?

Chapter Eight

Arden stared out the truck window, suppressing the need to ask for another stop this soon after the last one. Garrett's parents were expecting them for lunch. *At the rate we're traveling, we might make it to the ranch in time for a midnight snack.*

He pointed at a green exit sign. "I'm gonna get off here. Help me look for a place to stop."

"Don't do that on my account," she managed to say, her tone brittle. As much as she appreciated that he'd come over to help with packing and dinner last night, it was a tad humiliating. On top of having to cancel paying jobs this weekend, she couldn't accomplish basic tasks? Not being able to ride for ten minutes without needing to scout out another restroom intensified her mounting frustration.

"Oh, this isn't for you, it's for me. Old junior rodeo injury." He tapped his side. "My hip jams sometimes. Need to stretch my legs."

The corner of her mouth quirked. "You expect me to believe that load of horse manure?"

He grinned, unabashed. "Hey, I'm trying to salvage your pride here. The least you could do is play along."

When he winked at her from beneath the brim of his black cowboy hat, she couldn't help but laugh.

They changed lanes to make their way toward the exit ramp, winding up behind a huge truck that said Lanagan Brothers across its back doors. "Speaking of brothers," Garrett said, "what did yours say about our little road trip?"

She bit her lip.

"You *did* tell them? We'll be gone three days, and I know you wouldn't want them to worry."

"I was planning to call them from the road," she said brightly. "At a safe distance. Like maybe your parents' driveway."

He smirked. "That explains why I didn't find Justin at your front door this morning. I half expected to see one of them waiting with a duffel bag and the announcement that he was tagging along."

"With time, I think you could all become friends." Her words came out with less conviction than she'd hoped.

"Don't sweat it. Everyone's families come with their own peculiar baggage. Mine especially."

She saw the way his fingers tightened on the steering wheel, and her heart ached for him. One of the reasons she'd agreed to this trip was because she knew he'd been avoiding his mother in Cielo Peak. Arden didn't want to provide an excuse for him to stay away from home, away from his problems. Still, the thought of his parents made her uneasy. She'd been astonished that Garrett was bringing her to meet the Frosts without first warning them that she was carrying their grandchild. She hoped this wasn't, on a subconscious level, petty retribution—him springing this shock on his mother after she'd dropped her own bombshell. *Bound to be the most awkward introductions in the history of Colorado.*

When she'd tried to suggest giving them a heads-up would allow his parents more time to adjust, he'd become prickly, so Arden had dropped the subject, aware that he already had ample reason to be irate with her. Other than that, he'd been the perfect travel companion, thoughtful and funny with decent taste in road-trip music.

"Aha!" Garrett indicated a billboard for a family-owned place that was both a diner and a country store.

They followed the directions and reached a building that looked like an adorable stone cottage on steroids. There were two separate entrances at either end. Garrett parked near the door leading into the shop.

He unbuckled his seat belt. "Want a souvenir for your collection?"

This had been his running gag for the day. The first time they'd stopped, she'd remarked that she hated to use an establishment's restroom without buying something. So he'd jokingly purchased her a shot glass while he waited. At the following two places, he'd presented her with a postcard and the gaudiest ink pen she'd ever seen in her life, closer to the size of a rolling pin. It was a feathered monstrosity that played bird calls when you pressed buttons on the barrel.

He'd looked inordinately proud. "I've outdone myself. How am I going to top this?"

She'd pursed her lips to keep from giggling. "You are only allowed to buy me bottled water for the rest of this trip, you lunatic."

As they strolled up the sidewalk, she reminded him firmly, "Just water. Got it?"

He tipped his hat at her. "Yes, ma'am."

They stepped inside, and a blonde woman behind the cash register called out a friendly hello. Arden headed for the sign that said restroom, smiling inwardly when she heard Garrett ask the blonde to point him in the direction of the bottled water. A few minutes later, Arden reemerged and discovered that the blonde had come around the counter, abandoning her post to stand much closer to Garrett. She was practically draped across him as she laughed at something he said.

To be fair, Arden assumed the woman needed his proximity for body heat. After all, the tiny little thing was wearing a cropped sweater with low-slung skinny jeans. Exposing so much midriff, she must be chilly. Beneath the fluorescent lights, a dark orange jewel winked in her navel. A pierced belly button and a flat stomach. Arden sighed, recalling her own reflection in the ladies' room mirror. She felt like a bloated, overripe tomato in the bulky coat she wore—its bright red color had been so appealing in the store, but now...

Garrett suddenly turned, as if sensing her presence. "There you are. I got the water. Anything else you need?"

Only to get out of here. She shook her head. "Ready when you are."

The blonde pursed her lips in a pout, laying her hand on Garrett's arm. "Leaving so soon? You should stay and have some lunch at the diner. The bison burger is my favorite, but we also have a wonderful Denver omelet and green chili."

"Actually, we already have lunch plans," Arden said, sidling closer to Garrett. Since she'd made a beeline for the restroom when they walked in, it was probable the blonde hadn't gotten a good look at her yet. Once the cashier realized Arden was pregnant, would she assume Arden and Garrett were a couple?

Whether the woman noticed her or not, she didn't put any space between her and Garrett. She managed to reach for the business card holder on the counter without ever taking her eyes on him. "Next time you come through this way, give me a call. Maybe we can have that lunch together."

He didn't take the card. "Appreciate the offer, ma'am, but I'm not in these parts often."

His refusal should have mollified Arden, but her temper was still smoldering when they got back into the truck. Not that she had any claim on Garrett, or cared who he found attractive. But wasn't there a code between females, an inherent rule that you didn't flirt with another woman's guy right in front of her? Garrett wasn't hers, of course, but the blonde hadn't known that. The rational conclusion, after seeing them together, was—

"I got you something to go with the water." Garrett rustled the brown paper bag in his hand, and she wondered what he would pull out of it. Snow globe? A decorative plate featuring the Sangre de Cristo Mountains?

A squeak of excitement escaped her when she saw the familiar gold wrapping. "Are those what I think they are?" Manners temporarily forgotten, she lunged for the package. "They're my favorite! How did you know?" These particular caramel-filled, individually wrapped chocolate medallions weren't always easy to find. She never would have thought to look in a kitschy little market on the side of a low-trafficked road.

He grinned, clearly pleased with himself. "There were some in the candy dish on the coffee table at your house. I recognized the logo when I saw it again in the store."

"Oh, these are the *best!* I could kiss y—" She broke off abruptly, then wished she hadn't. It was just a stupid expression. By stopping midsentence, she gave the words more weight than she should have had. "Thank you."

"You're welcome." But he didn't start the truck. He was watching her, and she could feel the heat in his gaze.

A shiver of awareness ran through her. For the first time, Arden wondered if she'd gotten in over her head when she'd agreed to this trip.

In spite of the circumstances under which he'd left, driving through the wrought-iron archway of the Double F filled Garrett with the same sense of joyous homecoming it always had. He loved his home, these sprawling ranges of short-grass and sand-sage prairie where generations of Frosts had made their living. His grandparents now resided in an assisted-living home in the nearby town, but Brandon brought them here at least one weekend a month for Sunday supper. During some visits they all fished at the spring-fed lake, other times they simply played cards on the wraparound porch that circled the two-story brick house.

Garrett lived farther back in a modest one-story. He

experienced a wave of excitement mixed with nerves as he imagined showing Arden his place. When he'd left, he certainly hadn't been expecting to bring someone back with him. Would she like his house? Would she be cataloguing all the potential dangers to a baby? The good news was he didn't have stairs. But when he considered all the other possible hazards, it made his head spin.

"I'll buy outlet covers the next time I go to town," he announced. "That's a standard part of baby-proofing, right? I'm completely open to making whatever changes necessary. Just let me know what needs to be done."

She was quiet, the silence heavy around them. Was she thinking about all she still needed to do to prepare? He knew she'd hoped to take care of the baby registry this weekend and that she was worried about how fast time was flying. Or was her pensiveness caused by the idea of the baby being here with him and, by default, not with her?

His parents' house was directly in front of them. "Do you want to stop here, or would you rather come back after we've had a chance to drop off our bags at my place and freshen up?"

"We've already made them wait long enough. Let's get out here." But her tone was bleakly unenthusiastic as she shrugged back into her coat.

Garrett had a sudden paralyzing moment of doubt over his decision to bring her. Was it too stressful, meeting his parents like this? What kind of selfish idiot subjected a pregnant woman with dangerously high blood pressure to a nerve-wracking situation? "We don't have to do this, sweetheart. We could turn around and—"

But Brandon and Caroline were already hollering their greetings as they hustled down the porch steps. Obviously, someone had been keeping watch for his truck.

Arden's smile was sad, her tone wistful. "They sure are eager to see you."

She was unmistakably missing her own parents. His reservations about this trip evaporated. Even though he and Arden weren't dating, they were still linked by the baby. Given time, his parents, the only grandparents her child would have, could become like Arden's honorary extended family.

They climbed out of the truck just as his parents reached them.

"'Bout time you got your butt back here," Brandon chided with gruff affection. "I'm too old a man to be running this place by myself."

Garrett blew out his breath in a rude noise. "Good thing we have half a dozen employees, then, huh?" He threw his arm around his dad's broad shoulders and hugged him. Looking at him now, with a fresh perspective, Garrett wondered why he'd never noticed there was no resemblance between them. Brandon had brown eyes and sandy-blond hair, though it was liberally streaked with silver under his ubiquitous Stetson. His build was more compact than Garrett's, his features blunter.

If Garrett hadn't inherited his mother's coloring and facial characteristics, would the truth have come out sooner?

He nodded to Caroline, using introductions as a way to put off embracing her. "Dad, Mom, I want you to meet someone very special. This is Arden Cade."

As she lifted her hand in a timid wave, her coat slid, giving them a much clearer look at her figure.

"Oh, sweet mercy," Caroline breathed, her hand flying to her mouth. She impaled Garrett with a gaze full of impatient questions. "N-nice to meet you. I'm Caroline Frost."

Arden shook the woman's hand. "I've heard a lot about you."

Garrett was impressed at Arden's warmth. There'd been no irony in her tone despite all she knew about his mother.

"And you," Arden said, turning to his dad with a broad smile, "must be Brandon Frost. Your son really looks up to you."

Brandon cleared his throat twice, then hugged Arden with almost comic gentleness, as if he were worried she might break. "So, um, how long have you and my son known each other?"

"We met at Hugh's wedding," Garrett said. "About six and a half months ago."

Pink swept across Arden's cheeks, and she shot him a reproving glare. Was she annoyed that he'd told the truth? He glared back. His father was being lied to enough without Garrett further prevaricating.

Brandon glanced between the two of them, then dropped his arm around Arden's shoulders in a protective manner. "It's cold out here today. Let's get you inside, young lady." He steered her toward the house, their heads close together as if they'd known each other for years.

Caroline whistled under her breath. "Wow. He's a

good man, but I'm not sure I've ever seen him take to someone *that* fast."

Garrett had no intention of lagging behind and being forced into conversation with his mom. She'd no doubt have questions and opinions regarding his pregnant guest. It was only on the top step of the porch that he temporarily slowed, his gaze straight ahead, his voice low.

"Do you know if Will…has his condition changed?"

"No," Caroline said from behind him. "Dialysis and prayers are still the status quo."

He acknowledged her words with a curt nod and stepped inside the house, trying not to feel as though the life he'd known there had been an illusion.

ARDEN HAD EXPECTED a polite interrogation, but Brandon wasn't asking her any questions. Was he waiting until they were seated at the lunch table, or until he'd had a chance to discuss the facts with his son first? At some point, Brandon or Caroline would ask Arden how far along she was or when she was due and they'd be able to piece together that Arden had jumped into bed with him immediately after meeting him. Would they mentally brand her a shameless hussy? Would they assume it was typical behavior of hers, sleeping with men she didn't know? Might they even worry she was some kind of gold digger who'd schemed to entrap a cattle baron?

Oblivious to her inner monologue, Brandon Frost seemed content to squire her through the long hallway leading to the dining room. The walls were covered with pictures of Garrett through the years. The Frosts obviously doted on their son.

Her mood brightened when she spotted an eight-by-ten of Garrett in elementary school, grinning at the camera with that mischievous smile Arden knew. In the photo, the smile revealed that his two top front teeth were missing. "That is so cute! He's adorable." Since she had no idea whether she was carrying a boy or girl, she rarely imagined what her child might look like. But suddenly she had a visual. Oh, how she'd love to have a miniature version of this face glowing up at her as he told her about his day.

"Adorable?" Garrett echoed from down the hall. "Hale, hearty cowboys such as myself are not *adorable*."

She tapped the frame. "This picture says otherwise. I may have to start calling you cutie-pie."

"You may also have to walk back to Cielo Peak," he responded.

Brandon clucked his tongue. "No talk of leaving yet! You two just got here." He gave Arden a knowing smile. "When he took off last week, with very little explanation, I wondered what was so important in Cielo Peak. Guess now we know. Reckon you've been meeting him on those periodic weekend trips he takes?"

"Actually, no," Garrett said. "There's nothing romantic between me and Arden."

Her face flamed. She'd entertained the far-fetched notion that springing her on his parents like this was minor revenge for his mother's affair. It was slowly dawning on Arden that she might have had the right idea but the wrong target. At the moment, it seemed an awful lot like a vindictive response to her hiding the pregnancy.

She wasn't the only person who'd gone red in the face. Brandon's expression had also grown ruddier. "Oh. But I thought…" His gaze, full of confusion, fell to her stomach.

"It's your son's baby," she confirmed, raising her chin imperiously. Irritation with Garrett bolstered her confidence. "Perhaps the more accurate statement would have been there's nothing romantic between us now." Or ever again. She blasted Garrett with a fulminating glare, then—proud of how serene she sounded—told Caroline, "Something smells wonderful."

"She made Garrett's favorite," Brandon said.

Seeming eager to move on and dispel the tension, he led them into the dining room. A dark cherry oval table had been set with plates and silverware. Goblets of ice waited to be filled with beverages, and the sweet buttery aroma of cornbread wafted from the woven basket at the center of the table.

"I'll get the sweet tea while Caro checks on the casserole," Brandon said pointedly. He might as well have held up a sign declaring that he was giving Garrett and Arden a moment alone.

She wasted no time. Maybe some women employed the silent treatment, but she'd been raised by two brothers who'd taught her how to stand up for herself and, when the occasion called for it, swear like a sailor. "You ass," she hissed. "Is this why you didn't want to tell them ahead of time that I'm pregnant? Because you thought it would be more fun to make everyone uncomfortable and paint me as some kind of skank with loose morals?"

"Fun?" he echoed in an incredulous whisper. "Explaining a baby I knew nothing about until this week to a mother I can barely look in the eye and a father who's no relation to me? Yeah. Good times, Arden. Fine, maybe I could have used a smoother approach—"

She snorted.

"—but I will not lie to them about us. They deserve better. And so do you," he said unexpectedly. "I could mislead them about our relationship, but, trust me, you don't want that. Feeling like someone's secret, waiting for the other shoe to drop…"

Her anger slipped a notch. Garrett had been wonderful at the doctor's yesterday and for most of today. She'd known this homecoming would be challenging for him. Maybe it shouldn't have caught her off-guard that his terse explanations had been so graceless.

"And nobody who spent as much as thirty seconds with you could think you're a skank," he said earnestly. "I meant what I said to my parents. You're special. My dad never takes to people that quickly."

Bemused, she took her seat at the table while Brandon filled everyone's glass with tea. Sometimes there was such tenderness in Garrett's tone, yet other times, contempt flashed in his eyes. She recalled what he'd told her after the dinner with her brothers, that he didn't want to be a bitter, angry man. She could see him wrestling with the ways he'd been wronged. She hated that she'd contributed to that inner struggle.

Caroline returned with some kind of cheesy chicken casserole that made Arden's mouth water. The two women sat across from each other, while Garrett and his father sat on either end. Both men had removed their hats for the meal and set them on a side table.

Settling her napkin in her lap, Caroline looked at Arden. "I probably should have thought to ask before now—you don't have any food allergies, do you? Or foods you can't tolerate during pregnancy?"

"I'm avoiding shellfish and a few other items for the time being, but mostly, I can eat everything. And this looks delicious."

"Thank you." Caroline ladled a portion of the casserole onto her husband's plate and passed it back to him. "There are so many people in our church now with dairy or nut or gluten allergies. I never know what to bring to potluck anymore."

"I feel terrible for the Sunday school teacher, Bess Wilder," Brandon said. "Poor woman's allergic to chocolate. She's never once been able to eat Caro's award-winning brownies. Our friend Will has it worse. Diabetic." His expression grew shadowed. "'Course, now he has more to worry about than just missing out on dessert."

Arden noticed that Garrett had gone stock-still, his entire body rigid. And Caroline's gaze darted between her husband and son—she looked like a trapped animal that didn't know where to run. Garrett had said his biological father was diabetic and a family friend. Her heart squeezed in sympathy. It couldn't be easy to bite back the truth whenever Will's name was mentioned.

She wished she was sitting closer to Garrett so she could hold his hand or rub his shoulder. A silly impulse, perhaps, since patting his shoulder would do nothing to improve his circumstances, but she wanted to lend him strength. The way he had at her doctor's appointment yesterday.

Arden couldn't help stealing glances at Garrett throughout the meal. He'd barely eaten a bite, even though the recipe was supposedly one of his childhood favorites. Brandon ate almost absently, spending most of his time studying his wife, a concerned frown creasing his brow.

It seemed up to the women to make conversation, and Arden wasn't surprised when the first question came.

Caroline set her fork down. "So, the two of you met at Hugh's wedding? Are you a friend of—what's his wife's name?" She glanced toward Garrett, who acted as if he hadn't heard the question.

"Darcy," Arden related.

Brandon chuckled. "Freckled Hugh Connor, the kid who used to squeal in terror if his folks tried to make him ride a pony at the fair. Can't quite picture him as a married man."

"Well, he's grown now." Ostensibly, Caroline's reply was for her husband, but her gaze was locked rather desperately on Garrett. "His pony phobia was *years* ago. The past isn't always relevant to the present. I'm sure he's a much different person." Her every sentence and gesture seemed an attempt to reach out to her wounded son, who continued to silently stonewall her. It was painful to watch.

Arden wondered what the future held for her and her own unborn child. Would she ever do anything her son or daughter couldn't pardon? That would cut a mother to the quick. "I wasn't actually there as a guest," she told Caroline. "I was the photographer."

"Photographer, huh?" Brandon asked. "That an interesting line of work?"

"Some days, it's more interesting than I'd like. I learned early on that any portrait sessions including children or animals tend to be unpredictable."

"And do you like working with children?" Caroline asked. Her voice was tinged with sadness. Because of the current strain between herself and her now-grown child?

Arden squirmed in her chair, trying not to dwell on her tortuous afternoon with the Tucker twins. "I love it." *Mostly.*

"If you don't mind my asking, will this be your first child?"

"Yes, ma'am."

"*Our* first child," Garrett said unexpectedly. "I should have figured out sooner a better way to tell you that I'm going to be a father. To be honest, I'm…still adjusting to the idea myself."

"Well, becoming a father is momentous. And becoming a grandpappy?" Brandon looked delighted at the prospect. "Hell, Caro, we're getting old."

"Speak for yourself." She sent him a mock scowl, and he grinned back at her. Despite today's undercurrents of tension, it was evident the two of them were crazy about each other.

"How about your folks?" Brandon asked Arden. "Are they excited to have a baby on the way? Do they have grandchildren already?"

Her eyes burned with emotion. "My mother died when I was five, and my father followed her into heaven a few years later."

"Oh, you poor dear." Caroline's tone was distraught. "You're all alone, then?"

"Not completely. I have two older brothers. I'm sure they'll be good uncles." Assuming Colin was around. His growing restlessness scared her. What if he jumped on that damn motorcycle and disappeared, convinced his siblings were better off without his gloom and damaged psyche?

"We'll love the baby enough for two sets of grandparents!" Caroline vowed.

"We plan to register for baby stuff soon," Garrett said, "so you'll have opportunities to start spoiling your grandchild even before he—or she—gets here."

"You don't know the gender?" Caroline asked. "How soon can they tell that?"

"I wanted to wait until the baby's born to find out," Arden said. "I don't care if it's a girl or boy, as long as the little peanut's healthy."

Brandon nodded. "I'm proud to have a son to carry on the ranch and the family name, but I would have loved a daughter, too." He gave Arden a smile so welcoming that her throat constricted. For a split second, she felt a wave of utter belonging.

She was confident these two people would love her child, and she wanted that for the baby. The chance for grandparents was a gift she wouldn't have been able to offer as a single mom. But it hurt, the Frosts' acceptance of her. It was a cruel tease, showing her something she hadn't had in a long time but couldn't keep.

Or was she, as Layla would say, borrowing trouble? Life was short. Perhaps she should try to appreciate the blessing of this day and take the future as it came.

"Caroline, can I help you with the dishes?" she offered, wanting to repay their hospitality.

"Absolutely not!" Garrett objected. "There were multiple reasons I brought Arden home with me this weekend, but a major one was to keep an eye on her and make sure she doesn't overexert herself. Dr. Mehta says her blood pressure is too high. He didn't go so far as putting her on strict bed rest, but she's supposed to stay off her feet."

Brandon studied her, seeming to sense her frustration. "Don't you fret. Maybe I can't give you the standard walking tour of the ranch, but we can take the Gator."

She stared at him blankly.

"All-terrain vehicle," Garrett clarified. "We've got several kinds of transportation on the ranch, from tractor to snowmobile, but my favorite mode has always been horseback. I'm getting up early tomorrow to ride the perimeter and check fencing. See if there are any repairs we need to make before the serious winter weather rolls in."

"I've never been riding," she said. "I think I sat on a horse to get my picture taken at a birthday party when I was little, but that's about it." Justin and Colin had loved skiing and snowboarding. They'd been more eager to get her on the slopes than in a saddle.

"After the baby comes, maybe we—" Garrett stopped, catching himself. Whatever the future held, Arden doubted his girlfriends down the road would be thrilled about him spending recreational time with his former one-night stand. Even if—especially if—she was the mother of his child.

He recovered admirably, making it look as if he'd interrupted himself to say something else. "Hey, Dad gave me an idea. You wanted to register for baby gifts, but the doc said to stay off your feet. Don't most big stores have those motorized carts now? You can drive from one end of the store to the other."

She knew he meant well, but the suggestion highlighted the grating powerlessness she'd felt ever since the doctor said she had to cancel her jobs this weekend. It was mortifying to feel helpless, prohibited from simple tasks like dishes and shopping. Plus, though she was reluctant to admit to such pettiness, motoring around on one of those carts would chafe her ego. She was a young, comparatively athletic woman in the prime of her life! It had been bad enough standing next to Garrett while that crop-topped blonde with the bejeweled belly button flirted with him. She could just imagine following him around like some giant parade float while lissome salesgirls fawned over him and offered their assistance.

"Another option," Caroline said, "is to register online. We like not living in a city, clogged with traffic and malls, but I have to admit, being able to use the internet for shopping makes it a lot easier."

"Oh, yeah," Brandon grumbled good-naturedly. "She can whip out a credit card and buy anything her heart desires at any hour of the day. Hurray."

"So I suppose you want me to cancel those gifts I ordered for your birthday in November?" Caroline teased. She swung back to Arden. "Speaking of November, do you have plans for Thanksgiving, dear?"

"Only if you count having a baby," Arden said, trying not to gulp. She couldn't wait to meet her child, but thinking about the birth process was still daunting. She kept trying to skip over that part in her mind and look forward to Christmas. Last year had been the first holiday season since Natalie's and Danny's deaths; Arden hadn't even dredged up the energy to put up a tree. She and Justin had exchanged gifts and toasted each other with heavily spiked eggnog. Colin had insisted on being alone. This year, she planned to celebrate the biggest gift of her life.

"I've read all the recommended books," Arden said, "and I'm signed up for classes through the hospital, but I'm a nervous wreck."

"I understand completely," Caroline admitted. "The whole time I was carrying Garrett, I was convinced something would go wrong again."

"Again?" Arden asked.

"Oh! I...is that what I said?" Visibly shaken, Caroline bolted from her chair and carried her plate to the kitchen.

Brandon excused himself, gathering up more dishes and leaving to check on his wife.

Arden glanced at Garrett, who seemed confused. Had Caroline been pregnant before she had him? "Do you know what that was about?" she asked softly.

He shrugged. "Not a clue."

"Maybe we should give them some space," she suggested.

When Caroline returned a few minutes later to ask if anyone had room for dessert, Arden shook her head. "Actually, I'm more tired than hungry. I was just asking Garrett if we could take our stuff to his house. I may stretch out and take a nap."

"Of course. You two just come back when you're ready this evening. We'll have dinner and maybe play some card games." Her smile lacked its previous luster, but she was obviously trying to project cheer. "Have you ever played pinochle, dear? Brandon and I are formidable. Regional champs."

"Never tried it, but good to know I'll be learning from the best," Arden said.

"Thank you for lunch, Mom." But Garrett didn't so much address Caroline as the pale blue wall over her left shoulder.

As they left, Arden snuck one last glimpse at Mrs. Frost, who stood alone in the center of the dining room, shoulders slumped in dejection. She was staring down, so Arden didn't get a look at her expression, but her body language was clear. She was a woman with a broken heart.

"My house isn't very big." Garrett pulled their bags from the truck, feeling foolish for having stated the obvious. His house had always been more than adequate, focused on the exact luxuries he wanted and none of the unnecessary extras his mother had given up suggesting—like vases or "curio cabinets." What the hell was a curio? "It's kind of like yours, actually. So the peanut should feel right at home."

In his peripheral vision, he saw Arden flinch.

"Does it bother you, when I talk about having the baby with me? I'm not trying to separate you from Peanut, you know. I just want to be a father." His throat tightened. "Do you know how many milestones I'll miss? It's unlikely I'll be there for the first step or the first word. At best, they'll probably be blurry videos I get to see weeks later on your phone." If she'd had her way, he wouldn't have even experienced those.

"Garrett…"

There wasn't a damn thing she could say to change the circumstances or take back what she'd done. Shaking his head, he strode toward the house.

He unlocked the door and held it open for her, letting her step into the living room first.

The look she gave him over her shoulder was wry. "So this place is like mine, huh?"

Granted, she didn't own a big-screen television or a leather sectional sofa, but the analogy wasn't completely off-base. "Maybe without some of the homier details," he admitted.

On the mantel he had a framed picture of himself with his parents and grandparents and a much smaller photo of his favorite horse. They were the only photographs displayed anywhere in his home. He suddenly felt self-conscious about that, given Arden's profession. But mountains and spectacular sunsets and countless stars winking down at his porch were part of his daily existence. Why miniaturize them for capture in insignificant pewter frames when he could experience them firsthand?

"The good news is, I have plenty of room for baby paraphernalia," he joked.

The furniture was sparse, but that helped keep the modest-size house uncluttered. His philosophy was that he didn't need much, so for the belongings he *did* purchase, why not buy the best? He'd spent most of his budget on the high-end sectional sofa but skipped over a kitchen table. Between bar stools at the counter, folding TV trays and meals at the main house, he figured he was covered. Did Arden see an indulgent bachelor pad? He had to admit, his style of living wasn't necessarily compatible with having an infant or toddler in the house.

He scratched his jaw. "Guess I need to change more than just the outlet covers, huh?"

She hesitated as if there were something she wanted to say but thought better of it.

"Arden?"

"I actually am tired. Is there a place I can lay down for a while?"

"Right this way." He took her to the master suite. Something potent jolted through him. He'd always been sexually drawn to Arden, but having her here by his bed made the desire more primal. More possessive.

She took in her surroundings. "This isn't a guest room."

"Don't have one anymore. This house was over seventy years old. I did a complete remodel, including knocking out the wall between two small bedrooms. Figured less was more. Literally. You'll sleep in here, I've got the living room. The middle section of the sofa pulls out into a surprisingly comfortable double bed. Bathroom's right this way."

"Whoa." She gaped at the spacious tub. Its hot-water jets were perfect for easing sore muscles after days of sunup to sundown labor. "That's big enough for two people, easily."

The mental image was vivid and instantaneous. He tried not to groan at the thought of slicking soap over her dewy skin. The morning they'd woken up together in that Cielo Peak hotel, he'd hoped she'd join him in the shower. Instead, she'd stolen away without a backward glance.

He cleared his throat. "Unless you need anything else, I'm headed to the barn to help my dad." Putting much-needed space between himself and his alluring houseguest. "I've got my cell phone with me."

Although Garrett truly loved the ranch, he didn't think he'd ever been this eager to tackle menial chores. There was a specific calm that came with the familiar tasks—cowboy Zen his dad had called it once.

He found Brandon starting the tractor.

"About to haul hay," the older man called. "Wanna lend a hand?"

"Sure." Garrett stepped up onto the platform step and held on. The tractor chugged toward the round bales they would use to stock feeders. Sometimes the two men rode in companionable silence. Garrett knew today would not be one of those days.

Brandon came out swinging, raising his voice to be heard over the engine. "You gonna do the right thing and marry that purty gal?"

"Dad, I told you, it's not like that between us. We aren't dating." Relationships required trust. These days, Garrett was feeling pretty cynical about the institution of marriage in general. But that wasn't something he could discuss.

"I don't know what you mean by *dating,* but whatever you did was enough to get her pregnant." Brandon made a derisive noise. "You were brought up in a good home, with parents who loved each other. Didn't think you were one of those men with dumb-ass priorities, the ones too afraid to grow up and settle down."

"That's not it at all," Garrett said, defending himself. "And you're making an awfully big assumption that even if I asked her, she'd say yes. Arden...has been through a lot. She told you she lost her parents. About a year ago, she also lost her best friend and young nephew in a car crash. She's...in a delicate place emotionally, picking up the pieces."

A wholly unexpected stab of guilt twisted Garrett's insides. Whether he'd known it or not, Arden *had* been emotionally vulnerable the night he'd slept with her. He hadn't meant to take advantage of her loss. All he'd known was that the beautiful stranger made his blood boil with need. Hell, she still did.

Arden had said she wanted them to be friends. Did she have any feelings for him beyond that? She'd kissed him at her house but had been quick to blame pregnancy hormones. Had she been trying to tell them that her body might want him, but, aside from the ungoverned chemical reaction, she wasn't interested?

"Caught your momma and me off-guard," Brandon chided, "springing Arden on us like that. Don't get me wrong. We're happy to meet her. She seems like good people. But your momma... Long before we had you, there were miscarriages. Caro's tough enough to hold her own against a coyote or a snake, but she wasn't emotionally prepared to spend the afternoon with a pregnant woman."

Garrett didn't know what to say. "How come neither of you mentioned any of this before?"

His dad shrugged. "Never saw the need. Why dredge up old pain when it's in the past?"

They reached the bales and began the process of lifting them for transportation to the feeders. For now, conversation was over. But his dad's words kept replaying through Garrett's mind. Did Brandon truly believe it was better for the past to lay undisturbed? Caroline Frost insisted that telling her husband about her long-ago indiscretion would cause him pointless grief, that it was a fleeting mistake with no consequence on the present.

Except that wasn't true. Garrett was the consequence. Brandon always talked about the Double F as if it were the family legacy. But right now it felt as if their legacy was comprised of unintentional pregnancies and women who kept secrets.

Striving to push aside the doubt and questions—at least for one afternoon—Garrett threw himself into the familiar rhythm of feeding the cows. He envied the herd their simple existence. As far as his own life was concerned, it felt as if no decision would ever be simple again.

Chapter Nine

Arden suppressed a yawn, staring out the window at hundreds of twinkling stars. "I may have to spend the night in the truck. I'm too stuffed to move. Not that I'm complaining."

"I have to say, my mother went all out. She must really like you."

Was he really that blind? *Arden* wasn't the one Caroline was trying so hard to win over. "I would've said it was more a case of slaughtering the fatted calf to welcome home the prodigal son. In this case, literally." The Frosts' freezer was full of prime beef they themselves had raised. Had it been strange for him as a boy, eating a steak that might have had a name only a few months ago?

"I'm not that *prodigal*. I was only gone for a week."

"Nonetheless, she's happy to have you home. Happy and scared. She's afraid you won't forgive her."

"You think I *want* to be angry with her? I didn't ask for any of this. Waffling between all these emotions sucks. It's confusing. And exhausting." As they walked toward the house, a motion-sensor light flooded the yard.

She took the opportunity to steal a better look at his

expression. Did he classify her in the "any of this" he hadn't asked for, one of the factors currently screwing up his life? She would never, ever wish away the baby, but for the first time, it occurred to her to wonder what would have happened if she hadn't been pregnant when she'd encountered Garrett in the grocery store. Would they have met for a drink, maybe? Reexplored their physical connection? Would there have been a chance for them to develop something more?

"I know what you mean about the emotional exhaustion," she said. "When Natalie and Danny died, I was livid. But maintaining that level of outrage over the unfairness of it all left me depleted. Listless. It was a long, slow climb up out of that pit." Her night with Garrett had been a major catalyst in that process. She only wished there was more she could do to help him with his own personal crisis.

Inside, he asked, "Ready to turn in?"

"No. I slept too long this afternoon," she said ruefully. His bed was impossibly comfortable. "But if you're tired, I can read or something."

He didn't answer at first, and she wondered what he was thinking. Would he prefer the solitude of his own company? Or was he as reluctant to say good-night as she was? "How about we look into that online registry idea?" he suggested finally. "My computer's in the bedroom."

Fifteen minutes later, as Arden wiggled her bare toes and sipped from a steaming mug of generously honeyed chamomile tea, she decided that Caroline Frost was a genius for having thought of this. Arden had changed into a pair of pajamas, and Garrett was stretched out next to her in a pair of plaid flannel pants and a well-worn charcoal T-shirt, his muscles delineated beneath the thin cotton. This was *so* much better than rolling alongside him at a retail warehouse like his fat cyborg friend.

They hadn't gotten to any of the fun stuff yet—the actual scrolling through products and clicking on anything and everything that looked useful. Garrett was still inputting their basic information, listing her as the main contact and her address for shipping. She thought about what he'd said earlier, that his wanting to spend time with the baby was nonmalicious and that she was welcome to spend time here, too. After tonight, she could almost imagine doing so. Caroline and Brandon had entertained her with stories of Garrett's childhood and ranch life; they'd coaxed her to talk about herself and said her brothers sounded like absolute princes—which had earned a sarcastic guffaw from Garrett.

She nudged his ankle with her foot. "You have a strange surname."

"Frost? That's not weird."

"It is for a family this warm. Thank you for bringing me here. Your parents are wonderful people. *You're* wonderful." When the time came that her child was spending weekends and holidays and summers here without her, she would always know that the kid was in good hands.

But now was not the time for such bittersweet thoughts. She wanted to distract herself with cute onesies and colorful board books, not dwell on the challenges to come. "Maybe I should've typed," she mocked him. "Even with swollen hands, I could go faster than you."

"Not my fault," he grumbled, moving his fingers in an inefficient, hunt-and-peck fashion. "Your pajamas are distracting me."

She blinked. "My pajamas?"

"They're sexy."

The sky-blue drawstring shorts printed with bright yellow rubber duckies and the voluminous matching top? "Are you on crack?" A walking lingerie ad, she was not.

"Rubber ducks are for the bathtub," he said, as though this made something resembling sense. "Ever since what you said earlier...I might have pictured you in the tub once or twice."

A sweet, piercing heat flooded her. "Oh." He'd pictured her there? She was surprised by the intensity in his tone, how much he wanted her. True, they'd had incredible sex together, but that had been months ago. Before she'd damaged his trust. Before her body had morphed to its current shape. "Did you, um, picture yourself in the tub with me?"

He jerked his head up, looking startled by the question. Then he set the laptop on the comforter and leaned very close. "Yes." His breath fanned over her skin. "Would you like to hear the details?"

"I... No, I..." Frankly, she'd rather have a demonstration. But no matter how loudly the reckless words echoed in her head, she couldn't bring herself to voice them.

"I understand." He picked up the laptop again as if nothing had happened. She tried not to hate him for that.

Her breathing was shallow, her palms were clammy, her nipples were hard points. He resumed the uneven staccato of his typing.

Arden gulped her tea as if it were a miracle cure for lust, and immediately cursed.

"Whoa. Some language." Garrett looked impressed at her imaginative vulgarity.

"I was raised by older brothers," she said by way of explanation. But since she'd burned her tongue, it came out as *I wath raithed by older brotherth.* Very sexy. No wonder a gorgeous cowboy who could probably have his pick of any woman in the state spent time fantasizing about her. *Sheesh.*

"Okay, all done filling out the online form," Garrett declared. "Do you have a checklist of everything we need?"

"At home. I didn't pack it this weekend. But we can get started and always add items in later." She scooted closer so she could see the screen better and directed him to consumer reviews and safety reports on the car seats that interested her the most. It took them over forty minutes of research and debate to decide on a seat, a crib and a high chair.

He hesitated, his hand hovering over the mouse. "Should we register for two cribs?"

It was a fair question, and she tried not to balk. "How about this? We register for a playpen. It's basically a portable crib that you can fold up and throw in the back of the truck. Not only would it work well here at your place, you could easily schlep it over to your parents' for a few hours in case you wanted to visit with them or they offered to babysit."

After a number of big items had been selected, they began surfing the site just for fun. "Why are there no baby cowboy hats?" Garrett demanded. "That's a travesty!"

She had a sudden mental image of a little boy with Garrett's shimmering gray eyes, a too-big cowboy hat dipping comically low over his forehead.

"Oh, dear Lord." His befuddled tone snapped her out of her reverie. "Now I've seen everything."

"What is it?"

"Baby Booty Balm. Then there's another brand called Butt Spackle. Can't these people just call it diaper rash ointment? Leave the poor kids some dignity."

A succession of memories drifted through her mind—mental snapshots of Danny dressed like a bunny at Easter when he'd only been four months old, him covered in mud after he'd discovered a puddle in the yard, and streaking bare-assed through a dinner party once when he'd emphatically decided his father was *not* going to change his diaper.

"Hate to burst your bubble," she said, "but I'm not sure infancy and toddlerhood come with a lot of *dignity*."

"You never know," he quipped. "Our kid could be special."

Of that, she had no doubt. They made a few more selections, and she realized that the soothing chamomile had done its job. A peaceful lassitude was seeping through her bones. With Garrett next to her, making jokes about their son or daughter, she felt more tranquil and lighthearted than she had in weeks. Not wanting the moment to end, she tried to smother her yawn, but he noticed.

"Why don't we shut this off for now?" He clicked on an icon to bookmark the page, and she noticed some of the other sites in the "favorites" library. Most of them were about kidney transplants and living donors.

"Interesting reading," she remarked. She didn't want to pry, but she hoped that by giving him an opening, he'd know she was available to listen.

"Kidneys are among the most common organ transplants," he said. "And, if I read this one article right, doctors don't actually remove the bad kidney to replace it. They leave it in there and do some kind of…I don't know, arterial rerouting? Like when someone used to hack their neighbor's cable. So whenever Will gets a new kidney, he'll be walking around with three of them inside." Garrett frowned. "Three's an awkward number."

"How do you mean?"

"What was your impression of my parents together?" he asked. "As a couple?"

The question surprised her, but it meant a lot to her that he valued her opinion. "From my perspective as an outsider, it looks as if they're crazy about each other. I can't imagine why your mother was ever with someone else, but if she says it ended years ago, I'd believe her."

Garrett jammed a hand through his hair. "You may be right. I mean, I certainly never saw anything when I was younger to make me suspicious. I always thought my parents were devoted to each other, a shining example. I wanted, someday, to find what they had."

Was he angry not just that Caroline had betrayed

her husband but that she'd betrayed Garrett's long-held ideal? Parents were human beings, too. Yes, his mom was flawed, but he was still lucky to have her.

"I think the affair bothers me more because Will Harlow never married," he said. "He'd bring an occasional date to dinner, but I've been racking my brain and can't remember his ever having a serious girlfriend. It makes me wonder if his feelings for my mother were as platonic as she'd like to claim. Did he ever really move on? And does it matter? Even if he's been pining for my mother her entire marriage, is that a reason to deny him a kidney?"

She gave in to the impulse she'd had earlier today to comfort him. Now that they weren't separated by his parents' dining-room table, she put her arm around his midsection and hugged him tightly, resting her head on his chest. He went very still at first, but gradually relaxed, dropping one arm over her shoulders and stroking her hair with his other hand. It was very quiet in the room, only the whir of his laptop providing background noise.

Finally, he broke the silence. "You know I have a consultation scheduled for Monday? That's the first step, followed by several days, up to a week in the hospital. There are physicals, blood tests, psych evaluation…" He sounded overwhelmed.

"I could go with you on Monday," she ventured. "You know, for moral support."

"I'd rather you stay here."

She sat upright. "Are you sure? I know hale-and-hearty cowboys don't admit weakness, but it might be easier for you with someone there."

"Just the opposite. My dad really likes you."

What did that have to do with the price of skis in Denver?

"I already despise that I can't tell him where I'm going," Garrett said hollowly. "Bringing you with me would be like a double betrayal, making you an accessory to the crime."

"Garrett, you may end up saving a man's life—a man your father cares about deeply, by the way. That's hardly a crime." She decided to lighten the mood. "If you end up spending a week in the hospital, can I at least come visit you? Feels like it should be *my* turn to see *you* in one of the embarrassing paper gowns that covers essentially nothing."

He arched an eyebrow. "Here I thought you were being compassionate and supportive, but really you were angling for a look at my ass?"

"Is there a law that a woman can't be nurturing and ogle at the same time?"

He laughed at that, and his smile made her feel as if she'd won the lottery. Their gazes held a fraction of an instant too long. If he asked again whether she wanted to hear the details of his scandalous bathtub daydreams, she'd say yes this time. But he did the sensible thing and held his hand out for her mug.

"I'll wash these out. You can go ahead and brush your teeth, then I'll take my turn."

He gave her plenty of time. She was already in bed with the covers pulled up to her chin when he disappeared into the bathroom. Listening to him gargle mouthwash, she giggled in the dark. She'd lived alone for years and was unaccustomed to sharing the mundane, yet somehow poignant, intimacy of these daily routines.

The bathroom door opened, and Garrett shut off the light. Her eyes needed a moment to readjust—she could hear him but not see him very well. The man had a fantastic voice, rich and addictive like caramel.

"I'm not going to wake you before I saddle up in the morning," he reminded her. "No reason for us both to be up at the crack of dawn. Dad bought me some pastries when he went to town this morning. They'll be out on the counter. There's also a bowl of fruit and plenty of milk and juice. Mom used her spare key to stock the fridge when she heard I was bringing a guest. If you want anything more substantial for breakfast or need company, give Mom a call at the house. Dad bought her a used golf cart a few years ago so she can zip between all the buildings on the property as long as there's no snow on the ground.

"On the other hand," he continued, "if you feel like taking advantage of the opportunity to sleep in, no one would blame you."

"Feels a bit antisocial," she said. "To come all this way to meet your family, then waste half the day in bed." Plus, Brandon still owed her that tour he'd promised. He said the spring-fed lake was particularly beautiful. And he wanted to show her the spot on this very ranch where, thirty-six years ago, he'd proposed to Caroline.

The mattress dipped as Garrett sat next to her. "I think your obstetrician would see it as 'resting,' not 'wasting.' And you're nearly seven months pregnant. Being a little antisocial is your prerogative, okay?"

"Yes, sir." She gave him a jaunty salute.

He sighed. "Why are you mocking me?"

"Force of habit. I grew up with two well-meaning but domineering brothers, so irreverence tends to be my default mode whenever a man tells me something that's for my own good. Not that you were domineering. You're being considerate."

"I try. It hasn't been the easiest thing this week, but I do try. The considerate thing now is to leave you alone so you can sleep."

For a bare second, she thought he might kiss her good-night. Instead, he brushed his thumb over her bottom lip, tracing the sensitive outer edge and doubling back to curve across her top lip. Unable to help herself, she caught the pad of his thumb between her teeth, biting gently. He sucked in his breath, the gasp unnaturally loud in the stillness.

"Arden." That warm caramel voice spilled over her, making her toes curl beneath the sheets. "Even if I wanted to act on the attraction to us, I'm not sure it would be safe for you."

He had a point. In the unlikely event that her blood pressure didn't go back down and Dr. Mehta diagnosed her with preeclampsia, she needed to exercise caution for the duration of her pregnancy. The last thing she wanted to do was risk Peanut's safety.

She felt ashamed. "I'm sorry."

"Don't be." There was so much banked heat in his eyes, she imagined she could see them glowing.

When he headed for the doorway, she succumbed to a moment of weakness and called him back. "Garrett? I know we shouldn't...do anything stimulating. But do you really have to sleep on the couch? We've shared a bed before." She'd slept in his arms over six months ago and hadn't had that kind of closeness with anyone since. Once the baby came, she would have her hands full. It could be a *very* long time before she was serious enough about another man to spend the night with him.

The thought gave her a pang, as if imagining a hypothetical man in Garrett's presence was disloyal. What if…what if she'd already found the man she wanted? *Then you probably shouldn't have elected to cheat him out of the news that he was a father, especially not at the same time he was grappling with the most important woman in his life being a liar and adulteress.* With his scars and trust issues, she almost felt sorry for the next person to date him.

"You want me to stay?" he asked.

"I do." She held her breath.

"Then scoot over, and don't hog the covers."

"Can I put my icy cold feet on you?" she asked sweetly.

"Not unless you want to hear a grown man shriek like a little girl," he said as he slid beneath the sheets.

She rolled to the other side, fluffing her pillow and smiling at his nearness. Then she chuckled. "Figures. He does this every night—it's half the reason I never get decent sleep anymore." She reached for Garrett's hand and placed his palm over her abdomen. "Peanut seems to be gearing up for the 2028 Olympic gymnastics team."

"You called the baby *he,*" Garrett noted. "So you're thinking men's gymnastics, then? Maybe we should have registered for an itty-bitty set of parallel bars."

"It was just a slip of the tongue, not true maternal instinct." The power of suggestion—she'd been visualizing their child as a boy ever since seeing all of Garrett's baby pictures. By the time they'd returned to the main house for dinner tonight, Caroline had pulled out even more albums for Arden to peruse. "We should register for equipment used in both women's and men's gymnastics. Think that site we were on has anything in a miniature vault?"

"They'd better. If they've neglected to stock cowboy hats for newborns *and* essential gym equipment, we may have to take our business elsewhere."

She laughed and, as though responding to the sound, the baby rolled beneath Garrett's hand. "Peanut seems happy," she said. In fact, she herself felt dangerously content.

Snuggled against Garrett now, it was difficult to remember that he was the same person who'd baldly announced to his family earlier today that there was "nothing romantic" between him and Arden. He'd admitted that he was trying extra-hard to be considerate, and he knew from her visit to Dr. Mehta that she shouldn't be exposed to extra stress or conflict. Garrett was humoring the pregnant lady. Just because he'd agreed to her request to stay with her tonight didn't mean anything had changed long-term, that he'd forgiven her.

Still, despite what her logical mind knew to be true, her last absent thought as beckoning oblivion enveloped her was *my family*.

CAROLINE FROST MUST have been standing at her back door, keys in hand, just waiting for Arden's call. Scarcely three minutes after Arden phoned to say she was awake and showered on Sunday morning, Caroline appeared on the porch.

Garrett's front porch wasn't nearly as elaborate as his parents' wraparound veranda, but it was wide enough to accommodate a white swing and two padded chairs. In the spring, it was probably a beautiful place to enjoy the breezy sunshine and watch birds and small animals flit across the pasture.

"Come on inside," Arden welcomed Caroline. "Although, I feel a little foolish issuing the invitation, me being a temporary guest and this house having belonged to your family for generations."

They walked into the living room, where Arden had set out a pot of decaf coffee and pastries on the table.

"I hope you won't think of yourself as a mere guest for long." Caroline settled onto the couch, her expression earnest. "I'll admit, when Garrett told me he was bringing you home this weekend, I had mixed feelings. Nothing personal, dear. I only questioned the timing. But now I'm delighted you're here. I saw the way he looked at you last night. You may be exactly what he needs."

Suddenly Arden wished she'd taken Garrett's guidance about sleeping in this morning. This was the most carefree she'd seen his mother since they arrived, and Arden was about to rob her of her optimistic happiness. "Mrs. Frost—"

The woman harrumphed an unsubtle reminder.

"Sorry. Caroline. I appreciate the compliment, but you know your son and I aren't dating."

"Maybe not at the moment," she said knowingly.

"Maybe not ever. I lied to him. About the baby."

Caroline looked startled. "How do you mean?"

"I never called to tell him he was going to be a father. I'd planned to be a single mom with him none the wiser. And, frankly, I'm not sure he'll ever forgive me. That's not to say he's nurturing a grudge or being unpleasant to me," she was quick to add. "He's been…wonderful, very conscientious about my health and not upsetting me unduly. But there's a barrier between us. I don't know that it will ever completely go away."

"I see." Caroline's hand trembled slightly as she poured two mugs of coffee. "My son's certainly been through a lot. I wish I could promise you that forgiveness will come, but I'm the last person who can say that. Did he tell you that we had…not quite an argument, but a difficult conversation before he left?"

"He told me. About you and Will."

Caroline covered her face with her hands. "What you must think of me!"

"If there's one thing I've learned, we all act rashly at one time or another," Arden said wryly.

"I wanted to explain the whole story to him, my frame of mind at the time—not that it excuses what I did. But he was too damn mad. When he left the ranch, I had no idea how long he'd be gone or what he'd say to Brandon when he returned. I love my husband, Arden. With my heart and soul! I hate myself for what I did to him…but how do I regret having Garrett? My other pregnancies— Oh, but this isn't an appropriate story for a young woman expecting her first child. I don't want to frighten you."

Arden appreciated her thoughtfulness, but Caroline

Frost seemed as if she desperately needed a friendly ear. "I can probably take it. I grew up with the acute awareness that bad things happen. Often without rhyme or reason. One person could live a charmed life and the neighbors next door could lose their grandmother and their dog and have their house burn down all in the same week. I'll try not to let your misfortunes make me paranoid." *Try* being the operative word.

"You're sure?" Caroline licked her lips nervously. "Oh, if you weren't in a family way, I'd pour a healthy dollop of whiskey into both our coffees. Brandon loves this ranch almost as much as he loves me. He grew up here and planned to run it with his two brothers. But one was killed in Vietnam. The other overdosed."

Arden sometimes forgot that tragedy could be just as prevalent in other families as it had been in hers.

"When we got married, he talked all the time about having children. I think he hoped our kids could recreate the dream he lost when his brothers died. I wanted a big family, too," Caroline added with a sad smile. "We hadn't been married a whole year the first time I got pregnant. We were beside ourselves with joy. I lost the baby in the first trimester."

"I'm so sorry." Miscarriages in early pregnancy weren't uncommon, but Arden could see in Caroline's gray eyes—so like her son's—that the memory still haunted her.

"I was devastated, but the doctor assured me it wasn't a sign we'd done anything wrong or couldn't have children. After some time passed, we found out I was expecting again. This time, we didn't tell anyone. I wanted to safely pass that three-month mark first. We never made it that far."

Arden wanted to weep for her. It was easy to imagine the excited young bride and her groom with their dreams of children filling the brick house, playing hide-and-seek in the stables, gallivanting through the pastures, chasing after bunnies and chipmunks.

"Brandon and I never fought while we were dating," Caroline continued, "and we've rarely fought during our marriage. But that was a terrible time for us. Tension was so high. We didn't know—should we try again? Every time we came together as husband and wife, I was torn between half hoping we had conceived and praying we didn't. Then it happened. I was pregnant. I made it all the way to five months." She stopped, hiccupped, tried to catch her breath and stave off the gathering tears.

"You don't have to tell me the rest." Arden felt like hell for encouraging her in the first place. "Really. It's none of my—"

"No, it's okay," Caroline said bravely. "I should have talked this all out with someone a long time ago. You're doing me a favor. That last miscarriage was the worst. The doctors weren't even sure I could have a baby after that. Brandon was enraged, having lost his brothers and repeatedly losing the babies. I was despondent. We barely spoke, neither of us knowing what to say or how to make it better. The only time either of us laughed was when his friend Will joined us for dinner or to play cards. When the doctor told me it was okay to have relations again, Brandon wouldn't touch me.

"Looking back, I think it was fear. He was afraid to

cause me more physical or emotional damage. At the time, it felt like rejection, like I was defective. A piece of livestock he'd sell off because of inherent flaws. We had a horrible argument one night, and he took off."

Arden was so caught up in the tale she forgot to breathe. Even though she'd seen firsthand that the Frosts had overcome their tribulations, it was easy to imagine how scared and alone the woman had felt so many years ago, wondering where her husband had disappeared to and if he would be all right.

"Turns out, he'd holed up in a friend's hunting cabin to think. That's one thing about Frost boys, sometimes they have to go out on their own before they can figure out how to be with the ones they love. This was before the days of cell phones, and I was inconsolable. Bad storms swept into the area the next day, and Will came to look after me. Tornadoes in the area knocked out the power. Will and I lit some candles and made up pallets in the basement, planning to spend the night down there. We talked about Brandon and I cried, afraid he didn't want me anymore. Afraid no man would want me because there was something wrong with me. I…" She broke off on a wail.

When she'd regained a measure of composure, she finished. "It just happened. I know that sounds awful, like I'm not taking any responsibility, but I know I betrayed the man I love." She sounded lost.

Arden handed her one of the napkins from the table, taking another to dab her own eyes.

"The storm was the impetus Brandon needed to come home. As soon as the roads were cleared, he raced back to check on me. Will begged me not to tell Brandon what we'd done. He said that with everything Bran and I had already suffered through, he could never forgive himself if *he* was the straw that broke our marriage. For years, he wouldn't even come to dinner unless he had a date with him—a buffer, I guess. After Brandon and I made up, it took time to coax him back into our bed. He's a man. He doesn't pay attention to details like gestational calendars, unless it's calving season, but the timing didn't line up."

"You knew he wasn't the father," Arden observed.

Caroline nodded. "After the delivery, my doctor did a procedure to keep me from having more kids. He'd formed a theory that Bran and I were…incompatible, medically speaking. We're so blessed to have Garrett. He's ours in every way that counts. I never would have told him otherwise if it weren't a matter of life or death." Her voice was a naked plea, an entreaty for forgiveness that wasn't Arden's to bestow.

Tears were streaming down both their faces, and Arden hugged her tightly. They sat like that for a while, two mothers both understanding the compulsion to do right for your child amid a minefield of possible wrong choices.

Caroline straightened. "I've wondered, at times, if Will had an inkling of the truth, but we didn't speak of it through my entire pregnancy. As an infant, Garrett once had to go to the E.R. because his fever was too high. I realized there may come a day when there was a medical necessity for Will to intervene. Maybe donating blood or answering questions about patient history, whatever. For the sake of my son, I had to talk to Will, to make sure we were on the same page in case there was ever a future crisis. I never imagined it would be the other way around, that *he* would be the one needing assistance. Garrett may be too angry to see it right now, to remember it, but Will Harlow is a good man."

"I don't think I can convince Garrett to help Will," Arden said apologetically. "That's a deeply personal decision. But I will seize any opportunity to persuade him to forgive you. For his sake and yours. The time we get to spend with our loved ones can be too brief." If anything happened to Caroline without Garrett first absolving his mother, he would never find peace again.

"Thank you. I'm probably the last person in the world who should give another woman advice, but I'll do it, anyway. As you may discover, Frost men are not always easy to love. But loving them is worth any trials along the way."

Long after Caroline left, her words remained.

Arden could picture them hovering over her like cartoon thought bubbles. *Love Garrett?* That would be total folly.

Feeling suddenly claustrophobic in the house, she wrapped herself in a thick blanket and went out to the porch. Arden had thought herself in love once or twice in the past, but those men were dim memories now. She couldn't imagine a time when Garrett would be a "dim" anything. The larger-than-life cowboy had made more of an impression on her in one week than a past boyfriend had made in a year. The pregnancy muddied the issue. Her feelings for Garrett were tangled up in the love she had for their baby.

If they'd met and dated without this automatic bond between them, would she even be having this mental

debate? Was she falling in love, or was she simply overcome with gratitude? Not only had he given her Peanut,
but this weekend he'd also given her a sense of home
and family she hadn't experienced in a long time.

Much as she adored her brothers, their family was
undeniably fractured. She was increasingly frustrated
by Justin's glib refusal to let people get close to him,
and it felt as though Colin were growing more detached
every day.

Motion caught her eye, and she lifted her head, focusing. In the distance, a black horse galloped past, its
rider clad in a dark brown duster and a familiar cowboy hat. Even at this distance, her body quivered with
yearning, making a mockery of her deliberations.

Whatever she felt for Garrett Frost, it was a hell of
a lot more than gratitude.

Chapter Ten

If Arden had thought she was discomfited on the trip to the Double F, with the ordeal of meeting Garrett's parents looming large in her mind, it was nothing compared to the drive back to Cielo Peak on Tuesday morning.

Garrett had returned from his donor consultation the day before more withdrawn than she'd ever seen him. He'd told his father he wasn't feeling well and asked Brandon to fetch Arden to the main house for dinner. At bedtime, he'd gone straight to the fold-out sofa and she hadn't bothered to issue another request that he join her. He obviously craved space, and she refused to be that needy.

What had Caroline said on Sunday? That Frost men had to work through things alone?

Men were fools. Colin was also a believer in solitude over catharsis, but she couldn't see that it was working out for him. Arden would have lost her mind years ago without Natalie and, more recently, Layla. Even Caroline, who'd only just met her, had said her talk with Arden left her feeling more unburdened than she had in a long time.

"I had a long chat with your mom." Breaking the

silence in the truck was far more jarring than she'd intended. Like a loud crash at midnight in a perfectly still house. Grimly determined, she plodded on. "It was very enlightening. I think if you heard what she had to say—"

"I'd what?" His head swiveled toward her, his tone lethal. "Stop caring that she betrayed her husband and her vows? Stop caring that I'm another man's bastard?"

"Well, no." She gulped, clinging to her resolve. "Arden, I don't want to talk about this."

"Maybe not, but you should, anyway. You can't just let it eat at you."

"Actually, I *can*. I don't answer to you."

Perhaps his scornful tone would have deterred another woman, but she'd had a lifetime of practice with stubborn males. She continued as if he hadn't spoken. "You know she messed up. What you don't know are the extenuating circumstances, what she was going through at the time."

"Yeah, you're an expert at justifying deception and questionable decisions. No surprise you're siding with her."

Anger boiled up in her. She'd been sincerely trying to help, and he'd thrown it back in her face, not even bothering to see the big picture. "Do you even know how freaking lucky you are to have a mother who loves you? Who's knocking herself out to win your forgiveness? Maybe I am siding with her—I'm *glad* she had the affair. Otherwise, you wouldn't be here. And I care about you, you jackass."

That stunned him into silence. The admission had come as a bit of a surprise to her, too.

After a moment, he snickered. "'I care about you, jackass'? You steal that from a greeting card?"

She tapped her head against the window. "I guess it's safe to conclude our child is gonna have something of a temper."

"A fair bet." A few minutes later, he added, "I shouldn't have taken your head off. The donor consultation yesterday left me in a foul mood. That's not your fault, and neither is what my mother did."

He didn't address the other part—when he'd accused her of deception and bad decisions. No matter how well they might get along at times, she was fooling herself if she allowed herself to believe for a second that what she'd done was behind them.

"I have to figure out what I'm going to tell my father if I check into the hospital for days on end. I *hate* having to lie to him. That's the part I can't forgive, you know. If she'd made an isolated mistake thirty-odd years ago, I'd like to think I'm a big enough person to let it go. But this isn't an obsolete aberration, it's ongoing. It's my life. We're lying to him every damn day. You think I'm a jerk because I haven't forgiven her yet? Well, I'm having trouble forgiving myself, too."

She squeezed his hand. "Garrett, you haven't done anything wrong."

"Really?" He flashed his teeth in a humorless smile. "Because it sure doesn't feel like I'm doing anything right. What would Dr. Mehta say about my arguing with you when we're supposed to be decreasing your blood pressure?"

"I promise not to rat you out," she said solemnly.

"You'll call me after the appointment Thursday,

won't you?" Garrett asked. "Put me out of my misery? Otherwise, I'll worry. Arden, I…care about you, too."

She wished he sounded happier about it, but, for now, she'd take what she could get.

ARDEN ALMOST THREW her arms around Dr. Mehta in an enthusiastic hug. Was that outside the bounds of an acceptable doctor-patient relationship? "So the baby and I are fine?"

Being a medical professional, he was hesitant to give a clear yes or no. They probably had to attend lawsuit avoidance seminars that trained them how to be so evasive. "Your blood pressure's still elevated above what I would like," he said, "but it's gone down since last week. We'll keep monitoring, but given the significant improvement, this probably isn't a serious condition. Get plenty of sleep and hydration, and watch your salt intake. Don't overexert yourself, and try to minimize stress."

They talked about her being scheduled to work a bar mitzvah Saturday afternoon, and he cleared her to proceed as scheduled, as long as she tried to take it easy for the first half of the day. Garrett's prediction that all she needed was a restorative weekend at the ranch may have been right on the money.

Once she reached her car in the parking lot, she scrolled through her contact list to find Garrett's name, grinning in anticipation of sharing the news.

"Hello?" He yelled the salutation over the considerable background noise of some kind of motor. "Arden, is that you?"

She pulled the phone away from her ear, raising her

voice so he could hear her. "Yep. Calling with important news. Guess whose blood pressure is down? This girl's!"

Even with the background motor noise, she clearly heard his sigh of relief. "We definitely have to celebrate when I come to town next week."

They'd decided that it made sense for Layla to remain her official labor coach since she lived locally and due dates were difficult to pinpoint. However, Garrett wanted to be part of the process and was planning to visit Cielo Peak to attend a couple of the birth classes. Arden couldn't believe how badly she was looking forward to seeing him. How was it possible to miss him so much after only a couple of days?

Even sleeping alone was more difficult after the two nights she'd spent cradled in his arms. He'd rubbed her back when she couldn't sleep, spoke to her in a low, drowsy murmur that seemed to even soothe the baby, taming some of Peanut's wilder, 3:00 a.m. somersaults. Would it be a mistake to tell Garrett he could stay with her instead of the Connors? Hugh and Darcy had generously offered their guest room on an as-needed basis for the duration of Arden's pregnancy.

"Thanks for taking the time to let me know," he told her.

"Hey, we're in this together." And not just the pregnancy. On Friday, she sent him several non-baby-related texts after a hilariously chaotic photo session with a family of seven. Then around eleven on Sunday night, Garrett texted her to find out if she was awake because he couldn't sleep. Upon discovering she was up, too, he called.

Arden lit a few candles in her otherwise dark bedroom and curled up in bed with some caramel-flavored hot chocolate and the phone.

"Is it too late to take you up on the offer to listen if I needed to talk about that kidney thing?" he asked.

Only a guy would call the generous act of giving part of yourself to save another human being's life *that kidney thing.* "The offer stands," she assured him.

"I've scheduled my check-in date for testing the week of Halloween. It's going to require time away from the ranch. Would I be a terrible person if I let Dad believe I was coming to see you?"

Understanding how much the dishonesty bothered him, she knew it had probably cost him something to ask. "I'm happy to be your alibi if you need one."

"Thanks. There's only so much lying I'm willing to do, though. I've made a decision, and I need a second opinion. If, after they finish the blood work and paperwork and mental evaluations, they conclude I'm not a good candidate, then I'll keep Mom's secret. Why hurt Dad with the truth? But if I go through with this organ donation, she's got to tell him. I could be looking at up to six weeks of not being able to do my usual activities around the ranch, and Dad's gonna need a reason. Kidney and cornea transplants are pretty commonplace, there's minimal risk to me."

For her own peace of mind, she'd needed to hear him reiterate that. If anything were to happen to *Garrett*...

"The possibilities of rejection and dangerous infection are on Will's end, but still, this is a major procedure. I can't lie to my father about it."

"I understand that. I imagine Caroline will, too. She knows more than anyone the kind of man she raised."

"It doesn't sound like extortion? You can have my kidney, but only if you bow to my wishes?"

"No. Just…try to be gentle with her. No one can go back in the past and undo their actions."

There was a long pause, and she squirmed inwardly, trying to picture his expression. Was he wistful? Bitter?

"If you *could* go back," he said, "would you have done things differently? Found me, told me about the baby?"

She bit the inside of her cheek. The easy answer was yes. Now that she knew what kind of man he was—and how lucky her child would be to have him for a father—of course she'd say yes. But she hadn't known then. "I can't change what happened, Garrett. I can only hope you forgive me."

He was silent, not the response she'd hoped for deep down, but an honest one.

Changing the subject, he asked if Peanut had settled for the night or was awake and active. "Would it be weird to hold the phone to your stomach and let me say good-night?"

"Yes. I'd feel like a fool."

He talked her into doing it, anyway, and she was smiling when they disconnected their call, mentally counting down the days until she'd see him again.

ARDEN'S FIRST BIRTH class was on a Wednesday evening, and she was touched that Garrett was making the trip even though he'd have to immediately turn around and go back. He and his father were driving to another ranch the next day to look at their herd and discuss trading some cattle. Garrett called her from the road to say he was running a few minutes behind and would meet her at the hospital.

True to his word, he pulled into the parking garage a few car lengths behind her. Her pulse stuttered in anticipation, and she smacked her palm to her forehead. She hadn't even seen him yet—was she really so far gone that she was reacting to the front bumper of his truck?

He came to her side while she was pulling out a duffel bag of supplies and a large pillow from home.

"How long's this session?" he teased, taking the duffel bag from her. "You look like you're planning to spend the night here."

"There are floor exercises. It said in the brochure to bring a blanket and pillow." They fell into step with each other and headed for the maternity wing. "Look, Garrett, I really appreciate your coming with me. I just hope you don't find these classes…silly. They're supposed to cover multiple types of birthing methods and new-age relaxation techniques. Some of it might get pretty touchy-feely."

He shot her a wicked grin. "Some of my favorite pastimes are of the touchy-feely variety."

She laughed, appreciating his easy, cheerful manner. He seemed far more himself now than when he'd brought her home last week. "Have you had a chance to talk to Caroline yet about your proposed compromise?" Maybe he was feeling lighter because they'd reached an agreement.

"Nope. Dad and I have actually been really busy, and since I won't have test results until November, there's not much to say to her on the subject." He reached forward to open the door for her.

"Things on the ranch must be going well. You seem pretty chipper," she observed.

His gaze met hers. "Maybe my good mood is just because I get to spend the evening with you."

And ten other couples, all of whom would be lying on the industrial-carpeted classroom floor, practicing pelvic positions and breathing. She grinned. If that was enough to put a spring in his step, then maybe she wasn't the only one falling hard.

The classroom was plastered with informational posters and smelled faintly of bleach. About half the pairs were already present and the instructor encouraged students to mingle and get to know one another. "No one can fully comprehend what new parents are going through quite like other new parents," she reminded them. "Make friends, compare notes."

Garrett and Arden were the only couple in this particular session who weren't husband and wife. Arden explained that Garrett was the baby's father and would be present for some of the weekly classes, but that her friend and labor coach Layla would attend the others. As they began the first set of exercises, Arden realized that it was going to be a little awkward with her friend here.

They did a take on "passive massage," where the men were supposed to lay their hands on their partners and visualize healing, supportive energy leaving their bodies and filling the mother's. Accompanied by the somewhat cliché recording of soft jazz interspersed with the sound of rolling waves and seagull cries, it could have been comical. But Garrett's touch made it an altogether different experience. She'd begun to crave his nearness the way some pregnant women ravenously craved peanut butter.

The exercise where she was supposed to mentally link with her cervix, however, was far less sensual. Finally, it was time to watch the evening's birth video. There would be one at every class, including footage of a water birth.

"Be warned, this may be pretty graphic," she whispered to Garrett as the instructor dimmed the lights.

"Not to compare you to livestock, but I have witnessed plenty of births. I know what to expect."

Yet ten minutes later, he was ashen. "It's different with cows," he mumbled when the class was dismissed. "I've never really thought about that happening to *you* before."

He seemed to be taking this hard—but this was nothing compared to what she imagined Layla's reaction would be to the explicit videos. *I'd better bring smelling salts with me next week.* She poked him in the shoulder. "Aren't I the one who's supposed to be a basket case?" she asked.

He looked chagrined. "Guess I wasn't really student of the week. Give me another chance?"

As many as it takes. "Of course. Besides, you did way better than that guy in the back who hyperventilated. Thanks again for coming with me. I owe you."

"Funny you should say that. I was actually planning to ask you a favor. Darcy's been requesting, rather insistently, that we consider a double date with them Sunday night."

Arden lost her footing for a second and grabbed his

arm to steady herself. She stopped on the sidewalk, turning to face him. "Now, when you say *date*..." There were so many butterflies in her stomach that there was hardly room left for the baby.

"I know we're coming at this a little backward, but what if we actually tried dating? It seems like the sensible thing to do for our kid, and we do like each other." His grin was lopsided as he tucked a strand of hair behind her ear. "That's how we found ourselves in this position, right?"

She'd admitted to herself that she was developing romantic feelings for him. Were those feelings mutual?

Maybe not yet. He'd said he *liked* her and that dating would be *sensible,* but that was a foundation, wasn't it? Could they try building a relationship and see where it led?

And if it doesn't work out? They would be linked together for their child's entire life. The stakes were considerably higher than when her brother had broken up with a waitress and made it temporarily uncomfortable to have lunch at his favorite barbecue house.

"C'mon, sweetheart," Garrett coaxed. "Is the idea of going out with me that repellent?"

Not repellent. Beguiling.

She nibbled at the inside of her lip. Was this wise? She tried to imagine what guidance she'd give to Layla, or Justin or, years from now, her own child. Strategic retreat, or embrace the possibilities?

"All right, you're on," she decided. "It's a date."

Chapter Eleven

"I think it's so romantic that you're dating now!" Layla winced when a string of hot glue adhered to her finger. "Of course, most women don't wait until they're seven months pregnant to enter a relationship with the baby's father, but you're a unique individual."

"Thanks, I think." Arden was watching her friend in morbid fascination. So far, Layla had burned herself twice and cut herself with a pair of extra-sharp craft fingers. "It might be premature to say we're *dating* since our first date isn't until tomorrow night."

"But you've talked every night this week."

True. She'd already been mentally filing funny observations from her morning with Layla to entertain him with during their conversation tonight. "Why again are you the one who has to make these—what do you call 'em?"

"*Calavera* masks. For the multicultural performance the drama students are doing. I can't tell you how thrilled I would be if the theater teacher got transferred to another district," she huffed. "Just because she had some minor parts in a couple of movies out in California, the principal and PTA indulge her every whim. Don't get me wrong, I'm all for the performance, but everyone else ends up rushing to do the work whenever she has one of these last-minute 'brainstorms.'"

Arden laughed at her friend's sequined air-quotes. Sparkly beads and bits of feathers clung to Layla's glue-scarred hands.

The two women sat at Layla's kitchen table, and a dozen skull masks covering the painted wood surface. Of the four that were already adorned, Arden had finished three of them.

"You really saved my butt, agreeing to do this," Layla said. "I asked two of my honors students, Melissa and Phillip, to help. They've been dating since freshman year. They're so inseparable, they have one of those unified monikers—you know, where people mash their names together? Philissa."

Arden carefully brushed glitter onto the swirling pattern she'd created with glue. "So where are they?"

"Officially, Melissa remembered an SAT prep class she had to attend this morning and he woke up with a fever. Unofficially? I overheard some arguing in the hall at school. She accused him of hitting on a JV cheerleader. Note to self, don't rely on hormonal teenage couples." Layla stopped abruptly. "Hey! If you and Garrett make it work, your name will be Garden."

"*This* is the thanks I get for spending my Saturday making arts-and-crafts skulls?" Arden asked dryly.

"What you have against gardens? Seems fitting to me." Layla chortled. "You guys are obviously fertile."

"You know what I just remembered? *I'm* supposed to be at that SAT prep class, too."

"If you stay," Layla declared, "you get to taste-test

the batch of Mexican wedding cookies I'm baking for after the performance."

"Done." Arden knew from experience that her friend's cookies were small, sugar-coated bites of heaven.

"Good, because there's something else we have to— damn it."

Laughing, Arden got out of her chair and reached for the hot glue gun. "Give that to me before we have to call 9-1-1."

"I have many impressive skills," Layla grumbled. "This just doesn't happen to be one of them. Okay, so about this other thing I wanted to discuss? Now that you two crazy kids have registered, I want to throw you a baby shower!"

"You do?" Arden was touched.

"Duh. That's what friends do for each other. That and make Day of the Dead masks, even though Day of the Dead isn't technically until November first. It sounds like Garrett enjoys being involved in planning for the baby, so I thought he'd like to come. But I don't think it should be specifically a couples' shower, since that would count me out. And both your brothers."

"You want my brothers to attend?" Arden asked skeptically. Colin would be visibly uncomfortable, a pall on the festivities, whereas Justin would be like a kid in a candy store, unabashedly flirting with any female guests. Too bad she couldn't invite his ex-girlfriend Elisabeth. She and Arden had been close until the breakup.

"Your brothers are your family. I know how critical family is to you."

That was indisputable. "Okay, so they go on the invite list. Who else are we thinking? Vivian Pike, for sure." Viv managed the personalized print store next door to Arden's studio. She specialized in customized stationery and cute business cards. "And Hugh and Darcy Connor." Not only had they been the reason Arden and Garrett met in the first place, but it would also be nice for Garrett to have some friends there.

Thinking of Garrett made her question the timing. In late October, he would be in the hospital. If he decided to through with the donation, she had no idea what the potential timetable for the transplant was. If they were going to have this shower, sooner might be better than later.

"Layla, I know it doesn't give people much notice, but if we keep it on the casual side, is this the type of thing that could be put together in a couple of weeks?"

"Are you kidding?" Her friend swept a hand majestically over the table. "Last-minute rush jobs are my specialty. As long as I don't have to hot-glue anything for your party, we're golden."

GARRETT COULDN'T REMEMBER the last time he'd been nervous picking a woman up for a date. After all the time he'd spent with Arden, it was insane to feel nervous now. *No more insane than taking the mother of your child on a first date.* Maybe "sane" wasn't really their thing.

He parked his truck in her driveway, thinking that his dad was partly to blame for his anxious tension. Before Garrett had left the Double F, his father had resumed hounding him about marrying Arden, urging Garrett to hurry.

"I don't get why you're dragging your feet," Brandon had scolded. "She's a great gal, and you know it. Do you want your kid to be illegitimate?"

Why not? Garrett had thought sourly. *I was.*

Garrett had always assumed he'd get married someday. He just wanted to find the right person, the way his parents had. It was sobering to think that, as many years as they'd been together, as much as they loved each other, Caroline had been unfaithful. How could a relationship between two people with such a solid foundation go so wrong? He was glad he and Arden were going to give a relationship a try, but that didn't mean he was naive. He knew there were bound to be mistakes and regrets lying in wait for them.

Which was hardly the right attitude to begin their date.

He pasted a polite smile on his face that became a real one as soon as she opened the door. God, she was lovelier every time he saw her. He suddenly wanted to kick himself for not bringing flowers.

Her gaze swept from his head to his feet, and she beamed at him. "Wow. You clean up well. Not that you aren't equally attractive in a coat and cowboy hat, but... wow. Am I underdressed?"

"No. You're perfect. And my clothes aren't *that* dressy." Okay, he'd swapped his usual jeans for black slacks and got a haircut yesterday, but it wasn't like he'd shown up in a tie.

She wore an ankle-length maternity dress in deep green. The color made her eyes damn near mesmerizing.

"You look gorgeous," he told her as he stepped inside. The words weren't very suave or creative, but there was enough ragged appreciation in his voice that she couldn't doubt his sincerity.

"Well, I'm glad we were both in the same ballpark. When I told you to surprise me with our destination, I didn't realize I was making my wardrobe choice so difficult."

"You could have called to ask for hints, like whether we were going to be outside or whether the venue was formal."

"That felt like cheating somehow." She tilted her head. "So where *are* we going?"

"You'll see. Hugh and Darcy are meeting us there." Part of him worried that adding another couple made the evening less romantic, as if he wasn't trying hard enough, but he wanted Arden to get to know the Connors better. He liked the idea that they could look in on her if Garrett were unable to come to town for long stretches.

"Don't let me forget to tell them about our shower! Official invitations will go out later."

He frowned. "Shower?"

"Ah, I jumped ahead—sorry. Guess I temporarily forgot to invite you to the baby shower. It's on my list of things to talk about tonight."

He laughed. "You have a list?"

"Um…" She stared at the floor. "I'd like to say that was a figure of speech, but if someone were to check the memo section on my phone, they might find actual bullet points. You don't understand what pregnancy brain is like! I had to fill out a form the other day, and I blanked on my own address. So, yeah, I may have jotted down a few reminders of things that happened this week I thought you'd get a kick out of. It made me feel calmer, like I had some backup ammo in case we hit any awkward silences. Does this make me sound like a lunatic who doesn't know how to be spontaneous?"

"It makes you sound well-prepared and thoughtful." Qualities that were going to make her a great mom. Scratch that—qualities that made her a great person. They'd been so fixated on the pregnancy lately, their excitement for the baby, that he had to remind himself to stop and just enjoy *her*. Starting with tonight.

He stepped behind her to help her into her coat and resisted the urge to pull her body back against his. Her soft curves were tempting, but this was their first date and he wanted to be on time for meeting the Connors. "Ready to have a wonderful time?"

ARDEN WAS SO busy absorbing her surroundings that she didn't hear the hostess the first time she offered to take their coats. "Oh! Yes, please." She shrugged out of the red wool jacket.

She and Garrett had arrived first. They were spending their evening at a dinner theater called the Twirling Mustache Tavern. Arden had been here once, years ago, to see a musical with Natalie. But the Tavern was actually known for its uproariously over-the-top melodramas. Audience participation was strongly encouraged.

Theatergoers were expected to cheer loudly for the hero, yell catchphrases along with the actors and greet any romantic moments with a synchronized "aww." But according to the playbill she'd been handed, the villains got the lion's share of the attention. Patrons could not only boo and hiss when a mustache-twirling bad guy tied a heroine to the train tracks or evicted a little old lady from her farm, but each table was also given a huge bucket of popcorn they were supposed to throw at the stage during evil deeds. House rules asked that customers *only* throw the popcorn, and not the actual bucket. It all sounded like a blast and, despite her emergency list of topics in case of awkward silence, she doubted silence of any kind would be a problem.

They explained to the hostess that friends would be joining them shortly and were escorted to a table for four very close to the stage.

"I don't know how well you got to know them when they hired you for the wedding, but I think you'll really like Hugh and Darcy. Although, word of warning?" Garrett said. "Darcy is a dedicated—one might even say, zealous—bird-watcher. If the subject happens to come up, we may be hearing about it for a while. Like, until November."

Arden chuckled. "So no mentioning birds, even in passing."

"To be extra safe, we probably shouldn't order the duck or chicken. But other than that one tiny quirk, the Connors are great."

"It would be pretty hypocritical of us to judge anyone for being quirky." She gave him a rueful smile. "We're not exactly the poster children for normal. How many men take a woman home to meet his parents before he's even been on a date with her?"

He brandished a piece of popcorn at her. "Are you saying I'm abnormal?"

"Psst!" Hugh Connor stopped at their table, his voice

a faux whisper. "I know you said you were out of practice at this, buddy, but generally speaking, it's not chivalrous to throw things at your date."

Behind him, Darcy was nodding in agreement. "I suppose you could make a possible exception for rose petals, but even then she might find it odd." She craned her head around her husband and waggled her fingers in hello. "A pleasure to see you again, Arden."

It turned out that Darcy and Hugh were regulars at the Tavern, and they recommended some of their favorite entrees. The food was delicious, but Garrett's smiles throughout the dinner were far more tantalizing than anything on the menu. Arden had enjoyed her time at the Double F with Garrett and his family, but there was no denying that being around his parents had caused him stress. Here in the presence of an old friend, no secrets to be kept or emotional baggage to overcome, Garrett was relaxed and witty.

What am I going to do? The more she saw of Garrett, the more she discovered to love about him. Her heart went out to the taciturn cowboy who was struggling with his sense of loyalty to each parent. But her heart absolutely melted for the charming date who knew all the right things to say and never failed to signal the waitress if Arden's glass of water was even close to getting empty. He was gallant and funny and caring. She couldn't think of any qualities she might want in a man that Garrett Frost didn't have in abundance.

Except maybe forgiveness? Against her will, she recalled how icy he'd been when Arden had tried to broker peace between him and his mother. While he seemed to be making gradual progress, it was slow. How long would it take his anger to fully dissipate? And what about Arden herself? He'd asked the other night if she'd do things differently, and he hadn't seemed pleased with her answer.

But those were needless worries. For now, they were having a fantastic evening together, and there was no reason to dwell on negative issues he might be well on his way to resolving.

During a particularly "dastardly" scene in the play, Garrett heckled the villain louder than anyone else in the audience, mercilessly pelting him with pieces of popcorn since he was at such close range. Without ever breaking in dialogue, the actor stepped down from the stage and upended the bucket of popcorn on Garrett's head. Arden and Darcy both burst into laughter, and Hugh choked on his beer.

Garrett laughed as hard as any of them, and the amusement in his silvery eyes gave her hope. He didn't look like a man consumed with anger.

Once the play ended, Darcy asked if they wanted to join her and Hugh at a coffeehouse that was open late and featured independent musicians. Arden thanked her for the invitation but admitted she was tired, then told the Connors she looked forward to seeing them at the baby shower.

The ride home nearly lulled her to sleep, but when Garrett walked her to her door, she was instantly, eagerly, awake. Her heart thundered. Surely he'd kiss her good-night? They'd kissed each other even when they *weren't* dating.

"Did you, um, want to come in for a drink?" she asked breathlessly.

He shook his head. "No drink necessary, but the gentlemanly thing would be to see you safely inside." The wolfish grin he gave her beneath the front porch light made her think *gentlemanly* wasn't what he had in mind.

Once they made it to the foyer, he tugged her into his arms, his lips greedily claiming hers as if he'd been waiting to do this all night. She certainly had. Exquisite sensation blossomed inside her, hot and liquid. He speared his tongue into her mouth, making her light-headed with pleasure. When he pulled back, she almost whimpered in protest.

"I promised myself I would kiss you good-night and leave," he confided.

"Already?"

"If we keep this up, sweetheart…" With a groan of surrender, he took her mouth again. Her jacket hit the floor, and his hand slid down from the curve of her shoulder to cup her breast. She sucked his lower lip in fervent approval.

And the baby picked that moment to kick—although it felt more like a cannon blast than a foot motion.

Arden could feel her cheeks reddening as she stepped back. *Way to kill the mood, Junior.*

Garrett's eyes glowed with humor. "Is that kind of like the kid walking into the room and catching his parents making out?"

"Pretty talented, considering ours can't even walk." She managed to laugh in spite of her frustrated libido.

He palmed her cheek. "I should go."

"You don't *have* to. We spent the night together at the ranch," she reminded him.

"Not after kissing like that, we didn't. I stay, you might not get much sleep."

Sounds good to me. She knew her need for him was clear on her face—not to mention pulsing through other parts of her body.

He swore under his breath. "I'm not made of steel. We agreed to date, and I want to do this right. You pointed out the steps we've skipped, how we've done everything out of order up until now, and I think it's too important to be rushed. I want to send you roses tomorrow to thank you for a great time, start planning where I can take you next, call you during the week to let you know I'm thinking about you. I want to court you. You deserve that."

She let out a dreamy sigh. "That is the most romantic rejection I have ever heard in my life."

TRUE TO HIS word, Garrett did call her all during the next week—often right around bedtime. It quickly became her favorite part of the day. Hearing from him always gave her that little rush of exhilaration, but it was different at night, more intimate, less hurried. She curled up in the dark, closed her eyes and lost herself in his voice, pretending he was there with her.

He wasn't able to come to Cielo Peak the following weekend because he was managing the ranch while his parents were in Denver. Caroline was shopping in the city while Brandon attended a conference on winter grazing. Who knew there were such things? Arden had always pictured ranchers giving each other sage advice over fence lines, not holed up in the conference room of a Denver hotel, reviewing PowerPoint presentations about sod, rye and clover.

"But next weekend, when I come to town for the shower, I'll make it up to you by staying several nights," Garrett promised.

The Friday night before the shower, he called to tell her he couldn't wait to see her the next day. "I miss you."

"Want to prove it? When you stay in town this weekend, stay with me," she pleaded. "I don't want to be alone after the shower. I'll be all weepy over cute little outfits, and there will be nursery equipment I'll be impatient to assemble. I know you don't want me attempting to build furniture on my own."

He chuckled. "That's blackmail."

"Mmm, actually I think it's coercion," she said unrepentantly. Then, more seriously, she asked, "Will you at least think about it? Spending the night here could be your shower present to me."

"What makes you think I don't already have a present?"

"Really?" She spent a few minutes trying to wheedle clues out of him while he taunted her in classic juvenile I-know-something-you-don't-know fashion.

"So tell me again who's on the guest list for this shower?" he asked. "It feels surreal that I'll be celebrating the arrival of our baby with some people I've never even met."

"But you'll know the Connors and Layla, plus my brothers will be there." She got momentarily sidetracked. "I *wanted* to invite Elisabeth Donnelly. She's Justin's ex-girlfriend. They were great together, but she was the godmother for her college roommate's daughter.

When her former roommate passed away, Elisabeth got custody of the little girl. The situation was too intense for my brother. I adore Justin, but he needs to grow up. If he had any sense at all, he'd get her back. I asked him if I could invite Elisabeth but he refused. I should have just asked her to come and not told him."

"You would've blindsided him? In the middle of our shower?"

"For his own good. You don't understand. He makes jokes all the time, but his happiness is superficial. Deep down, in his own way, I think he's nearly as miserable as Colin. He could benefit from someone scheming on his behalf."

"But not telling him she was coming would be the same as lying to him." Garrett's tone had taken on an edge. "You can't deceive someone just because you think you know what's best!"

She inhaled sharply, stung by his anger.

"If we're going to be in a relationship, Arden, I have to know you aren't going to rationalize away my right to the truth whenever it suits you."

"And *I* have to know that you can get past this!" She could only apologize so many times. "You had every right to be upset that I kept the pregnancy a secret, but I can't change that. And we weren't even discussing us, we were talking about my brother. I know my family a lot better than you do."

"Oh, really? Because you keep trying to pin Colin down and make him stay put. You don't seem as interested in what he needs as you do in keeping him close because it's what you need."

The implication that she was selfish sent her reeling. She adored her brothers and wanted the very best for them. Especially Colin! How many eighteen-year-old boys put their lives on hold to raise an annoying kid sister?

"You don't understand what it's like to have brothers or sisters," she shot back. "And you sure as hell don't seem to understand *me*."

With a muttered "Guess not," he told her he'd see her at the shower and ended the call.

"OH, HOW I WISH the punch was spiked," Arden lamented.

"If it was," Layla reminded her, "you couldn't have any."

"Maybe we could use it to sedate Garrett. Assuming he's even coming."

Layla paused in the middle of removing a plastic baby bottle from its packaging. "He'll be here. You guys had a fight—it happens. You're pregnant, with a hormonal probability of turning cranky, and it was late at night. He could've been tired and overreacted. Honestly, it was one argument. That's nothing compared to the kinds of things the two of you have endured. Together and separately."

"Lord, I hope you're right." Arden had lain awake for hours last night, rotating between crying jags, righteous fury and the almost visceral need to call him back.

"Of course I'm right! Now help me open the rest of these bottles."

"Why are there so many?" Arden asked. "Don't tell me these are what the guests will be drinking out of."

"Ha! No, these are for baby bottle bowling. Because

yours truly is a genius, I planned all games where the equipment needed is actually extra baby supplies for you guys. Once I've got these all opened, where can I set up my lanes?"

They'd discussed having the shower at Layla's house, since she was the hostess and didn't want to create any extra work or cleaning for the mommy-to-be. But they'd decided it was silly to have everyone bring presents to her house when Arden and Garrett would simply have to load them back up for transport home. So Layla had come over bright and early to help Arden tidy up— and to listen to her vent about last night's catastrophic phone call.

"It started off so well," Arden said in disbelief. "He was as happy to be talking with me as I was with him. How did we make such a mess of it?"

"Sometimes phone conversations are more difficult than face-to-face. Long distance is hard, but you guys will get the hang of it."

How? After the baby was born, she'd be exhausted from middle-of-the-night feedings and barely be able to stay awake for their nocturnal chats—and that was assuming that a crying infant didn't make it impossible to hear. She'd adored her nephew, Danny, but when he'd been an infant, some of his ear-splitting crying spells had gone on for thirty minutes straight. Even if she and Garrett eventually mastered long-distance dating... to what end? What was their ultimate goal here? That she'd live in Cielo Peak, he'd work the ranch all week and they'd only be a family on weekends? Her memories of her own parents were faded with time, but she remembered two people very much in love.

Family was the most important thing in the world. Didn't her child deserve more than parents who were in a part-time relationship?

"Hey!" Layla snapped her fingers. "I know that look. Guests will be here within the hour. This is not a good time to fall apart. Besides, you know that if Justin and Colin get here and find you red-eyed over Garrett, they'll use it as an excuse to pick a fight with him."

"Good point." Telling herself that Layla had gone to a lot of trouble to make today special, Arden got busy slicing up cucumbers for the cucumber-and-cream-cheese appetizers. The *whack whack whack* of the knife against the cutting board was cathartic, and by the time the doorbell rang, she no longer wanted to cry. Much.

She found Garrett at her front door, holding an armful of gold bags—her favorite chocolate and caramel medallions.

"I bought out three different stores," he told her. "Can you forgive me? I know you love your brothers, and you were only speaking hypothetically."

"Only if you'll forgive me, too. I should've been more tolerant of your point of view." She threw her arms around him, although he was holding too much candy to return the hug. "I'm so glad you're here. I was afraid you'd change your mind."

"And miss today? This is our first real family event. Wild horses couldn't have kept me away. Now, would you like to relieve me of some of this chocolate? Because I still have to unload all the real gifts from the truck."

As he brought in prettily wrapped pastel packages and gift bags, Layla mouthed a gloating *told you so* in

Arden's direction. Arden merely laughed. She'd never been so elated to be wrong.

Shortly thereafter, Justin arrived, asking if there was anything he could do to help. He made jokes with Layla and Arden and was even passably friendly to Garrett. But when he and Arden were alone in the kitchen, his good-humored mask fell away, revealing sorrow.

"Don't shoot the messenger," he said. "But I bring tidings from our brother."

"He isn't coming?" She was as unsurprised as she was disappointed.

"I tried for over an hour to talk him into it, telling him it's what our parents would have wanted—for him to be here since they can't—but nothing worked."

"Thanks for making the effort. Maybe…maybe it is better for him not to be here." She didn't want to flaunt her burgeoning new happiness in front of Colin, and the baby shower she had once thrown for him and Natalie would probably have been etched in his mind all day. Replaying Garrett's words from the night before, she tried to focus on what her brother needed for his mental well-being. Maybe some men were like wounded animals, needing to skulk off on their own before they could heal. She resolved to stop smothering him with her worry.

The Connors' arrival was a welcome distraction. As it turned out, Darcy was nearly as besotted with babies as she was with birds. She cooed over the decorations, the planned games, the adorable gift tags on the presents that were piling up in front of the fireplace. And she kept reminding Arden and Garrett that after the baby was born, they had a ready and waiting babysitter.

"And that is officially the last time I say the *B*-word," Darcy vowed as she handed a diaper pin over to Layla. One of the ongoing shower games was that everyone fastened a diaper pin to their clothes, and if they were heard saying the word *baby,* another guest could claim the pin. Whoever had collected the most by the end of the party won a mystery door prize.

The final guests showed up, including Vivian Pike and Nurse Sonja from the hospital. As with all parties since the beginning of time, everyone ended up gathered around the snack table.

Justin grinned at the nurse he'd briefly dated. "Good to know that if this shindig gets too wild, we have a medical professional on the premises in case of emergency."

When Sonja asked Arden if she was sticking to her guns about not learning the gender ahead of time, Darcy followed up by saying, "Are you making lists of potential girls' names *and* potential boys' names?"

"I can help with that," Justin volunteered. "The name Justin, for example, is majestic and traditional. Teachers won't misspell it, kids won't pick on it. Also good are Justine and Justina for girls."

Garrett made a show of leaning toward Arden and whispering much too loudly, "Remind me why we invited him."

"Because we feel sorry for him." She smirked. "He's alienated all the women in a hundred-mile radius and thus has no social life."

"That is patently untrue," Justin argued. He turned to Vivian, who fell into the rare category of both being single and having never dated him. "For instance, have I alienated you yet? Justin Cade, nice to meet you."

They followed bottle bowling with an entertainingly ridiculous scavenger hunt and a baby-changing relay race where team members had to strip one outfit off of a baby doll and get a completely different one all snapped into place as quickly as possible.

"And Arden gets to keep all these clothes," Layla added. "I went with gender-neutral colors like yellow, which is just as easily masculine as feminine."

"The hell it is," Garrett whispered for Arden's ears only. He obviously didn't think buttercup-yellow would be suitable attire for a son.

From across the room, Justin gave them a thumbs-up, as if he knew what Garrett had said and agreed whole-heartedly. It was the first sign of real bonding Arden had witnessed between the men, and it was heartening to think they might not kill each other, after all.

Layla sliced up the decadent cake she'd ordered from Arden's favorite local bakery, and the guests found spots in the cramped living room to enjoy dessert while watching her open gifts.

The Connors had purchased an adorable play mat labeled a "baby gym," and Arden laughed. "Did Garrett tell you our child is already an Olympian in training?" Garrett's parents went overboard with their gifts, which included both the stroller and the playpen from the registry. Arden rolled her eyes at Justin's present, infant shirts with slogans like Cuteness Runs in the Family. You Should Meet My Uncle.

"You are *not* using my kid to scam women," she said. He laughed, then handed her a card with Colin's handwriting on it. "He asked me to deliver this." He lowered his voice. "I know he hates himself for not being here. He just couldn't."

Oh, what she wouldn't give to wave a magic wand and erase Colin's pain. If Colin needed to go somewhere else in order to eventually find his way back to them, she would support that. As she read the card he'd signed, sentimental tears welled in her eyes, then she gasped when she saw the amount of the gift card he'd placed in the envelope.

Garrett was equally startled. "Whoa. Is this to help pay for newborn provisions, or is he single-handedly trying to put the kid through college?"

After everyone else's presents had been unwrapped, Garrett handed her a gift bag that he said was from him. "Nothing off the registry," he said. "Just a little something all kids should have."

She reached inside and pulled out a baby-size super-soft, red cowboy hat that inexplicably made her cry. It would be adorable on either a little boy or girl. There was also a chocolate-brown floppy plush cow.

"These are the sweetest things I've ever seen." She sniffled. She hugged the plush stuffed animal to her chest.

"Took me a while to find one that wasn't black-and-white. They shouldn't all be Holsteins!" Garrett complained. The man was serious about his cows.

She thanked him with a hug, but had other ideas about how she wanted to thank him once they were alone. It was Darcy Connor who seemed to guess Arden's feelings and subtly began directing guests to leave. Justin left with Vivian, and Arden didn't know whether to be amused or irritated. Finally, only Layla was left.

As the two of them straightened the kitchen, Arden told her, "You outdid yourself with the food. No one who was here will need to cook dinner tonight."

In between his trips carrying all the gifts to the eventual nursery, Garrett thanked Layla with a hug and a kiss on the cheek, flustering her.

"Sorry," Layla whispered to Arden. "I know he's yours, but damn, he's hot."

Finally, *finally,* it was just Arden and Garrett. Alone at last after she hadn't seen him for two weeks. Taking his hand, she led him to the couch but didn't sit with him.

"You never actually gave me a straight answer when I asked you on the phone. Are you staying tonight?" she asked shyly.

He nodded, his gray eyes intense. "The entire drive to Cielo Peak, I worried that I'd lost my chance to build something with you. I need to hold you, feel you with me."

Leaning forward, she kissed him tenderly. "Then we're definitely on the same page. Wait here?" she murmured near his ear.

Battling the impulse to race to her closet in an undignified sprint, she sauntered out of the room, giving him a sassy wink over her shoulder.

As often as she thought about him during the days and nights when he wasn't in town, she'd had ample time to play this out in her mind. While she didn't think of herself as specifically vain, any woman seducing a man wanted to look her best. No way in hell was she letting him peel industrial-strength maternity under-garments off of her. At least, not for their first time.

And, in a way, this would be their first time.

What seemed like a lifetime ago, she'd had sex with a good-looking and very kind cowboy who'd changed her life forever. But now, she was about to make love to Garrett, the man she'd come to know over the past month, the man who worked hard and knew how to make her laugh, the man who cherished family as much as she did, the man who acted as if he'd do battle to defend her honor but looked completely at home holding a snuggly stuffed cow.

She'd purchased a very simple nightgown. The silky material was midnight-blue and fell from spaghetti straps to hit right above her knees. It wasn't ornate or lacy or sheer, but it made her feel sexier than she had in months.

Wearing nothing but the nightgown, she returned to the living room. Her senses were so heightened that the mere brush of satiny fabric against bare skin was arousing.

Garrett sat bolt upright, shock and pure masculine hunger playing across his face. "This may have been a strategic mistake on your part," he cautioned. "If this is what I get after we argue…well, I may be picking a lot of fights."

She smiled but didn't say anything as she continued her unhurried approach.

He leaned toward her, catching her waist in his hands and tipping her almost off balance as he pulled her forward. She thudded against him, soft and curved in all the places he was hard, and his heat went straight through the thin material.

He threaded one hand through her hair, angling her head to deepen their kiss until it felt as if they were fused together. Sensation built in the very core of her. Dazed, she realized that she'd begun rocking against his lap. He bit her earlobe, not hard enough to hurt, but just enough to penetrate the sweet hazy fog of desire enveloping her.

"Are you sure about this, sweetheart?" He took her chin in his hand, meeting her eyes and seeking assurance.

"Completely. All the stuff we unwrapped earlier is wonderful, but this is the only gift I really wanted today."

Needing no further urging, he reached down to tug off his belt while she fumbled with the buttons on his shirt. When he was stripped down to dark boxer-briefs, he repositioned her on his lap, kissing her like a man in a frenzy, leaving her mouth only to skim kisses across her sensitive collarbone. Meanwhile, his fingers traced maddening circles over her breast, not yet touching the sensitive peak. Without warning, he replaced his hand with his mouth, suckling her through the silky nightgown.

She cried out, her inner muscles clenching, tension already spiraling through her, pooling low where she was wet and wanting. Under his skillful attention, it wouldn't take long for her to detonate in his arms. *"Garrett."* She clutched the back of the sofa with one hand, crushing the upholstery in her fingers as she ground against him. He was hard as stone beneath her.

"Right there with you, sweetheart." As he shifted the hem of her nightgown to position himself, the straps slid down her shoulders. He tugged them farther, exposing her breasts to the cool air as he flexed his hips upward to enter her. He went slowly at first, not penetrating completely, savoring the moment and giving her time to adjust. But then he gripped her hips and thrust, wrenching another ecstatic scream from her. Her nerve endings were on fire with need. Using the back of the couch for leverage, she moved with abandon until the mounting tension began to ripple and spasm and finally exploded outward with such force it nearly blinded her for a second.

With a shout, he plunged into her one last time, then cuddled her against his chest.

Eventually, she realized she was practically panting and cursed herself for not having the forethought to place a glass of water nearby. "That..." She couldn't quite catch her breath enough to finish her sentence. But that was okay. There were no words adequate enough to capture what they'd just shared.

Chapter Twelve

Pale October sunshine stole through the window, and Arden experienced a childish urge to hide underneath her sheets. She resented that it was morning already and expressed her opinion with a rude noise along the lines of a raspberry.

Next to her, Garrett propped himself on one elbow. "You don't have to get up yet, you know. I realize some insensitive SOB kept you up half the night."

More than half, but that wasn't why she was feeling peevish. "I'm not tired. I just don't want… You're like a living, breathing sci-fi anomaly."

His eyebrows drew together. "Is that some sort of compliment on my performance? If so, I'll take it. But I don't get it."

"I think you disrupt the flow of time somehow. Whenever you're around, time flies so quickly it's unnatural. Then when you're gone…it feels like whole civilizations rise and crumble in the days when I don't see you."

He sifted his fingers through her hair. "I miss you, too."

When he climbed out of bed to take a shower, he invited her to join him, but she was feeling too blue to thoroughly appreciate the experience. He paused in the bathroom doorway. "You *are* going to be here when I get out, right? No running off and leaving me a note?"

That succeeded in drawing a smile. "One of the benefits of having sex with a woman in her own home is that she's unlikely to flee afterward. Of course, one of the drawbacks is that there's no room service."

"Don't be so sure," he told her. "I saw eggs in your fridge last night. You stay put, and think about what you want in your omelet. I owe you a breakfast in bed."

Thirty minutes later, he made good on his promise. He sat against her headboard, shirtless and barefoot, while she snuggled next to him in her favorite robe. She only had one breakfast tray, so both of their plates were balanced on it, giving them an excuse for extra closeness.

She moaned her appreciation at the fluffy, perfectly seasoned eggs. "This is terrific. How am I going to let you leave?"

"Maybe you don't have to. I did a lot of thinking while I was cooking. Dad always said I was stubborn, but I guess his lectures are finally sinking in."

She wasn't exactly following his train of thought, but as soon as he'd said maybe he didn't have to go, her heart had thumped happily. "You don't need to return back to the ranch soon?"

"No, I do. It's my job, and my life. I explained it wrong. When I leave, what if you came with me? My dad's been telling me since the day he met you that if I had the brains God gave a turnip, I'd take you off the market once and for all."

She gave him an incredulous look. "Off the market?"

"Marry you. And he's right."

"You can't be serious." Her brain whirled. What had happened to "let's not rush this" and "you deserve to be courted"? Okay, yes, they'd taken a big step forward last night, but she hadn't realized it was tantamount to getting engaged.

"Of course I am. I wouldn't joke about this." He swung his feet over the side of the bed, and she knew he'd be pacing within minutes. "Our baby received so many presents yesterday. Wouldn't the best gift be a stable home, a mother and father under one roof? We both know how important family is. Don't you want to provide that for the little one?"

She resented that line of reasoning. It sounded too much like he was trying to guilt her into the biggest decision of her life.

"It's the smart thing to do," he pronounced, irritating her even more.

"So if I don't say yes, I'm dumb *and* a bad mother?"

"What? How the hell did you make that leap?" He narrowed his eyes. "Wait, why wouldn't you say yes? We've both wondered how we're going to make this work long distance. You're alone here. At the Double F there's someone who can share the middle-of-the-night changings, built-in babysitting so you can keep working. Or you could stop working. I'll take care of you."

Now she shot out of the bed, too. It was a reminder of everything intimate they'd shared during the night— back *before* she'd wanted to throttle him—and she didn't want to acknowledge those memories right now. "I'm not alone here! I have Justin and Layla and my studio. And, yes, I plan to keep working. I love being a

photographer, and I spent a lot of time building a professional reputation and cultivating word-of-mouth mar-
keting. You would expect me to drop all of that without
a second thought?"

Apparently, he would. He *had*.

He ran a hand through his hair, making it stand on
end. It looked as stressed out as she was feeling. "Is this
really so out of the blue, so unthinkable? In less than
two months, you're having my baby. In a perfect world,
we'd have more time to plan and discuss, but we didn't
go about any of this perfectly."

Irrational tears burned her eyes. Last night had
seemed pretty damned perfect. For that matter, she'd
accumulated a number of "perfect moment" memories
in Garrett's presence, even when it had been something
as small as laughing until her face hurt over the world's
ugliest souvenir pen. But to hear him tell it, he'd merely
been making the best of a bad situation.

Suddenly devoid of energy, she sank back down to
the mattress. "You said your father's been goading you
to get married since the day he met me? We weren't
even dating then."

"True, but he knew we were about to be parents. If
we get married before Thanksgiving, our child will—"

"*Before* Thanksgiving?" Was he delusional? They'd
never even discussed this before now, and he wanted to
throw together a wedding in five or six weeks? Tears
burned her eyes. He'd gone from telling his family there
was "nothing romantic" between them to insisting she
become his wife. Obviously marriage meant very different things to each of them. "Garrett, why do you
want to marry me?"

"I told you. The baby des—"

"My answer is no."

GARRETT HAD LEFT Cielo Peak in a raging bad mood that did not improve on his drive to the ranch. Arden had been unreasonable. She'd admitted she was miserable without him, but she refused to take the logical step so that they could be together. Even though it would make them both happy. Even though it was best for the baby.

Despite knowing his parents would want to hear about the shower and ask how she'd liked their gifts, he drove straight past their house. He needed to be alone. But fate had something different in mind. He'd barely removed his boots when his doorbell rang. He held his breath, debating how to proceed. He couldn't really ignore his own parents the way one might a door-to-door salesman.

"Son?" Brandon called. "We need to talk to you. It's important."

It had better not be about Arden. He'd had enough of his father's unsolicited advice on that front. *I tried, Dad.* She'd trampled his proposal with all the violence of a stampeding herd.

Years of ingrained obedience won out, and he opened the door for his father. Garrett did a double take, noting that his mom had been crying and that even his father's eyes were puffy. He experienced a moment of emotional vertigo— Oh, God. Had Will Harlow lost his battle with renal failure? "C-come in." Garrett cast his hand out to the side blindly, looking for something that would steady him.

They filed into the living room, no one speaking,

until finally, Caroline said, in a voice so small it was almost inaudible, "Your father suggested that we invite Will for Thanksgiving next month. He has no family, and he's been so ill. It would be the charitable thing to do. And I just...couldn't. I couldn't go on not telling him anymore."

This wasn't about a downturn in the man's health? This was about Thanksgiving? Garrett's gaze dropped, zeroing in on his parents' joined hands. They were here as a unified front? Brandon hadn't driven into the mountains to process news of his wife's duplicity?

"You're not mad?" Garrett asked without thinking. "You don't care?"

"Of course I care, son. Especially for you. Your momma tells me you've been going through hell this last month, and I've never been prouder of you. You want to help a man who's critically ill, despite your anger. You tried to protect your momma by keeping her secret, but through it all, you've felt a strong pull of loyalty to me? We raised you good. And you had reason to be hurt. But only the two people *in* a relationship can truly understand what's happening between them."

Sometimes even fewer than two. Garrett, for one, had no idea why Arden had thrown away what could have been an amazing future.

"You don't know what that time was like for Caro, what I was like. I have a son, and Will may be dying. In light of those facts, holding a grudge seems pretty pointless. We just wanted you to know you don't have to hide it anymore. And we both fully support whatever you decide about the kidney donation. Suffice to say, Will Harlow won't be joining us for Thanksgiving.

Not that I suppose it makes much difference to you. We figure you'll be in Cielo Peak."

With Arden, they meant. It was going to be difficult to feel thankful after her rejection.

Despite his relief over Brandon finally knowing the truth and his admiration that his parents had managed to weather such a significant betrayal, Garrett felt hollow. How could he be this bereft? When he'd first learned about Pea—about the baby, he'd assumed he and Arden would parent separately and platonically. It was only very recently that he'd begun to believe they could have more. They'd been on *one* date. How could he mourn the loss of something he'd never truly had?

His gaze went involuntarily to his parents' still-linked hands. Just because he'd never had something didn't mean he couldn't recognize the value of it.

THREE TEENAGERS POSED against a pumpkin-patch backdrop in Halloween costumes ranging from zombie cheerleader to a two-headed mummy. But the scariest thing in the studio was Arden's unshakable gloom. What was the point in a soon-to-be mom taking a principled stand on her right to keep working if she chased off all her clients with her morose attitude?

"Great shots, girls." She put the camera away, trying not to think about when she and Natalie had been that age, the silly moments like these—funny BFF photos, staging "chance" run-ins with boys they liked, never having any idea the twists and turns their lives would take.

After the giggling teens had chipped in their money and selected the photo they wanted for their joint package, Arden was alone—free to put her head on her desk and cry her guts out. Except she couldn't. The woman who'd cried at greeting cards, soup commercials, random puppies she passed in the park and internet banner ads was completely empty. She'd been dry-eyed since Garrett stomped out of her house last week, unable to wash away the memory with cleansing tears.

Although she hadn't spoken directly to Garrett, Darcy Connor had suddenly discovered numerous reasons to call. The woman was obviously checking on Arden and the baby and making covert reports.

"Knock, knock." Layla stood in the doorway. As the teenage girls had happily announced, today had been an early release day for local schools. "This is an intervention."

"What?"

"Today, we close the studio early, go to your place and eat chocolate-covered caramels while we watch action movies with lots of car chases and explosions. Then, tomorrow, you start shaking this off, or I think your brothers are taking a road trip to the Double F and doing some damage. You remember your brothers, right? Big strapping guys who love you and are worried sick?"

"I'm not trying to worry any of you," Arden said apologetically. "I just…hurt."

"Oh, sweetie." Layla came around the desk to give her a hug. Then she pulled a caramel-filled chocolate medallion out of her pocket. "Here, want to get a jump start on the gorging?"

"No." Arden swatted the candy away. It made her

think of Garrett. *Big surprise.* Everything made her think of Garrett.

"If you miss him so much, you could call him."

"And say what? Layla, the guy expected me to marry him without ever mentioning his feelings for me. He thinks it's rational to get married for the baby's sake, and, you know what? He may be right. There are probably people who do that and make it work. But I'm holding out for more than *rational.* He made it sound like a good mother would want her child to have a loving home with both parents, and I *do.* Enough that I'm willing to wait for the right situation, for a man who actually does love me. A man who gives his future with me the due consideration it deserves. I can't just pack up and leave Cielo Peak!"

Layla narrowed her eyes at her, lips pursed.

"What?"

"Don't scream at me...but are you *sure* you can't?"

"Hey! You're one of the reasons I'm staying. Do you want to get rid of me?"

"What I want is to see you happy. I know we couldn't go out for spur-of-the-moment pizzas if you left, but even living in the same town, we spend half our time on the phone. You'd be moving to a ranch, not the far side of the moon."

"I have a business I started from scratch. And the thought of leaving my brothers..."

"Maybe you'd be setting a good example for them," Layla suggested quietly. "Colin can't seem to find his way back to happiness, and Justin is too afraid of being happy to give it a fair shot. If you seized happiness with Garrett, it could give them hope, a blueprint to follow.

I agree the man's proposal sucked, but let's look past that for the moment. Do you think he could make you happy?"

Arden stared into space, recounting all the small and not-so-small ways he'd done just that, the unexpected joy he'd given her.

"C'mon, you can think it over on the ride to your house." Layla had already picked up Arden's purse and was bringing the red wool coat to her. "You said Garrett goes in for testing next week? Maybe you can call him Sunday night, after you've both had a chance to calm down and reflect. Wish him luck on the medical stuff and see how you feel talking to him."

Conjuring a ghost of a smile, Arden stood. "You're a very wise woman."

"That's what I tell my students. Let's go. Bad action movies await."

"I don't think so." Arden gasped, gripping the edge of her desk. "My water just broke!"

ALL THE OTHER ranch hands had called it a day. Garrett should, too. It was cold and dark. But where else would he go? His house was too quiet, too lonely. And up at his parents' house, Caroline's admission seemed to have brought her and Brandon even closer. With the weight of her secret lifted, Caroline was practically giddy. She danced around the kitchen to her old records while baking, a constant smile on her face. The house was full of the cinnamon-spiced aroma of pumpkin pie and happiness.

He'd rather be out shivering in the barn.

The cell phone in his pocket rang, and he had to remove one glove to answer it. He almost ignored the call since he didn't recognize the number. "Garrett Frost," he announced himself.

"Frost? This is Justin Cade."

Garrett groaned. Was the man planning to kick Garrett's ass because he'd displeased Arden? "Look, if you're calling to bust my chops, you should know I *tried* to do the honorable thing."

"I'm calling because she's in the hospital." The swaggering man had never sounded so fragile. "How soon can you get here?"

BY THE TIME he reached the hospital, it was all over. Garrett was ravaged with self-blame. Why hadn't he been here with her? Had this happened because they'd had sex? Between all the machines in the hospital interfering with cell phone reception and Garrett driving through several "dead spots," he hadn't been able to stay in constant contact with Justin. Those moments of not knowing what was happening had been sheer hell.

What he did know was that Arden's membranes had ruptured a month too early. The doctors had given her antibiotics and had considered a drug to discourage labor as well as steroids to help speed development of the baby's premature lungs. But ultimately they'd decided the safest thing for both mother and child was an emergency C-section.

When he'd last spoken to Justin, that was all the man had known. Garrett burst into the maternity waiting room, frantic. Layla rose from a chair and ran to hug him.

"Tell me she's okay," he implored.

She nodded. "With the type of C-section they did, they had to knock her out. She's still asleep, but she should be fine. The baby was having a little bit of trouble breathing on her own, but she's on a ventilator in the NICU and—"

"She?" Garrett grabbed Layla's shoulders. The errant tears he'd fought since he'd jumped into his truck spilled over unchecked. "I have a daughter?"

Layla nodded emphatically. "Four pounds even. Name yet to be determined. Come on, her uncles are already upstairs watching her through windows."

Four pounds? Lord, she was smaller than a bowling ball but already had so many people in her life who already loved her. He followed Layla to the elevator bank. Now that the adrenaline in his body was starting to ebb, his legs felt too rubbery to take the stairs. The doors parted, and he was about to step inside the elevator when a nurse behind them called, "Family and friends of Arden Cade?"

He spun around. "Is she awake? Is she all right? Can I see her?"

The woman lowered her clipboard and gave him a patient smile. "Slow down there, sir. She's awake, but groggy. She'll experience some discomfort over her recovery period, but right now she's on some pretty strong painkillers. And, yes, you can see her. Only one at a time in the room until she's had a bit more rest."

"I'll go tell the guys." Layla squeezed his arm. "You tell Arden we all love her."

We all love her. God, he'd been an idiot. Why hadn't he dropped to one knee the last time he'd been with her, told her he'd never felt this way about another woman and begged her to marry him? He'd been cynical lately about matrimony and fidelity and honesty, but was that the kind of world he wanted to raise his daughter in? A place where people saw the worst in each other and didn't take risks with their hearts?

The nurse led him to a dimly lit maternity suite with a couple of guest chairs and a hospital bed angled so that Arden was reclining but not flat on her back. She was connected by IV to several different apparatuses and monitors. Wearing an unflattering hospital gown, tubes sticking out of her arms, plastic bracelets encircling her wrists, her damp hair sticking to a face bloated with the fluids they'd given her, she was easily the most beautiful woman he'd ever seen.

She blinked in confusion, as if trying to decide whether she was dreaming. "Garrett?" Her voice was slurred. "That you?"

"It's me." He came to her side, wondering if she'd let him hold her hand. Unable to stop himself, he leaned down to kiss her forehead. "Congratulations, I understand you have a beautiful daughter. But no way is she as beautiful as her momma."

"I need to hold her!" Splotches of color rose in her cheeks. "They put me under, I only glimpsed the hospital blanket and a blur and—"

"The nurse who brought me in here said they'll wheel you upstairs soon. They need to check some vitals first."

That seemed to calm her. She swallowed audibly, the sound dry and cracked, and he looked around for a pitcher of water.

"How'd you get here so fast?" she asked.

Fast? Under other circumstances, he would have

laughed at the irony. "Sweetheart, those were the slowest, most agonizing hours of my entire life. I felt like I was stuck in another dimension and couldn't reach you. It was a living nightmare."

Her eyes slid closed once again. "You're here now."

AFTER A NIGHT that passed in a fragmented series of narcotic impressions, Arden woke the next morning with a sense of awe. *I have a baby girl.* It seemed almost a dream, except for the pain in her midsection and the still-vivid memory of the fear she'd felt when the doctor had said they needed to do an emergency Caesarean.

Trying to remember how much of what she recalled was real, she turned her head to identify the source of snoring. She half expected to see Justin or Colin, but it was Garrett, his jaw covered in stubble, his legs hanging off a chair that transitioned into a twin bed about a foot too small for him.

"Garrett?"

He came awake immediately, his expression as chagrined as if he'd fallen asleep while he was supposed to be keeping watch. "I only closed my eyes for a minute."

She started to chuckle, but it hurt, tugging her insides in opposite directions. "You're allowed to sleep. How is she?"

"Healthy. She's upstairs in an incubator, but they say she's doing incredibly well for a preemie. She may have to stay in the hospital for a few weeks, but she should be home by Thanksgiving. My parents called about an hour ago. Would you mind if they come see you?"

"No, they should be here. Family's the most important thing in the world."

"Then you must be my family." He stood, coming to her side. "Because all I could think when I hauled ass to the hospital yesterday was that you're the most important thing in the world to me. You are my world. I'm sorry I didn't articulate that clearly enough until now."

She didn't know what to say. Could she trust what she was hearing, or were the drugs in the hospital very, *very* good?

"I can't wait to celebrate our first Thanksgiving as a family," he said. "And Christmas! I'll put so many lights on the outside of the house the baby thinks she lives in Times Square."

"You...sound like you plan to spend a lot of time at my house. Don't they need you at the ranch?"

"I don't want to be here just for your recovery—or hers, no matter how much I love her. I want you, Arden. If I have to, I'll ask Dad to give the foreman extra responsibilities, hire some extra help. I'll stay in Cielo Peak as long as you want. If you'll have me," he said brokenly.

"But the Double F—"

"What's one ranch compared to the entire world?"

"Arden, is this bum bothering you?" Justin's teasing voice came from the door, and Arden was glad to see his familiar face—although it looked as if it had gained several new worry lines in the past twenty-four hours.

"I'm not sure," Arden began, "but he *might* have been proposing."

"In a hospital room with no ring?" Justin snorted. "Frost, my sister deserves a string quartet and a five-star meal."

"As soon as she's all better and you volunteer to

babysit your niece, I'll take her out for those things. Right now, I'm improvising." He turned to Arden. "You asked me before why I wanted to marry you?"

She held her breath, almost afraid to hope.

He took her hand, his heart in his eyes. "Because I love you and always will."

"I love you, too." Joy filled her, and for a second she felt no pain at all. "And I'd like nothing more than to marry you."

Epilogue

Arden stood by her daughter's hospital crib, watching her sleep. "I hate that I'm going home without you, but I'll visit every day. And going home just means I can supervise Daddy while he gets your room set up perfectly," she whispered. "I'll tell you a secret, you've already got Daddy completely wrapped around your finger. Be careful with him. He may be a big, strong cowboy, but he's got a tender heart."

She couldn't believe he'd really been willing to move to Cielo Peak for them. She'd informed him that under no circumstances would she allow such a sacrifice. But they *would* have to remain for at least a few months, as their daughter got stronger. They'd relocate to the ranch sometime after New Year's and were hoping to get married around Valentine's Day.

Her husband-to-be was waiting for her in the hall, having already said his temporary goodbye to their daughter. As soon as the drugs had begun to wear off and Arden started having longer stretches of lucidity, Garrett had asked if she'd decided on a name for a baby. During her pregnancy, she'd toyed with the notion of perhaps naming a daughter for Natalie. Or after her own mother. But those both felt off the mark now. There was nothing wrong with honoring the past, but Arden wanted to focus on the bright, bright future ahead of them. They'd christened their daughter Hope.

"Everyone's waiting downstairs," he told her, putting his arm around her shoulders. "If you want to change your mind, I can tell Mom that—"

"No, we agreed. Caro's going to stay with me while you finally get that testing done. You already had to postpone because of me. I don't want this hanging over your head, Garrett. The nurses are giving Hope the best care possible, and you know your mom will look after me and call you with daily—possibly hourly—updates."

"I just hate to leave you."

"I know, but we have a whole lifetime ahead of us. We can spare a week of that to find out whether you can help Will."

During the days she'd been in the hospital, Garrett had told her all about how Brandon had forgiven his wife's transgression. And Arden had thought about the many rich blessings she and Garrett shared. If they could bless someone else with a second chance...

Even though she was able to walk by herself, hospital policy dictated that she be taken to the exit in a wheelchair. Apparently, there was a waiting list for the chairs, because the nurse who said she'd be right back had yet to reappear. The elevator doors parted, but it wasn't the nurse who stepped off the conveyance. Both her brothers were loaded down with her belongings, ready to take them to Garrett's truck, and they were accompanied by Layla and the Frosts.

"We just wanted one last peek at Hope through the window before we go," Layla said sheepishly. "I can't wait until you can bring her home, and I get to hold her as much as I want."

"Sorry, honey," Caroline said. "I've got grandmother's prerogative. You'll have to wait in line."

"Her parents get first dibs," Garrett said firmly.

Affection and gratitude filled Arden. How was it possible she had ever felt alone? She looked from the group assembled in the hall back to her beautiful daughter, then up into the eyes of the man who loved her. *My family*. Hope didn't know it yet, but they were the luckiest two ladies in all of Colorado.

* * * * *

*Be sure to look for the second book
in Tanya Michaels's*
THE COLORADO CADES *trilogy—
SECOND CHANCE CHRISTMAS*.

MILLS & BOON®
are delighted to support
World Book Night

Georgie Lee

The Secret Marriage Pact